ABOVE THE BAY of ANGELS

Center Point
Large Print

Also by Rhys Bowen and available from
Center Point Large Print:

In Farleigh Field
The Victory Garden

**This Large Print Book carries the
Seal of Approval of N.A.V.H.**

ABOVE THE BAY of ANGELS

A NOVEL

RHYS BOWEN

CENTER POINT LARGE PRINT
THORNDIKE, MAINE

This Center Point Large Print edition
is published in the year 2020 by arrangement with
Amazon Publishing, www.apub.com.

Originally published in the United States by
Amazon Publishing, 2020.

The text of this Large Print edition is unabridged.
In other aspects, this book may vary
from the original edition.
Printed in the United States of America
on permanent paper.
Set in 16-point Times New Roman type.

ISBN: 978-1-64358-589-5

The Library of Congress has cataloged this record under
Library of Congress Control Number: 2020930517

This book is dedicated
to the real Mary Crozier.
While not a marquise,
she has a house almost as
lovely as the villa in Nice,
and she gives the most
amazing tea parties.

CHAPTER 1

London, September 1896

If Helen Barton hadn't stepped out in front of an omnibus, I might still be sweeping floors and lighting fires at an ostentatious house in St John's Wood. But for once I had followed my father's advice.

"Carpe diem" was one of my father's favourite sayings. Seize the day. Take your chances. He usually added "because that might be the only chance you get." He spoke from experience. He was an educated man from a good family, and had known better times. As the son of a second son, he could expect to inherit neither a title nor the property that would have come with it, and was sent out to India to make something of himself, becoming an officer in the Bengal Lancers. He had married my mother, a sweet and delicate creature he met on one of his visits home. It was soon clear that she couldn't endure the harsh conditions of Bengal, so Daddy had been forced to resign his commission and return to live in England.

From what Daddy told us, it had been made evident to him as a young man that he could expect no financial help from his uncle, the earl. He never told us why, or what rift had occurred within his family, but he was clearly bitter about it. However, he had finally fallen on his feet in a way and had acquired what was considered a prestigious position: he was in charge of guest relations at the Savoy, London's new luxury hotel. His ability to speak good French and mingle with crowned heads had made him popular at the hotel. He had patted the hands of elderly Russian countesses and arranged roulette parties for dashing European princes, for which he received generous tips. We had lived quite happily in the small town of Hampstead, on the northern fringes of London. My younger sister Louisa and I attended a private school. We had a woman who came to clean and cook for us. It was not an extravagant life, but a pleasant one.

Until it all came crashing down when the demon drink overcame my father. He worked at an establishment where the alcohol flowed freely amongst the guests. When invited, he took a glass, as it would have been rude to refuse. So who would notice if he later finished off a bottle?

I remember the first time he came home drunk.

"Roddy, where have you been?" my mother asked him when he arrived home at ten o'clock. "We waited dinner for you. I was worried."

"None of your business, woman." He spat out the words.

My mother winced as if he had struck her. My little sister grabbed my hand. We had never seen our father like this. He was normally so amiable and adored my mother.

"Roddy, have you been drinking?" Mummy said coldly.

"Just being sociable with the clients. Part of the job, don't you know," he said. Then he added, his voice rising aggressively, "I have to work for my living, or have you forgotten that? After all, it was because of you that I had to give up my commission in India and take a menial job bowing and scraping to those who should be my equals. Now where's my dinner?"

I saw my mother's horrified stare as she blinked back tears. After that day nothing was the same. It felt as if we were walking on eggshells. We never knew when he'd come home or what kind of mood he'd be in. Sometimes he was as jovial and affectionate as ever, but other times it was as if he'd turned into a monster I didn't recognize. Louisa and I spent a lot of time hiding away in our bedroom. Mummy tried hard at first, begging him to stop drinking and think of his family, but nothing she said reached him, and in the end she just seemed to give up and fade like a wilting flower. She had never been strong to begin with.

I suppose we had all been dreading what happened next. My father arrived home in the middle of the afternoon announcing that he had been dismissed from his job. "All because of some stupid Russian woman who said she'd seen my helping myself to a little sip from a bottle of Scotch. They took her word against mine. Can you believe it? Who'd want to work at a place like that? I'm well rid of it."

"But Roddy, what will we do?" my mother asked. "How will we pay the rent?"

"I'll find something else, don't you worry," he said breezily. "A chap like me—I'll be snapped up in no time at all."

But he wasn't. He tried in vain to find another position, but without a reference no respectable establishment wanted him. We watched him sink lower and lower into depression and drunkenness. We gave up our servant. I tried to be grown-up and take over the housework as Mummy seemed to have no energy for even the most basic of tasks. Daddy seemed genuinely concerned for her, but it didn't stop his visits to the public house.

It was a bitter winter that year, and the price of coal had gone up. We spent our evenings around the kitchen table where the stove provided warmth. Mummy developed a nasty cough. I thought she should see a doctor, but Daddy dismissed the idea. "It's just a bad cold, Bella. Your mother always likes to dramatize things, you know that."

It might have started as a cold, but it turned into

pneumonia, and three days later she was dead. I couldn't believe she was gone. Neither could my father. "My precious darling Winnie," he said. "It's all my fault. It's all my fault." And he actually wept. He and Louisa and I hugged each other while the tears flowed. My mother was a genteel and sweet person who adored my father. They said she died of pneumonia, but I think it was of a broken heart.

We moved to a squalid two-room flat above a butcher's shop, with only cold water and an outside lavatory. Father occasionally picked up work writing letters for the illiterate, tutoring in French, but nothing kept the wolf far from the door. I suppose I had no idea how bad our situation really was until one day, just before my fifteenth birthday, he announced he had found a position for me. I was to leave the school that I adored and become a servant in a big house, so that I'd earn money to feed father and Louisa and someone else would have to feed and clothe me. I was more than shocked. I was mortified. We might not have been rich, but I was from a good family.

"A servant? You want me to be a servant?" I could hardly stammer the words.

"I feel as terrible about it as you do, my darling child," he said, "but the truth is that I can't afford to feed you. We'll be out on the street if someone doesn't pay the rent, and I can't seem to find a

11

position. So your sister and I are relying on you at this moment."

I wanted to shout at him, to tell him that we might have enough money to scrape by if he didn't visit the public house so frequently, but I'd been brought up to be the good child, to obey my parents. I was doubly shocked when I found out that the house where I would be sent to work belonged to a nouveau riche man who had made money in the garment business. His factories turned out cheap blouses for working girls. He and his wife were loudmouthed and commonly ostentatious.

I stood outside, staring up at the gables and turrets of an incredibly ugly house. "Daddy, please don't make me do this," I pleaded. "Not a servant to these people. I realize I must leave school, but there must be something else I can do."

"It's only for a short while, Bella," he said, patting my hand. "I promise you as soon as I'm on my feet again I'll bring you home. Until then you are helping to make sure that your little sister does not starve."

What could I say to that? I realized then that he had always been a great manipulator, using his charm to get my mother to agree with whatever scheme he had in mind at that moment.

So I went to work for Mr and Mrs Tilley at the ugly house in St John's Wood. They kept a butler, a parlour maid, a footman, two housemaids, a cook and a scullery maid. As the lowest housemaid, I was responsible for rising at five in the morning, lighting the copper and the stove, then carrying heavy scuttles of coal to the bedrooms to make sure that the family awoke to warmth. It was backbreaking, soul-destroying work. I had to share a bed with Poppy, the scullery maid, in a freezing attic room. Mercifully I was so tired that I fell asleep instantly every night. It felt like a nightmare from which I couldn't wake up.

Then one day Mrs Tilley was entertaining. She liked to entertain frequently: coffee mornings and tea parties and extravagant dinners. All of these events meant extra work for us servants. We went through a frenzy of polishing silverware, making sure there wasn't a speck of dust on the mahogany table that seated thirty and, in my case, ensuring that the fires were supplied with enough coal to keep them burning brightly. On this occasion it was a tea party. Cook had been baking all morning: scones and sponge cakes and shortbreads so that the kitchen was full of wonderful aromas. And all afternoon she had been making little tea sandwiches—cucumber, egg and cress, smoked salmon. After Elsie, the parlour maid, had gone up to the drawing room with the tea things, Cook noticed that she had forgotten to put the macaroons on to the tray. She thrust them into my hands. "Quick. Take them up before Mrs T notices, or there will be hell to pay," she said.

I ran out of the kitchen with the dish, up the stone steps and through the green baize door that separated the servants from the real world. Female voices were coming from the drawing room. I crept in. Elsie had already put the tray on the trolley and was pouring tea. I hesitated, unsure what to do next, when Mrs Tilley spotted me.

"What do you want, girl?" she asked.

"I've brought the macaroons, ma'am," I said. "They weren't quite ready when Elsie carried up the tray."

She heard my refined accent and frowned. "Are you trying to ape your betters, girl?" Her own accent still carried an undercurrent of her East End upbringing.

"No, ma'am. I've always spoken this way. My father was a gentleman."

"Then what in God's name are you doing here?" one of the other ladies asked.

"My mother died. My father became too ill to work, and I need to support my little sister," I replied. "There are not many jobs available to a fifteen-year-old."

"You poor child," the woman said. "Life can be cruel."

Then she took a cream puff from the plate and bit into it. "You'll never believe what I heard about Sylvia," she said, her upper lip now lined with a delicate moustache of cream.

"Do tell." The ladies leaned forward. And I was instantly forgotten.

You might have thought that my lot would have improved after that moment. It did, but only slightly. I still had to get up early to light the fires, but when Mrs Tilley was entertaining, she'd make sure I served them in the drawing room. "Her father was an aristocrat," she'd say in a stage whisper. "Her parents died. I took her in, poor little thing."

I'd stand there like a statue, determined to keep my face a mask of stone to show them I didn't care. I wanted these self-satisfied, patronizing ladies to know that whatever they said they could never break me. "One day," I would whisper to myself. I wasn't sure what I meant by it. Only that if I could just hang on long enough, then I'd find a way to escape. And I'd make something of my life.

The only good thing about the Tilley household was that Mr and Mrs Tilley loved to eat. They ate very well. So well that I was able to take home leftovers to Daddy and Louisa on my afternoon off every week. My father loved his food. He would have been a gourmet if we could have afforded it and spoke fondly about banquets he had attended, as well as Indian feasts, country picnics, Christmas at the family seat. His eyes would light up when he saw my weekly offerings, wrapped in a clean napkin.

"My, my," Daddy would say. "Roast pheasant. That takes me back to my childhood. I remember a banquet with the old earl once. We'd been out shooting. I'd bagged a couple of pheasants. My God, they were good. And smoked salmon. My dear, you are a miracle worker, a lifesaver."

He'd take my hands and gaze up at me adoringly, the way he used to look at my mother. I'd try to smile back at him, although I wanted to scream. I wanted to shout at him, "Your childhood was full of banquets. Do you know what mine is like? Have you ever scrubbed floors so that your hands are raw? Or lugged coal up four flights of stairs? You have no idea what you are putting me through." But he had become so thin and pale that I couldn't say anything to hurt him. He had called me a miracle worker, a lifesaver, and I think I really believed to begin with that I could make him well again if I brought home enough good food to fatten him up. I tried to find bottles hidden around the flat and dispose of them. After a while, however, I realized it was hopeless. He was going to drink himself into the grave. I knew I had to stay where I was, enduring Mrs Tilley, until Louisa could be somehow taken care of.

Mrs Tilley boasted about having the best cook in London. "I lured her away from titled people," she used to say. "It's true what they say, you know. Money talks. I pay her much more than she was getting. And I'm told we have the best table for miles around."

We also ate well in the kitchen, and I found that I had inherited my father's palate and appreciation of good food. Our cuisine at home had always been rather basic, even in the days when we had a cook, and I became fascinated with the process of creating such wonderful flavours. "Show me how you made that parsley sauce, those meringues, that oyster stew," I'd say to Mrs Robbins, the cook. And if she had a minute to spare, she would show me. After a while, seeing my willingness as well as my obvious aptitude for cooking, she suggested to Mrs Tilley that her old legs were not up to standing for hours any more and that she needed an assistant cook. And she requested me. Mrs Tilley agreed, but only if she didn't have to pay me more money and I should still be available to do my party piece whenever she entertained.

And so I went to work in the kitchen. Mrs Robbins found me a willing pupil. After lugging coal scuttles up all those stairs, it felt like heaven to be standing at a table preparing food. We had a scullery maid who did all the most menial of jobs, like chopping the onions and peeling the potatoes, but I had to do the most basic of tasks—mashing the potatoes with lots of butter and cream until there wasn't a single lump, basting the roast so that the fat was evenly crisp. I didn't mind. I loved being amongst the rich aromas. I loved the look of a well-baked pie. The satisfaction when Mrs Robbins nodded with approval at something I had prepared. And of course I loved the taste of what I had created.

Now when I went home to Daddy and Louisa, I could say, "I roasted that pheasant. I made that apple tart." And it gave me a great rush of satisfaction to say the words.

"You've a good feel for it, I'll say that for you," Mrs Robbins told me, and after a while she even sought my opinion. "Does this casserole need a touch more salt, do you think? Or maybe some thyme?"

The part I loved the best was the baking. She showed me how to make pastry, meringues that were light as air, all sorts of delicate biscuits and rich cakes. After a year under Mrs Robbins's tutelage, I realized that I could now start to spread my wings. I could get a job as a cook, with the money and respect that went with it. I made the mistake of telling Mrs Robbins of my ambition, and she told madam. And madam didn't want to lose me. She loved the status that her aristocratic servant gave her. "Go on, tell them about your dad in India," she'd say when the ladies came to call. "Tell them about your great-uncle the earl and that blooming great palace of a house he lives in."

When she heard that I might be thinking of leaving, she called me into the drawing room and told me that if I was ungrateful enough to want to leave, she wouldn't give me a reference. She smiled as she said it. Smirked, actually, knowing that nobody would hire me without a reference. I was stuck whether I liked it or not. I tried to think of ways to escape. I could go to America maybe. They'd be impressed by my upper-class English accent and noble background, wouldn't they? I could become a cook there, or work in a high-class shop, or become a lady's companion. The only fly in that ointment was that every penny I earned went to Daddy and Louisa. I had no way to save up for my fare. And of course I couldn't leave them.

My father died the autumn I turned twenty. This did not come as a great shock to me, and I have to admit I did not feel the grief a daughter should feel. I had learned to shut off all feeling the moment I became a servant. Mrs Tilley gave me a day off to arrange for his funeral, and Louisa and I stood together at his grave.

"Well, that's that, I suppose," Louisa said. "I'm rather glad it's over, aren't you?"

"Glad our father died?" I asked.

She gave an awkward smile. "I don't mean it like that. After all, he was our father and I suppose we loved him once, but it was like holding our breath, waiting for the end to come."

"Yes, it was," I agreed. "But I'm worried about you. What will happen to you now?"

She was almost seventeen, had shown little interest in her schooling and was recently apprenticed to a milliner. It suited her well as she had always been the sort of girl who admired herself in the mirror and longed to be fashionable one day, while I was interested more in my books and less in a way of life I could never have.

"You like your job?" I enquired. "And your employers?"

She nodded, tentatively. "They are very kind."

I enquired whether she could live in with the family who owned the shop. She actually blushed and said that wouldn't be necessary. She had been holding off until Daddy died, but she had had a proposal and was going to marry.

"Marry?" I stared at her in disbelief. "But you're only a child."

"Nonsense. Many girls marry at seventeen," she said. "And Billy will take good care of me. I won't have to work."

I was more than shocked when I found out that the boy she wanted to marry was Billy Harrison, the son of the butcher above whose shop we lived. "A butcher boy? Louisa, you can't marry trade. Daddy would turn in his grave."

She regarded me haughtily. "As if our father did anything for us, Bella."

"He did his best," I said, not believing those words. His best hadn't been good enough.

She put her hand over mine. "Billy is a good catch, Bella. His father owns three shops, plus a pig farm out in Essex. He plans to hand one of the shops over to Billy. We'll live with his parents in a nice house on Highgate Hill until Billy can find us a house of our own. You can stop being a servant and come and live with us. I'm sure Billy won't mind."

I can't tell you what anguish I went through that night. Of course I wished my sister well and wanted her to be happy. But here I was, stuck in domestic drudgery, having toiled for five years to support her, when she had no idea of the life I lived. I had wanted her to be educated, to have more chances than I. And now she was going to marry, and I . . . I was still a prisoner at the house of Tilley. Life seemed bitterly unfair.

Then it struck me that I'd no longer be responsible for her. My wages were now my own. I'd save up and be able to buy my ticket to America. This cheered me so much that I decided to treat myself on my next day off. No more coming home with leftovers from the Tilleys. I'd go up to the West End and look in the shop windows, maybe buy myself a new comb or even some rouge for my too-pale cheeks and maybe take tea in a tearoom. So I caught the Metropolitan Underground railway to Baker Street, then the

Bakerloo Underground to Oxford Circus. It was horribly hot and smoky, and I was so relieved to come up into the fresh air again.

I felt a flutter of excitement when I emerged to a different world. Smartly dressed women, big beautiful shops. I walked along Oxford Street until I came to John Lewis's wonderful department store. I gazed at all the windows, with their smartly dressed mannequins and realistic country scenes. In one window there was even a motor car. "A jaunt in the country" was written across the backdrop. Then I reached the front entrance and took a deep breath before I went in. It looked so beautiful it was almost like stepping into a palace. I approached the cosmetics counter and let the lady apply a little rouge to my cheeks before buying a small tin. Feeling very daring I came out again and turned down Bond Street.

I paused at Fenwick's department store, then gazed in the windows of the jewellers, hat-makers, leather goods merchants and china shops until I emerged on to Piccadilly. Then a really extravagant thought struck me. I remembered my father relating how he had been taken to tea at Fortnum and Mason when he was a child. I spotted the name across the street and decided that I, too, would have tea there, just this once. I stood at the edge of the curb, waiting for a break in the seemingly incessant stream of hansom cabs, omnibuses, delivery carts, and even occasional motor cars. Then right behind me I heard a scream, shouts and a police whistle, and my life changed in that instant.

CHAPTER 2

I spun around to witness a horrible scene. An omnibus stood beside the curb, its horses dancing nervously. Beneath its wheels lay the body of a young woman.

"She stepped out right in front of me," the driver shouted as he climbed down to calm the horses. "We were going too fast. I had no chance to stop."

"Is there a doctor in the crowd?" Two police constables had arrived at the scene.

"Too late for that, mate," a male voice said. "I reckon she's a goner all right."

"Poor thing," a woman beside me muttered. "I'm not surprised. Many's the time I've had to sprint for my life as one of them omnibuses comes charging at me. The traffic is getting awful these days. You're not safe to cross the road."

The omnibus driver was backing up his horses cautiously as the constables tried to move the girl. I couldn't take my eyes off her broken body. She was not much older than I. She reminded me of a rag doll I had had as a child. My sister had stuck scissors into it in a fit of temper, and let the sawdust run out so that the doll lay in a crumpled heap. As I looked on with pity and horror, I saw the girl's eyes flutter open, looking around her with surprise as if she couldn't believe what had just happened to her. Without hesitation, I stepped forward and knelt beside her, putting a gentle hand on her shoulder. "It's all right. You're going to be all right," I said, gently, although I didn't think this was true. "I'll stay here with you until a doctor comes."

She tried to focus on my face. "Palace." The word came out as a whisper I could barely detect. "Palace. Tell . . ."

She tried to move her hand, and I saw that she had been holding an envelope in it. I took it from her. "Don't worry. I'll tell them," I said, although I had no idea what she meant. Clearly it had been troubling her because the worried expression left her face. She gave a little smile and a small sigh, and her eyes closed. It almost seemed that she had fallen asleep, but a big hand touched my shoulder.

"There's nothing you can do for her now, miss." I looked up to see a constable standing behind me. "Were you a friend?" He helped me to my feet.

"No. I didn't know her. I just didn't want her to think she was alone. It was so awful."

"You're a kind girl. I expect she appreciated that," he said.

Several men were lifting the girl's body on to

the pavement. Someone was covering her with a rug. I had no reason to stay any longer. I pushed through the crowd that had gathered, blinking back the tears that were welling in my eyes. I was still so much in a state of shock that I had crossed the street towards the park before I realized that I was holding the girl's envelope. Something in it was so important to her that it was her one concern as she lay dying. I stepped into a shop doorway, out of the stream of passers-by, and looked down at the envelope for the first time. It bore a crest—an impressive crest—and yet the girl was clearly from the working class, judging by her clothing. Curious now, I opened it and took out the letter inside.

To Miss Helen Barton, Sowerby Hall, Near Leeds, Yorkshire

From Her Majesty's master of the house-hold

Dear Miss Barton:

We are in receipt of your application for the position of under-cook at Buckingham Palace. The references you submitted are most satisfactory. Please present yourself at the palace on September 25th for an interview, and should you prove in every

*way suitable, we will be happy to offer
you the position.*

My heart was beating so fast that I couldn't
breathe. My first thought was today was
September 25th. My second was that she would
no longer be needing the position. It would
remain vacant, to be filled by someone else.
I could apply in her stead and impart the news
that she had met with a tragic accident, but that I
was equally qualified to do the job. But then, of
course, I realized that, unlike Helen Barton, I had
no satisfactory references. That was when the
preposterous idea came into my head. I would
present myself as Helen Barton. She was from
Yorkshire, after all. Nobody here would know
her.

As I kept walking down Piccadilly in the direction of Buckingham Palace, the enormity of what
I was proposing threatened to overwhelm me.
Did I dare to do this? And I heard my father's
voice: "Carpe diem, Isabella." It was indeed my
one chance to escape from my present drudgery,
and I couldn't let it slip away. And it was almost
as if Helen Barton had wanted me to have it. She
had begged me to take the envelope. Was this my
one gift from heaven, to make up for all that I
had suffered?

When I reached the edge of Green Park, I sat
on a bench, feeling the warm September sunshine

on my face, and went through the ramifications. I was not hurting anybody. I was not depriving anybody of a job. In fact I'd be doing the palace a good turn because they would not have to advertise again for the position. And I knew I was a good cook.

I stared down at the letter in my hand, and it dawned on me that this might be the only means of identifying Helen Barton. She might have had a handbag with her, but it may not have contained her address. Without this letter, her dear ones would not know she was dead. She would be buried in a pauper's grave. I couldn't let that happen, however much I wanted the job. "Stay calm, Bella," I told myself. "There must be a way." I thought it through logically. I would write to Sowerby Hall and inform them that I had witnessed the tragic death of Miss Barton. I would only sign the letter *A well-wisher.* At least her nearest and dearest would know where to apply for her body if they desired. However, I suspected she would not have any close relatives in Yorkshire. After all, she had been planning to move to London, and she would not have done that if she had an aging mother or a sweetheart living nearby. I told myself that she was probably an orphan. And her employer obviously knew she was applying for this position as she had provided a reference. I made up my mind. In spite of all the risks, I was going to do it. I was going to seize the day, just as my father had told me.

I tucked the stray wisps of hair under my hat and realized that I now had rouge on my cheeks. That would never do! I took out my handkerchief and scrubbed at my face until, I hoped, every trace had been removed. I wished I had a looking glass in my handbag. I crossed Green Park and came out to the Mall, and there was Buckingham Palace ahead of me. My heart started racing again. If I was found to be an imposter, if I was caught trying to deceive the queen, did that count as treason? Did they still behead people in the Tower? I hesitated, looking at that imposing facade and the tall wrought iron gates. Did I really dare to go through with this?

Then it was almost as if I could hear my father's voice. "What have you got to lose, Bella?"

That's right, I thought. How would they ever find out I was not Helen Barton? She was from a house in the wilds of Yorkshire and presumably knew nobody in London. The queen required a cook, and I was good. The palace would be happy with me. Having bucked myself up in this way, I strode out, then hesitated again as I approached those imposing gates with the sentries standing in front of their boxes. Surely a servant would not enter in such a grand manner? Even Mrs Tilley in St John's Wood had a servants' entrance. It must be off to one side, in a discreet place, but where? I sidled up to one of the sentries.

"Excuse me, but could you direct me to the servants' entrance?" I whispered. "I'm here for an interview."

His gaze did not falter. He continued to stare straight ahead of him, and his mouth didn't move either, but between his lips he muttered, "Off to your left, miss. Door in the wall."

I thanked him and saw the ghost of a smile twitch at his lips. Off I went, past the front of the palace and around to the side, where a tall brick wall ran around what was presumably the palace grounds. And there in the wall was the small, almost invisible door. I opened it and was met by another guard.

"Miss Barton to see the master of the household in regard to the post of under-cook," I said in my most efficient-sounding voice. As I said it, an awful thought struck me. What if Helen Barton had already had her interview and was on her way home when the accident occurred? What if the master of the household informed me that he had already conducted the interview and demanded to know who in heaven's name I was?

Again it was a risk to be taken. If she had already had her interview, why was the letter still clutched in her hand? No, she had to have been on her way to the palace! At least the guard at the side gate didn't react in any way. He escorted me down a narrow path to an ordinary-looking door in a brick wall. He rang a bell. A young man appeared—a footman, I supposed, although he was not dressed in splendid livery but in a white shirt and black trousers.

"This young lady to see the master about a job interview," the guard said.

I held out the letter for him to scrutinize.

"Follow me, please, miss," the footman said. At least he hadn't looked at me in surprise and commented that I was the second young lady to present herself for the position that afternoon, which must mean that Helen Barton had been on her way to the palace. I think I let out a little sigh of relief. Along a plain white plastered hallway and up a flight of wooden steps we went, then into a slightly larger corridor. The footman tapped on a door.

"Enter," came a deep voice from within.

"A Miss Barton to see you, Master," the footman said.

"Send her in," said the deep voice.

My heart was racing. I took a deep breath to calm myself and stepped into the room. It was not fancy, just a big mahogany desk, bookshelves and a window looking out on to the garden. The man at the desk had impressive grey whiskers and deep frown lines on his forehead. He wore a military uniform with lots of braid and was clearly the sort who expected to be obeyed with no nonsense.

"Miss Barton." He held out a hand to me.

"I am Colonel Pelham-Clinton, Master of Her Majesty's Household. Good of you to come."

"How do you do? It's good of you to see me, Colonel," I replied, reaching forward to shake his hand.

The frown on his forehead deepened. "I expected a Yorkshire accent," he said. "You are not from that county?"

"Yes, sir," I replied. "My father was an educated man who had fallen upon hard times. I was raised to speak properly." I decided to stick to the truth as much as possible.

He nodded. "And where is your father now?"

"He died. Both my parents died when I was a child. That was why I had to go into service. I no longer have anybody."

"I see." He nodded again. "You have the nice red cheeks of a girl from the countryside. I'm afraid you'll soon lose those in the smoky air of the city."

I tried not to smile as I realized that the red cheeks were a result of my scrubbing off the rouge.

"And you're younger than I expected."

"I'm told that I look young for my age," I replied, wondering how old Helen Barton had been. She hadn't looked much older than I—had the advertisement stipulated over twenty-one?

He picked up a paper from his desk. "Your letter of reference is commendable," he said.

"It seems you were prized at Lady Sowerby's."

I was wondering what reason I could come up with for wanting to leave Lady Sowerby when he went on. "The housekeeper says you are honest, sober and willing to learn."

"Yes, sir. I am," I replied, while a voice whispered that I was not being honest at this moment. I almost gave in and confessed to my deception, but he was already continuing. "It seems that Lady Sowerby is of advanced years and is closing up her household to live with her son, is that correct?"

"So I understand, sir," I replied.

"And what made you decide to come all the way to London?"

"There is nothing to hold me in Yorkshire, and who wouldn't want to jump at the chance to serve Her Majesty?" I said.

He actually smiled. "I think you will do well here, Miss Barton, but first I have to introduce you to our maître de cuisine, Mr Angelo Romano. He is most particular about who works under him, down to the lowliest scullery maid. Allow me to escort you to the kitchens."

We went down the stairs, along a tiled hallway this time, and opened a swing door on to a vast kitchen. I think I swallowed back a gasp. All along one wall, rows of gleaming copper pots hung on hooks, in ascending size from one pint to several gallons. Beneath them was a row of stoves on which stew pots were bubbling, sending out an enticing aroma of herbs. I noted that the stoves were mostly modern gas burners, with a couple of old-fashioned coal-fired ranges for good measure. Around the room, scrubbed pine tables were arranged, and at each of these cooks were at work. A whole army of cooks, it seemed, dressed all in white, some in tall hats, others in caps, and all busy chopping piles of vegetables or mixing things in bowls. Actually, as I examined them more closely, I noticed nearly all of them were male. Only a couple of older women amongst them. No other young girls.

The master hesitated at the door. "Mr Angelo, might you be free for a moment?" he asked.

A man with a curled black moustache and a most superior expression came over to us. He wore an immaculate uniform and a toque on his head. From the way he walked, I could tell he thought a lot of himself. "What is it, Master? As you can see, we're up to our eyes at the moment."

I had expected an Italian accent, but he sounded like any other Londoner.

"This young lady has applied to be an under-cook," the master said. "Her references seem satisfactory, and she has a pleasant manner, but of course the final say is up to you."

Black Moustache was looking me up and down as if I were an unsavoury piece of meat. "You know my feelings about having a young woman in the kitchen."

"I do, but we also know Her Majesty's sentiments, don't we? And it is not up to us to dispute the wishes of our employer."

Black Moustache hadn't taken his eyes off me for a second. "So what cooking experience do you have, young woman?" he asked.

"Only plain English cooking, sir," I replied. "And of course I've only been allowed to assist, not compose the dishes myself. But I am familiar with most cooking methods."

"You have experience with game? Her Majesty is most fond of game."

"I've worked with pheasant, sir. And squab."

"And sauces?"

"I can make a smooth white sauce, sir, and a brown sauce . . ."

"White sauce?" He was looking down his nose at me. "To what kind of white sauce are you referring? Velouté? Béchamel? Supreme? Pascaline? Ravigote?"

"I'm afraid that I am not familiar with foreign terms. The cook who taught me was adamant that English food was as good as any and she wasn't going to cook any 'foreign muck,' as she called it."

As I said the words, I wished I could un-say them. Angelo was obviously an Italian name, although I detected no trace of an accent in his speech. Actually, I thought I detected a hint of cockney, and there was certainly a smile at the corners of his lips.

"I think I might be inclined to agree with you. Nothing is superior to a first-class joint of roast beef and Yorkshire pudding, but Her Majesty likes her food to be fancy. Not necessarily foreign, but pleasing and tantalizing to the eye, as well as good to taste. Some of our dishes take all day to prepare." He paused, and sucked through his teeth for a long moment before he asked, "What would you say was your forte?"

"I'm told I have a light hand with pastry, sir."

"We have Mr Roland, who is our pastry chef and takes care of the items for the queen's tea and any pastry items on the pudding menu. Her Majesty is very fond of her tea—and the cakes and scones that go with it. Never misses her tea, no matter where she is or what she is doing. But you may be called upon to make a meat pie for the servants' dining room."

"Oh yes, sir. I can make a good meat pie."

"That remains to be seen," he said, "but I can tell you're willing and eager to learn, and you've a nice manner to you, so I think we'll give you a trial. When can you start?"

"Since my employer is closing down her household, I could start as early as next week, if that's convenient, sir."

"Splendid," he said. "You understand that

this will not be glamorous work, don't you? Occasionally we have to cater for state banquets, and then it's fancy food and all hands on deck. But most of the time you'll be chopping vegetables and preparing meals for the staff, and you will be at the bottom rung of our ladder here. You will take orders from me and from the other cooks who are older and wiser than you."

"I understand that, sir."

He gave me a brief smile and a nod. "I'll hand her back to you, Master. I have six pheasants waiting to be boned."

I followed the master of the household back to his office.

"Mr Angelo is a firm taskmaster, you will find. He expects hard work and perfection all the time." He turned back to address me. "But you could not learn more from any chef in the country."

"He is from Italy?" I asked. "He doesn't seem to have a foreign accent."

"No, as English as you or I. London born and bred. His ancestors came from that country, several generations ago. Her Majesty selected him because she had previously had another chef with an Italian last name, of whom she was very fond. And that has given her the impression that all Italians are good cooks."

He opened the door to his office and ushered me inside, waiting until he had taken up position at his desk before addressing me again. "Your starting wage will be fifteen shillings a week, all found," he said. "You will be provided with your uniform and laundry service, as well as your board and lodging." He looked up, waiting for me to say something.

"Thank you, sir. That sounds most satisfactory," I said, although in truth it wasn't much more than I had been making at Mrs Tilley's. But the thought struck me that at least the money would now be my own, not going to my father and sister. I'd be able to save for my future, with precious little to spend it on.

"And you will be required to sign documents of confidentiality, Miss Barton. Nothing that happens inside these walls is to be discussed with anyone, not even your closest friends. Nothing is to be removed from the palace, not even extra food. Is that clear?"

I nodded. "Yes, Master."

"And walking out with a young man is frowned upon."

"I have no young man, sir," I said, "but I couldn't help noticing that there are no other young women in the kitchen."

"That is correct. Until recently, Her Majesty's kitchen was nearly exclusively composed of male chefs. But Her Majesty is also forward-looking. She feels that, with the new century approaching, we should create more opportunities for young women—since she herself has proved what a young woman can achieve, given the chance."

I wanted to say that not many of us have the chance to inherit a monarchy, but stayed wisely silent.

He went on, "I have to confess that I do not share her enthusiasm. In my experience, it is a waste of training to take on young women as they have a habit of going off and getting married."

"I have no intention of doing that for a long while, sir. I am passionate about becoming a better cook."

He actually nodded with approval. "Splendid. I can see we chose well. Then if you'll just sign here . . ." He produced a document, a pen and inkwell. I dipped, prayed it wouldn't blot and hesitated before I remembered to sign *Helen Barton.*

Then he held out his hand. "Welcome to Her Majesty's service, Miss Barton."

CHAPTER 3

I came out of there in a daze. I started to walk across St James's Park. Faster and faster I walked, while my mind tried to come to terms with what had just happened. I had been raised by my mother to be truthful and to always behave in a way that brought credit to my family. And yet I had just obtained a position by lying. Could I live with myself?

Then I was reminded that my family hadn't exactly done much for me. My father had sold me into near slavery, humiliated me in the worst possible way. My sister would not make use of the precious education she had been given, thanks to my back-breaking work. I owed nothing to nobody. I was a free woman, taking my life into my own hands for the first time. I was now an under-cook at Buckingham Palace. My future looked bright. I'd work hard, and maybe after a year or so, I'd have enough saved up to go to America, where I would be hired immediately as someone who had cooked for royalty. Or I'd even open my own restaurant one day. The possibilities seemed endless. Perhaps I really had been born with my father's optimism after all. It was just that those four years with Mrs Tilley had almost crushed it.

As soon as I reached Mrs Tilley's house, I rushed up to my room, took out my writing paper, pen and inkwell, and began to write the letter to Sowerby Hall. I had composed it many times in my mind on the Underground journey home.

To whom it may concern:

I am sorry to inform you that I witnessed a tragic accident in London this afternoon. A young woman was struck and killed by a speeding omnibus. I helped to gather her possessions from the street and found an envelope, addressed to a Miss Helen Barton. So I can only conclude that this is the woman's name. I thought I should write to you in case the London police do not see fit to inform you of her death, and she has any next of kin who would want to know of her fate . . .

Then I added, *I have also informed the master of the household at Buckingham Palace of her tragic death.* That should surely stop anyone in Yorkshire from having a need to contact the palace. I signed it, *A well-wisher.* I put it into an envelope, licked it shut and I went out again, straight to the nearest pillar box, where I posted it. I was still feeling most unsettled when I came back and could hardly eat a morsel of the delicious rabbit pie that Cook had prepared.

"Stuffed yourself with tea at a café, I've no doubt," Cook commented, and I didn't refute this. I went up to my room as soon as I had helped clear away supper and stood, staring out of my attic window at the skyline of chimney pots. I still couldn't quite believe what I had done. All I knew was that I would finally be able to escape.

It was with great satisfaction that I presented myself to Mrs Tilley the next morning and told her that I would be leaving at the end of the week. Her plucked eyebrows rose in astonishment.

"Going? Walking out on me after all I've done for you?"

"That's right." I didn't say, "Yes, ma'am."

"But where do you think you're going? What person of quality would take you on without a reference, I'd like to know?"

I would love to have told her that I'd be working at the palace. I so wanted to tell her that, but I knew that the spiteful old witch would be likely to write to the palace with false complaints about me. So I had come up with a perfect excuse on the Underground ride home.

"I won't need to work any longer," I said. "My sister is about to marry well, and I've been invited to go and live with her husband's family."

This was partly true. Louisa had invited me

to live with them. The offer was still open. It's just that I had declined it. Maybe the second falsehood is not as hard as the first. I saw Mrs Tilley blink a couple of times. Then she said, "Well, lucky for some, isn't it? And since you've fallen on your feet, I don't suppose you'll be needing your last pay packet, will you?"

"I most certainly will expect to be paid money I've earned," I said, "and I'm sure my sister's husband will want to make sure that I get what's due to me. His family is not without influence, you know."

Those piggy little eyes blinked rapidly again. She got up and strode over to her purse. "Take it and get out. Ungrateful girl," she said and flung the coins at me. I wanted to be dignified enough not to pick them up, but I bent and retrieved them before making my exit. I found that I was shaking and had to have a glass of water in the kitchen. I couldn't wait for the end of the week.

My next task was to meet with my sister. She wanted to close up the flat, dispose of the contents and move in with her future in-laws. We stood together in that damp and depressing living room while slanted evening sunlight shone on the threadbare rug through grimy windows.

"Oh, Sissy, I feel so badly for you," she said. "I will be leading a life of happiness and luxury while you are still slaving away for that monster. Will you not change your mind and come to live with us?" She took my hand. "You could resume your studies. You always were the bright one. You know how much the teachers thought of you."

I have to confess I had been tempted when she had brought this up before. But I wasn't about to be beholden to anyone. And I had come to realize I had a passion for cooking. So I had to invent another lie—only a half-truth this time.

"You are very sweet," I said, "but I've managed to find a better job, away from that awful household."

"You have? That's good news. Where is it?"

"I can't tell you where it is yet."

"You can't tell me where it is?" Her sweet face clouded over. "Bella, is it somewhere shady? You are not becoming a dance hall girl, are you? Or even worse?"

I had to laugh at the thought of me becoming a lady of the night. "No, no. It's quite respectable, I promise you."

"Then why can't you tell me?"

I frowned. Should I just lie to her and say that I was going abroad? But then I'd never see her again, and she was the only family I had. I'd have to think this one out and come up with a way I could explain that I was now Helen Barton.

"We haven't quite sorted out the details of my position yet," I said.

She squeezed my hands. "You won't go too far

away, will you? I'll miss you so much. You are my only relative in the world."

"Don't worry. I will come to visit you on my days off." I smiled at the worried frown on her face and realized that perhaps she might be having some reservations about marrying and moving in with a strange family. "And when you have children, I'll be an adoring aunt."

The worried look deepened. "I'm not so sure about that side of things." Her voice dropped to a whisper. "One hears such awful rumours. I have let Billy kiss me, and that was actually rather nice, but beyond that . . ."

"I know little more than you, I'm afraid," I confessed. "But I'm sure you'll come to enjoy it with someone you love. Mother and Father were in love all their lives until he broke her heart, weren't they?"

"But what about childbirth?" She was still whispering, even though we were alone. "Women die all the time, don't they?"

"You're a strong and healthy girl, Louisa," I said. "And you are marrying a rich man who can afford the best doctors."

She gave me a hopeful little smile. "I hope you find someone who will love you soon, Sissy. I want so much for you to be happy."

"That would be nice," I said. "But in the meantime, I am going to enjoy the challenges of my new position."

"Is it far from London? You said you'll be able to visit . . ."

"Don't worry. I'll be close by, and I'll let you know as soon as I have an address you can write to."

Fortunately, she dropped the subject, and we went around the flat, Louisa deciding if she wanted to take my father's few remaining good pieces of furniture with her. There was an inlaid writing desk he had had made in India for my mother and had refused to part with. I told Louisa to take it. The rest of the items would be sold.

"Please keep all the money. I shall be well provided for," she said.

I shook my head. "No, you take the money for your wedding dress. We do not need to be beholden to Billy's family for everything. I shall be earning a good wage."

A smile flashed across her face, making me realize how very young she still was. "All right. I was worrying a little about my dress. And we shall choose yours as my maid of honour. Peacock blue, don't you think? It would look so startling with your red hair."

We held hands and gazed at each other, both realizing that nothing in our lives would ever be the same again. Before we parted, I was formally introduced to her intended—a pleasant enough young man I had seen coming and going from his father's shop, and clearly smitten with my sister, but of a manner and speech that my parents would not have considered suitable as a prospect for a son-in-law. On the way home, I tried to examine my feelings. How could I afford this snobbish judgement of my sister's future husband when I was a servant? I was lower down the social scale than he, and yet my father had ingrained into us the belief that we belonged in the rarefied air of aristocrats. Would I have to accept that a lower-class husband was my lot someday? Louisa didn't seem to notice his London accent or lack of vocabulary. And she was happy. That was all that mattered, I told myself firmly.

On Saturday morning, a man came with a cart to take away the last remnants of my former home. They were sold, and on Monday morning, I moved into the palace. That sounds like a very grand thing to say. The reality was not quite as glamorous as this sounds. I was assigned a room of my own on the top floor. Quite spartan, decidedly chilly, with a narrow iron-framed bed, a white painted chest of drawers with a mirror over it and two hooks on the wall to hang up clothes, but at least I would have some privacy. I was fitted for my all-white uniform, a blouse and skirt with a big apron to cover me, and a pillbox hat under which all my hair had to be hidden. I was told firmly that the apron was to be changed the moment there was any stain on it. I was always to look immaculate, in case Her Majesty or one of her higher officials chose to pay a visit to the kitchens. I stood looking at myself in the mirror, a ghostlike apparition in my white uniform, and gave myself a brave little smile. "It's going to be all right," I said to myself. "I'm Helen Barton, and I'm a jolly good cook."

"Ah, the new girl's here." Mr Angelo looked up as I entered the kitchen. "Good news, as we've just had a luncheon sprung on us. Her Majesty's daughter Princess Helena and her granddaughter Princess Thora are visiting. Here's the menu: consommé aux fines herbes, cheese croutons, poached fillet of sole with parsley sauce and potatoes à la crème, puree of squab à la chasseur, creamed celery, pork chops with apples, red cabbage and duchesse potatoes, iced pudding à la Prince Albert, canary pudding with vanilla sauce, anchovy toast. Mr Francis, you'll take the fish course, Mr Roland the puddings, I'll handle the squab and pork chops and Mrs Simms, you'll be on consommé. I'll add the new girl to your team for now. What was your name again, my dear?"

"It's B—it's Helen, sir." My heart was thumping. I'd almost committed my first faux pas.

"Well, Helen, you call me Cook, not sir. I am officially maître de cuisine, but that's a mouthful, isn't it? Simple Cook will suffice. Everyone else you address as 'Cook'—apart from those apprentices. Is that clear?"

"Yes, Cook."

He nodded. "Off you go. Table by the window. And chop-chop, everybody. We don't have that much time."

I went to the station I was assigned. "You can cut the veg," Mrs Simms said. She was a round, comfortable-looking woman who didn't look nearly as fearsome as the men in the kitchen—who all had a most superior look to them and seemed to be regarding me with displeasure if not outright loathing. "Make sure you peel them well. No scraps of skin left on those carrots."

She pointed to several baskets full of various vegetables.

"How many do we need?" I asked.

"Enough to serve eight," she replied. "They're only for garnish in the soup, and Her Majesty isn't that keen on her clear soups anyway, so it will probably all come back."

I took a deep breath and selected some carrots, a turnip, a bunch of parsley. I checked the other baskets. "I don't see any onions," I said.

Mrs Simms frowned. "Her Majesty does not use anything that could make her breath smell," she said. "No onions, no garlic, no foreign spices."

"I see." I went to work peeling the carrots, then started to chop them.

"Don't do that," a voice whispered in my ear. I turned to see a tall, lanky boy with hair even

49

brighter red than my own standing right beside me. He had the sharp features and cheeky expression of a typical cockney. "We always julienne the veg for soups."

"Oh, thank you." I gave him a tentative smile. I wasn't really sure what "julienne" meant. Mrs Tilley's cook never used foreign terms. The boy must have seen my hesitation because he took a carrot and sliced it longways into tiny, even slivers. "This is how they like it here."

The smile was truly grateful this time. I nodded and got to work.

"I'm Nelson," he said. "Nelson Biggs."

He paused, all the while still cutting slices of bread into cubes. "Did you say your name was Helen?"

I nodded, wondering how I could ask them to call me Bella instead. "Welcome to the kitchen then, Helen. You'll find Mr Angelo runs a tight ship here. Ever so picky, he is, and quite temperamental, too." He had lowered his voice for this last phrase. "But on the whole the work's not too demanding, unless we have a big state banquet, then it's crazy. And we eat well, let me tell you that. This skinny body is not a result of undernourishment." And he grinned.

"This certainly is a large amount of food for a luncheon," I said. "All these courses. Does Her Majesty not take a proper dinner? Is this her main meal?"

"On the contrary," he replied. "The dinner is even more courses. Her Majesty likes to eat. You'll soon notice that. And if you actually catch a glimpse of her one day, then you'll see where all that food goes."

"Enough of your comments, young man," came Mrs Simms's voice from the other side of the table. "It's not up to you to judge what Her Majesty does or doesn't do. If she likes her food, I say good health to her. There's precious little else left in her life to give her pleasure." She wagged a chubby finger at us. "Now more work and less talk over there, or we'll be running behind. And you're setting our new girl a bad example."

Nelson winked at me as we went back to work. It felt so much better to have an ally, and by the end of the morning, Mrs Simms had found nothing to complain about in my work. In fact, she said, "I'm sure you're going to do just fine here, my girl."

"I feel rather strange amongst so many men," I whispered to her. "Did you also start here as a young woman?"

"Oh no, dearie," she said. "I only came here a few years ago. Her Majesty was visiting Lady Malmesbury's, where I was cook, and she expressed great satisfaction with the food that was served. Of course, Lady Malmesbury had no alternative but to offer my services to the queen, who readily accepted. Although funnily enough, when I got here, I was relegated to working under the men, and only allowed to do the simpler of the dishes."

"Do you miss your former place of employment?" I asked.

"I do, sometimes. I'm a country girl, like you, and I feel hemmed in in the big city, but the likes of us don't have much say over what happens, do we? I have to admit it's a pleasant enough atmosphere most of the time, and the work's not too hard—although I must say it's nice having a young woman to chat with. The men keep to themselves, and Mrs Gillespie's not exactly a little ray of sunshine."

I glanced over at a far table where the grim-faced woman was chopping celery sticks with the violence of an executioner.

As I was taking off my apron, Mr Angelo came up to me. "If you want to know what it takes to become a proper cook in this establishment, I suggest you study some of our cookery books on that shelf during your spare time. You can start with the one written by my fellow countryman, Charles Francatelli. He was chef to the queen and Prince Albert and invented many of the dishes that have become her favourite. Take it and start making notes. You can begin with your white sauces."

"Yes, Cook," I murmured and went to retrieve the heavy tome from the shelf. After our supper,

I sat under the electric light in our common room and started to read. Oh heavens above! I had thought, in my ignorance, that I had become quite a fair cook. Now I realized how much I had to learn. I thumbed through page after page: over fourteen hundred recipes, many involving things I had never heard of, and so complex, so complicated.

Page after page of sauces. Page after page of soups. Bisque of snipe à la bonne bouche. Bisque of crab à la Fitzhardinge, which included adding a pint of boiling cream. Puree of asparagus à la St George involved three dozen small quenelles of fowl and half a pint of small fillets of red tongue. Mercy me.

I flicked on. What on earth was ragout of cock's kernels à la soubise, or ragout of ox palates? At the Tilleys' residence, we rarely ate offal. Mr Tilley was fond of liver and bacon, but Mrs Tilley saw offal as food of the lower classes, for those who could afford nothing better. So our meals were good old-fashioned roast beef, leg of lamb, chops and steaks, with the occasional steak and kidney pie. These recipes looked horribly complicated: *Put about half a pound of cock's kernels, with cold water, into a stewpan, let it stand by the side of a slow fire to remove the little blood they contain, taking care that the water does not become too warm.*

I read on. *As soon as they whiten . . . pat of*

butter . . . simmer . . . drain them on a napkin . . . small stewpan, with a ragout-spoonful of Soubise sauce and a little Allemande sauce . . .

Good heavens. I looked up from my book. The rest of the cooks were sitting around the common room, reading the newspaper or writing letters. How had they learned to master all these dishes, I wondered. Who had instructed them, or had they learned from observing? I couldn't imagine any of those superior-looking men taking the time to tell me how to make a soubise sauce. I went back to the book, feeling more overwhelmed with every page. The recipe for turtle soup began with procuring a 120-pound live turtle and then included three pages of instructions on how to kill and de-shell it. I certainly hoped I'd never have to do that. I didn't think I'd be good about killing things. I'd even been squeamish about dropping lobsters into boiling water.

How would I ever learn all this?

Little by little, I told myself. I was an under-cook. I would learn as I observed. If the others in the kitchen could cook all these dishes, then so would I.

CHAPTER 4

By the end of the next day, I had started to breathe a little easier. I had handled all the tasks given to me and had even received a couple of small compliments—on the smoothness of my gravy and mashed potatoes, for instance. But there had been precarious moments. The first was when Mrs Simms asked me to pass her a cup of flour. At least what she had said was, "Helen, get me a cup of flour."

I had been mashing potatoes and didn't react.

"Helen!" she said sharply now. "Wake up, girl. A cup of flour."

Nelson, working beside me, gave me a little nudge. I looked up, my cheeks flaming, and realized she had been talking to me. "Oh, so sorry," I said and rushed to get it.

"What were you daydreaming about?" Mrs Simms said as she took the cup from me. "Some young man, no doubt."

"Oh no, Cook," I said. "I was concentrating on getting all the lumps out of these potatoes."

"Well, you do do a good job on the spuds, I have to give you that," she said.

I went back to my work, cringing with

embarrassment. The problem was I hadn't realized she had been talking to me. I had to learn to answer to my new name, rather like a dog who goes to a new home. Then, a little later that day, Mrs Simms asked me about Yorkshire, where her sister now lived.

"Where exactly is this Sowerby Hall?" she asked. "I went to visit my sister once. She lives in Filey. Nice little seaside town, but oh so cold with that east wind off the sea."

I remembered the address was near Leeds and told her. "Oh, that's a good way away, isn't it? Up near the moors."

"That's right," I said. "And equally bleak when the wind blows."

"I'd imagine it would be." She gave me a commiserating smile. "And snow in winter, no doubt."

"Lots of snow."

"I don't like the cold weather myself," she said. "Bad for my chilblains. In fact, I'm glad we don't ever go to Balmoral in the winter. Osborne House is where the queen usually spends Christmas, and that's on the Isle of Wight. Nice, pleasant climate there."

I was just taking in the implications of this. "Do we travel with the queen when she goes to her different palaces?"

"Some of us do. She takes a pared-down staff with her because there is usually not much entertaining to be done at Osborne. It's strictly family there. And Balmoral, well, she uses local servants mainly. She takes Mr Angelo and a couple of others with her because he knows what she likes to eat."

"And what happens to the rest of us when she's away?" I asked.

Mrs Simms nudged me. "When the cat's away, the mice will play, eh?" Then she corrected herself. "Not that we're allowed any high jinks, mind you, but we have a nice, easy time of it. We feed the remaining staff, we experiment with new dishes the queen might like. We take our own dinner early and put our feet up. Mr Williams plays the piano if he's with us, and we have a sing-along sometimes. Or one of us reads to the rest. It's quite pleasant."

In my narrow bed that night, I wondered how I might persuade them to call me by my real name. I dared to mention it to Mrs Simms when we were working together cutting up stewing steak for a meat pie. "You don't think it would be possible to call me by my pet name that I was called at home, do you?"

She looked up, the cleaver still in her hand. "Your pet name? What was it?"

"Bella," I said, blushing now.

"Bella? That's hardly a name for a servant, is it? How long ago were you called this? Surely not at Lady what's-her-name's?"

"Oh no. Not at Lady Sowerby's," I said quickly. "I just always liked Bella better than Helen. Helen's such a harsh name, don't you think?"

She sniffed. "We can't choose what name we were christened with, can we? My own is Mildred, which I confess I'm not fond of either. But I'm afraid you're stuck with Helen, my dear, until you become a cook like me, and then you can call yourself Mrs Barton."

So I had to put any notion of being called Isabella aside and simply train myself to become Helen. After a few days, I had learned to answer to my new name. Other than that worry, the work was not arduous. If we were not on breakfast duty, we rose at seven thirty, and our breakfast was served at eight. It was porridge and bread and jam, sometimes with scrambled eggs or bacon. I was assigned basic tasks, all of which I could handle with ease—apart from a blunder with an artichoke. I had never seen one before and did not realize I should have snipped off the sharp spikes before serving. Luckily my mistake was caught before I poked the queen's eye out!

The tasks I was assigned were well within my capabilities, but I couldn't help gazing in awe at some of the dishes that were being composed around the kitchen. Something that looked like a pineapple on a fine crystal dish turned out to be a salmis of partridges in aspic. It was an absolute work of art.

Mr Angelo usually made the most complicated dishes himself. I spotted him working at a table that was full of tiny bones.

"What is Cook making?" I whispered to Mrs Simms.

She glanced across at his table. "Oh, he's making a lark pie," she said and went back to trimming her beef.

"Lark pie? You mean larks? Little birds?"

My mind went back to a day on Hampstead Heath with my father, when he had paused, a look of rapture on his face, and pointed at the sky. "Listen," he said. "A lark is singing."

"That's right," Mrs Simms said, as if this was an ordinary matter for discussion. "Forty Dunstable larks are needed for that pie, and they all have to be boned first. I'm glad it's Mr Angelo doing it and not me. There is hell to pay if one of the royal guests finds a bone."

"I had no idea they made pies of little birds," I said.

Mrs Simms grinned. "Oh yes. The queen's very fond of her larks. Sometimes it's blackbirds, too."

"You mean like four and twenty blackbirds baked in a pie?" I was astonished.

"They say they're quite tasty, but you can only eat them in the winter months for some reason. And, of course, they line the pie with a layer of beef scallops, and that makes anything taste good."

She went back to her work while I digested that I'd one day have to learn to bone little birds if I wanted to call myself a master cook. This made me pause. Would I ever rise through the ranks in this kitchen where men clearly ruled the roost? Did I want to be one?

One step at a time, I decided. At this moment, I was happy learning my trade.

For that first week, I would not have guessed that I was working in a palace. Every morning we walked down uncarpeted back stairs to the kitchen and worked in our own little universe. Light came in through high windows, but we saw only sky, only the slightest hint of the weather outside. Every morning we heard marching feet and barked commands, and sometimes sounds of a brass band as guards marched on their way to the forecourt. But that was our only hint that we were not in an ordinary house. We certainly saw no royal persons. If we stepped outside the palace, it was through the plain little gate on to Buckingham Palace Road. But the weather had turned inclement, and during the hour we had off after serving luncheon, I had no wish to go into the outside world. In fact, I only went out once during the week, and that was to find the nearest post office, near Victoria Station, where I arranged to have any letters held in their poste restante. Now at least Louisa would have a way of contacting me.

By the end of that week, I had almost worked out who was who in the kitchen. The maître de cuisine was Mr Angelo, the cockney Italian. Under him were Mr Francis and Mr Roland, the pastry chef. They were considered master cooks. Mr Francis was an older man, with bristling grey eyebrows and a perpetual scowl. Mr Roland was French, and highly strung, I was told. Then there were four that were known as "yeoman cooks": Mr Phelps, Mr Williams, Mr O'Rourke and Mr Fitch. Four men of indeterminate age, clean-shaven, pasty-faced. It was hard at this stage to know which was which, as none of them seemed to acknowledge my presence. The only females were two older cooks: Mrs Simms and Mrs Gillespie. I couldn't tell whether they were above or below the yeomen in rank. They certainly weren't allotted the more complicated dishes. Nelson was an under-cook like myself. Then there were three apprentices, Arthur, Jimmy and Fred, all lanky and cheerful chaps about my age.

There were also three kitchens and a scullery where two scullery servants, a man and a girl called Ruby, did things like peel potatoes and wash pots. Most of us worked in the main kitchen. This had both coal and gas stoves, a spit for roasting and a charcoal burner for finishing, so it was always rather warm. On one of the stoves was a giant stockpot, and all the bits and pieces went into it. I was told it had been going non-stop for twenty years!

Mr Roland had his own smaller kitchen for cakes and pastry, and there was a funny old Monsieur du Jardin, who was the confectioner in his own kitchen. I understood he had been in the palace since the queen was young and was famous for his works of art with chocolate, but his primary job was to make the ices the queen so adored.

As well as the queen's intimate circle, we also had to cook for the members of her household—the various secretaries, gentlemen-at-arms and ladies-in-waiting who ate in their own dining room, and finally the servants who ate in the cavernous, draughty servants' dining hall. This meant essentially preparing three meals, although the members of the household sometimes shared what the queen was eating. For the rest of us, it was plain and simple food in the extreme: a thick soup, a meat pie or pudding, macaroni and cheese, toad-in-the-hole—anything that made use of leftovers and cuts of meat that could not be served to royal persons. Mrs Gillespie was in charge of this and was very creative in what to do with the parts that nobody wanted.

At mealtimes we had to serve the other ser-vants—footmen who took off their livery before they came to the table, maids of various ranks, and others who held strange and wonderful positions: master of the boots, mistress of linens and others that were not clear. For the most part, these latter ignored us. We were lowly kitchen staff. Rank was all-important. We had to serve them in order of precedence, and we were not allowed to eat until they had been served. One particular woman, grander than the rest, came in one day and sat apart at one end of the table. As I served her a helping of stew, she looked up at me. "You're new here," she said.

"Yes, ma'am," I replied.

She smiled then. "You don't need to call me ma'am. I'm a servant here, like you. Only a few rungs up the ladder. I'm Her Majesty's personal maid and dresser. You call me Miss McDonald. I usually take my meals apart, but Her Majesty had a fitting for a new gown all morning. It took longer than expected." She examined me. "You're a pretty little thing, with a nice manner to you. You should go far, only watch yourself. There are those who are lured by a pretty face and a slim ankle like yours. And you're not exactly in a position to say no."

I glanced around the room, wondering to whom she might be referring. And when I was back in my bedroom that evening, I examined myself in the mirror. "A pretty little thing," she had called me. I had always thought of myself as the scrawny, skinny girl I once was. The idea that anyone might find me attractive was new to me.

Mrs Tilley's staff had been nearly exclusively female, apart from the gardeners, the groom and the coachman, who were older and paid me no attention. Now I saw that I might have good bone structure. And wide green eyes. And I knew that Nelson was showing interest. Maybe there was hope for my future.

CHAPTER 5

On Sunday afternoon, I went to visit my sister at the home of her future in-laws. I wouldn't describe this as an ordinary house either. A great monstrosity—that's what my father would have called it! It was a red brick replica of a medieval castle, complete with leaded windows, curly chimneys and a turret in one corner. Inside there were more knick-knacks and aspidistras than at Mrs Tilley's, and swags and swathes of red velvet. But Louisa seemed happy enough; Billy's parents seemed to have made their future daughter-in-law very welcome. I got the impression that Billy's mother considered her quite a catch. She would no doubt love introducing Louisa to her friends— her dear new daughter, related to aristocracy, no less. She also seemed to take to me, making me sit beside her and taking my hand.

"So, my dear, do you have a young man? Any wedding bells on your horizon?"

I shook my head. "I'm afraid not."

"It's not right that the younger sister marries before the older," Billy's mother said. "We'll have to do something about that, won't we?" She glanced across at her husband. "Bert, get your thinking cap on. Who do we know with a young, unmarried son—a nice eligible boy, mind you?"

"Off the top of my head, I can't think of no one," Bert said, "but I'll put my mind to it, like you say."

"Oh really, that's not necessary," I said hastily. "I'm making my own way in the world just fine."

"And what is it that you do, young woman?" Bert asked me. "Louisa said you was working as a house servant. That's no life for a nicely raised girl like you."

"Now I'm working as a cook," I said. "And I really enjoy cooking. I hope to become a head cook someday."

"Louisa says you used to be smart with your books, when you were both in school."

"I was," I agreed.

"So you should be thinking of a way to better yourself. Not cooking for people. But don't you worry. Like the missus said, we'll put our heads together. Come up with a young man with good prospects, eh?" And he gave me a wink.

"Next time you come, we will have a fitting for your dress," Louisa said as she escorted me to the front door. "I can't wait to try on mine. You should see the fabric, Bella. I shall feel like a princess. And yours shall be quite grand, too."

"I'm so happy for you," I said. "I can see they are already fond of you."

"They are, aren't they?" She beamed. "It is so

66

nice to have a mother again. Father was no substitute, was he?"

I gave her the address to which letters could be sent. She frowned when she saw it. "But why to a post office, Bella? I felt so awkward to admit you were a house servant in front of my in-laws, and you won't even tell me where. Are you ashamed of where you are now?"

"Not at all. It's just that . . ." My brain had already worked out another lie, but I couldn't tell it to my sister. "It's simpler this way. Don't worry."

I came back to the palace feeling strangely unsettled. I had a good position. I had a chance to rise in my profession, but apart from that, I had nothing. Nowhere to call home. Nobody who cared whether I lived or died. I put this feeling aside as I joined my fellow cooks in the servants' dining room, around the big fire.

"Been out visiting, have you?" one of them asked.

"Yes, I've just been to see my s—" I started to say "sister," then swallowed it back. Helen couldn't have a sister in London.

"My fellow servant from Lady Sowerby's house who has moved to London," I finished the sentence.

"That's nice for you, having a friend down here," Mrs Simms said. "It can be terrible lonely in a big new city, especially when you're a girl from the countryside in the north like you."

I nodded but wisely said nothing.

"Come and sit down and have some hot chocolate," Nelson called, patting the bench beside him.

"You've made quite an impression on our Nelson," Mrs Simms muttered, giving me a little nudge. "You could do worse."

I helped myself to hot chocolate and sat perched on the bench beside him. Heavens, I hoped I hadn't been leading Nelson on. He was a nice enough lad, but I was afraid that I retained enough of my father's inborn snobbery to want better for myself. Maybe in a year or two, I'd come to terms with my current position in life and be glad to step out with a boy like Nelson. He gave me an encouraging grin. "Quite nippy out there today, wasn't it?"

I nodded, wrapping my hands around the mug of cocoa, feeling the warmth of the fire spreading through me. Enough of snobbish thoughts, I decided. This was my new family. I was welcome here. I was starting to belong.

The next morning I had to run back to my bedroom to retrieve a forgotten handkerchief. While I was there, I glanced out of my window. It was a clear, bright day, and my room looked out to the palace grounds. To my astonishment, I spotted a pony cart. In it sat a round little old woman. On her head she wore a black cap, and a black cape was draped around her shoulders. It dawned on me that this must be the queen. I had seen her picture often enough, and her image on pennies. But even more surprising was the person standing at the pony's head, leading it. He was a swarthy man, dressed in extraordinary oriental garb, a bright-pink silk tunic, green baggy pants and a canary-yellow turban. It was almost the costume of a stage performer, and I wondered what on earth he was doing there, alone with the queen.

Then I remembered that I had dashed upstairs to get my handkerchief and would be in trouble if I didn't return instantly. I ran all the way down those flights of stairs and slipped into my place in the kitchen. But I couldn't put what I had seen out of my mind.

"I've just seen the most extraordinary sight," I muttered to Mrs Simms, who was filleting plaice beside me. "An oriental man in bright colours, leading what I think was the queen around the grounds."

She made a face. "That darned munshi," she said, giving a disparaging sniff.

"Munchy?" I had no idea what the word meant.

"That's what they call him. I think it's what they call Hindustani clerks or language teachers back in his country. Abdul Karim is his name. Her Indian friend," she replied. "Have you not heard about him? He was sent over here as a gift from her subjects in India to be a table servant, but he's wormed his way into her favour. Now he seems to think he's a secretary and acts as if he's above the rest of us. Apparently, he can do no wrong in her eyes." She shook her head. "She always did have her head turned by a handsome young man—although this one is neither particularly young nor handsome, in my opinion. But she was looking for someone to replace John Brown after he died, and this one seized his chances. Now she thinks the sun shines out of his head. He obviously presents one face to her and another to the rest of us."

She glanced around to see if anyone was close enough to overhear, then lowered her voice. "He comes in here, giving orders like he's one of her senior advisers, not a blasted table servant. Tells us how to cook his special food—the cheek of it. Won't touch pork. Wants to know how the animals have been killed. I ask you! Nobody can stand him except for her, and of course she's the only one who counts, isn't she?"

I had an encounter with him myself later that week. I was escaping for a few minutes of solitude after we had finished clearing up the luncheon. I had taken down the famous cookery book again from its shelf and was planning a few moments of note taking. I had moved beyond sauces and on to soups. I had just reached that famous turtle soup recipe, but decided to skip over it as I was sure it would not appear on menus too frequently. And I was not going to slit the shell of a 120-pound turtle and remove its innards.

I came out of the kitchen, and a figure loomed in front of me in the dark hallway. I think I must have gasped. I saw the flash of jewels on cerise silk and a bright-blue turban. Queen Victoria's munshi was before me, looking down at me with contempt.

"You, girl," he said. "You are a kitchen maid?"

"No, I'm a cook," I replied.

"That is no way to speak to your betters. You address me as 'sir,' " he said. He had a strong Indian accent, and he smelled of a cloying perfume.

"I'm sorry, sir," I said, with overemphasis on the last word.

"Now, I do not wish to go into that kitchen because it is a place where pork is prepared," he went on, "but you are to go immediately and tell the head cook that I am most displeased. I requested a curried chicken and a dal when I wanted to entertain a fellow countryman of mine. I wished to make a good impression, but alas I was embarrassed. The chicken had no flavour, and the dal was made of split peas, not the correct lentils."

I waited. He waved an elegant hand at me, a hand with several rings on the fingers. "Go now.

Tell this cook, and return to me with the answer of how he plans to remedy this."

I swallowed hard as I went back into the kitchen. Mr Angelo had finished working, and I found him in the servants' dining room, sitting by the fire in the one good chair, reading the newspaper. I apologized for interrupting his rest and reported what I had been told. He slammed down the newspaper.

"He had the nerve to say that, did he? Doesn't he know you can't make a good curry without onions to seal in the spices, and I couldn't allow the risk of that fellow breathing onion and garlic breath at the queen, could I? And what's more, I don't see why I should put my staff through extra work to make special food for one blooming servant. We don't do it for her private secretary, who is a proper gentleman. We don't do it for her ladies-in-waiting, who are all titled people and English to boot, so why in God's name should we do it for him? And lentils? We don't use lentils, do we? Split peas are good enough for us and should be good enough for him."

I stood there, feeling rather sick, accepting this tirade. "Should I go and tell him this, Cook?"

"Of course you shouldn't." He stood up. "I don't allow my cooks to be subjected to abuse. I'll tell him myself and tell him that if I had my way, he'd be eating with the rest of the palace servants, in this dining hall. Strutting around like a bloody peacock! Giving himself airs and graces. The old lady needs to wake up and see the truth. I wouldn't be surprised if he was robbing her blind. We'll find the crown jewels missing soon, you mark my words."

He stomped out of the room. I was dying to follow him and see the encounter myself. I heard raised voices, and soon Chef returned, his face bright red. "I told him a thing or two," he said.

"Aren't you worried about being given the sack?" I asked. "I'm told he does have the queen's favour."

"Ducky, she likes her food better than she likes him," he said with a grin. "I think I'm quite safe. And when I next get a chance to talk to the master of the household about menus, I'll mention that he was trying to force me to cook onions and spices, and I knew she wouldn't want the smells seeping into her own food and the curry taste impregnating her pans."

We didn't receive another visit from the Indian, and I didn't spot the queen on the grounds with him again, as the weather had become blustery, sending leaves flying from the trees behind the palace and occasionally peppering my window with rain as I lay in bed. But we did have an interesting visitor in the kitchen later in the week, a distinguished-looking older man with a neatly trimmed beard. I had seen pictures of the Prince of Wales and wondered for a moment if this was he. I was about to curtsy but noticed none of the others reacted in this way.

"The queen's physician, Sir James Reid," Mrs Simms whispered as all work stopped at the entrance of this visitor.

"Mr Angelo," he said. He had a deep, quiet voice with a trace of a Scottish accent. "A word if you don't mind."

"Certainly, Dr Reid." The chef wiped his hands on his apron as he approached the doctor. "Would you care to sit down? I can fetch you a chair."

"Not necessary, thank you. What I have to say won't take long." He cleared his throat.

"It's about Her Majesty's diet. I'm sure you've noticed but she's eating far too much. Gorging herself, that's what she's doing. And not taking any exercise either. She says her legs will no longer support her. 'Of course they won't,' I told her. 'There is too much body above them.' " He paused and smiled. "The result is that she's becoming fatter and fatter. If this goes on, she'll develop heart failure, dyspepsia, diabetes and all kinds of unpleasant diseases, and be facing an early demise." He looked around, noticing that the rest of us had abandoned our duties and were listening eagerly. He frowned, and we pretended to go back to work. "She said she had little to live for, and only her dear Abdul brought her joy."

I heard a sniff from Mrs Simms.

"Did she really want to die, I asked her. She did

not. She had no intention of dying, although the thought of being reunited with her dear Albert was an enticing one. She said the reason she intended to stay alive was that she did not want her son to become king. He was weak with too many vices. He would run the empire into the ground."

He finished speaking, and the only sound was that of a knife on the chopping board.

"What do you want me to do about it, Doctor?" Mr Angelo asked.

"Make changes to her diet."

Mr Angelo sighed. "I meet with the master of the household, and I can sometimes make suggestions on the menus, but mostly they come directly from her. My job is to cook what I'm told to prepare and do it well."

"Quite." Dr Reid nodded. "But maybe you could surreptitiously cut down on the cream and butter in the sauces and mashed potatoes. And if you do get a chance to make suggestions— maybe to replace a heavy pudding with a baked apple?"

Cook gave a derisive chuckle. "Does she listen to your suggestions, Doctor?"

"Not often, I have to admit." The doctor grinned.

"And you a qualified medical man with the highest degrees. She's certainly not going to take advice from a mere cook. All we'll get is complaints that the mashed potatoes weren't up to the usual standard if we withhold the cream."

The doctor nodded in agreement. "It will not be easy, I agree. But maybe at every meal, we cut back just a little of the richness. Cut out one fattening item. I'm sure every little bit helps at this stage, and we don't want our beloved monarch to die, do we?"

"We most certainly do not," Mr Angelo said emphatically. "We'll do everything we can, Doctor. The trouble is that she is set in her ways. She knows what she likes, and she's not willing to try anything new."

Dr Reid patted him on the shoulder. "Do your best, Mr Angelo. We can only try."

Then he departed.

CHAPTER 6

After Dr Reid had gone, we had a meeting. Mr Angelo was sceptical that we could alter Her Majesty's diet without causing wrath to fall upon us.

"Any suggestions?" he asked.

The others stood there, tight-lipped and not willing to stick a neck out. I raised my hand tentatively. "Roast chicken. Does she like that? It's supposed to be healthy and not fatty."

"You've been reading our bible, I notice," he replied, frowning down at me. "The former chef's cookery book. Did you observe that any of the dishes could be described as simple? If it's a roast chicken, then it's stuffed. Take a look at the book and see what is in the stuffings: oysters or forcemeat or even some smaller fowl inside it."

I nodded, suitably chastened, but couldn't resist adding, "What about rabbit? That's another lean meat, isn't it?"

"Rabbit?" I was regarded with scorn. "That is food for the masses, my dear."

"A rabbit pie can be very tasty," I said. "She may not even know it's rabbit."

"You would try to deceive the queen?" He looked horrified.

"Not deceive, Cook. Unless she asks what is in the pie, you would not need to tell her."

He wagged a finger at me. "I can see you are a wily young woman under that innocent exterior. Let me think on this. And any other suggestions while you have the floor?"

I glanced around. The other cooks were watching me with interest, probably waiting for the axe of doom to fall upon me. I took a deep breath. "I was thinking that meringues do not contain any fat. Tiny ones for Her Majesty's tea, perhaps?"

He nodded. "Except she likes the cream to be oozing out between them. But maybe we could get away with less cream . . . Do you know how to make meringues?"

"I do, Cook."

"Very well. You can try a batch this afternoon. We'll see how well they are received."

I felt rather pleased about this—pleased but a little scared, too. I was being noticed in my new position. I was being given a chance to prove myself.

My meringues were a success. I was told that if I dared to make the rabbit pie, Chef would offer it one lunchtime. I did, and we heard that the chicken today was particularly succulent in the pie. We said nothing to contradict that.

On my afternoon off, I met with Louisa, her mother-in-law and the seamstress who was to make our dresses. I found they had picked out a gorgeous blue velvet for my dress. It was to have a cape trimmed with white fur. I could not have been happier. I was secure in my position; my sister was happy and settled. All was right with my world. Did we not learn as children that pride comes before a fall? We were in mid-morning preparation when a footman appeared in the doorway. He stood, looking around, until one of the cooks noticed him.

"What is it?" the cook asked.

"There's a visitor for a Miss Barton," he said.

I looked up from chopping stewing steak for our lunchtime pie. My heart did a rapid flip.

"Miss Barton?" Mr Angelo frowned. "Miss Barton does not receive visitors during working hours. She should know that."

"I am sure there must be a mistake, Cook," I said. "Nobody knows that I work here now. And I know nobody in London."

"The young man says he is her brother, and it's urgent," the footman said.

"Brother? You have a brother? I understood you were without family." Mr Angelo was frowning at me now. It was rather alarming.

I felt the colour drain from my face. Was it possible that Helen had a brother in London?

Was that why she decided to seek employment in the south? I tried to think of excuses as to why I shouldn't see him, but realized that I would have to. "I am an orphan, Mr Angelo. Both of my parents died long ago. And I had no idea my brother was in London, or knew that I was here. We have not seen each other in a long while."

"Well, I suppose you'd better go and speak to him," Mr Angelo said impatiently. "Only make it snappy. Tell him you'll have time to see him properly on your afternoon off."

"Yes, Cook," I said and followed the footman out of the kitchen and along the hallway.

My heart was racing, and I tried to control my panicked thoughts. He couldn't know that his sister had died. I would have to break the truth to him gently and tell him why I had stolen Helen's identity. I would have to make him understand somehow and appeal to his better nature.

The walk down the hallway seemed to take forever. Bright sunlight streamed in from the open door. The footman leaned closer and said quietly, "He's waiting outside. I didn't want to let him in without permission, but if you want to bring him in . . ."

"No, I'll speak to him outside," I said rapidly.

"I'll leave you to it, then," the footman said and retreated.

I took a deep breath and stepped out into the brisk autumn day. He was standing off the path, to one side, watching for me—a skinny young man, dressed in a rather flashy manner. He came forward warily.

"You're Helen Barton?" he asked. I disliked him from first glance. He had a thin, vulpine face with darting eyes and a cocky expression. I imagine this would be how a fox would look if a chicken strayed too close to his den.

An idea struck me. Helen Barton would not be an uncommon name. I could tell him that he had come about the wrong Helen. Not his sister. I was the one who was offered the job. I was still forming these words in my mind and wondering how his sister had received a letter from the palace that was meant for me when he said, "So how come you don't give your brother Ronnie a kiss?"

"You're not my brother," I replied.

"Blooming right I'm not," he said. "I'm Helen Barton's brother. Helen Barton. The one who applied for this job. The one who should have got this job, only . . ." He left the rest of the sentence hanging. I took a deep breath.

"Perhaps you haven't heard the terrible news, sir," I replied. I addressed him in this way even though I was quite sure he didn't deserve the title. I heard my voice take on the upper-class tones that my father used when he was under moments of stress. "Your sister was killed by an omnibus in Piccadilly. I happened to witness the accident.

It was terrible to behold, the poor thing. I tried to comfort her as she was dying, and she had an envelope in her hand. She was in distress and begged me to take it to the palace and tell them. I promised I would. After she had died, I found it was a letter inviting her to be interviewed for the position of under-cook at the palace. By sheer happenstance, I am also a cook, and I was looking for a way to escape my own servitude at that time. This seemed like a gift from heaven to me. Your poor sister would no longer be needing the post, and I could do it well."

"And so you applied in my sister's name," he said.

"I did. I know that was not an honourable thing to do, but I couldn't bring your sister back to life, and the position needed to be filled. I am sorry to be the bearer of such tragic news about your sister."

He shrugged. "As it happens, I was still working at Lady Sowerby's house in Yorkshire when we got the news that she'd been killed. After our mother died, Helen and I both decided to look for positions down in London, try our lot in the big city, you know. Helen getting the chance to interview at the palace was an incredible stroke of luck. We talked about her finding a way to secure me a position in a royal household, too. And then we heard she had been killed." He paused, sucking through his teeth. "Imagine my surprise when I arrived in London and heard that a Miss Barton was now working at the palace. I thought I had better come and see for myself."

"I'm sorry if this was distressing to you, sir. I meant no harm. Your sister was dead, and I am a good cook. They are most satisfied with my work."

"So why not tell the truth and give your own name?"

"Because I was working for a spiteful woman who valued my services and didn't want to lose me. She told me that if I tried to leave, she'd give me no reference. I was trapped in an unpleasant situation. This seemed like a miracle. Finally a way out for me. Surely you understand that?"

He was still almost smirking at me. I decided his face was more weasel than fox. Nasty, spiteful little dark eyes, darting as they examined me. "And you've never told them the truth here?"

"How could I? I'd be dismissed."

"So what do you think would happen if some-one else told them?"

I stared at him for a long moment. The wind had whipped up leaves, swirling them around the forecourt and threatening to snatch my cook's hat. I put up a hand to secure it.

"You are the only person who seems to know the truth," I said.

"That's right." He really did smirk then. "I am,

aren't I? And what's to stop me from marching right in there and telling them?"

I frowned. "I don't think I understand you. Why would you want to do that? I'm truly sorry about your sister, I really am. I was shocked when I saw her body lying there. But I can't bring her back to life, and I haven't taken anything from her."

"Are you sure?" He raised an eyebrow. "You know what's going through my head at this moment? I'm thinking you might not have been the bystander you claimed to be, but you actually pushed her under that omnibus."

I stared at him, open-mouthed. "What a ridiculous thing to say. I didn't even know your sister. I never even met her, and I'd certainly never do anything to harm another person."

He folded his arms across his chest. "You see, I'm thinking that maybe Helen came down to London, and maybe you sat side by side in the same café. And she was excited about her job and told you why she had come. And you decided to take your own chances. You followed her to Piccadilly, and at the right moment you gave her a shove."

I fought back anger and panic. "How dare you suggest such a thing? I told you, I never met your sister. Why would I lie to you?"

"You've already told one pretty big lie recently, so it seems." He smirked again now. "I think the police would be very interested to hear my story, don't you? You kill my sister, and then you take her place—working at the palace under false pretences? And if I happened to come up with a witness who saw you push her? Well, I reckon it would be nothing less than the noose, don't you?"

My heart was racing so fast I could hardly breathe. I fought to stay calm, at least to give him the appearance of being calm. "I don't understand. Are you trying to threaten me? To blackmail me? Because I'm afraid you'd be wasting your time. I have no money, no family and no connections. I was a penniless servant girl like your sister."

"You don't sound like it. In fact you don't sound like a servant at all."

"My father was a gentleman, my mother a lady, but they died, and I had to fend for myself. I was put into service when I turned fifteen. I worked as a maid and then became a cook. I've had a hard life, just like you, and you can't blame me for taking the one chance I might ever be given, can you?"

"No, I don't blame you," he said.

"Then what do you want from me?" I heard my voice, taut and shrill now.

"I was thinking there might be ways you could be helpful to me—to advance my own ambitions."

I gave a nervous laugh. "I'm the lowest

assistant cook, Mr Barton. I have no influence at all. Are you also a cook?"

"Me?" He shrugged, sticking his hands into his pockets. "I've been several things. I started off as boot boy, worked my way up to footman and then valet, but I've a mind to work in a royal household, too. I wouldn't mind starting off in a lowly position again, if necessary. I'm not too proud. Actually, I've a fancy to work for the Prince of Wales. He seems like a man after my own heart. Free with the cash, too, so they say."

"So why not apply to his residence to see if there might be a vacancy?"

He shrugged. "Unlike my sister, I don't come with glowing references. A small misunderstanding about some silver. She was the golden child of the family, always did everything perfectly. Me, not so much. So you see, Miss whatever-your-name-is, you and I can help each other. I can keep quiet about your little deception, and you can put in a good word for me to get me a post with the royals."

"I've told you, Mr Barton," I said, "I have absolutely no seniority. I've never even met a member of the royal family. How do you expect me to put in a good word for you?"

"You'll find a way," he said. "I'm sure you will. I'll give you until the end of the year, and then I'll go to the palace with the truth. I may even decide to go to the police with my version of what happened to my sister." He pulled his hand out of his pocket, now holding a piece of paper. "This is where I'm staying," he said. "If I change my address, I'll write to you, care of the palace. And I look forward to hearing good news from you in the near future."

"And if I call your bluff?" I said. "If I go in there and say there is a man who is pestering me? He claimed to be my brother, but he really isn't. He's a young man who has designs on me, and he won't take no for an answer, and now he's trying to cause trouble for me. Who do you think they will believe?"

He went to say something, opened his mouth, then shut it again. "I think they'd believe me," he said.

"Oh, and why is that?"

He smirked again. "Because I come with proof. I happen to have a photograph of Helen and me, taken outside Sowerby Hall. And my sainted mother has written on it: *Helen and Ronnie, the day they started work for Lady Sowerby.* One look at that photograph, and anyone can see that you look nothing like our Helen." He turned and started to walk away. "End of the year at the latest. I'll be expecting good news."

He didn't look back as he pushed open the little gate in the wall of the forecourt and let the wind slam it shut behind him. I stood for a moment in the cool stillness of the hallway, trying to compose myself. I think I had known from the first instant that what I was doing was wrong. I was so desperate to escape that I had not listened to my conscience. I had half expected to be punished for my lie, and now judgement had fallen upon me. "Beware your sins will find you out." That's what they taught us in church when I used to attend with my mother. It had seemed like such a harmless deception, too. As I said to Ronnie Barton, I had not hurt anybody; in fact, I had done the palace a service by finding them a good cook. And now I was truly trapped again. If he went to the police and told them that concocted story, they might well believe him, and I'd be arrested and tried for murder.

If I couldn't do what he wanted, but told him I had tried my best, would he be satisfied with that? The trouble was that I suspected he had no better nature I could appeal to. He was clearly the sort who was never quite straight. Maybe he had been a thorn in Helen's side, which was why she came all the way to London to escape him. But what he wanted was impossible. I could go to the master of the household and tell him that my brother was looking for a job, but they would not take him on without the highest references, even if I spoke up for him. At least I had until the end of the year. Almost two months to come up with a plan of escape.

I took several deep breaths, straightened my

cap and went back into the kitchen. Chef glanced up but said nothing as I took my place back at the table beside Mrs Simms.

"You look as white as a sheet, my girl," Mrs Simms said. "Is everything all right?" When I didn't respond instantly, she went on, "Were you not pleased to see your brother?"

"Not exactly," I muttered.

"You were upset to see him." It wasn't a question.

"I haven't seen him in a long time," I said. "And we didn't exactly get along well."

"So what did he want, money?"

"No, nothing like that. I just wasn't very happy to know he'd followed me down to London, that's all."

"At least he can't bother you here," she said. "You're as safe as houses at the palace."

I gave her a weak smile.

"If anyone tries to bother you, Miss Helen, you just tell me." Nelson stepped closer. I hadn't realized he'd overheard.

I gave him a grateful grin. "You're really kind."

"Not at all. We're family here. We watch out for each other. I don't care if he is your brother, he's not going to upset you, or he'll have to deal with me."

A wonderful thought came into my head. I could send Nelson, and maybe some of his sturdier friends, to intimidate Ronnie Barton into leaving me alone. But then Ronnie would tell them the truth, and Nelson would know he'd been lied to. And that might change how he felt about me. I went back to work, chopping so fast that the pieces of potato flew across the bench, as if every piece was Ronnie Barton's neck.

That night I found it impossible to sleep. Rain peppered my window, and the wind howled through the chimneys. It was as if the whole world was caught up in my turmoil. I did have a way to escape, of course. That was what I told myself. I could accept my sister's kind offer and move in with Billy's family. Ronnie Barton didn't know my real name. He'd have no way of tracing me. Besides, I'd be of no use to him if I was no longer at the palace. I examined this thought. Could I really tolerate that life? I'd be the spinster sister, the one to be pitied. Billy's mother would make it her mission to find me a suitable husband, and her idea of suitable was not mine. But was that preferable to finding myself in court, trying to prove my innocence in the death of Helen Barton when I would already be known to the jury as a liar and a cheat? I lay staring into complete darkness, but no solution would come. They were not bad people, Billy's family. They weren't of my original class, but neither was I any longer. Louisa had accepted her diminished social status quite happily. Why did I find it so hard to admit that we were now working class and not aristocrats?

I could resume my education, I thought. Louisa had suggested as much. I could train to be a teacher. That thought cheered me a little until I reminded myself that I had found my métier in cooking. I loved to cook. I was really happy in my current position. I did not want to abandon it, and with it any chance of furthering my education in the kitchen. And most of all, I hated to let a slimy weasel like Ronnie Barton get the better of me. I was not going to go down without a fight.

CHAPTER 7

I tried to put all thoughts of Ronnie Barton out of my mind and threw myself into my work with zest. Both Mrs Simms and Mr Angelo complimented me on my efforts. After the success of my meringues, Mr Angelo suggested to Chef Roland that he might want me as an assistant with the cakes and pastries. I had already noticed that Chef Roland was a highly strung individual, a Frenchman who easily took offence. He was now regarding me as if I was something unpleasant he had found under his shoe. He tossed his head petulantly. "Are you now suggesting that I am past my prime, Chef, and therefore in need of someone to assist me?" he demanded.

"On the contrary," Mr Angelo said. "I was merely thinking that this young woman shows promise in terms of becoming a pastry chef and could learn much from your expertise."

The expression softened a little. "Ah well, in that case . . . I suppose I could teach her a thing or two. As long as she doesn't get under my feet."

"Oh no, Mr Roland," I said in my most respectful voice. "I really want to learn and will be most grateful."

He stood looking at me for a long time, then he sniffed. "Well, let's give it a try, and we'll see how it works out."

"I don't envy you, working with him," Nelson muttered when I returned to my place at the table beside him. "He's a right little prima donna, that one. But it's good that Mr Angelo thinks you have potential."

I blushed, realizing that my transfer meant he had been passed over. "Oh, I'm sorry. I didn't mean to push myself forward," I stammered. "I'm sure I did nothing to ask for any favouritism."

He laughed. "Don't be upset yourself. I know my own limitations, and a light hand with pastry is not something I'll ever have. So good luck to you." He leaned closer to me. "You're a really special girl, you know. Look, how would you like to come for a stroll with me next Sunday afternoon? We might take tea somewhere, eat something we didn't have to cook?"

He was looking at me hopefully. What was wrong with me, I thought. He was a nice boy. How could I afford to be too proud to accept his offer?

"I'd really like to, but . . . ," I began and watched his face fall. I was about to say that my sister was getting married and I had to have a fitting for my maid of honour dress. I swallowed back those words at the last second. Of course Helen Barton didn't have a sister.

"It's all right. I understand," he said quietly.

"No, you don't." I looked up into those light-blue eyes. "I have a friend getting married," I went on, trying to stay as close to the truth as possible. "I'm helping her with her preparations. She relies on me."

"I didn't realize you had anybody in London," he said, still looking uneasy. "I thought you came down from the north."

"She was one of the things that made me want to be in London," I said. "She's one of the only people in the world I'm close to. We were children together, and when I knew she was getting married here, I took the big chance . . ."

I saw his expression relax. "I see. And when is this wedding?"

"In two weeks. After that, I'd be delighted to spend an afternoon with you."

"You would?" His face lit up.

"I would," I repeated.

He was still grinning to himself as he returned to his work. *What have I done?* I wondered as I got on with my own peeling and slicing. Louisa seemed happy enough with her future. What right did I have to want something more for myself? Then I decided that it wasn't as if he wanted to marry me. Perhaps he, too, just wanted some pleasant companionship on his days off. It was lonely working away from home. I might even enjoy an afternoon out with a friend.

• • •

Louisa's wedding took place on a rainy afternoon in November. We were whisked under umbrellas from the carriage to the church, while the wind threatened to turn those umbrellas inside out. Louisa looked lovely and absurdly young in her long veil. The way she smiled up at Billy relieved any worries I might have had. She loved him. And he was looking down at her with the same adoring gaze. Suddenly I felt a pang of jealousy that no boy had ever looked at me that way. What did it feel like to be in love? I wondered. How would I ever have a chance to meet someone who would mean everything in the world to me?

As I watched the wedding ceremony proceed, I found myself overwhelmed with a great surge of conflicting emotions. I had locked my feelings away when I was sent into service. All except anger, that is. Anger and betrayal. I had felt that my father had let me down in the worst way, robbed me of my childhood and my dignity. He had not tried to find a humble sort of job himself, I had thought. He was not going to sink below his rank, but he was quite willing to sell his daughter into slavery. I felt tears welling up in my eyes. Maybe I had judged him too harshly. Maybe he had been sicker than we knew, and the alcohol had already poisoned his liver. I found that I could feel forgiveness, and love for Louisa and even a spark of hope for my own future. I was going to become a first-class cook, and maybe one day I would meet someone who looked at me the way Billy was gazing at my sister at this moment.

After the ceremony had concluded, the rain had eased enough to have a photograph taken on the steps of the church, before we were taken back to Billy's house for the wedding breakfast. I was glad that I had not succumbed to my fears and asked to live with Louisa's in-laws when I found that I was seated beside Billy's cousin at the long table. He was a skinny, pimply boy called Algernon, whom Billy's mother referred to as "our Algie." Memories of my schooldays told me that algae was something that floated on top of ponds. I found him equally unappealing, especially when he slurped his food and chomped loudly.

"Our Algie's doing very nicely as a bookkeeper for the railways," Billy's mother said, giving me a little nudge. "You could do worse."

I could do a lot better, I thought. I made the excuse of needing to help Louisa change into her going-away outfit. Then she was off in a carriage to Paddington Station and going on her honeymoon to a hotel in Torquay.

"Have a lovely time," I said as I hugged her.

"I hope so," she whispered. "I'm terrified, actually, but I expect it will be all right. Billy's kind, isn't he? He'll be gentle with me."

"Of course he will. And you'll have time to get to know each other better."

"Yes." She took my hands. "After this, nothing will ever be the same again, will it?"

"No, it won't," I said. We stood, looking at each other with wistful smiles, she probably remembering, as I was, those days as children when our mother was still alive and we curled up beside her while she read a book to us, or when she played the piano while we danced. How long ago it all seemed.

So Louisa went off on her honeymoon, and I went back to the palace, slipping away while everyone was outside throwing rice after the departing couple, and before I had to face Algie again. It was dark and raining heavily by the time I approached the servants' entrance. I was walking, my umbrella tilted forward as I battled the wind, when somebody stepped out in front of me. All I saw were legs and feet. I stopped, expecting the person to step aside. When he didn't, I looked up and saw Ronnie Barton smirking at me.

"Had a nice day out?" he said. "Carrying a valise with you? I wonder where you went, when you said you know nobody in London."

"It's none of your business," I replied. "Please step aside and stop bothering me."

"The end of the year's getting closer," he said, ducking to step under my umbrella to put his face inches from mine. "I hope you've been working hard on your little assignment I gave you."

"Go away and leave me alone." I was tired, and angry. I tried to shove him aside.

He gripped my wrist with unexpected strength and twisted it back. "Don't you try to brush me off, my girl." He almost hissed out the words. "Don't you ever forget I hold your life in my hands. Have you ever seen the Old Bailey? How about Holloway prison? Not very pleasant, I'm told. And of course that noose is even less appealing. But at least it's quick. Drop. Snap. Goodbye."

"Helen?" I hadn't heard the footsteps behind me. I spun around.

"Nelson," I exclaimed.

Ronnie stepped out from under my umbrella.

"Are you all right, Helen?" Nelson asked. "Is this man bothering you?"

"I'm really glad to see you, Nelson," I said. I slipped my arm through his. "Would you take me inside, please?"

"Of course." Nelson looked over at Ronnie Barton, who had backed off a few paces. "Leave her alone, understand me? Go on. Beat it."

"All right. Keep your hair on. I'm going, for now." Ronnie sized himself up against the much taller Nelson and turned to leave. Nelson took my valise from me, opened the gate and allowed me to pass through ahead of him.

"Has she told you the truth yet?" Ronnie called after us. "I bet she hasn't."

The gate closed. We reached the door, I closed my dripping umbrella and we went inside. I found I was shaking.

"Who was that man?" Nelson asked. "A rejected suitor?"

"No, my brother," I replied. "He and I don't exactly see eye to eye. I try to stay well away from him."

"What did he want? Asking you for money, was he?"

"No, not money," I said. "He was asking me for a favour I can't deliver. Being quite persistent about it."

"Don't worry, you're quite safe from him here. You're amongst friends," he said.

Then he added, as we made our way along the passage to the stairs, "What did he mean about telling the truth?"

What could I say? It passed through my mind that I could tell Nelson exactly what I had done. He would understand. But I realized I couldn't burden him with a secret that couldn't be shared with the rest of the cooking staff. And I might even compromise his position if it ever came to light that I had lied. No, I had to keep my secret to myself.

"It's something I can't tell you at this moment," I said. "Nothing shocking. Nothing bad, I promise. But just something about my past life that I can't share with you yet."

He was looking at me earnestly, those clear blue eyes troubled. "Are you in some kind of trouble, Helen, because if so . . ." His voice trailed off.

"Not trouble in the way you are thinking," I said. "Just something that's awkward and needs to be sorted out. Something that involves my brother. Please trust me, Nelson. I have not done anything that would make you think less of me, I swear."

"Of course you haven't. You're a nice, refined girl with high standards. I saw that from the beginning." He paused. "So will you come out walking with me next Sunday?"

"I'd like that very much," I replied, and realized that I was telling the truth. I needed a friend and an ally. And it was rather gratifying to have someone who thought I was special. His whole face lit up with such a sweet smile that I found myself smiling back.

CHAPTER 8

It was strange that, having seized one opportunity, following my father's advice, I should have the chance to seize another. I had been making good progress with Chef Roland, to the extent that he actually called my shortbread passable and my cream puffs "not bad at all."

For my part, I was relishing the chance to make such an assortment of cakes, biscuits and pastries, even if I did have to endure his temperamental nature. One day he was chopping candied peel very finely when he sneezed. He turned his head away, of course, but the knife sliced into his finger. He let out a stream of French, including some curse words which were outside my childhood vocabulary.

One might have thought he had been attacked with a hatchet instead of just cutting his finger by the way he was carrying on. I rushed to get a wet cloth to stop the bleeding. "Calm yourself, please," I said to him in French. "It is not so bad, I assure you."

"Not so bad?" he wailed.

Mrs Simms had heard the outburst and came

over to assist. "Whatever has happened, Mr Roland?"

"I'm doomed, my career will be ruined." He pulled his finger from the cloth and held it up, while blood dripped down.

"Nonsense, it's just a little cut. It will heal," Mrs Simms said, not showing much sympathy. "We'll bind it tightly. Go and get the first aid box, Helen."

"No, I must go to the hospital right away," he insisted. "It needs stitches before it's too late."

He wouldn't listen, and in the end a hansom cab was called for him, and off he went.

"It will be up to you to finish Her Majesty's tea, my girl," Mr Angelo said. "I see he's done the eclairs, but the scones have to be made fresh. Can I trust you with the scones? You make them just before they are to be carried in, so that they are still warm. And you know that she doesn't like raspberry jam. Just strawberry or apricot, and the cream whipped very thick. Got that?"

"Yes, Cook," I said, feeling both scared and excited at the same time. It was up to me to feed the queen. Mrs Robbins at my former establishment had made very good scones—at least they had tasted good to me. So I made them just the way she did—with very cold butter, double cream, a dash of vanilla extract. I brought them out of the oven when they were just turning golden on top and wrapped them in a napkin. Off they went on the trolley with the rest of the tea things.

I realized that Chef Roland might not return in time for the queen's dinner and asked Mr Angelo if I should start preparing one of the puddings.

He looked at me quite kindly. "Luckily, it's a quiet night with no guests at dinner except for Princess Louise," he said. "I think we can get away with a Bavarian cream, don't you? I'll send Mr Williams over to help you. He's not bad at puddings."

And one of the yeoman cooks was dispatched to my table. He didn't look too pleased at the thought of helping me, when I was clearly his junior, but I smoothed things over by saying, "I'm very grateful you have the time to show me how to do this. I would have been a bundle of nerves if I'd had to create a pudding for Her Majesty by myself."

He grinned. "Put enough cream and sugar in it, and she doesn't care," he muttered. "Oh, and a good splodge of brandy. I don't know how she eats the way she does. And drinks, too. Do you know she has a different wine with each of the courses? And sherry before the meal and port after it. And she's going on eighty, too. She must have a cast iron stomach."

"Miss Barton?" I looked up to see Mr Francis beckoning to me. I thought that we had been over-heard gossiping about the queen and expected a rebuke, but as I walked over to him, he said, "Take off your apron at once. You've been summoned."

"Summoned?" I looked at him in horror, my first thought being that Ronnie had gone to the police.

"Upstairs," he said. "A footman has been sent down to fetch you."

"Upstairs? You mean to the queen?"

"So it would seem," he said.

"Oh gracious, what have I done?" My heart was beating so fast that I could hardly breathe.

"You'll find out when you get there, I dare say," he went on. "Get on with it, then. Don't keep Her Majesty waiting."

My fingers would not obey me as I tried to undo my apron strings. I hung it up on the wall, smoothed down my skirt and went out into the hallway. A footman in black velvet livery was standing outside the door.

"You're the one, are you?" he asked in surprise.

"I've no idea," I stammered. "I can't think what the queen would want with me."

"She sent me down to fetch the cook who made the scones today. That's all I know."

"That was me," I agreed.

"Come on, then. Follow me." He led me at a great pace along the hallway, through a heavy door and out into a different world. A great marble staircase curved up ahead of us, with a red carpet going up its centre. Up we went, so fast that I had to pick up my skirts and was out of breath by the time we reached the top. Then he hurried me along a broad gallery where portraits of former monarchs frowned down at me, and there were statues in niches. There was a thick Axminster carpet underfoot, and the walls were covered with rich brocade. I hardly had a moment to take this in as the footman came to a halt before double doors, then opened one cautiously.

"The pastry chef that you requested, Your Majesty."

With that, I was almost pushed inside. I stepped into a large sitting room. It was a pleasant sort of room, not too grand, with tall windows that opened on to the grounds at the side of the palace. Velvet sofas and armchairs were arranged around a marble fireplace in which a healthy fire was glowing. In one of the high-backed chairs, a little old woman was sitting. I had seen pictures of her aplenty, of course, but she seemed even smaller in person, her feet resting on a footstool. In truth, up close for the first time, she looked like anyone's grandmother, a white shawl around her shoulders and a lace cap upon her head. She looked up in surprise as I entered.

"You're a girl," she said.

"Yes, Your Majesty." I attempted a curtsy.

"I thought all my cooks were men," she replied. "Where is my pastry chef?"

"I am only an under-cook, Your Majesty," I replied, "but Mr Roland, who normally makes your pastries, met with an accident this afternoon, and I had to step in and take his place. I am sorry if my efforts did not measure up to your usual standards."

"An accident? I trust it was not too severe?"

"He cut his finger, Your Majesty. But he felt that the cut required stitches, so he was taken to a local hospital. However, I expect he will be perfectly fine by tomorrow and able to resume his activities."

She was looking at me critically. "You're nicely spoken for a servant girl. What's your name?"

Oh dear. I was about to lie to a queen. Images of the Tower and dungeons swam into my head. "It's Helen, ma'am. Helen Barton."

"Well, Helen, I've summoned you today because we found the scones to be particularly delicious. We both commented on them."

That was when I noticed that she was not alone. A portly man with a neatly trimmed grey beard was sitting in a high-backed chair across the fire from her. I'd seen images of him in newspapers. The Prince of Wales. He was looking at me appraisingly.

"Mama, you did not tell me that you were employing young women in the kitchen these days," he said.

"I thought it was about time that the palace was

forward-looking," the queen replied. "The new century is coming. Young women should have a chance to make something of themselves. Heaven knows that most of the cooks in the great houses around the country are women. It's a natural art for us females." She stirred herself in her chair and looked around the room. "Frankly, I've been thinking for some time that the kitchen is in need of new blood. My dear munshi complained to me that apparently my cooks cannot produce even the simplest of Indian dishes for him. He was entertaining a fellow countryman, and the chicken curry was quite unpalatable. He is a Muslim, poor Abdul, and has quite strict dietary requirements."

"I don't know why your kitchen staff has to go to any great lengths for a fellow servant," the prince said shortly.

"A fellow servant?" The queen frowned. "He is my one companion and solace, as you very well know. I value his advice, even if he can be rather bossy on occasion. But I like that. It reminds me of when my dear Albert was alive. And he clearly worships me." She gave a heavy sigh. "Life would be quite meaningless if Abdul was not here."

"The chap is a bounder of the worst kind, but you are too blind to see that because he fawns and flatters."

The queen now sat very upright and gave him

the haughtiest of stares. "As monarch of this country, I think I have the right to choose my own courtiers and my own friends," she said. "You will do well to remember that, Bertie. If and when you become king, you will be able to do the same. And I expect there will be many in the country who will criticize your choice of companions."

She reached over to the serving tray, took the last piece of shortbread and popped it into her mouth. Then she seemed to remember that I was standing just inside the door. "We shall not discuss such matters any further," she said. "I am the one who makes the rules in my own household. I have decreed that I want to introduce young women into my kitchen, to bring in new life and vigour. And you see I was right in my prediction. This young lady steps in and bakes us the most delicious scones. We finished the plate between us, and I dare say we could have attacked a second plate had one been offered."

"I can go down to the kitchen and make you a second batch if you wish, ma'am," I said, but she held up her hand and smiled.

"One does not want to spoil one's appetite for dinner," she said. "As my dear Baroness Lehzen used to say, 'Enough is as good as a feast.' "

She waved a hand in my direction. "Run along now. I expect you are needed for the dinner preparations. But I shall look forward to scones made by you every afternoon from now on. You are to tell Mr Angelo that I have made this request of you."

"Yes, Your Majesty." I curtsied again and attempted to back out of the room, praying that I wouldn't bump into any precious object on the way. I reached the door successfully and stood for a moment in the hallway outside, trying to calm myself. It was indeed a heady moment, and I wished that I had someone to share it with. Instead I was dreading informing Mr Angelo and more especially Mr Roland of Her Majesty's instructions. They might not take kindly to an upstart girl pushing herself forward like this.

I looked around for the footman who had escorted me, but not seeing him, I started to make my way back along the hall. I was halfway down the grand staircase when I heard footsteps behind me. I paused and glanced around to see the Prince of Wales following me. I flattened myself against the wall, allowing him to pass, but instead he drew level with me.

"What's your hurry, bright eyes?" he asked. He was looking at me with a sort of half-smile.

"I have to get back to my duties, Your Royal Highness," I replied, my voice scarcely more than a whisper. "I have to make the puddings for dinner."

"Nonsense." He chuckled, a deep, throaty chuckle. "Nobody can complain if the queen kept you, can they? Or even if the Prince of Wales kept you." He took a step closer to me. Rather too close to be comfortable. "What a delightful little creature you are." He raised a hand and stroked my cheek. "Do I detect a wisp of auburn hair under that severe white cap?" And before I could do anything, he had whipped the cap from my head. To my mortification my hair tumbled over my shoulders. The prince's eyes lit up. "I was right." He picked up a curl and toyed with it. "I have a distinct softness for red hair. Red heads are supposed to be fiery and passionate, aren't they? Are you fiery and passionate?"

"No, sir," I mumbled. "I'm sure I'm a most quiet and well-behaved young woman."

He laughed, tugging on my hair. "That's because you haven't met the right man to wake you up yet. I bet you'll be a little tiger one day."

I could feel my cheeks burning, trying to think how I could possibly get away. But he had me pinned against the wall, and one can hardly give the heir to the throne a good shove.

"Please sir, let me go," I whispered. "I really should get back to the kitchen."

"I'll wager you have more talents than making scones," he said. His eyes were challenging me.

I could sense what he was hinting at, but I replied, "Perhaps I do, Your Highness. I am told I have a light hand with pastry."

This made him throw back his head and laugh

heartily. "What a sweet innocent you are. I can't wait to—I can't wait to taste your pastry, young woman. Or experience your light hands. Why don't you come and cook for me? I'm sure we can find you a position in my household. More money, too. And other privileges. I'd enjoy getting to know you better."

My cheeks were burning, and my mouth was so dry I could hardly force out the words. "I couldn't do that, Your Highness. I am only newly hired by the queen. It would be rude and disloyal to leave now, when she has given me such a wonderful chance."

"Enchanting and honourable, too," he said, letting the strand of hair fall to my shoulder, tracing the line of my neck with his finger, down to where the top of my dress prevented further exploration. "But think it over, my sweet. You would not find your duties onerous in my employ, I promise you. And I travel abroad. The Riviera in the spring is most delightful . . ." He gave me a playful little smile.

"I'm sure it would be an honour to work in your household, sir," I replied, "but I owe a great debt of gratitude to Her Majesty."

"I suppose I will accept rejection, for now," he said. "I will go home dejected and with a heavy heart."

I had been so confused and embarrassed that all coherent thoughts had vanished from my head.

But now something hit me with blinding clarity. "There is one favour I might ask, Your Highness," I stammered out the words. "My brother. He is recently come to London with me and is a great admirer of you. If you could find him a place in your household—"

I hadn't finished the sentence, but he grinned. "Then you would have to come and visit him frequently, wouldn't you, bright eyes? Sisterly duty, don't you know." When I said nothing, he nodded. "What is the young man's name?"

"It's Ronnie, sir. Ronald Barton."

"And is Mr Barton also a cook?"

"No, sir, but he has held several positions in a great house in Yorkshire and knows the protocol. He would welcome the chance to be a footman, I am sure."

He stroked my cheek again. "Have him come to see my butler. I'm sure we can find a place for him, if his sister promises to visit him."

"You are very kind, sir," I muttered, not promising anything. "He will be so grateful, I assure you."

"I suppose I'd better let you get back to your kitchen. And I also have an appointment for which I am running late." He backed away from me. "However, I look forward to seeing you again before too long, when we both have a little more time." The way he looked at me made me feel so uncomfortable that I blushed again, making him laugh. He patted my cheek and walked past me, down the stairs, across the foyer and out through the great front doors. I fled through the pass door, back to the safety of my part of the palace.

CHAPTER 9

The moment that great door swung shut behind me, I stood alone in the empty hallway, trying hard to compose myself. It had never occurred to me before that I might be in any way desirable to a man. No man had ever looked at me in that way before. Actually, I had had little contact with men before coming to the palace. It was almost all female staff at the Tilleys' household, apart from a groom, a coachman and a couple of gardeners, who were all elderly. It was true that Nelson seemed interested in me, but he was a harmless sort of chap, and I took his interest more as friendship than anything of a sexual nature. I had heard of the Prince of Wales's reputation, of course. He was mentioned in newspapers as having been spotted with this woman at a race meeting or dining with yet another woman. It was said he always had a mistress. And now it seemed he had set his sights on me.

Don't be ridiculous, I told myself. The prince wasn't really interested in me. He was enjoying making a young servant uncomfortable. But one had heard whispers of masters who had designs on their servant girls, who used their power to have their way. And it was the girl who suffered the consequences, while the man walked away whistling. But how did one say no to a prince? There was an obvious answer: make sure I avoided him. That was when I remembered something else: I had fulfilled my obligation to Ronnie Barton. I was free of him. He could take up a position with the prince, and it was up to him what he made of it. However, I certainly didn't plan to visit him at the prince's palace. I was sure that by then the prince would have forgotten about me anyway.

I tucked my hair hastily back into my cap and hurried back to the kitchen. Eyes turned to watch me as I entered.

"Well?" Mr Angelo demanded. "Spill the beans. Did you put too much bicarb in the scones? Are you getting the boot?"

"No, Cook. The queen complimented me. She thought the scones were delicious, and she has instructed me to make them for her every afternoon."

"Well, that's a turn up, isn't it?" Mr Angelo raised an eyebrow. "Mr Roland isn't going to be happy with that news when he returns."

"I'm sorry, Cook," I said. "I really am. I did nothing to push myself forward, I promise you."

"You can't help being a good cook. Make the most of it."

As I started back to my station, he took my arm.

"Are you all right? You look white as a sheet, girl. I imagine being summoned to Her Majesty for the first time was quite terrifying for you, but you came through with flying colours."

"It wasn't that, Cook," I said. "She was kind to me. It was just that . . ." I broke off, now not willing to talk about it.

"Come on, spill the beans. What did you do? Break a precious ornament? Trip over the carpet?"

"No. The Prince of Wales was there, and he—" Again I couldn't go on.

"He got a little too friendly, did he? Not the first time he couldn't keep his hands off the servants. But don't worry. He's not that fond of his mama, so he won't be turning up too often, and when he does, you make sure you stay in the kitchen." He gave me a brisk nod. "Now get back to work, or there will be no pudding for the queen's dinner and you'll be out of favour again."

I was still blushing bright red as I headed back to my table. Nelson looked up from the potatoes he was peeling and gave me a wink. "Going up in the world, aren't we?" he said.

"It wasn't funny. It was terrifying," I replied.

"So what's it like, out on their side of the palace? Very fancy?"

"The staircase and the hallways were very fancy indeed," I replied. "Lots of paintings and statues and vases. But the sitting room was quite ordinary. Just like you'd see in any large house."

"And the queen? What was she like? I've never actually seen her in person, apart from through the window."

"Small and round. She didn't look at all queenly. And she was very kind to me."

"Well, you made her food that she liked. They say the way to a man's heart is through his stomach, but the same applies to the queen. Eating is her one comfort, so we've heard."

"Enough of that gossip, young Nelson, or those spuds will never be boiled in time," Mrs Simms said, looking up from the steak she was trimming. As I went past her to my own table, she murmured, "You might want to watch yourself, dearie. There are those here who take offence easily."

"Because I was summoned to the queen?"

"Because you're below them in the pecking order and you've suddenly found favour."

"I'm really sorry. I didn't mean to offend anyone."

"Of course you didn't. But a closed environment like this isn't healthy. It breeds jealousy and suspicion. For my part, I say congratulations and good luck to you, but there are others who might not be above sprinkling a little salt into your puddings. So be on your guard."

"Thank you. I will." I went back to work, separating egg yolks into a basin. As I worked, I glanced around the kitchen. Which of them might want to get back at me? Mr Francis, the second in command, clearly disliked me and made it clear that no woman should be anywhere near him. The other woman, Mrs Gillespie, was not exactly friendly. There were the four yeoman cooks, who regarded me as a necessary nuisance, and the three apprentices, who were easy to get along with. In truth I hardly knew them. We chatted at meals, and they seemed friendly enough. The only other girl was Ruby, a scullery maid and therefore beneath me. I was sure that Mr Roland could easily carry a grudge, and I'd have to think carefully about how to break this news to him.

He returned that evening, just as we were assembling the trolleys to be wheeled up for the queen's dinner.

"So sorry to have left you in the lurch," he said to me, "but am I glad that I went to the hospital. They told me my cut could have become infected and festered and I could have died from blood poisoning." And he held up a heavily bandaged hand. "So I'm afraid it's all up to you tonight. I hope you haven't attempted any puddings beyond your scope."

"Oh no, Cook . . . Mr Angelo instructed me to just stick to a simple Bavarian cream, as the queen is only dining with Princess Louise."

"*C'est bien*. Very good. I hope that the tea service went smoothly?"

"It did, Cook. In fact, the queen let it be known that she found the scones tasty."

"Did I make the scones before I left? I can't remember, but I do not think so."

"No, Cook. I made them. They were one of the few things I learned to do well from my old cook. She had a particularly good recipe."

"So you saved the day. I'm in your debt."

"Since the queen seemed to enjoy my scones, I wondered if this might be a task I could undertake every day, if you were agreeable, Cook."

He frowned for a moment, then nodded. "Why not? It would let me be free to make the more complicated cakes that she so loves."

So that was that. I had done it! As soon as I completed the pudding, I rushed up to my room and wrote a letter to Ronnie Barton.

Today I met with the Prince of Wales. He is willing to find you a position in his service. You are to report to his butler and mention that you are my brother, and the prince is willing to give you a chance. I have thus fulfilled my obligation to you and do not wish to hear from you again.

Then I slipped out after our supper and deposited the letter in the nearest postbox. I did not receive an answer, but I had done what he had requested, and he could have no more reason to bother me.

That Sunday I went out walking with Nelson. It was a bitterly cold and miserable day. The wind threatened to tear my bonnet from my head. Nelson offered me his arm, and I was glad to take it as we were swept along the street. Nelson suggested that this was no day for a walk in the park. I agreed. We walked down to Victoria Station, then took the Underground to South Kensington and paid a visit to the Natural History Museum. What an imposing building that was, more like a palace than Buckingham! We spent a pleasant afternoon examining the exhibits—the dioramas of wildlife from around the world, the dinosaur skeletons and the collection of rocks and minerals. These latter I found the most fascinating . . . I suppose every woman is naturally drawn to precious stones!

As we walked, we chatted amiably, although as always I was on my guard not to say the wrong thing. I almost did when I suggested that we visit a certain gallery, and Nelson was surprised. "You've been here before?" he asked.

I was about to say that my father took us to all the museums when we were children but stopped myself at the last minute. "No, I saw the arrow on the wall, directing us this way," I said quickly. After that, the pleasant atmosphere of the afternoon seemed to have vanished, at least for me.

Nelson still acted as if nothing had changed. "How about that?" he said as we stood before the exhibit of the African plains and saw a giraffe. "I wonder how long it takes to swallow if your neck is that size?"

When I didn't answer right away, he said, "Is everything all right, Helen? I hope you don't find my presence too boring or offensive."

"On the contrary," I replied. "I'm sorry if I'm a poor specimen of a companion today. It has been a worrying week." And I told him about my encounter with the Prince of Wales.

Then he was most solicitous. "I've heard about him. I thought you looked quite unsettled when you came back to the kitchen but assumed it was the shock of meeting the queen."

"I'm just praying that he is the sort who likes to make servant girls uncomfortable and flirts with every female," I said. "I don't know what I'd do if he did request that I be sent over to his household, or if I found myself alone with him."

"Give him a good kick where he'd remember it," Nelson said, then realized this might be too offensive a remark to a young lady. "I'm sorry. I shouldn't have said . . ." He broke off in embarrassment.

I laughed. "On the contrary, it was the perfect suggestion." And he joined me in laughter.

"You're such a splendid girl, Helen," he said. "I know I've no right to ask, and of course I'm only an under-cook like yourself and not in any position to think of the future, but is there a chance you'd consider me as someone who'd like to court you properly?"

Oh dear. I did like him. I did enjoy his company, but he was a mate, a pal, nothing more.

"Nelson, I was told in no uncertain terms that stepping out with a fellow was frowned upon," I said. "I don't want to lose my job."

I saw his face fall.

"I really do like you," I said. "I'm having a grand time this afternoon with you, and I'd certainly like to repeat an outing with you. But let's take things one step at a time, shall we? As you say, neither of us is in any position to make any plans for the future, beyond what we have to cook for tomorrow's meals."

He grinned. "You're right about that."

"The only thing I can promise you is that there's no one else in my life."

"That's good then." He gave a satisfied little nod. "Shall we go and see if they've a tearoom here? I could do with a hot cuppa and a bun, couldn't you?"

I agreed. Over tea, he told me about his family—his mother the matriarch and his six brothers and sisters. His father had met with an accident while working on the railways when

Nelson was twelve, and he had gone into service right away to support his family. "Boot boy to start with," he said. "And worked my way up to under-cook. Found I liked the cooking part."

"Just like me," I said. "I started off as a housemaid. Up at five to get the boiler going and light the fires."

"We've got such a lot in common, it's no wonder we get along so well," he said. And I realized that yes, we did have so much in common. Was I wrong to have ideas above my current station about the man I'd like to marry someday? And I remembered the promise I had made at my interview—that I would not have any suitors. That would be a convenient excuse if Nelson began to take our friendship too seriously.

CHAPTER 10

I heard no more from Ronnie Barton, so I had to presume he had applied for the position with the Prince of Wales and been granted it. After that, I found that I could finally breathe more easily. I did everything required of me, I made my daily scones and in the evenings I studied those recipe books, wondering if I would ever be able to produce a soufflé or Mazarin to the queen's satisfaction. Christmas was approaching, and we were informed that the queen would be departing for Osborne House on the Isle of Wight, where, as was her custom, she would join other members of her family for the holiday. She would be taking with her Mr Angelo and several senior members of the kitchen staff—all men. It was explained to me that they did not like to include women in the party because of the travel arrangements. It was not seemly to stuff one woman into a third-class carriage with seven men, or to have to use the same facilities when nature called.

It was also imparted to me that we who were left behind would be cooking for the palace household members—a simpler sort of menu altogether—and would be allowed to join our families for Christmas Day if we wished, since there would be enough cooks with no family ties to put together a Christmas dinner. Did I want to join Louisa and her new family? I wasn't at all sure, but I thought it might be churlish of me not to do so. She had returned from her honeymoon, and I made the journey to Highgate on my next day off. She looked different somehow—immediately more poised and grown-up. Her hair was perfectly piled upon her head, and she was wearing a dark-green high-necked dress. She held out her hands to me as I was ushered in.

"Bella, how lovely to see you. You don't know how often I thought of you while we were away. Do come and sit by the fire, and we'll take some tea." She turned to the hovering maid. "Please tell Cook that my sister and I will take tea now and not wait for your mistress."

"Very good, Mrs Harrison," she said and retreated.

I studied her with interest. Did one month of marriage turn a girl into a confident grown-up woman? As soon as the door was shut, Louisa looked at me and gave a very girlish, impish grin. "It's rather fun, isn't it? I do like having people to wait on me. It's been for so long that I've had to do everything for myself. I even have my mother-in-law's maid to do my hair."

"It looks very impressive," I said. "So how was your honeymoon?"

"The hotel was most agreeable," she said. "It had a glassed-in conservatory that faced the promenade, so on inclement days we would sit, and Billy would read the newspapers, and I'd read the women's magazines, and we'd take tea."

I was still studying her face. Was she trying hard to put on an act, or had she really turned into a remote stranger?

"That wasn't what I meant," I said. "How was your honeymoon?"

She glanced around, then leaned closer to me. "It was rather awful to start with," she said in a whisper. "I mean, I had no idea what to expect. Do you know exactly what it entails? It's shocking, Bella, what men like to do to our bodies. Why were we never told?"

"Our mother died."

"But could you see her informing us of such things? She was always so refined. I bet she wouldn't have said a word either," Louisa said. "But I have to say that Billy was very patient with me, and now I've quite learned to endure it."

"Endure it? Are you not supposed to feel more positive than that?"

She gave a little shrug. "I have to confess that I don't enjoy it in the way that Billy seems to. I mean, all that bouncing up and down and panting. But I suppose it is a necessary obligation for a married woman, if one wants children, and I may

126

come to enjoy it more as time passes. Although frankly, between ourselves I think it's rather silly. And annoying when I'm tired at the end of the day and I'd rather be asleep."

She broke off as the door opened and the maid came in pushing a tea trolley. We allowed her to pour cups for us. The little cakes, I noted with satisfaction, were not up to our standards at the palace.

"About Christmas," I said. "I have good news. I'm to have Christmas Day free if I wish."

Her face fell. "Oh dear, Bella. I'm so sorry, but we're to go to the family farm for Christmas. To Billy's grandfather, out in the country, and we'll be gone for a whole week. Do you think your employer would give you a week off to come with us?"

"I'm afraid not," I said. "Just Christmas Day."

"I'm so sorry," she said again. "It won't seem like Christmas without you."

"That's all right," I said. "I'm sure I'll have a jolly time with my fellow servants."

She reached out and took my hand, squeezing it. "Bella, I can't bear to think of you as a servant while I enjoy all of this. It's not right. It's not fair. Won't you change your mind and come to live with us?"

"You are very sweet, Louisa, but I have no wish to be the spinster sister with your mother-in-law making it her mission to find me a suitable husband." I smiled at her. "I really like my place of employment, and I'm doing very well. I've been promoted to assistant pastry chef."

"Oh, so it must be a very large kitchen if there is a chef just for pastry, and an assistant, too. We only have one cook and one scullery maid here."

"It is. Very large."

"Ah, so it must be a hotel or restaurant." Her face lit up. "I was worried before that it was something not quite proper."

"Very proper, I assure you. I'm just not allowed to tell you. Company rules."

"I see." She looked happier now. "I'm glad you are in a good position, although I wish you did not have to earn a living."

"But I enjoy it," I said. "I'm becoming quite skilled."

"And you will meet someone soon, I'm sure," she said. "Someone who will make you as happy as Billy is making me."

"I hope so." We sat there, our hands still clasped together.

Christmas approached. The queen and her retinue departed. We stood lined up in the foyer to give her a proper send-off. She hobbled past on the arm of her Indian munshi, using her stick to walk with, but nodding to us. When she spotted me, I saw recognition in her eyes, and she gave me a little smile. Then she was helped into the carriage, more like lifted and bundled, actually, and off they went. Mr Angelo wished all of us a merry Christmas and said that the wine steward had been instructed to open a bottle of claret and a bottle of port for our celebrations. He departed, too, along with other senior cooks, leaving Mr Francis in charge and the two ladies and we juniors to hold the fort.

It was a pleasant few days. Meals consisted of big soups and stews followed by suet puddings that were easily made and easily cleared up. On Christmas Eve it snowed, and we went out into the grounds for a snowball fight. Even Mrs Simms joined in, shrieking when a snowball hit her, although Mrs Gillespie clearly disapproved. She was a strange woman, polite enough but quite reserved and never really friendly. That evening one of the apprentices brought in a Christmas tree, and we decorated it with candles, glass balls and paper chains. Then we sat around the tree singing carols.

I was just making my way up to bed when I heard someone calling, "Helen." I turned to see Nelson behind me in the hallway. "I just wanted to say Happy Christmas," he said. "I'll be taking off early tomorrow to go home for the day, and spend it with my old mum and the family. But I didn't want to go without giving you this. I didn't want to give it to you in front of the others," he said. "They might get ideas." And he handed me a little box. "It's not much," he said, "but I wanted to give you a token."

I opened it, praying that it wasn't jewellery, especially not a ring. Inside was a lavender sachet, prettily embroidered with flowers.

"I had my sister make it for you," he said. "She does embroidery for a seamstress."

"It's beautiful." I felt embarrassed because I hadn't bought anything for him. He must have realized this.

"No, don't say it." He held up his hand. "It's the done thing that a young man should shower his special girl with gifts, never the other way around."

"It is very sweet of you, Nelson, and I really appreciate it," I said. We stood alone in that hallway, rather close to each other.

"I should take this up to my room and put it away safely."

"Before you go," he said and put a hand on my arm to restrain me. "You should look up."

I did, wondering what he was talking about. We were standing in the spartan hallway, which had no adornment of any kind.

"Well, what a surprise," he said. "Mistletoe. I wonder who put that up there."

A sprig of mistletoe was hanging from the overhead electric light. Before I knew it, he had taken me into his arms and was kissing me. I didn't struggle or try to push him away. I let him kiss me. When we broke apart, he was beaming at me.

"Best Christmas ever," he said. "I'll remember this for a long time."

I went on up to bed, trying to come to terms with what had just happened. Should I have stopped him? Had I now given him too much encouragement? For a first kiss, it had been gentle, not at all alarming, but wasn't I supposed to have felt something? In truth all I was aware of was his slightly cold lips pressing against mine. Not unpleasant, but certainly not the divine sensation written about in romance novels. I lay in bed, listening to the wind rattling the window panes, trying to come to terms with what had happened. I had known he was keen on me, but this had taken it one step beyond friendship. The trouble was that I wanted more. I wanted to fall in love, to feel my heart skip a beat every time he looked at me, to live happily ever after. And I couldn't picture a life ahead with Nelson and his old mum and noisy siblings in the house behind the gasworks. In spite of everything that had happened to me, I suppose I hadn't learned to discard my aristocratic roots. Maybe I'd have to someday.

I fell asleep eventually and awoke to the distant sound of church bells. "Christmas Day," I muttered, and thought of Christmas Days in the past, when Mama was still alive. A stocking beside my bed with an orange, a chocolate mousse, maybe a book and a new pair of gloves. Never anything extravagant, but exciting just the same. For the past few years, Christmas Day had meant up at dawn to light fires, and later a rush to get the stuffing made and the turkey into the oven. At least there wouldn't be too much work for us today. And at least I had a present to unwrap as well as one already given.

I had bought a diary with a lock and key for Louisa and sent it off in good time before she departed for the country. A parcel had arrived from her, but I waited until Christmas morning to open it. First we had to attend church service in the palace chapel, but then we came back to a big breakfast with sausages, eggs and bacon. The birds were stuffed and went into the ovens. After that we gathered around the tree. Everyone received a little gift from Her Majesty. It was a royal medal with her likeness on it. And also a gift from Mr Angelo. This one was more practical and was a new handkerchief for each of us. Finally, I opened Louisa's gift. It was a pretty necklace of amethyst beads, a warm scarf and a golden guinea. I felt tears coming to my eyes. It had been years since anyone had bought me anything nice or special. I found myself feeling guilty. I had judged her so harshly for wanting to marry when I had funded her education, and for not seeming to appreciate my sacrifice. Now I saw that she did care for me.

The Christmas feast started at one o'clock. We joined the other members of the household staff in the servants' dining hall. The tables were laid with white cloths and decorated with holly and ivy. There were crackers beside each plate. Two turkeys and four geese were carried in, their skins nicely browned and glistening. Mr Francis and Arthur carved for us while tureens of roast potatoes, chestnut stuffing, sage and onion stuffing, bread sauce, Brussels sprouts, cauliflower with a white sauce, cabbage and gravy were passed around. Claret was poured. We pulled our crackers, put on paper hats, read the silly mottos and riddles and demonstrated our toys and puzzles. Then we said grace and ate until we couldn't stuff in another bite.

There was a blast on a bugle, and the Christmas puddings were carried in, flaming with brandy and with a sprig of holly stuck in them. I had helped to make these on Stir-up Sunday back in November, and most of them had been sent with the cooks to Osborne House. But there were plenty for us, served with the custard and brandy butter I had prepared. There were even several silver threepenny pieces inside, and I was lucky enough to get one of them.

"Make a wish," the parlour maid sitting

opposite me instructed. I wasn't quite sure what to wish for.

"Let the new year be favourable for me," I whispered to myself. "No unpleasant surprises, please."

After that mammoth meal, you might not have thought that anyone would want to eat again for weeks, however, we served tea, a little later than usual. Mr Roland had insisted on making the Christmas cakes for this tea. Ours was indeed a work of art. It had sat on the shelf resplendent in royal icing and waiting for the china figures to complete the snow scene. Now it was decorated with sledding figures, snowmen and children throwing snowballs.

After tea we sat around the fire, too full of food to do much. We played some party games—the Minister's Cat and charades. Later, for supper, we put out plates of cold turkey and goose, pickles and bread, but I couldn't face any. Nelson had said that it was his best Christmas ever. All I could think was that it was the nicest Christmas I had spent in years.

CHAPTER 11

The new year dawned, a year that promised the great excitement of the diamond jubilee—sixty years on the throne for our queen. But it didn't start with great jubilation. The queen returned from Osborne House suffering from a horrible cold and in a foul mood. We were instructed to make all kinds of medicinal broths, as well as the standard calf's foot jelly. Her Majesty sent most of them back, declaring them to be disgusting and useless. There was no entertaining, and we under-cooks spent our time practicing new and complicated dishes from the library of cookery books, only to have to send them to the ladies and gentlemen of the household or eat them ourselves. It was murmured around the palace that the queen's health was deteriorating and she might not even survive to celebrate in the summer.

"Don't you believe it," Nelson whispered to me. "She's a tough old bird, and stubborn, too. She'll hang on just to make sure she rides in that coach down the Mall."

To my relief, Nelson and I had settled back into our comfortable relationship. It had snowed heavily just after Christmas, and walking outside was treacherous, so we had not ventured out much. I had heard from Louisa that her Christmas in the country had been excessively dull and that Billy's grandfather drank far too much, but I hadn't had a chance to visit her in person to hear the details. However, I was secretly glad I had not been able to attend. Cooped up in the snow with Billy's relatives would have indeed been a penance.

I did not have a chance to visit Louisa until the end of January. I went to the big house in Highgate on my afternoon off and thought that there was something strange about Louisa. Something different. Then it dawned on me.

"Are you pregnant?" I asked.

She shook her head. "Not that I know of. No, there is something else that I have to tell you. Something I'm not quite sure about." She paused, twisting the long strand of jet beads she wore around her neck. Then she blurted out, "Billy wants us to move to Australia."

I certainly hadn't expected that news. "Australia? Isn't that where they send convicts? Whatever for?"

"These days it's a prosperous part of the empire," she said. "Lots of good land, and they are dying for people to go and settle it. Billy's father has told him he'll set him up with all he needs to start a sheep or cattle farm. He can get thousands of acres. And we can export the sheep and the wool to England. We have a chance to be really rich, Bella. We'll be somebodies. And in Australia they don't care if your father was a butcher or a chimney sweep."

I was lost for words.

"Say something," she said at last.

"I'm very happy for you, if that's what you want, Louisa," I muttered at last.

"That's just the problem. I'm not at all sure it's what I want, Bella. I mean, I want Billy to have the chance to get on and make something of his life. But Australia is so far away. I was wondering . . ." She paused and looked up at me. "If you'd come with us. You're all I've got, Bella. And when it comes to childbirth and things, well, I'd be scared to be all on my own." And she reached out and took my hand. "You will come, won't you? Billy will take care of everything."

Thoughts whirled around inside my head. I didn't want to abandon my only sister, but what would there be for me on a farm thousands of miles away from home? The chance to marry a farmer and be stuck in the middle of nowhere. And what of my cooking ambitions? The chance to lead my own life? It struck me that for the first time I had to put myself first.

I shook my head. "I'm sorry, Louisa. But I can't. I have dreams of my own. I want to become a good cook—a proper chef. I want to make my own way in life, not be a hanger-on, the poor unmarried sister in your life."

"I've heard there are plenty of unmarried men in Australia," she said.

"Farmers and cowhands and uncouth, uneducated men. I want more for myself, Louisa."

"And you think being a cook will get you the respect and status you desire?" she said sharply. "A cook is also a servant." Then I saw tears well up in her eyes. "I'm sorry. That was stupid of me. It's just that I don't want to move so far from you."

I shook my head. "I'm sorry, too. I don't want you to move so far away, but I have found a place where I feel that I belong, Louisa. I love my work. I'm learning more every day. You should see the cakes I can make now."

I gave her an encouraging smile, but she turned away, still upset. It crossed my mind that she was a little like my father, who also sulked when he couldn't get his own way. But in this case, it was not over a trifle. A move to Australia would be overwhelming for anyone.

"Maybe when you are settled and you can tell me what conditions are like and how far you are from towns, I'll consider it. I may even come for a visit," I said. "But not now. Not when I'm just beginning to find a place for myself in the world."

"Very well," she said stiffly. "Then you had

better hug your little sister one last time because we may never see each other again."

"Are you leaving so soon?" I asked, horrified.

"No, not until the summer at the earliest," she said. "Billy's father has a land agent working to find the best farmland, and we have to secure a passage."

"So of course I'll be seeing you again, you silly goose," I said. "Do you think I'm not going to visit you between now and the summer?"

She gave a sad little laugh. "Of course you are. It's just that once we say goodbye, it will really mean goodbye." She took my hands and squeezed them tightly. "Do think it over, Bella. My mind would be so much more at ease if I knew you were going to be with me in that far-off land."

"I will think it over, Louisa," I said, although my mind was already made up.

I felt guilty when I saw the hope in her eyes. "It could be a wonderful adventure, you know. They have kangaroos and koala bears and all sorts of funny things."

"Louisa, I can't marry a kangaroo," I said, making her laugh and easing the tension.

I spent a miserable few days feeling alternately guilty and angry that she had put me in such an untenable position. Of course I didn't want to go to Australia and live on a farm. But I saw the fear in Louisa's eyes, and she was so very young. Then I reminded myself that I had put my family first since my mother died. I had endured years of humiliation and servitude for Louisa. Now I wanted to become an expert cook—but more than that, I wanted to be an independent woman with the means to live life on my terms. Now it was time for me.

I threw myself with enthusiasm into improving my cooking skills, even creating what might become signature dishes, while we waited for daily bulletins on the queen's health and her recovery from her current illness. Then one day at the beginning of February, when the snow had turned to slush, making walking outside even more unpleasant, Mr Angelo summoned us all together. He had an announcement from Her Majesty. The queen felt that she was not going to get better as long as she stayed in London. She was anxious to go to the Riviera immediately. Apparently, she had spent her winters on the Mediterranean coast several times before. In the past she had stayed at hotels or villas belonging to other high-born people and only taken her personal maids and attendants. However, this time a brand-new hotel had been built specifically for her. "It's called the Excelsior Regina, if you can believe it," Mr Angelo said with a grin. "A whopping great place with a whole wing for the queen and her retinue. So this time she plans to take a good portion of her household."

"Does that include kitchen staff, Cook?" Jimmy, one of the apprentices, asked.

"It does, although I can't see us taking you, boy. You'd get into too much trouble in the hot climes of the Riviera with those French girls." And he grinned again.

"Don't they have chefs at hotels?" Mr Phelps asked.

"They do, but the queen prefers her meals prepared the way she likes them, cooked by people she knows. And she's suspicious of foreign cooking, as you well know."

"So who will you be taking?" Jimmy persisted.

"Not me, I firmly hope," Mr Francis said quickly. "I am near retirement and too old for such a strenuous journey, besides, I can't take the heat any longer."

"It's only Nice, Mr Francis, not the Congo," Mr Angelo replied, "but I will respect your wishes. It will only be a small contingent. We will mainly be cooking for an intimate party of her relatives. Should she decide to hold a bigger banquet, the hotel chefs are at our disposal. So who would like to go? I should like to take your wishes into account."

He looked around the kitchen.

"I don't think you'd want to take us ladies," Mrs Gillespie said. "It wouldn't be right for us to travel with the men, or to go out unescorted in foreign parts."

"Quite right, Mrs Gillespie," Mrs Simms said vehemently. "The tales one hears about those Frenchmen and Italians. No sense of decorum at all. They pinch bottoms."

"I am a Frenchman and I resent that," Mr Roland said. "I am as well behaved as any Englishman—better than most."

"I'm not saying all Frenchmen, Mr Roland," Mrs Simms said hastily. "Anyone can see that you are a proper gentleman."

"Of course we'll be taking Mr Roland," Mr Angelo said. "How would Her Majesty survive without her cakes and puddings?" He gave a nod to Mr Roland. "Added to which we'll need someone to interpret for us and to communicate with our French kitchen workers." He looked around at us. "I think we should take two cooks—Mr Phelps and Mr Williams, as the senior men, if neither of you has strong objections?"

"Not at all, Cook," Mr Phelps replied. "I think the air on the Riviera would be most agreeable for my rheumatics."

"And I, too, don't mind getting away from the winter rain," Mr Williams added.

"That's that, then," Mr Angelo said. "Plus one of you young upstarts to do the basic prep. Nelson? You seem to be the most advanced in your skills."

I glanced across at Nelson, who had turned bright red. "If you please, Cook, I'd prefer not to go so far from my mother, who is not in the best of health and relies on me, not having my dad around, you see."

Mr Angelo sighed. "Very good, Nelson. I respect that sentiment. So I suppose it better be Jimmy instead, as the senior apprentice. In spite of my misgivings about temptations with French women . . ." There was a general chuckle from the assembled group. "Unless he has family obligations he can't bear to tear himself away from."

There was a big grin on Jimmy's face. "Oh no, Cook. I've been dying to travel and see the world. Sign me up. I'm your man."

"Well, that's settled then. Myself, Mr Roland, Mr Phelps, Mr Williams and Jimmy it shall be. Those of you who are left will be catering for the members of the household who do not travel with Her Majesty."

"And a nice pleasant time we'll be having of it, too," Mrs Simms muttered to me as we went back to our stations.

As I went to join Mr Roland in our part of the kitchen, he seemed quite put out, and I had to remind him that he had already added two teaspoons full of baking powder to the sponge.

"Thank you, my dear," he said, which in itself was strange. He wasn't known for his gratitude and usually took full credit for anything I had baked. He had certainly never called me "my dear" before.

"Is something wrong, Mr Roland? Or are you just excited that you will be visiting your native land again?"

He looked around, then leaned closer to me. "Au contraire, Helen. I am not looking forward to it one bit. I dread the sea crossing. I suffer badly from mal de mer."

"Surely the sea crossing is quite short? It is only an hour at sea from Dover to the French coast, so I've been told."

"Not the way she travels." Again he glanced around to see if anyone was close enough to hear. "She takes the train to Portsmouth, then the royal yacht to Cherbourg. That's an overnight of being tossed around. I know. I did it once. Never again. And to be frank with you, I do not have any great love for my countrymen from the south. Those people in Nice, they are more Italian than French. Scoundrels and brigands the lot of them."

"But think of the lovely sunshine and the fruit and flowers."

"Like all young girls, you are a romantic. Me, I think of the bad drains and the typhoid."

I laughed. "I can see you are not at all a romantic, Mr Roland," I said.

"I have learned that life is hard and dreary, Helen. We are born, we work, we create things of beauty that are devoured in a few seconds . . . and then we grow old and die."

I was still smiling, and in a way flattered. It was the first time he was talking to me as if I was a person and not an underling. "I hope there is more to life than that," I said. "I must admit my own experience until now has not been wonderful, but I am hopeful about the future."

"You will no doubt find a young man, fall in love, marry and leave me—just when I have found an assistant who is not impossible to work with and who actually seems to have some talent."

"Thank you, monsieur. I am honoured that you think so," I said in French. "But I have no intentions of falling in love until I have learned to be a good pastry chef."

He frowned. "How is it that you know my language? Have you ever been to my country?"

"No, monsieur," I replied. "I was educated as a young girl. I came from a good family, and my father spoke excellent French. But he and my mother both died, and I had to go into service."

"So you see, life is hard," he agreed. "But now I remember. When I cut my finger and I uttered a few choice words in French, you understood, did you not? You told me to calm myself."

I nodded. "I didn't know the exact meaning of some of those words, but I understood the sentiments you were expressing."

"Now that I know you speak my language, I shall enjoy having a chance to converse occasionally. I find that I'm losing the facility, having not spoken it for so long."

"You have been in this country for a long time?" I asked.

"I came as a child," he said. "My father was a pastry chef before me in Paris, and then he was invited to London to work at a Gunter's as a confectioner. I learned my profession from the best."

"You certainly did," I replied. "Your petits fours are exquisite. I hope to learn many things from you when you have time to show me. How long do you think Her Majesty will be away?"

"She usually stays for at least two months. Two months of bad water and hay fever from all those blossoms." And he sighed.

I went away rather stunned. I had seen Mr Roland as a difficult individual who saw me as a necessary nuisance. Now it seemed as if I might have a chance of a real relationship in the future, even a modicum of friendship!

After this, the kitchen was in a hustle and bustle of preparation for the grand voyage. Mr Angelo agonized over which of the cookery books should be taken with him, as well as his particular favourite pots and pans. "I must have all my recipes. That is obvious. And I know they tell us they have a well-stocked kitchen," he said, "but will they have a mould just right for Her Majesty's favourite blancmange? Or a turban for that game terrine? And my fish poacher? Do they know how to poach fish in France? And how do I know what kinds of fish will be available in the local markets?" The pile of equipment he could not do without rose higher and higher. I wondered how they'd manage to carry it.

There was a discussion about what they were going to wear. It was no doubt warmer in southern climes. The men complained they only had dark suits for their days off. How could they acquire linen suits? Mrs Simms and I watched it all with amusement.

"Like a pack of women, they are, wondering what to wear and whether they'll look fashionable in France," she muttered. "But I'm that glad we're not going. I wish they'd be gone and we could get back to peace and quiet and our proper routine again."

As it happened, they found out they were to leave sooner than they expected. Her Majesty, or rather one of her secretaries, decided that it would be a good idea if her cooks went ahead so that the kitchen was up and working by the time she arrived. So there was added panic that they had to leave in two days. The good news was that they were to take the usual boat train to Dover and then cross the Channel to Boulogne by the shortest route. This would remove the long sea crossing, but instead it would be an extended and uncomfortable journey to the South of France by train if you were sitting up all night in a third-class carriage.

I felt they were rather ungrateful to complain. They'd be going abroad, seeing the world, actually travelling through Paris. I lay in bed that night, picturing what it would be like to travel. My father had been to the Continent as a young man, before being commissioned into the Indian Army. He had seen much of the world. Maybe someday . . .

I came downstairs the next morning to find the kitchen in a state of panic.

"What on earth is happening?" I asked Nelson, who was busy stirring the porridge for the servants' breakfast.

"It's Mr Roland," he whispered. "He's had an accident. He was going to the—you know—in the middle of the night, and he tripped over the suitcase he had open on his floor. He's fallen and twisted his ankle so badly he can't walk on it. He may have broken it."

"Oh, poor Mr Roland," I said. "If he can't walk, how can he possibly travel to France?"

"That's just the problem," Nelson said. "He can't. Cook is in a right state."

Even as Nelson uttered these words, Mr Angelo stormed into the kitchen. "Of all the stupid things to have done," he blustered. "Can't walk. Can't travel. What are we going to do now? That's what I'd like to know. We don't have a pastry chef. None of us knows a word of French beyond the names of dishes we have to cook. That's not going to cut the mustard, is it? How are we going to make our way across France, eh? And who is going to order for us at the market and talk to those foreign blokes at the hotel?"

"Excuse me, Cook," Nelson said, "but Helen here speaks French."

There was an instant silence in the kitchen. Eyes turned to me. I felt my cheeks burning.

"You do?" Mr Angelo asked. "You actually speak French, more than *la plume de ma tante*?"

I nodded, finding it hard to make myself speak. "Yes, Cook. I speak quite good French."

"Was one of your parents from that country?"

"No, Cook. But my father was well travelled and well educated. I learned French at school, and we sometimes spoke it at home."

"Well, blow me down with a feather," Mr Angelo said. "Young woman, you are full of surprises. You seem to have a bit of talent when it comes to pastry, and you speak French. I see no alternative: we'll have to take you with us."

"Me, Cook?" I could hardly get out the words.

"Yes, you. Go on then. You'd better go and pack your things."

I almost flew up the stairs with excitement. I

was going to France. It was only when I reached my room that the truth hit me. If one went abroad, didn't one have to carry a passport? I didn't have one, and if one had to be procured for me, how could it possibly be in the name of Helen Barton? Surely I would need to produce a record of my birth before they'd give me a passport. I'd just have to come up with some reason why I couldn't travel. A sudden case of the grippe . . . That's when it occurred to me that that was just what Mr Roland had done. He had made it clear he hadn't wanted to go to France, and miraculously he'd hurt his ankle badly enough that he couldn't go. How convenient for him.

I went downstairs again and found Mr Angelo wrapping blancmange moulds in newspaper, before putting them into a crate. "This one is her favourite," he said, looking up at me. "I doubt they'll have a mould in the shape of a rabbit, and she's liked this one since she was a girl."

"Cook, I've just had a worrying thought," I said. "I presume one needs a passport to travel abroad. I don't have one."

"Neither do any of us, ducks," he said. "But we don't need it. We have a letter of passage to say that we are part of the queen's retinue and they are to let us pass without hindrance. I'll have to have them add your name to it, but apart from that, Bob's your uncle. Now get cracking. We don't have any time to waste."

CHAPTER 12

I was going to France! And not just France, but the French Riviera. It seemed almost too good to be true. I half expected someone to tell me that a mistake had been made and a female servant was not allowed to travel after all. I retrieved my valise from under my bed and started to pack my pitiful wardrobe. Nothing I had was vaguely suitable for a fashionable resort or a warm climate. I had my uniform, one winter dress, one cotton shirtwaist (now a little tight), one summer skirt that had been let out from the days before I became a servant, my one good outfit from Louisa's wedding and a winter cloak. That was it. For a moment, I wondered if I could pay a rapid visit to Louisa and see if she had any extra clothing she could lend me. I had seen her trousseau, and it was quite generous. But I reminded myself she was shorter than I, and also I was too proud to ask for favours. But she had given me a golden guinea for Christmas, which was still tucked away in my purse, and I had my earnings since October in a savings account. Maybe when we reached France, I could find a dressmaker and have some suitable clothing made.

I didn't think there would be an occasion for a blue velvet dress, but I packed it anyway. Now that I fully believed that miracles could happen, I wanted to be prepared for another one. I was told that we'd be leaving on the eleven o'clock boat train the next morning. The queen and her party would follow two days later. I wrote to Louisa, telling her that I'd be going abroad, so she wouldn't hear from me for a while, then faced the driving sleet to pop the letter into a postbox.

I don't think I slept a wink that night, I was so excited. A little worried, too, if you want to know the truth. I had become passably competent at making cakes and pastries, but nothing like Chef Roland, and always under his supervision. I knew how fond the queen was of her pastries. What if mine were not up to her standard? I reassured myself that there would be French chefs at the hotel and I could ask them for advice. Also that Mr Roland would presumably recover in a week or so and be sent out to join the party.

When we assembled for breakfast in the morning, I could tell that the others in our party were as jittery as I was. "Not the day I'd choose to cross the Channel, is it now?" Mr Williams was muttering to Mr Phelps. They broke off as I came to join them at the table, regarding me with glances that indicated I was an interloper and they did not welcome my presence.

Rain beat against the high windows and the

wind howled through the chimney so that Mr Angelo went to ask permission to use the carriage portal, where we could load in our baggage without getting soaked. We were just carrying out the many crates and boxes that Chef deemed necessary when the queen's munshi appeared to say Her Majesty would like a word. Up the grand staircase we went and were ushered into a formal breakfast room where Her Majesty sat at a long table, a plate piled high with eggs, kidneys, bacon and poached haddock in front of her. Her Indian servant went to stand behind her, giving us a haughtily disapproving frown. The queen looked up from her food.

"I just wanted to say bon voyage to my loyal servants. I hope you have a safe journey and that everything is made ready for my arrival."

"It will be, Your Majesty," Mr Angelo replied.

"Very good. Off you go." And we were dismissed again, hearing the queen saying, "Hand me some of that marmalade. No, not that one. The ginger."

When the last pieces had been strapped on to the back of the carriage, we made ready to depart. The other servants had come to see us off. Nelson touched my arm. "Safe journey. Have a good time, Helen. But don't go talking to any strange Frenchmen, understand?"

I laughed. "I can hardly spend time in France without talking to any Frenchmen, Nelson."

"You know what I mean," he said, lowering his voice. "I understand that Frenchmen can be very persuasive. I wouldn't want your head turned."

"I promise you nobody is going to turn my head," I said. "Take care of yourself until I come home."

"I will." He took my hand for a second and gave it a squeeze. Then he assisted me into the carriage, and off we went. The five of us were packed in with boxes of kitchen equipment on our laps. Mr Phelps was clearly uncomfortable sitting so close to me. I realized that in the months I had been in the kitchen he had never addressed a word to me.

"Don't worry, Mr Phelps, I won't bite," I said. Jimmy chuckled.

"I have nothing against you personally, Miss Barton," Mr Phelps said primly. "But I think it is a mistake to take a female person on a long and arduous trip like this. What if you should become ill? If you should faint?"

"I assure you I am in the best of health and have never fainted in my life," I said. "And I promise that I will do my best to make sure you are not inconvenienced in any way."

"You can't say fairer than that, Mr Phelps," Jimmy said, giving me a wink. I hoped the wink was just a friendly one. I didn't want any complications on this trip.

We arrived at Victoria Station, and Mr Angelo

bossed the porters as they loaded the luggage in the guard's van. We found our seats, the whistle blew and off we went. It was not an auspicious start as we chugged out of the station. Rain peppered the windows, sending streaks of grime running down. The backyards we passed looked dismal. But it was my first real train ride, my first time going out of London, and I was determined to enjoy every moment. By the time we arrived at the port of Dover, the weather had not improved. We were soaked and windswept as we negotiated the gangplank on to the ship and had to compete with other passengers for a corner of dry space in the second-class saloon. The crossing was indeed choppy, and I could see why Mr Roland had dreaded it so much. We were crowded together on the bench that ran around the wall. The boat lurched and rolled, making it impossible to stand. Mr Phelps moaned. Mr Williams had gone very pale, and even the normally cheeky Jimmy was silent. Strangely enough, I felt just fine.

"Don't worry, Mr Phelps," I said. "Not long now."

"I don't think I shall survive to see France," he groaned. There were beads of sweat on his forehead. Suddenly he had to get up and rush through the crowd in the direction of the lavatories. He did not return for some time, and when he did, he looked positively green.

"Let me get you a glass of water," I suggested.

I forced my way to the bar and came back with the glass, having only spilled a little. He nodded gratefully. As the crowd parted, I looked out through the saloon window, and there, ahead of us, was the coast of France. What's more, the rain had stopped. I left the others and went outside on to the deck. The sea was still flecked with whitecaps, but the waves had now subsided to a gentle roll. I could see brightly painted houses lining a harbour, and white cliffs like the ones we had left behind. We passed a fishing boat, and the men on board looked up and waved. They were all wearing bright-blue smocks and made a colourful contrast to the red sails of the boat. I felt that I was bubbling over with elation. Here I was, Bella Waverly, former housemaid, lowliest of servants, and I was now about to set foot on the Continent. I was going to make the very most of this opportunity.

We were whisked through French customs, thanks to the letter from Her Majesty, and escorted to our train. The gentlemen seemed to have recovered, and Mr Williams produced cold beef sandwiches he had made just in case there was no proper food to be found on the journey. We ate them gratefully. I couldn't stop staring out of the window. Everything was so different: the brightly painted shutters on the windows of houses, the lines of poplar trees along the roads, the great yellow horses working in the fields and the peasants in smocks. I was dying to get my first glimpse of Paris, but darkness had fallen by the time we approached the outer part of that city. I peered out of the window as we passed through backstreets, then through the dark haze I caught a glimpse of it. Taller than any building I had ever seen, rising impossibly high into the night sky.

"There it is, Mr Angelo," I blurted out. "Look. The Eiffel Tower."

The others crowded to the train window, but then we passed between buildings again, and the view was lost. We came into the Gare du Nord about seven o'clock that evening, only to find it was eight o'clock in French time. We had to hire a wagon to take us across the city to the Gare de Lyon, from which our train to Nice would depart. Seeing as I was the only one who spoke French, I had to pluck up courage and hire the transportation. But the driver was used to carrying English visitors, and I really didn't need to say more than "Gare de Lyon, how much?" I had no idea if I'd struck a fair price. The wagon driver certainly made a great show of complaining about the amount of luggage we carried with us. Again we were crammed in with our luggage behind us, and I only got the occasional glimpse of tall, elegant houses, shutters at the windows, cafés with bright awnings and tables out on the pavement. But enticing smells wafted towards us: tobacco smoke that smelled quite different from the pipes and cigarettes at home—herbier, spicier and more attractive, I thought. And good culinary smells: onions and garlic and coffee roasting. And there were strange and different sounds too: the sound of an accordion, a woman's voice singing came to us and later a loud argument from an upstairs window, all serving to remind me that I was in a different land.

Jimmy was peering out into the night. "I'm a bit disappointed," he said. "The people look just like Londoners."

"What were you expecting, boy? Savages wearing loincloths?" Mr Phelps said acidly.

"No, but you hear things about the French, don't you? You know—ooh la la. Cancan dancers and fishnet stockings?"

"Hardly in the middle of winter on city streets," Mr Phelps retorted, making me smile.

At the Gare de Lyon station, Mr Angelo handed us each a packet containing French money. "Your weekly wages in francs," he said. "And don't ask me what the conversion rate is to our pounds, because I am as much in the dark as you are. So until we learn, be careful that nobody tries to trick you." We nodded, taking the packets from him. Then he suggested we should find something to eat, as there would be no dinner on the train for third-class passengers like ourselves.

"At least we can all read this much French,"

Mr Williams commented as we stood staring at the menu in the station cafeteria. "But I'm not quite sure what *grenouilles* are?"

"Frogs, Mr Williams," I replied.

"God forbid." He raised his eyes. "Don't tell me we've got to live on frogs for the next few months."

"There are other things, Mr Williams," Chef pointed out. "But I think we should stick to a bowl of vegetable soup, don't you? Just in case foreign food might upset our stomachs on the journey."

So we each had a bowl of soup at the station restaurant. It was rich and tasty, and the bread that accompanied it was delicious. Thus fortified, we found our seats on the train and settled in for a long and uncomfortable night sitting up on a hard seat. At nine o'clock we pulled out of the station. The carriage shook and swayed around a lot, making Mr Phelps look quite ill again.

"I bet the queen doesn't have to travel like this," Jimmy said.

"She does not," Mr Angelo agreed. "She has a private train meet her at Cherbourg, and she has two cars all to herself—a sleeping car with a proper bed and a sitting room. I believe the furniture comes from the palace, too."

"Do you know what I heard?" Mr Williams said. "I heard that she is having her own bedroom furniture shipped across to the hotel in Nice."

"Nice for some," Jimmy said. "I mean *neece* for some." He played on the word, making us all smile.

"Do shut up and let me sleep," Mr Phelps said. "I feel quite unwell again, and the sooner morning comes the better."

I closed my eyes and tried to sleep. We stopped at one station after another—Dijon, Mâcon—then we came into the city of Lyon and stayed there long enough to have coffee on the platform. I tried to sleep and dozed occasionally, only to have Jimmy's head fall on to my shoulder. There were no more stations for a long while, and I think I drifted off to sleep, until at first grey dawn we came into the big port city of Marseilles. The people on the platform here were quite different from the elegant men and women I had spotted in Paris. There were men in striped jerseys, berets on their heads, and women wrapped in bright shawls and colourful wide skirts. Their language was harsher with a strange twang to it. We pulled out of the station again on the last leg of our journey. The landscape became hilly and wild, then suddenly the sun came up, and we had our first glimpse of blue sea. I gave a little gasp of excitement. The colours were so bright! There were whitewashed houses with bright green or yellow shutters, red and orange flowers spilling over white walls. And in the distance, the sparkling blue of the Mediterranean. It was dazzling after the dreary days of the English winter. I couldn't wait to get to Nice.

Jimmy seemed more lively than the rest of us. He stood at the train window, staring out at the sea. "Who's game for a dip in the Med, eh?" he said.

"I think you'll find that the sea is rather cold, my boy," Mr Angelo said. "It is winter here, too, you know. Even if the sun is shining. And besides, I'm afraid the beach in Nice is all stones."

"Stones? No sand like Margate?"

"All stones," Mr Angelo said. "Nasty round little pebbles that make walking most uncomfortable."

"How do you know about the beach in Nice, Mr Angelo?" I asked. "Have you been there before?"

"I have, Miss Barton. I accompanied Her Majesty when she rented a villa a few years ago. But I have not stayed in the area of the new hotel. I understand it's in a quarter called Cimiez, up on a hillside, so it will be a learning experience for me as it will for all of us."

The rail line followed the seashore, stopping at one little station after another. I spotted fishing boats out at sea and amongst them a beautiful and sleek steam yacht. My travelling companions had been rather quiet all through the night, but now we had all revived.

"Would you look at that." Jimmy gestured at

it. "You know who that belongs to, don't you?"

"Would that be the Prince of Wales's yacht?" Mr Angelo asked.

"I reckon it is. I saw a picture of it in a magazine," Jimmy replied. "Not bad. I wonder if we'll be invited on board."

Mr Williams chuckled. "You've gotta hope, boy. He'll have his own complement of chefs and everything else."

"Including mistresses, I shouldn't wonder." Jimmy gave me a wink.

"Watch it, young fellow, we've got a lady present," Mr Angelo said.

"My apologies, Miss Barton." Jimmy gave me an overly effusive bow.

"I assure you I'm not easily offended, Jimmy," I replied.

Conversation lapsed as we watched the yacht. My pulse had begun to race. The Prince of Wales on the Riviera. All those worries I had managed to put aside since my encounter with the prince now came flooding back. I tried to tell myself that he would not even remember me if we met again. It had been one of his harmless flirtations, long forgotten. But the fact that his yacht was now on the Riviera was too close for comfort.

"Does he also stay with the queen in Nice?" I asked casually.

"No, he has his own villa in Cannes," Mr Angelo said.

"He wouldn't be caught near her," Jimmy chimed in. "She doesn't approve of his goings-on and lets him know it."

That made me breathe a little easier. I wasn't quite sure how far away Cannes was, but at least he wasn't going to be at the queen's hotel. I was all in favour of the Prince of Wales keeping his distance from the queen. Then another disquieting thought surfaced in my brain: Ronnie Barton. I had not even heard whether the prince had hired him, but if he had, surely he would be on the lowest rung of servants and therefore not accompanying his employer to France. But he would never find out that I was here, I told myself. And even if he did, I had fulfilled my part in the bargain. I hoped I had nothing to worry about.

CHAPTER 13

"One thing I should mention to you before we arrive at Nice," Mr Angelo said as the train began to slow. "The queen does not want to draw attention to herself while she is abroad. We are not to mention that she is Queen Victoria. She likes to refer to herself as Lady Balmoral."

"Really?" Jimmy looked amused. "How many people did you say she was bringing with her?"

"About forty-five, I think. That's not counting the royal relatives."

"She's got relatives coming, too?"

"Any number of them, so I've heard. Her daughter Beatrice of Battenberg and her children; Princess Helena, who is now Princess of Schleswig-Holstein, isn't she? Oh, and I believe there is a young German cousin included in the party, Princess Sophie of some German place I can't remember and probably couldn't pronounce, plus the princess's fiancé, Count something-or-other."

"And yet she wants people to think she is a simple, ordinary Lady Balmoral, with a house full of royals like that?" Jimmy chuckled. "Forty-five retainers, crowned heads of Europe. That doesn't give the local people a hint that she might be Queen Victoria? Added to which she is rather distinctive looking, isn't she? A little round dumpling of a lady wearing a veil."

"Don't be disrespectful, boy," Mr Angelo warned. "Whatever she chooses to do or say or be called is not for the likes of us to dispute."

"What about that dreadful Indian munshi fellow?" Mr Williams asked. "Don't tell me she's bringing him with her?"

"I rather fear she is, Mr Williams." Mr Angelo raised his eyes in despair. "And there has been a frightful row about that, in case you haven't heard."

"We hear nothing, shut away in the kitchen," Mr Williams said. "We might as well be in another world, might we not?"

"Well." Mr Angelo leaned closer. "The gentlemen of her household—real proper gentlemen, I mean—can't stand the bloke. They threatened to resign en masse if she brought the munshi along. She told them they could go and boil their heads, the munshi was coming."

"She didn't actually say that, did she?" Mr Williams looked aghast.

"Something along those lines." Mr Angelo managed a cheeky grin.

"And did they resign?" Mr Williams asked.

"They did not, so I understand. And the munshi

is coming whether we like it or not. But I have no intention of making curries."

"That should arouse the curiosity of the local people," Jimmy said. "With him strutting around in those outlandish clothes and looking like a peacock."

"It certainly may," Mr Angelo said, grinning with Jimmy. "Not to mention her Scottish pipers who always accompany her."

"Pipers? Playing bagpipes, you mean?" Mr Phelps sat up, now looking animated. "In their Highland dress? Kilts and all?"

"Kilts and all, Mr Phelps," Mr Angelo said.

"And we still have to refer to her as Lady Balmoral?"

Mr Angelo nodded. "I think the reason behind it is that her title denotes this is not an official visit, so dignitaries do not feel obliged to arrange formal welcomes and banquets."

"Ah, well that makes sense then." Mr Phelps nodded.

It didn't make much sense to me. Why try to claim you were an ordinary member of the aristocracy and yet bring a regiment of pipers with you and arrive on a private train? Surely the name Lady Balmoral would fool no one.

We steamed into Nice station at mid-morning. The sun was warm as we descended from our compartment and stood on the platform stretching our tired and cramped limbs while the engine hissed and puffed like a tired old gentleman looking forward to a rest.

"Off you go, Helen," Mr Angelo said, giving me a little shove. "Find us some kind of transport to the hotel."

It was my first real chance to try out my French. The first time they were relying on my skills, and I set off, a little apprehensive. It was true that my French had been quite good in school and at home with my parents, but I had never tried it with real French people. And it seemed the inhabitants of the south spoke with a strange accent—a twang not heard in the north. Nevertheless, I made for the station exit and located a string of open carriages. By the time the men joined us, followed by several porters with barrows piled high with our luggage, I had a vehicle waiting.

At the sight of our many bags and cases, the coachman let out a stream of rapid French, waving his hands in animation. I only just got the gist of it.

"He says that five people plus all these bags will be too much for his horse up the hill. We will need a separate cart for the bags."

"Very well," Mr Angelo agreed. "You'd better find us another vehicle for the baggage then, Helen."

That wasn't hard. Other drivers had gathered

around, interested in the group of foreigners asking for the Hotel Excelsior Regina. A fight broke out as they vied for our business.

"You are not royalty?" one of them asked me, looking at our attire.

"No, but we are with the party of a distinguished English lady . . . Lady Balmoral," I replied.

He laughed. "You come with your queen. We know that."

So much for her travelling incognito.

"They build the hotel expressly for her," he went on. "Millions of francs it cost. No expense spared. Better than a palace. You wait until you see it."

The last bags were piled on to a second open cart. We left the station and traversed crowded shopping streets, where donkeys jostled with smart carriages and even the occasional automobile. The streets were cobbled, and we bounced uncomfortably while the contents of our boxes rattled alarmingly. We came to a residential area, and the road started to climb. At first there were elegant apartment buildings, then, as we ascended the hill, we could see villas set amid gardens. There were blossoms on trees and shrubs, and the air smelled delightful: fresh and sweet, but with a hint of tang from the sea. The road got steeper, and I could see why the carter had objected to his horse carrying a heavy load.

We were now high above the town, with market gardens and olive groves between newly built villas, and in front of us mountains arose, clothed in green at this time of the year. I found it hard to contain my excitement. It was the first time I had seen a real mountain, an olive tree, a palm tree. I glanced at the men in the carriage beside me. If they shared my enthusiasm, they did not show it. In fact, Mr Phelps was looking alarmed. "And how are we supposed to get down to the city, that's what I'd like to know," he said. "Walk all that way down and then all the way back again?"

"I don't know if I'd want to be going down to the city myself," Mr Williams said. "Did you see the look of some of those people? Swarthy brigands, that's what they looked like. They'd rob you and cut your throat without thinking."

"Oh, surely not, Mr Williams," Mr Angelo replied.

"It's all right for you, Mr Angelo. You look like one of them," Mr Williams replied. "I look like a foreigner. I'd be a prime target for robbery."

"Look up there," Jimmy said suddenly. "I bet that's where we're headed."

We turned to look where he was pointing. A giant white building rose up from gardens, as big as a palace and just as elegant. It swept in what appeared to be a curve across the hillside, topped with turrets from which flags of many nations were flying. And on the front was the sign "Hotel Excelsior Regina." We had arrived.

Hotel porters came running out to greet the carriage. They became less enthusiastic when I explained to them in French that we were Lady Balmoral's servants.

"We know who she is," one said. "You don't need to keep up pretence with us. Why else would they build a hotel for her? Wait here, and I will summon the manager. I know he will want to greet you."

We waited. Mr Angelo watched with an eagle eye as the bags and crates were unloaded and then had me pay the drivers. It seemed they were asking for an awful lot of money, but I was unfamiliar with francs.

"What would be the correct amount from the station?" I whispered to one of the hotel employees. He told me, and I paid accordingly. The drivers did not look pleased, but they didn't argue either.

The manager appeared, looking as grand as royalty in his frock coat and high collar. He wore a really impressive black moustache. "Welcome, welcome, dear guests from across the Channel to Cimiez and to the Hotel Excelsior Regina," he said. "You are part of the queen's advance party?"

"We are her kitchen staff," I replied in French. "Mr Angelo and cooks."

"Ah." He didn't look quite so enthusiastic. "You are the interpreter for them, mademoiselle?"

"I am," I replied.

"And they do not speak French?"

"I'm afraid not."

"Welcome, dear friends and servants of Her Majesty," he now said in English. "Since the hotel is not busy at this moment, I shall be delighted to show you personally to your rooms."

"Very kind of you, monsieur," Mr Angelo said. He pronounced it *mon-sewer*.

We were led in through a grand entrance, the foyer carpeted appropriately in royal blue with a fleur-de-lis pattern.

"Is there not a servants' entrance we should be using?" Mr Phelps asked, glancing around nervously.

The manager shook his head. "Not for the queen's wing of the hotel. The entrance was designed so that she can come straight from her carriage to a lift and not have to walk up any steps. We understand that she is very lame and cannot walk."

We were now facing the lift, designed with an elegant ironwork facade. "The queen will occupy the whole of the first floor," he went on. "Her guests and her family members will occupy the floor above. Her military attachés and important household members on the third floor. Her secretaries and doctor on the fourth. Her lesser attendants on the fifth. You will have rooms on the top floor. I will take you up now in our new lift. In the future I am afraid that servants should use the staircase at the back, in case you run into a member of the royal party or inconvenience them by summoning the lift at the wrong moment."

A smartly dressed lift attendant leapt out and pulled back the wrought iron door, allowing us to enter. It was the first time I had ridden in such a contraption, and I felt a trifle apprehensive. I saw Mr Phelps glance at Mr Williams and realized they were similarly unfamiliar with lifts.

"And where are the kitchens?" Mr Angelo asked.

"They are situated on the ground floor, in the main part of the hotel, not in the part reserved for Her Majesty. You will be sharing kitchen space with the chefs of the hotel. However, a suitable portion of the area has been set aside for you, following Her Majesty's wishes." He paused as the lift gate snapped shut, and with a creaking, groaning sound, we began to ascend slowly. "I will be happy to introduce you to your fellow chefs when you are settled into your rooms."

Eventually we came to a halt with a jerk. The gate was opened for us. We came out on the sixth floor. "You gentlemen may select your rooms along this hallway, according to your rank," the manager said, standing aside to let us emerge from the lift. "The bathroom is at the far end. But you, mademoiselle, I think you should be on the floor below, with the queen's lesser secretaries and minor officials?"

"Oh no, monsieur, that would not be right," I said. "I am also one of the cooks, and junior to these men."

"All the same, I think you would prefer that you are amongst ladies of the household and do not have to share the bathing facilities with these men."

"Would that be all right, Mr Angelo?" I asked. I certainly didn't want to offend any of the men at this stage of our trip.

"I think that is quite right and proper, Miss Barton," he replied. "You should not have to share facilities with the men in the party."

Off they went to choose rooms, and I allowed myself to be led down a flight of stairs to the floor below. These stairs were by no means grand—narrow and made of stone. The room I was offered was also simple—an iron-framed bed, a chest of drawers, a narrow wardrobe and a washbasin. But the view from the window: I stood gazing out and found I couldn't breathe. The whole of the town of Nice lay below me, elegant white buildings along a waterfront lined with palm trees, pastel-coloured villas clinging to hillsides and beyond the sparkling blue curve of the bay. I had never seen anything as lovely in my life, and my thought was that I never wanted to leave.

CHAPTER 14

Reluctantly, I wrenched myself away and unpacked my belongings. Then I thought I had better find out about the kitchen arrangements so that I could report back to the other cooks. I did not presume to use the lift this time, so I walked down flight after flight, each staircase a little grander than the one before, until the last two were very grand indeed—made of marble with a red carpet at the centre. When I reached the queen's floor, I went in search of a door that might lead to the kitchens, but could not find one and did not want to poke and pry too far, in case I was accused of snooping or even worse. I paused in the hallway, thinking.

That's right. I remembered we had been told that the kitchens were situated in the main part of the hotel. I came out through the queen's porte cochère, looked around on the forecourt, then, not seeing any humble way in, dared to enter through the main doors. Nobody stopped me. I found myself in a breathtaking foyer, soaring two stories high—all marble pillars and with a grand staircase at its centre. The dining room was equally impressive, with white-clothed tables between more marble pillars, a dais for an orchestra and full-size palm trees. Fortunately, it was deserted at this time of the morning. Eventually my clear lack of status caught up with me.

"Mademoiselle, may I be of assistance?" a voice said behind me, and when I turned to look a very disapproving and very superior waiter was glaring at me. I excused myself and told him that I was part of Her Majesty's retinue and that I had been sent to locate the kitchens where the English chef would be working. Then he was genial and led me personally through the dining room, through an anteroom with warming tables and finally to a pass door that led to the kitchens. He deserted me at this moment, and I pushed open the door cautiously. I was greeted by enticing aromas and the clatter of pots and pans. The door opened into a long, modern room, brightly lit with electric light bulbs. Several men in white chef's uniforms were at work, and the smells from those pots on the stove were enticing. Nobody looked up as I came in.

"*Pardon, messieurs*," I said loudly.

The man who had been trimming a duck at the table nearest me looked up and started violently.

"Mademoiselle, what are you doing in my kitchen?" he demanded, coming towards me and waving his hands as if he was shooing away chickens. "You must leave at once. This is forbidden to guests of the hotel."

He was quite young, fit looking and clean shaven, with dark eyes that were now flashing dangerously.

"Pardon, monsieur, but I am a member of the queen's party. We have been sent in advance to be ready for her arrival, and we need to know where we are to establish ourselves. Are we to have a separate kitchen or to share this space with you?" I was glad that I had prepared the sentences in my head as I walked down the stairs because he was rather alarming, and my French was decidedly rusty.

"The queen's cooks?" he said with scorn in his voice. He turned back to his fellow chefs, who were all regarding me with interest. "We have been warned about this. We have been told the queen will send her own cooks from England because she thinks we French do not know how to prepare food."

The other men laughed.

"On the contrary, monsieur," I replied hastily. I could feel my cheeks burning, and tried to stay calm. "The queen is an older lady. She has to be careful what she eats. She wants to make sure the dishes are familiar to her and will not make her sick." This, of course, was an outright lie. The queen loved dishes that were quite wrong for an old woman's digestion, and she seemed to have a cast iron stomach, but I also suspected the French could be most sensitive about their famed culinary skills. I hoped this explanation had done the trick, but he was still glaring at me.

"Perhaps your queen does not know that a French chef can prepare any meal, even the most boring and mundane—although perhaps not quite as boring as English food."

Again there was laughter.

"Then I suspect you have not tasted English food," I replied. "I hope you will have a chance to taste some of our preparations while we are in residence here. Now, about the kitchen arrangements . . ."

He frowned. "You are their interpreter?"

"I am also one of the cooks," I replied.

"A woman as a chef?" He made a little "pah" sort of noise. "And what exactly will you be doing?"

"Cooking excellent meals, one would hope," I replied. "But as to that, I am not yet a chef. I am still learning the intricacies of the preparation of fine food." At least that was what I hoped I had said. I would need to expand my vocabulary beyond that of the schoolroom.

He was still looking at me with scorn. "The queen has to send a woman, an apprentice? Has she no proper chefs in her employ?"

"Plenty, but I am here as a member of the party because of my facility in the French language. None of the other chefs speak any French. Our Monsieur Roland, the pastry chef, who is French, was regrettably indisposed at the last moment, and I was sent in his place."

"As the interpreter, not the pastry chef, I would think."

I had a great desire to slap that smug face, but restrained myself.

"Actually both. I have been studying under Monsieur Roland, and while I am not at his level of perfection yet, the queen has expressed herself satisfied with my creations." I stood there, staring him in the eye. My fighting spirit was now aroused. I saw the expression of scorn turn to one of suspicion, maybe even of curiosity.

"This is normal in England to employ women to cook? Are the others in your party also women?"

"No, I am the only woman."

"Thank God for that. The queen has many women in her kitchens?" he asked.

"Very few. Two older women cooks and myself, newly hired because the queen believes that young women should be given chances to advance."

"So how is it that you speak the language? You were born in France? Your family came from our country?"

"No, monsieur. I was educated as a young girl. I was raised to be a lady. Unfortunately, both my parents died, and I was alone in the world and had to earn my living."

His expression had now softened. "And what is your name?"

I hesitated. "It's Helen," I said. "Helen Barton."

"Ah. *La belle* Hélène." He actually smiled now.

"And your name, monsieur?"

"It is Jean-Paul Lepin. Chef Lepin."

I could not stifle a grin. I thought he had said *lapin*, which is the French word for rabbit. "For a rabbit, you seem quite fearless."

This made the other chefs chuckle again, and I saw by the nod of a head that I had scored a point.

"Ah, very good." He looked amused now. "But alas my name is Lepin, not Lapin. But you are right. I am quite fearless."

"Pardon me, Chef, but do you want to taste the sauce before it is added to the timbale au crevettes?" one of the other cooks called out to him.

"I trust your judgement completely, Henri," Jean-Paul Lepin replied.

I was now staring at him with curiosity. "You are the head chef here?"

"I am."

"You are very young for a head chef," I commented.

"No, I am really fifty-five, but I have lived a good clean life," he replied, loudly enough that the other men in the room looked up again and laughed. He was smiling as he turned back to me. "As a matter of fact, I am only thirty, and

I am young to be a head chef, but I started in my father's kitchen when I was sixteen and learned my skills from the best. Also, the man who built this hotel is modern in his ways and forward-looking. All of us cooks are young and ambitious and will create new dishes to excite the international celebrities who will stay here."

"A great opportunity for you," I said.

He nodded. "And for you, so it would seem. Well, Mademoiselle Cook, I must get back to my duck breast, or our luncheon service will be behind. You asked about the kitchen facilities. As a matter of fact, we have been informed that we must share a kitchen with the queen's chefs. We have been instructed to do all we can to accommodate you and make your stay agreeable, since this hotel was built expressly with the intention of housing your queen, and thus hopefully bringing in many other noble and distinguished visitors. So the tables on the far side of the room are reserved for you, as are the stoves on that far wall. The pans hanging above are at your disposal. Please let me know if there is some article of equipment that you lack. I am sure it can be easily obtained."

I grinned. "When you see what our head chef has brought with him in the way of equipment, he was taking no chances. I just hope there will be space to store it all."

"He does not believe that we possess pots and

pans in France?" He was looking less friendly again.

"Of course he does. But Her Majesty is very particular in the way she likes things prepared, and he did not want to be caught out."

"I understand. As a chef, I prefer my own tools. One needs to know how a particular pan will perform."

"I thank you for your time, and for allotting us our space in your kitchen," I said. "I will bring down the chefs to introduce to you when you are less busy."

"Of course. My staff looks forward to making their acquaintance." He said this stiffly, as if he was only repeating what he had been told to say, and gave a little bow. "And, mademoiselle, we are very well aware that this kitchen, this hotel, would not exist if your queen had not decided that she wanted to visit Nice. Everyone in this city hopes that she will be what is needed to bring visitors from all over the world. She will turn our city into a fashionable wintering resort. And for me, personally, I will have the opportunity to demonstrate my skills to people of rank and money. Who knows, maybe an emperor or an American millionaire will invite me to come and work for him."

"You would want to leave Nice?" I exclaimed. "But surely it is the most beautiful place in the world."

"You are correct there," he agreed. "But I have a desire to see the world before I settle down." He paused, then said, in a more formal voice, "Now, if you will excuse me, I need to return to my preparations."

He went back to his work, and I made my exit. This time I found that there was a similar pass door at our side of the kitchen, which led down another narrow hallway to the queen's private dining room. I peeked inside. It looked like a room in any country house—not particularly grand, but the walls were decorated with suitably royal paintings, and the table might seat twelve at the most. Beyond it was another, larger dining room, where the royal household would take their meals. If the queen wanted to host a large dinner party, I had no idea how or where she would do this. Maybe take over the great dining hall of the hotel? Anyway, that was not my concern. I followed the hallway and came out behind the staircase. Ah, so that was how I had missed the door on the first occasion. It was cunningly concealed.

There I paused for the first time, catching my breath. I had found the encounter with Chef Lepin to be quite alarming. I hoped all Frenchmen would not be so belligerent and confrontational, also not as unnervingly handsome!

CHAPTER 15

I duly reported to Mr Angelo that I had located the kitchens and met with the head chef. I warned him that our presence was rather resented and not to expect to be welcomed with open arms.

He nodded. "I'm not surprised about that. I would not take kindly to a foreign chef being thrust into my kitchen. Don't worry. We'll probably get along once he sees the quality of our food preparation. Will you take me down now?"

"I think we should wait until after luncheon," I said. "They are rather busy at the moment."

"Of course. I forgot that this is also a working hotel. There will be other guests. And it's time we ate something, too. I presume there is a staff dining room where we should take our meals, or are we expected to cook our own?"

"I didn't ask about that," I said. "In truth, the chef was rather patronizing about us. I was anxious to get away."

"Then we will go out and find a café," he said. "We still have some of our travel money unspent. We'll have a good meal."

• • •

The others were summoned, and we went in search of a place to eat. After enquiring, I found that this area on the hill was all parks and villas and grand hotels. For an ordinary café, we would have to go down into the town again. "But there is the trolley," the hotel porter told us. "A new trolley line built especially for this hotel."

"Oh, that is good news," I replied.

He shrugged. "Unfortunately, it is apt to break down with regularity. Perhaps it will be working well today."

The trolley was working, and we made it safely down the long, steep hill into the town. We found a pleasant little café where the men selected a type of pasta, but I chose an omelette. I had always thought that eggs were for breakfast, so I had never tried one, and I was not disappointed. It came up light, fluffy and stuffed with tiny shrimp. Every mouthful was a delight, and I began to see that appreciation of food was a way of life in France. It was accompanied by crusty bread so fresh it was still warm, and sweet butter. I did make the mistake of asking for a cup of tea when we were offered a carafe of wine. It appeared that tea is not something the French have taken to, at least not as the English like it. It came up so light that it was just water with a slight scent to it, and with a slice of lemon beside it.

"I reckon it will have to be wine with meals

from now on," Mr Angelo said as he watched me sip with disgust on my face. "We can't drink the water, so I've heard. It's questionable. So it's wine or nothing."

"Wine? At midday?" Mr Williams asked. "You know I don't drink, Cook. I'm teetotal, like everyone in my part of Wales. I've taken the pledge."

"Then you'll have to stick to milk, or tea that looks like Helen's."

When we came to ride up the hill again, we were informed that the trolley had experienced one of its many breakdowns, and we had to trudge all the way up. We reached the hotel hot, tired and a little grumpy. The men declared they were going to have a rest and were in no hurry to meet the hostile French chefs. Since the queen would not arrive for a few days, we did not have to rush to prepare the kitchen for her, and we would not need to order food yet. Thus our time was our own. This was magical news for me. I couldn't even remember a time when I had had leisure, certainly not in such wonderful circumstances. I changed into a cotton blouse and skirt and went out exploring.

In front of the hotel, I had noticed the most wonderful gardens. The walkways were lined with massive palm trees, and their fronds whispered and crackled as they swayed in the stiff breeze that now came up from the sea. Even at this time of year, there were flower beds of bright flowers whose names I didn't know. Brilliant red-and-yellow climbing plants spilled over walls. There were arbours and fountains, a croquet lawn, a tennis court, a conservatory full of exotic plants and at the front of the garden a display that spelled out the name of the hotel in flowers. It was all so heady and enchanting for one who had grown up in London. It was true I had experienced the freedom of Hampstead Heath, but that was so long ago now it seemed as if it was in another lifetime, or even in a dream.

I walked the carefully raked paths, pausing to sniff when a particularly intoxicating smell came to me. Trees with yellow powder puffs of flowers had the sweetest scent. I sat on a bench under one such tree and looked around me, almost believing I might be in heaven. Then tiredness from the sleepless night on the train overcame me, and I must have drifted off to sleep because I heard a voice saying, in French, "Stay exactly where you are. Do not move."

I sat up, instantly alert, and found myself staring at a fashionably dressed woman. Although her face was flawless, I deemed her to be of middle age, maybe forty or so. She was dressed in a light-grey silk dress with leg-of-mutton sleeves, a slimline skirt and a pin-tucked front. On her head was a small, jaunty hat, and she carried a fringed silk parasol to ward off the sun's rays. Her stare was fixed on me, and I looked around to see if I might be in some kind of danger or even breaking a rule. It did occur to me that this garden was reserved for hotel guests, and that did not include servants. I fought back the urge to stand up, since she had told me not to move.

"Madame?" I asked in French. "Is something amiss?"

"Nothing," she said, coming towards me now. "In fact, it's just perfect."

"What is?" I was now beginning to wonder if she was perhaps a little touched.

"You are, my sweet child," she said. "You are just what I have been searching for."

Now it crossed my mind that she might be an elegant madam trying to recruit me for one of her houses of ill repute. She came to sit beside me. "Are you staying at the hotel?"

"Yes," I replied, "I have just arrived. I am a member of the queen—of Lady Balmoral's party, sent in advance to make sure everything is ready for her."

"Of course," she said. "Lady Balmoral, eh?" She gave me a knowing wink. "So silly when we all know her. So, you are English?" She had reverted to my language, and this confirmed my suspicions that she was a countrywoman of mine. Even though her French was flawless, there was a slight hint of foreignness to her accent.

"I am."

"Might one know your name?"

Could I tell her the truth? I wondered. She didn't need to know my masquerade. I'd probably never even meet her again. But the expatriate circle might be a small one. "It's Helen Barton," I said.

"Delighted to meet you, Helen." She held out a dainty gloved hand. "I am Mary Crozier."

"How do you do?" I shook hands formally. "Are you also staying at the hotel?"

"Oh no. I live here. You see that villa to our right? That is mine. The Villa Angelica. Silly name, don't you think? My husband's whim. He said the view was so pretty that angels would want to live here. He does get whims from time to time."

I looked down at the romantic villa set amid lovely gardens. I thought of her surname. "Your husband is French?"

"He is. Le Marquis de Crozier. A dashing Frenchman. My family thought him quite unsuitable when we met at a Paris ball. But I told them the best they could do for me was a mere baronet or possibly a viscount, and this was a marquis. And I have to say I've never regretted it. As dashing as he is, he has proved remarkably faithful, and I've provided him with four healthy sons. So all is well." She paused and gave a little sigh. "I do miss England from time to time,

London theatre, and scones with clotted cream, but now that the Riviera is becoming the place to winter, I can be amongst my own people again."

"I think it's wonderful," I said. "If I lived here, I'd never want to move."

"The French can be rather tiresome, you know," she said. "Lots of gossip and intrigue and who is sleeping with whom. Luckily Francois finds it as tedious as I do. That's why we escaped from Paris in the first place and built this villa. Which brings me to my current quest. Are you free this evening?"

Thoughts raced through my mind. I was a servant. Did she recognize that from my clothing, and was she asking me to help out at a soirée? But what if she was actually inviting me to be a guest? Could I accept an invitation from a marquise?

"Oh, please. Do say yes." She pressed her hand over mine. "It will be an interesting little gathering. Nothing formal, but you are desperately needed."

"Needed? For what purpose?"

She laughed. "Don't look so worried. Your hair, sweet child. You see, tableaux are all the rage at the moment, and I had my heart set on a tableau of Charles II and Nell Gwynne—you know, the orange seller he met outside the theatre and who became his favourite mistress. But Nell Gwynne was famous for her red hair, and alas I knew no redheads. And now you appear like a miracle. So do say you'll come. You will make my evening a success."

How could I say no? "Of course. I shall be delighted to, Marquise," I said.

She squeezed my hand even harder now. "You must call me Mary, as I know we shall be the best of friends." She was studying my face again. "Such a pretty little face. So English. You don't know what it's like, having a household that is full of rambunctious males. How I longed for a daughter like you." She stood up. "Oh, there are my wine merchants arriving now. I must go, or they'll put everything in the wrong place. Until tonight then. Come about eight so that we can have your costume fitted." She jumped up and hurried down the path as fast as those tight skirts would allow her.

CHAPTER 16

I waited until Mr Angelo had awoken from his afternoon nap and then took him down to meet his French fellow chefs. The meeting was brief and exceedingly polite. I hoped that things would thaw out as we worked together.

"Blimey, he's a rum one, isn't he?" Chef muttered to me as we made our way up the stairs. "I can see it's going to be a barrel of laughs working with that lot. But it should go smoothly as long as we stick to our side of the kitchen and they stick to theirs."

I nodded. Then I asked, cautiously, "So for this evening, am I free?"

"We're all free until Her Majesty gets here. Unloading the crates and arranging the shelves tomorrow, and getting the larder stocked for the first meals. Luckily, I brought a lot of the basics with me: condiments, herbs and good English tea, too, after what you went through today."

"So about this evening," I said. "Would you mind if I went out?"

He frowned. "I don't like the idea of a young girl wandering around a strange city at night. Not without a chaperone, and we are all too tired to go gallivanting."

"Oh, I don't intend to wander around the city, Chef. It's just that I have been asked by an English noble lady to go and help with her soirée."

"English noble lady? And how do you know her?" He was still looking suspicious.

"I met her in the gardens this afternoon. She owns the villa you can see on the right."

"And she doesn't have servants of her own for her soirées?"

"She does. But she doesn't want me as a servant. She's putting on a tableau, and she needed someone with red hair to complete it."

"What do you mean, a tableau?"

"You know, living people pose as a famous painting or a scene from history. She's doing Charles II."

"And she wants you for?"

"Nell Gwynne," I said.

He shook his head. "You know what she was, don't you? It wasn't just her oranges she was selling."

I had to smile at this. "Chef, I'm not going to act the part. All I have to do is to stand quite still for a few minutes. Then I'll come back. You don't object to that, do you?"

"I suppose not. Just watch out for those aristocrats, won't you? They think any pretty servant girl is easy pickings."

"Don't worry. I'll be careful," I said. "And I can assure you I'm not easy pickings."

He studied me for a moment, then said, "No, I don't think you are."

When it came to getting ready for the soirée, I was in an agony of indecision. I had brought my one lovely dress, the blue velvet one I had worn to Louisa's wedding, and apart from that, my clothes were plain in the extreme. But perhaps Mary Crozier had not expected me to be a guest, merely an entertainer, hustled in through the servants' entrance and then out again when my party piece was over. On the other hand, if I was introduced to any guests, I certainly wouldn't want to be wearing an old cotton frock. That settled it. I put on the blue velvet dress and left my hair down, knowing that it would have to be unpinned anyway for my part in the tableau. Lastly, I draped the matching cape, trimmed with rabbit fur, around my shoulders, and made my way down the stairs, through the foyer and out into the night.

The forecourt was well-lit and full of activity. Carriages were arriving and departing. There was the sound of an orchestra coming from the open front doors. I made my way without incident to the Villa Angelica. There was the villa's name on the gate, but I would have recognized it anyway by the bright lights streaming from every window and the bustle of activity as footmen waited in the forecourt to receive visitors. I came forward tentatively, not sure still if I should approach as a visitor or as part of the entertainment. But almost instantly a footman clad in black livery stepped forward. "*Bonsoir*, mademoiselle," he said. "This way, please."

And he escorted me in through the front door. Suddenly there I was in a room full of elegant people. How many times had I dreamed of this? When Papa told his tales of visits to the family seat, of banquets and balls in India and of parties at the Savoy, I would picture myself at one of them, and I'd mutter, "Someday, Bella." Now this was actually coming true, and I was terrified. I looked around the room—my dress was not quite right. There were no velvets, only silks as far as I could see. And the waists were much tighter, the necks much lower, the bustles much bigger. How at ease they all looked, laughing and talking, champagne glasses in their hands. They all belonged here, and I never would. I hovered at the perimeter of the room, and when a waiter came up to me with a tray of champagne glasses, I wasn't at all sure I should accept one. Still, it was something to do with my hands. I took the glass, and sipped, experiencing the delightful taste of bubbles.

Then I heard someone calling, "Helen!" Mary Crozier was coming towards me, arms outstretched. "You've come, my sweet child. How lovely. I was scared I might have frightened you off with my enthusiasm. And you've got a drink already. Wonderful. Come and meet some fellow countrymen." She took my arm and steered me to an older man, standing alone by the mantelpiece.

"Another English rose, Lord S," she said. "Miss Helen Barton. And of course you know Lord Salisbury, Helen."

I tried not to let my astonishment show. I was being introduced to the prime minister of England. The strange thing was that he was the one who looked a little out of place. His clothing could have done with a good pressing, and his hair had not been properly brushed. Against the other guests, he looked decidedly shabby. I only had a second to take this in before he gave a friendly nod. "Miss Barton. You are newly arrived on the Riviera?"

"Today, sir," I replied.

"And you have the stamina for a party after that dreadful journey? My, my. I admire the verve of the young. When I came to my villa, the first thing I wanted to do was take a nap. Did you get a chance to sleep well on the train? I find that even with the best of first-class compartments it sways around so much that rest is impossible."

"I confess that I did not get much sleep," I replied.

"And the crossing? You came by the short route through Boulogne, did you?"

"I did. And the weather was awful. But I think I must be a good sailor because I endured it better than most."

"That's the spirit. We English have hearts of oak, don't we? Born to be seafarers."

"Some of the gentlemen in my party would not agree with you on that sentiment, sir," I said. "They looked very ill indeed."

He threw back his head and laughed at this. "Delightful child," he said. "Are you staying with the Marquis de Crozier?"

"No, Lord S, she's with the queen's party," Mary interrupted. "Sent ahead as an outrunner and scout."

"So when does the queen arrive?" Several other guests had joined our group.

"Not for three more days," I replied.

"And have you determined that the new monstrosity will fit her needs?" a younger man asked.

"You mean the hotel? I think she will find it most agreeable," I said.

"She should," Lord Salisbury said. "It was designed expressly for her. Cost a fortune, so I'm told. Let's hope they can let out their rooms when she's not present or if she decides not to come to Nice again."

"She is elderly, isn't she?" the young man said. "At her age, one never knows."

"It's my belief she'll live forever." A large older woman, resplendent in purple and dripping in diamonds, gave a deep chuckle. "She doesn't want Bertie to take the throne."

"Well, would you?" the first man said, and there was laughter.

"Careful what you say, chaps," the young man said. "This young lady is probably her niece, and this conversation will be reported back, and we'll all wind up in the Tower."

"I say, you're not related to her, are you?" the large lady asked, peering at me through her lorgnette. "We're not supposed to be calling you ma'am?"

"Oh goodness, no," I said. "I am just a member of her household."

Mary Crozier put a hand on my shoulder. "I must spirit Helen away now. She has a little task to perform for me."

I was grateful to make my escape. "Do you want me to put on my costume now?" I asked.

"Oh no. Not until much later. Half the guests haven't arrived yet. But I did want to make sure you got something to eat before I need you. Come through here and help yourself. I know it's a trifle early for dinner, but we will be preparing our surprise while they eat."

She pushed open double doors trimmed with gilt. And there before me was the biggest table I had ever seen. Silver and glass sparkled in the light of a dozen candelabras. And on that table was the most impressive assortment of food: salmon mousse in the shape of a salmon; cold chickens; quail; a huge platter of oysters, shrimp and lobster claws; all kinds of salads; fruits and cheese. It was all so beautifully arranged that I hardly dared to touch it. At one end was a huge bowl of peaches. "Peaches, at this time of year?" I blurted out.

"From our greenhouse. Forced, of course. But Francois does enjoy his fruit." Mary thrust a plate into my hands. "Go on. Don't be shy."

I had had nothing to eat since our luncheon, and an omelette, while delicious, is not exactly filling. When I had enquired about meals for the cooks at the hotel, I was told that we were welcome to eat with our French chefs until we had our own kitchen set up and operating, but they didn't eat until after the guests had been served, usually around ten. Mary put a hand on my shoulder. "I'll leave you to it, then."

Although I was really hungry, I did not like to disturb the more beautiful creations and helped myself to a little salad, with lobster claw and shrimp, plus a slice of cold chicken. Then temptation overcame me, and I took one of those peaches.

"I say, jolly fine spread, don't you think?" said a voice behind me.

I turned to the speaker. He was young, probably

not much older than I, slim, with reddish-blonde hair and very English looking. He wore his hair quite long, and he had a frilly jabot at his neck, so the impression was of a romantic poet.

"It's magnificent," I replied.

"Oh, thank God, you speak English," he said and gave me an embarrassed grin. "My French is atrocious. My tutor despaired of me. I tried to persuade the pater to send me to Paris for a few months to work on my pronunciation, but I think he suspected I'd spend my time in less honourable pursuits."

"You'd be practicing your French, even at the least honourable places," I replied, and he burst out laughing.

"So I would, by George. What a splendid girl you are. How come I haven't seen you before? Are you newly arrived?"

"Yes, very newly. I arrived today."

"Are you staying with your parents or friends?"

"Neither. I am part of the queen's entourage, sent ahead to make sure everything is as she wants it."

"Gosh. What an awful responsibility. Is she as big of an old tartar as they say?"

"She's very particular in what she likes and doesn't like," I could say with truth.

"Rather you than me." He made a face.

"And who are you staying with?" I asked.

"I'm at a villa in Villefranche-sur-Mer, just

around the Corniche from Nice. Much nicer and with a proper beach that isn't all stones. My father had a bad touch of gout and decided we needed warmer climes. But I say, I should have introduced myself. I'm awfully bad at protocol. I'm Giles Waverly."

I took in a little breath. I was speaking with my cousin. I seemed to remember I had heard my father mention a Giles. At least he was not a close cousin. My father was an only son, so that must mean that our grandfathers were brothers. That made him a second cousin, didn't it? I could never get those things right. While I was doing this rapid calculation, he said, "And your name, unless you are travelling incognito for the queen?"

Wouldn't it have been lovely to tell him that I was Isabella Waverly, his cousin? I hesitated, weighing this. An image flashed into my head of being welcomed back into the bosom of the family, regaining my rightful place in the world, moving freely amongst those people at this party. But I remembered that my father had been denied assistance when he needed it. There had been some kind of awful rift, and I'd be risking my position with the queen if the truth came out. It was a risk I couldn't take. I took a deep breath. "How do you do, Mr Waverly? I'm Helen Barton."

"Helen." He shook his head. "That's too severe a name for a charming person like yourself. Do you have a pet name that you are called at home? I shall call you by it unless it's too, too silly, like Dodie or Bunnykins or something."

"Actually, I was called Bella at home," I said. "My parents are now both dead."

"Bella. That's splendid and quite appropriate. Bella it shall be. But I'm keeping you from your food. Please do sit and enjoy it." He indicated the chairs around the wall. I sank on to one of them.

"I might as well join you before the mob gets here," he said. He had just picked up a plate when Mary poked her head around the door. "Viscount Faversham, what are you doing, sneaking in to dinner early? This young lady has to eat now because I require her services later, but you, dear boy, will just have to wait until supper is announced after the performance."

"Oh, I say, Lady Crozier, you are a spoilsport. Here am I, dying of starvation, and just when I was getting to know this lovely girl."

"This lovely girl needs peace and quiet to eat." Mary took his arm. She gave me a little smile. "Don't believe anything this one tells you," she said.

Giles Waverly gave me a hopeful smile. "I shall see you later, shall I not?"

"Maybe," I said, "but once the queen arrives, I shall be at her beck and call, with not much free time."

"We'll jolly well make time," he said.

"Out," Mary said. "The poor girl needs to eat before our little surprise."

And she ushered him out. I could hardly swallow a morsel. Viscount Faversham. Not only my cousin, but a viscount. *Of course,* I thought. My grandfather's brother had inherited the earldom. I'd heard all about the Earl of Altringham and the estate at Kingsbury with its herd of deer. My grandfather had been sent out to the colonies, as always seems to happen to younger sons. My father had been born in India, spent his childhood in England where he attended Eton and Oxford as was proper for a young man, then sent back to India after his education with a commission in the Bengal Lancers. What a strange world we live in. An accident of birth order making the difference between plenty and pauper!

Anyway, I found I was excited to have met him, rather stunned that I was at a party and the son of an earl was actually interested in me. I wondered if I would have a chance to see him again after our tableau. Then I had to remind myself sternly that I was Helen Barton, under-cook. I did not move in the same social circles as a viscount. And I did not possess the wardrobe to move in those circles even if I could escape my duties from time to time.

"Do not get ideas above your station" was something all young girls were told. But it didn't hurt to dream, did it?

CHAPTER 17

As soon as I had finished eating, Mary whisked me up to a bedroom where a maid was waiting to help me into a costume. "Formidable," the maid exclaimed when she saw me. "Her hair, it is perfect. Where did you find her? Monsieur le Marquis will be so happy to have his Nell Gwynne."

"In the hotel gardens," Mary said. "I still can't believe my luck at bumping into her. Here, Helen, try on your dress."

As the maid removed my dress, she made tut-tutting noises. "Mademoiselle does not wear a corset."

"She's a young girl. She doesn't need one yet," Mary said. "Look at her neat little waist!"

"One must train the body early before the waist starts to spread." She helped me to step into the dress, lacing the front rather too tightly, I felt. As I saw myself in the mirror, the result was truly amazing, a brilliant peacock-blue fabric with big puffed sleeves and yards and yards of skirts. What's more, it fitted me as if it had been made for me. As I examined it more critically, I realized that it was quite revealing at the front.

"Should it not have another hook or button here?" I tried to indicate where it plunged between my breasts.

"Of course not," Mary said. "You're Nell Gwynne. You are selling your wares in Covent Garden, or was it the Strand?"

My dresser was nodding with approval. "That is good. She has nice firm, round breasts. See how the costume highlights them. The men will not be able to take their eyes off her."

This made me feel a little uneasy. I had never attended a party like this. I knew that the Prince of Wales and various aristocrats were roués. Had I been lured here for more than a tableau, at a safe distance from the audience? Was I fair game the moment the show was over?

Surely not, I told myself. *Mary Crozier seems like such a kind person, she surely would never let . . .*

"There, mademoiselle," the French maid said. "Now on to the makeup and the hair, and the transformation will be complete. Sit yourself here before the mirror."

I sat at a sumptuous dressing table on a burgundy velvet stool. A cloth was placed over my dress to protect it, and the maid started on my hair. She wound and pinned until she had it piled high on the head, with a couple of tantalizing curls escaping down my cheeks and into my cleavage. She started applying face cream. "You have good skin," she commented as she massaged the cream into my face and neck. "You have not done much damage by exposing it too much to the sun."

I laughed. "It's hard to find too much sun in London."

"The English, they do not understand," she went on as she applied rouge to my cheeks. "They come here, and they stroll on the Promenade des Anglais with no parasol. They look sunburned like peasants."

My cheeks looked unnaturally red, and when she applied kohl to my eyelids and a crimson gash of lipstick, I had to say something. "Is this not a little too bright?"

"Of course not," Mary replied. "You will be on stage, with bright lights. And you are a courtesan, after all."

I was now feeling more and more uneasy and regretted coming to a party unchaperoned. If some lord wanted to take me into a back room, who might come to my defence? Then I told myself that Giles Waverly would. I did have an ally here. Mary led me through corridors that were clearly the servants' domain, and we came out into a dimly lit ballroom. Lines of chairs had been placed around a dais with a red velvet curtain hanging in front of it. Several other people were standing around talking. They were dressed for the period, with long wigs and wide skirts.

"Here we are, my love," Mary called as we came closer. "You see, I have found you your Nell. Is she not perfect?"

A tall, dark man turned to us. Charles II with long curls over his shoulders and a brocade frock coat.

"Bonsoir, Nell." He took my hand and kissed it. "She is perfect. You are a genius, *chérie*."

"Just remember that it is only acting, Francois," Mary said, giving his hand a little slap. "Do not let yourself be carried away with any fantasies."

"As if I could when I have you." He paused, then added, "Watching me like a hawk."

And she laughed. They clearly had a good marriage that had been a love match.

We were led around to the stage. I gasped when I saw what lengths Mary had gone to in creating the scene. A proper theatre set had been built, to represent the streets of Old London. On one side was a barrow full of fruit for sale. It felt terribly authentic. We were put in our places, the design apparently having been taken from a painting. I was given a basket of oranges to hold on one arm, and I had to stand holding out an orange to King Charles while his entourage watched. We took our appointed spots. "I'll give you the cue when the audience is in place," Mary said.

King Charles winked at me, but it was an assuring wink. "Just do not scratch your nose or sneeze," he whispered. "We must be like statues."

We heard the scrape of chairs as the party-goers came into the ballroom, animated conversations in French and English. Then we were given the signal. I held up my orange and planted my feet firmly. The curtain was drawn back. Bright lights shone on us, making me blink. There was a round of genuine applause from the audience. I wished the marquis had not said anything about having to scratch my nose because it had now begun to itch. I forced myself to stay still, my arm unmoving as I held out the orange. I could hear ribald comments coming from the audience and pretended not to have heard them. The moment seemed to go on and on. *How long can I hold up my arm?* I wondered. Finally, Mary came on stage and asked the audience to thank us all for our magnificent performance.

"Is this not the best tableau we have seen this year?" she asked.

The lights went out. The curtain fell. I was escorted back to the dressing room, where Mary's maid removed my makeup, took down my hair and helped me back into my own dress. "You should choose another fabric next time," she said. "Velvet is not suitable now that it's almost spring."

"I'm afraid this is the only evening dress I brought with me," I confessed. I remembered my guinea, and, if necessary, my pay packet out of which I had no expenses. "Do you know of a good dressmaker, not expensive?"

"My mother. She is the best. I will give you her address. She lives in the old town. Find some fabric you like, and take it to her. Tell her that I sent you, and she will give you a good price."

I didn't like to ask if my meagre savings would be anything like enough to pay a good dressmaker, minus the cost of fabric, of course. I nodded instead. "Wonderful. Thank you."

I came out of the dressing room. There was no sign of Mary. I wondered whether I should rejoin the party or take this opportunity to slip away. I was tempted to see Giles Waverly one more time, and maybe have another glass of champagne. It had not chimed midnight; Cinderella was not yet ready to leave the ball and find herself back in the kitchen. As I emerged into the brightness of a large salon, I spotted Mary and Francois, still in his Charles costume, chatting with a portly man with his back to me.

"I'm so sorry you were too late, sir," Mary said in English. "If we'd known you were coming, naturally we would have waited."

"Small problem with the yacht," said the voice. "Delayed me. Most annoying, still it's all fixed now, and I'll move into my villa tomorrow. But I wish I'd had a chance to see you as my ancestor, dear boy. Actually, not my ancestor, but my forebear, right? I don't believe we Germans have Stuart blood. We are certainly not known for being parsimonious like the Scots." And he laughed heartily.

I ducked back rapidly behind a large potted plant. The Prince of Wales had come to the party.

"So I hear that Nell Gwynne was a luscious little wench," the prince said. "Anyone I know?"

"You may do. She's part of your mother's household," Mary said. "Let me go and find her and present her to you, although I'm afraid she is no longer wearing her costume."

"What, you mean no more oranges to squeeze?" He laughed again.

I looked around frantically for a way to escape. I retreated the way I had come. Through the open door, I spotted Mary's maid tidying up. Perhaps I could ask her how I could find the servants' entrance and escape that way? At that moment, I heard Mary's voice, coming around the corner. I had no time to think. I ducked behind a Roman statue in a niche. Mary came towards me.

"Claudette, have you seen Miss Barton?" she asked in French.

"Not since I helped her out of the costume," she replied.

"Drat and bother. I wonder where she can have got to." Mary turned, looking worried, and then she stared straight at me.

"Oh, there you are. I've been looking everywhere. What are you doing?" she asked, looking at me suspiciously. "Are you hiding?"

There was nothing for it but confession. "I was looking for a way to escape, if you want the truth. I saw the Prince of Wales had arrived, and I had a rather disturbing encounter with him once at the palace. He . . . he propositioned me."

"Oh, I see." She nodded. "Yes, that is awkward, isn't it? He's a naughty old devil. Can't keep his hands off beautiful women. So I take it you don't want to meet him again?"

"I'd really prefer not to."

She took my hand. "Then I'll show you the way out. Come on." She led me swiftly along the corridor, through a small door and into a servants' hallway. "That's the back door," she said. "You'll have to make your way around the house, but it is well lit."

"Thank you so much," I said, heaving a sigh of relief.

"We women have to stick together against the depravations of the male sex, don't we?" She squeezed my hand.

"What will you tell the prince?"

"That I couldn't find you and you must have gone home, not feeling well." Then her face fell. "Oh dear. I'm afraid I committed a blunder by telling him you were part of the queen's household. Let's hope he doesn't come searching for you there."

"I'm told he stays well away from his mother when he's at his villa as she doesn't approve of his lifestyle," I said. "So I hope I can avoid him."

"If not, just turn him down," Mary said. "A girl is entitled to say no and to choose her own suitors. Tell him you are engaged to a jealous Russian count who loves fighting duels!"

I had to laugh. "Mary, you are a card. Thank you."

"I must get back before they come looking for me," she said. "Off you go, then. We must meet again soon. Come for tea and we'll chat. I'd love that."

"That would be very nice," I said, "but as I said to Viscount Faversham, my time is not my own once the queen arrives."

"We'll make it happen. We're such close neighbours, and I do crave English company."

She gave me a little kiss on the cheek and almost pushed me out through the door. I made my way through the grounds, listening to music and laughter spilling out through open windows, reached the front gate and arrived back at the hotel without incident.

"Well, Bella," I said to myself. "All those years at the Tilleys' house when you dreamed of excitement, romance and a glamorous life. Now you are living it." It still didn't seem real.

CHAPTER 18

There was no sign of any of our cooks when I returned to the hotel. I presumed they must all have fallen asleep. I went to my room, undressed and opened my window. Down below me, the city twinkled with a carpet of lights. It was hard to tear myself away from that magical scene. "I'm really here," I whispered to myself. It wasn't a dream, tonight had really happened. I lay in bed enjoying the cool scented night breeze wafting in. Images of the evening flashed through my head: Giles Waverly smiling at me. Standing on the stage and hearing the applause. But then the prince saying, "What, you mean no more oranges to squeeze?" I might have been naive, but not so naive that I didn't get its true meaning. I just prayed he would stay away from his mother during his visit and that I could manage to avoid him. But he had been told I was part of his mother's household. Would he come searching for me? I just prayed a more suitable candidate for his affections would turn up rapidly.

I woke at first light to the sound of pigeons cooing on the balustrade outside my window. The sun was streaming in, and when I looked out of my window I could see the Mediterranean Sea sparkling as if it was laced with a thousand diamonds. I gave a deep sigh of satisfaction. Then I dressed and went to find breakfast. Mr Angelo and the two other cooks were sitting at a long pinewood table eating breakfast. They did not look very happy.

"So you got home safely, young Helen?" Mr Angelo asked. "I was worried about you. I felt guilty that I had let you go, unescorted."

"I was home really early. About ten o'clock," I said. "I left right after my tableau."

"Good girl," he said. "I was worried."

"We've all heard what these Frenchmen are like," Mr Williams said. "When Mr Angelo told us where you'd gone, we didn't think he should have let you go."

"I'm really quite capable of taking care of myself, Mr Williams," I said. "Besides, I was only part of the tableau. I had to get into costume and pose on a stage. That was all."

"Well, that's all right then," he admitted. "Help yourself to breakfast. And a lot of nourishment you'll get from it, too!" He sniffed derisively.

I looked at the long, thin loaves of bread, a dish of butter, one of jam and jugs of coffee and milk.

"That's what they eat," Mr Angelo said. "I tried to make that French johnny understand. Where was breakfast? But this is what he was eating.

No eggs. No bacon. No kidneys. Just bread. It's a wonder they keep their strength up."

"It's all that wine they drink," Mr Phelps said. "They are thoroughly pickled."

"So what is the plan for today?" I asked, cutting myself a large hunk of bread and helping myself liberally to butter and jam. "What would you like us to do?"

"Miss Barton, I'd like you to organize how we order in our supplies," Mr Angelo said. "I'll write you a list for grocer, greengrocer, butcher and fishmonger, and you can translate it and find out what purveyors the French chefs use in their part of the kitchen. Then you can take the lists down to the shops and arrange for delivery. Tell them the hotel will be paying the bills."

"Very good, sir," I said.

I finished my breakfast, actually enjoying the unfamiliar taste of coffee made with hot milk, then took the lists that Mr Angelo had made. I went to find Chef Lepin in the kitchen. He was not there, but the one he had called Henri was busy at work making a pastry dish.

"What is that?" I asked because he was stuffing puff pastry with a rich brown mixture.

"It is called tourte de blettes," he said. "A specialty of our region."

"What are *blettes*?" The word was unfamiliar to me.

"It is a green vegetable, like cabbage, only with

long green curly leaves," he explained, then he held a stalk up for me.

"Is that Swiss chard?" I exclaimed. "Then it is a savoury tart?"

"No, mademoiselle, it is for the dessert."

"But chard? That must taste bitter."

"Not at all. It is made with raisins and pine nuts and brown sugar, and when it is finished, I will save a small taste for you. You will see, it tastes not at all bitter. Quite delicious, in fact."

I asked him then about ordering supplies. He told me to present my lists to the hotel manager, and everything would be delivered. But then he added that Chef Lepin liked to choose his own meats and fish and vegetables. He was very particular about the quality.

"Do you know where he shops for these supplies?"

He looked amused. "In the market, mademoiselle. Where else is everything brought in fresh that morning?"

"The market in the town?"

"*Bien sûr.* In the old part of town near the waterfront. Take the tram down the hill and then turn to your left. But you should go early, or the best items are gone."

I thanked him and reported this back to Mr Angelo. He told me to go and investigate what sort of things could be found in the market. Meanwhile, he would make out a list of supplies for the hotel to order. He said we had been told that we could use any basic items from the kitchen, so we would not need to be concerned about staples.

"So go and take a look at that market," he said. "But don't buy anything. I'm not too sure about quality. And we don't want it to go bad before Her Majesty gets here."

"I won't, sir," I said. "Unless I find something we'd like to experiment with first."

"Good idea," he said and handed me some francs. "But don't pay too much for anything. They'll try to cheat you because you're a foreigner."

"Oh, surely not?"

"They are cut-throats and brigands here—everyone says so. And watch your purse."

I was smiling to myself as I set off. My father had travelled the world and had raised us with none of these prejudices. I was eager to experience life in another country for the first time, not just in the rarefied atmosphere of the hotel but down in the town where the real people lived.

I went upstairs to get my shawl, excited about this chance to explore Nice alone and about the new level of responsibility accorded to me. In the top drawer, I saw the scrap of paper with Claudette's mother's address on it. Claudette had said she lived in the old part of the city—maybe

I'd have a chance to find some fabric and take it to her, since Mr Angelo could have no idea how long it would take me to make the journey to the market and back. I took my purse and set off with great expectations.

The air was quite chilly at this hour, chillier than I had expected. I had to remind myself that even in this southern clime it was only February. I wrapped my shawl tightly around my shoulders as I made for the trolley stop. I waited, but after there was no sign of any trolley for a long while, I started to walk. The city was still waking up. Milk wagons were delivering to doorsteps, gardeners were raking paths, women were hanging out washing, children were walking to school with satchels on their backs. From a bakery came the delicious smell of bread baking. The sound of a bell tolling floated towards me, and then I came to a church to see people filing in for Mass. They were mostly women, dressed in black and wearing black headscarves tied under their chins. The bell echoed in the clear air above our heads, sounding so different from English churches where bells are rung in peals.

I followed the tram tracks until I came to a broad open area at the seafront. To my right was an impressive square, lined with pink buildings. Then came gardens with lawns and palm trees. At the water's edge, a long promenade stretched away as far as the eye could see, lined with more fine palm trees. A pavilion of some sort with an oriental dome jutted on a pier out over the water. Couples who could only be English by the look of them were taking their morning constitutional walk. It was all so civilized. I stopped at a booth selling tobacco and newspapers and bought some bright postcards. In truth I had been feeling guilty that I had dashed off that letter to Louisa in such a brusque manner. She must have worried when I said that I was going abroad, with no further explanation.

Then I did as Henri told me and headed off to the left where a hill, crowned with a fortress, rose up at the water's edge. At one point a small river entered the sea, its banks lined with washer-women, making such an interesting contrast to the opulence of that sparkling pavilion with its glass dome.

Here was a different Nice of narrow alley-ways, cooking smells laced with garlic, laundry hanging out of windows, donkeys piled high with sacks, and the not-too-savoury smell of drains. I had to be rather careful where I put my feet, as it was not very clean underfoot. I found myself glancing about as I negotiated narrow alleys. But eventually I found the market.

At this early hour, it was bustling with activity: women in brightly striped skirts and black fringed shawls haggled with stall-keepers and chatted loudly with neighbours in shrill voices.

Dogs slunk around and barked at cats. The noise level was intense as the sound echoed from tall yellow painted houses with their green shutters. And at the fringes of the crowd lurked gypsy children and scruffy young men. I remembered Mr Angelo's warning and clutched my purse firmly in front of me, hidden under my shawl as I entered the fray.

The fruit and vegetable stalls were a dazzling mass of colour: oranges and tomatoes that we rarely saw in England. Bright lemons and purple onions. Spiky artichokes I had only just learned about at the palace; giant cloves of garlic— wouldn't the queen be horrified to see those? And shiny purple vegetables shaped like fat, bulging cucumbers.

"What are they?" I asked the woman at the stall.

She looked at me as if I was a visitor from the moon. "Aubergine, mademoiselle. You have not tried them? They are very good. We make the ratatouille."

"And those?" I pointed to round red and yellow vegetables that looked so shiny they seemed to be made of wax.

"The peppers?" she asked in amazement. "You do not eat peppers where you come from?"

"I've never seen them before," I said.

"Then try," she urged. "And the aubergine, too. They are delicious stuffed."

She shook her head as if I was a creature to be pitied. I bought one of each, and one of the purple onions at her insistence, and went on to the next stall. This one had an array of olives. Olives were a rare luxury in England. I had never tried them personally, but here was a whole stall with olives of varying colours and sizes—fat green ones, slim black ones, some stuffed with something red, others with a white cheese, some in olive oil, some not. I told the stall-keeper that these were unfamiliar to me and could he make me up a small sampling of the various offerings. He was a rotund old man wearing a dirty striped apron, and he laughed at my request, but then gave me a more generous portion than I deserved. When I went to pay, he waved away my coin. "No need, mademoiselle. If you like them, you will be back."

I moved on to stalls selling herbs—big baskets of lavender, rosemary, parsley and other plants I couldn't identify. And then I came to the flower stalls, lingering by bunches of daffodils, freesias, jonquils and many others I didn't recognize, breathing in the heady scents. There were branches of the fluffy yellow flowers that smelled heavenly. I resisted temptation and made my way to the meat stalls. I realized here I was out of my element. Hearts and lungs and livers I knew. Tripe I hated. But what were those little round nuggets? Were those sweetbreads? And was that brain? And cockscombs? And what were the tiny birds? I decided that Mr Angelo would have to make his own meat selections or have the hotel procure them for him.

Closer to the waterfront, I came to the fish market. My nose led me to rows of stalls there. I realized that here, too, I was a complete novice. I knew what herring looked like, and whitebait. I knew a hunk of cod when it was put in front of me, and shrimp and lobster. But what were those fish with wings, and heavens—was that an octopus? I had only seen a picture of one before. It looked terrifying and disgusting—its tentacles draped across the slab. How could anybody . . .

"Bonjour, Monsieur Jontue," said a voice behind me. "I see you have a fine octopus for me today."

"Saved it especially for you, Monsieur Lepin," the stall-keeper replied.

I spun around to see Chef Lepin standing there, his basket already full. He looked at me in surprise. "Mademoiselle. You are up bright and early. I thought the English were late risers."

"Not the servants," I replied. "When I was a housemaid, I had to light the fires at five. This hour is a luxury for me."

"You also buy your food at the market?" he asked.

"I came to see for myself," I said. "In England the food is delivered to the palace."

"Then how does your chef choose the best cuts of meat, the freshest fish?" he asked in horror.

"I suppose he trusts those businesses that have supplied the royal household for generations," I replied.

"Oh, I forgot," he said in patronizing tones. "In England there is not much selection to be made. Always the mutton or the roast beef, and the boiled potatoes and the dreary cabbage, eh? Me, I would not bother to be a chef if all I had to do was to put a roast into the oven."

"May I ask why you are so hostile to all things English?" I demanded, feeling that I should stop but no longer able to. "I understand that we have invaded your kitchen, and that must be upsetting to you. I assure you that we have no control over that; neither have you. But this criticism and mocking of English food. What experience do you have of this? Have you ever been to England?"

He was a little taken aback at my belligerence. "I have not, mademoiselle. I have never left the South of France, I regret to say. I have not even been to Paris." He paused then, his swagger returning, and added, "But I can only repeat what one hears and see how the English who come to stay here behave. They demand the mutton and beef, and they want us to cook their vegetables until all the life goes out of them, so I assume all English like to eat this way."

"You will be surprised, Monsieur Le Chef," I said. "Her Majesty's food is most complicated. Sometimes a dish will take three cooks all day to prepare. It has to look exciting as well as taste good."

"Do you think her food tastes good?" he asked.

I thought about this for a moment. I had not had a chance to taste much of what went up to the royal dining room, but I found myself saying, "Between ourselves, I think they use too many rich sauces. One never gets the true flavour of the meat or vegetable. Her Majesty's favourite accompaniment to roast beef is a horseradish cream sauce that is so hot the meat must taste like paper. Most of the vegetables the queen eats are made into purees. And her meat is often turned into ragouts and terrines. Some dishes mix too many flavours. The queen loves butter and cream with everything. So bad for her." And I grinned.

He nodded as if he understood. "So you have a palate that appreciates the taste of good ingredients?"

"I do."

"And how did you develop this?"

"I must have inherited it from my father, who had lived well and appreciated fine food. I was apprenticed to a good cook who produced simple English fare—pork chops, roast lamb, roast pheasant, chicken, sole, lobster. There was a sauce to accompany them, but it never overwhelmed the flavour of the meat or fish."

He was nodding now. "You really wish to become a chef?"

"I would like to be in charge of my own kitchen someday, yes."

"I think you may have a problem there," he said.

"You don't think I'll be good enough?" I asked coldly.

"I don't think you will find a male sous-chef who will want to take orders from a woman."

"Perhaps I shall employ an all-female kitchen," I replied. "After all, who does all the cooking in private houses? Women know how to cook instinctively. Men must learn."

He laughed heartily at this. "Very good," he said. Then he grew serious again. "But you do not wish to marry? I thought all girls wanted a husband and a home and a family."

"Maybe one day," I said. I looked at him defiantly. "What about you? Are you married?"

He looked embarrassed. "Mademoiselle, I have a problem. I do not see how I can ask any girl to marry me. Who would want a husband who does not come home until midnight and who rises at dawn to go to the market? I am married to my profession."

"Monsieur Lepin. You wish me to wrap the octopus?" the stall-keeper interrupted.

"Please, *mon ami*."

"Tell me," I said. "How does one cook an octopus? It looks as if it would be slimy and rubbery."

"And so it will be, if one cooks it too long. Myself I prefer to grill it in the Spanish style. The tentacles can be cut into rings, or marinated and served whole, but always they must be cooked to the moment of perfection so that when one bites into it there is no resistance. You will try a piece when I serve it as an entrée tonight."

"Thank you, you are most kind," I said.

"I am not normally known for my kindness," he replied. "You must be having a bad effect on me."

Our eyes met for a brief second. There was something in the way he looked at me that made me feel uneasy—as if some kind of subtle contact had been made. So I said quickly, "I must not keep you from your commissions. You need to prepare the lunch menu."

"I do," he said. "*Au revoir*, Mademoiselle Chef. I will see you at the hotel. You and your fellows should dine with us tonight. I am making a bouillabaisse. You will sample the local cuisine."

"Thank you. I look forward to tasting it, and to learning new recipes if you are willing to share them."

"Until later, mademoiselle." He gave a little

bow and pushed his way into the crowd. I found myself staring after him, my heart beating rather fast. *Remember that the French are known for their flirtatious nature,* I reminded myself.

CHAPTER 19

After Chef Lepin had gone, I wandered into the
section of the market that sold household goods
and bric-a-brac and found a stall selling fabrics.
These were fabrics for the common people, no
silks or brocades amongst them, but I found a
length of a cotton weave that felt soft and pleasing
to the touch. It was in a pretty bluish green that
would go well with my hair and colouring, and
it seemed extraordinarily cheap to me. I added
a couple of yards of thin muslin lining, then I
went off to find Claudette's mother. After many
directions and pointings, I found her dwelling
up a flight of stone steps ascending the castle
hill. She greeted me cordially when I explained
that her daughter had sent me, and I handed
her the cloth. I found her extremely difficult to
understand—her local accent was so strong, and
she lacked most of her teeth—but the gist I got
was that the cloth was of inferior quality and she
didn't know if she could make a decent dress out
of it. I explained that I had very little money. She
said she would try and took my measurements. I
went away not feeling too hopeful. Had I wasted
precious money on something that would be

useless? But how was I to know? I had had no experience in selecting fabric for my clothes; in fact, I had not had new clothes for many years. At least it would be better than nothing, and if it didn't last, as the old woman had suggested, I didn't really care. And if I liked the quality of the woman's work, I would splurge and spend some of my hard-earned wages on a new wardrobe.

I reported back to Mr Angelo. We tried a dish using the aubergine, peppers and onion—sautéing them together with the forbidden garlic and tomatoes, then declaring it to be quite interesting. After my description of the market, Mr Angelo decided he would order his meat through the hotel, just to be on the safe side. "I know what I like," he said.

I also told him that we had been invited to join the French chefs at their dinner that evening. He thought it was quite neighbourly of them. I wasn't so sure. I suspected it was Chef Lepin's way of saying, "Look what we can do." A way of scoring points over the stupid English.

We got down to work, discussing what meals we should prepare for Her Majesty's arrival.

"She will have been travelling for two days and be tired," Mr Williams said. "A light meal, easily digestible. Maybe a soufflé? A fish dish? A roast capon?"

"I think she'll be starving," Mr Angelo disagreed. "There is no proper food served on the train. No dining car. They have to take it on at stations and keep it hot for her. I think we should tempt her appetite. Make her glad she's arrived. Give her some of her old favourites. We know she likes cream of rice soup, and whitebait, and lamb cutlets, and we'll order ices from the hotel confectioner. What else, do you think?"

As under-cook, I kept silent while the men added dishes, but Mr Angelo turned to me. "And for her puddings?"

I thought carefully before I answered. "She loves her rice puddings and her *mehlbrei*, doesn't she?" I suggested, using the term the queen always used for a German nursery custard. "All those puddings with milk and cream. Maybe I'll make a cold rice pudding, and custard tarts?"

"Good idea. Settle the stomach after the journey," Mr Phelps said. "If her stomach is anything like mine after all those hours on a train, she wouldn't want stodge."

I volunteered to go down to the market to purchase fresh whitebait the day of the queen's arrival. Mr Angelo cooked a couple of capons to serve cold with a veronique sauce and grapes. And at dinner that night, we joined the French chefs, eating at the kitchen tables. I have to admit it: the bouillabaisse was one of the most delicious things I had ever tasted. The rich broth, tasting of both fish and tomato, and with a spicy tang to it, and the little pieces of fish and seafood coming unexpectedly on to the spoon. And the crusty bread to dip into it? Heaven.

"How do you prepare the sauce?" I asked. When I found out they started with twelve cloves of garlic, Mr Angelo shook his head. "The queen wouldn't approve, would she? Nothing that would make her breath smell bad," he said. "You know she's always forbidden garlic."

"How would she know?" Chef Lepin asked. "If garlic is cooked well, it does not come on the breath."

Then he came over to me. "And I saved you a morsel of the octopus," he said. He stuck his fork into what looked like a piece of brown grilled meat and held it up to my mouth, as one feeds a child. The gesture was somehow so intimate that it startled me. I opened my mouth obediently and felt the explosion of flavour—saffron and garlic and a hint of spiciness and flesh so tender it almost melted. He nodded with satisfaction as he watched my face. "Someday I will teach you to cook octopus like that," he said.

I also found that Chef Henri had saved me a sliver of the chard tart. It was delicious, and one would never know that it had a vegetable in it. After dinner I went straight to my room and wrote down the recipe as well as I could remember it. Also the recipe for the fish soup. I had been keeping my own little notebook of dishes I liked, dishes I remembered from the days of Mrs Robbins, and ideas that had come to me to try one day. *Maybe I'll publish my own cookery book,* I thought, laughing at this absurd suggestion. Then it struck me that this wasn't such an absurd idea. A book of recipes from the South of France? How many of those were there in England? I would try to assemble as many recipes as I could, starting with the bouillabaisse and that strange tart made of chard.

That evening I sat in my room, watching the lights of the town twinkling below me, and wrote one of the postcards to Louisa.

> *My dearest sister.*
>
> *As you can see, I am in Nice. My employer decided to visit the Riviera for her health, and I was lucky enough to be taken to cook for her. Everything is so beautiful. Perhaps you will stop here on your way to Australia!*
>
> *Much love, your affectionate sister,*
>
> *Bella*

The next day work started in earnest. Her Majesty would arrive the next morning. Supplies were delivered. Crates were unloaded, and our many moulds and saucepans were washed and placed on shelves. Mr Angelo lamented spices and sauces that he hadn't thought to bring with him, also that he didn't have his stockpot. "How can I possibly make decent food without good stock?" he asked. "I can simmer veal bones, chickens and vegetables all day, but they are a poor substitute for a stockpot that has been going for twenty years."

I was relieved to find that I was not expected to go down to the market for supplies every morning. Frankly I would not have known what was good and fresh and what wasn't. Especially when I didn't recognize half of it. I had come to realize that my training had only just started. If I couldn't identify every cut of meat, every fish, every vegetable, I could never call myself a chef. Maybe one day when Chef Lepin had a little time, I could accompany him to the market, and he could identify those mysterious morsels that lay on meat and fish trays. And I have to confess that the thought of spending time with him was quite a heady one.

Be sensible, Bella, I warned myself. *There is no point in falling for an older Frenchman, especially when you are only here for a little while.* I assumed that Mr Roland would come out to take my place as soon as he could walk again, and I'd be sent home. And I realized I really didn't want to leave. I'd just have to prove my worth. That was a frightening thought. I had seen the quality and intricacy of Mr Roland's pastry creations, and I was nowhere near that level yet. But perhaps I could learn some local cakes and pastries to surprise the queen. I had heard she did like to be surprised.

I went to work earnestly that day, knowing that the queen would probably be expecting her usual teatime every day. I made a batch of sweet biscuits, a German recipe she liked that I had made before. Then I decided to make a coffee gateau. I needed to ask Chef Lepin for coffee and chocolate powder, but it came out as light and moist as I had hoped. I sliced the layers and spread the coffee buttercream and whipped cream between them. I was in the process of frosting it and wondering what kinds of decorations I'd find in the kitchen when I turned to see someone standing behind me. It was Chef Lepin.

"I congratulate," he said in accented English, then added in French, "Most attractive and pleasing to the eye."

"Thank you, Chef. I only hope it tastes as good as it looks."

"I'm sure it will," he replied. "I am impressed."

Again I was left feeling uneasy. When he said "pleasing to the eye," his gaze had left the dish on the table and travelled over me. Surely I was reading too much into this, allowing my fantasy to run away with me.

· · ·

The morning of the queen's arrival, we were up early. Her train was expected at the station at eleven, and she, with her party, would be at the hotel in time for luncheon. We had been handed the official list of personnel. It was quite daunting. All in all, there would be around forty people accompanying her. Two of her daughters: Princess Beatrice and Princess Helena, plus Beatrice's four small children. Also a young cousin from Germany, Princess Sophie of Mecklenburg, and Sophie's fiancé Count Wilhelm of Schlossberg-Hohenheim. One rank down from this were the ladies-in-waiting, the gentlemen-at-arms, the queen's secretary, her doctor, her personal maid, other maids, footmen, a guard of Highland pipers and Abdul Karim, the munshi. I studied this. So the Indian had triumphed after all. Those men with power and influence had not stopped him from accompanying the queen. I had to smile when I looked over the list: How could anyone believe that she was a mere Lady Balmoral when half of the English court was here with her, including a guard of Scotsmen in kilts?

Early that morning I went down to the market to buy the whitebait. I didn't spot Chef Lepin this time. I have to confess that I felt a twinge of disappointment about this. I wanted him to approve that I was following his example. I caught the trolley back up the hill with no problem, then set to work on my desserts. I made my rice pudding with slivers of almond, raisins and plenty of cream. I made the pastry and the egg custard.

By eleven o'clock, all was prepared. The lamb cutlets waited to be grilled, the garnishes ready, sliced beside their pots, the capons boned and lying on their platters. So all we could do was wait. We put on our best uniforms and went outside to join the welcome party, as was expected of us. Hotel employees were also lining up, including the manager, looking very smart in his long frock coat, wing collar and top hat. The sun became rather warm as we stood waiting. I saw that crowds were starting to gather outside the hotel grounds. Some carried Union Jacks.

At eleven thirty, the first of the wagons arrived, bringing the queen's furniture from the train.

"Blimey, would you look at that?" Jimmy whispered into my ear. "She's brought that ruddy great bed with her. And a wardrobe. Does she think the Frenchies don't have beds or something?" Then he grinned. "Perhaps she thinks French beds have fleas or bedbugs."

He was becoming rather too cheeky, I thought.

"You should watch what you say, or you'll find yourself in trouble with Mr Angelo," I muttered to him.

"I'm only saying it to you, Helen," he

answered. "We young'uns have to stick together, don't we?"

I could have pointed out that I was a fully fledged under-cook and he was only an apprentice, but I didn't. One should never make enemies where one might need allies. Men from the hotel went to join the footmen who had come on the wagons, and it was rather painful to watch as they tried to manipulate the queen's heavy bed and wardrobe down from the vehicle and in through the carriage entrance. There was much grumbling and cursing in French. I wondered if they would fit into the lift or if the furniture would have to be carried up a flight of stairs. More wagons pulled up, this time with maids accompanying the baggage. Crates were unloaded and carried inside. But still no sign of the royal party.

The servants came over to greet us when they saw us standing there. "Consider yourselves lucky that you didn't have to accompany her," a footman said. "It was an awful journey. That sea crossing—I thought we were going go down and I was going to die."

"So where is the queen now?" Mr Angelo asked.

"She's getting an official reception at the train station," one of the maids said. "She wanted to travel incognito and not be recognized, but there was a band playing and the mayor and town officials standing to attention and young women with arms full of flowers when the train pulled up. Silly old thing, she insists on travelling by her own private train. How can she not be recognized?"

"Hush, Maisie. It's not for you to comment on your betters," a senior footman reprimanded and got a grin in return. Maisie glanced around. "Well, I'd better go in and start unpacking her things. She'll want it to look like home by the time she gets here. And I'm ready to take a nap. I didn't sleep a wink sitting up crammed eight of us to the compartment."

One by one the items of furniture, her rugs and the crates were all carried into the hotel. The maids and footmen returned to stand in line with us. A carriage arrived, but it was gentlemen of her household. They looked a little the worse for wear after their journey, as if they, too, hadn't slept last night. They did not join us but went inside. I thought I heard distant cheering. The sound of bagpipes floated up the hill on the breeze, and then we caught sight of them. First came the pipers, striding ahead of the royal carriage. The crowd outside the gates was now considerable. They cheered. "*Vive la reine anglaise*," came the chant towards us. And the carriage came to a halt outside the main entrance of the hotel. In it was the queen, her two daughters and her grandchildren, looking very sweet. Attendants rushed forward to open the door and assist her down. But a second carriage had already arrived. It held the queen's doctor, Sir James Reid, and the munshi, Abdul Karim.

"It's that damned munshi," I heard Mr Angelo mutter beside me. "He certainly considers himself important these days. No wonder the queen's gentlemen have had enough of him."

More carriages pulled up, one with the queen's ladies-in-waiting and another with more gentlemen of the household—her secretaries, gentlemen-at-arms and whatever these strange positions were called. I watched with interest. So the queen's gentlemen, who were aristocrats, had to travel together in a carriage while the Indian had a carriage almost to himself, following the queen. I was sure that did not go down well in palace circles. The munshi jumped down and sprinted to the royal carriage to push the hotel attendants out of the way, prepared to help the queen descend.

The hotel manager stepped forward, carrying a huge bouquet of spring flowers. "Welcome, Your Majesty," he said in hesitant English. "A thousand welcomes. Your hotel has been built for you and now awaits you with joy."

Queen Victoria gave him a little nod while examining the hotel with a critical eye. "It's very large, isn't it?" she said. "And please don't address me as Your Majesty. Simple Lady Balmoral will do. I wish my stay on the Riviera to be that of an ordinary woman, enjoying the sunshine."

"Where is the entrance for Her Majesty?" Princess Beatrice asked in French as the queen prepared to step down. "I understood she was to have a private entrance. She is not able to walk far, you know."

"Of course. A thousand pardons, Your Highness," the manager replied. "A special entrance, direct from the carriage, is to your left. I will lead you there."

So the royal party sat down again. The carriage followed him and came to a halt beside a special entrance crowned with a blue awning. The munshi had walked beside the carriage and now helped the queen to descend. She smiled up at him as she took his arm. Then inside she went, leaning on him and using her stick. The princesses followed, first Princess Helena, and following came Princess Beatrice with her tow-headed children holding her hands and her older daughter and son following. I understood that Princess Beatrice had been staying with her mother since her husband, the well-liked Prince Henry of Battenberg, had died the previous year.

After that, a second carriage drew up. A pretty young girl with almost white-blonde hair braided around her head was riding in this one, along with a chubby man who looked around with distaste, as if this luxurious palace of a hotel did not measure up to his expectations.

"Who is that?" I whispered to the maid standing beside me. "Are they royal relatives?"

"I think she's Princess Sophie," the maid replied. "She's some kind of young cousin of Prince Albert's from Germany. She came to stay at the palace once. She was really nice. And the gentleman with her is her betrothed. They call him Villie. I don't know anything about him."

"She looks awfully young to be married, doesn't she?" I whispered.

"I think she's eighteen. I suppose that's a good age if you are royal," the maid replied, her voice a little louder now that the royals had gone into the hotel. "But you wouldn't catch me wanting to be tied down with a husband and children at least until I was twenty-five. I want to see a bit of life first."

"Quite right," I agreed and found my thoughts going to my sister, Louisa. Married at seventeen, what did she know of the world? Would she later come to regret that she had tied herself to this man and his family? I might be poor and have no connections, but at least I was free to choose my own destiny. This thought perked me up considerably as I made my way back to the kitchen to help with the luncheon.

CHAPTER 20

The luncheon must have been well-received because the dishes came back almost empty and there were no complaints, except for a visit from the lady of the bedchamber in charge of the royal children, giving us instructions on the nursery food. The children were to be served bread and milk for their tea, and their diet was to consist of nourishing soups and vegetables. Plain food, nothing spicy or foreign, we were told. Boiled eggs for breakfast and the occasional fish were also recommended. Jimmy was given this assignment.

"Cooking the nursery food?" he asked, making a face of despair. "How am I ever going to learn to be a proper chef if I have to make bread and milk? Even my old mum couldn't mess that one up, and she was the world's worst cook. It's a wonder any of us grew up without being poisoned."

"Then just make sure you create the best bread and milk ever made," Mr Angelo said, smiling at Jimmy's horrified face. "And eggs boiled to perfection. That is a task at which most cooks fail."

Shortly after the lady had departed, we received another visitor—the despised munshi in person. He swept into the kitchen with a swagger. "Her Majesty has sent me to inform you that she wishes to give a little dinner party this evening since the prime minister is staying nearby. Dinner for twelve. Make sure it is an interesting menu."

"Our menus are always interesting," Mr Angelo said, putting down the cleaver he had been using with a decided thump.

"I would not say so," the munshi replied. "Again and again, I request special food, knowing that my diet must be suitable for my religion, and what do I get? I get chicken with no flavour. I get a pea soup that you call a dal. And what am I to eat here, I ask myself."

"The same as the other servants, I should imagine," Mr Angelo said.

"You insult me. I am not a mere servant," the man said. "I shall report this to Her Majesty and have you dismissed."

Mr Angelo smiled. "I don't think so, mate. The one thing Her Majesty loves more than you is her food. I'm not going anywhere. You, however, should be careful if you want to stay around."

"What do you mean by that? Do you threaten me?" The man's eyes flashed.

"Not me," Mr Angelo replied, "but I can tell you that you don't go down well with the rest of the court."

The munshi gave a little snort of derision. "As if I don't know this. But they are jealous that I am the queen's favourite, and they can do nothing about it." He stalked out of the room. The other cooks broke into chuckles.

"Blasted cheek," Mr Angelo said. "We'll beat him at his own game. We'll make him a vegetable dish every meal and put so much spice into it that smoke will come out of his ears." Then he clapped his hands. "Well, you heard the man. Dinner for twelve."

This didn't seem to worry Mr Angelo one iota, but it sent me into a bit of a panic. Until now, I had looked upon this assignment as a lark, a challenge, a time to prove my worth. Now it struck me that I had to live up to expectations. A dinner party would not be satisfied with ices and rice puddings. I tried to think what Mr Roland would have done. At least an impressive gateau. I thumbed through the cookery books. Mille-feuilles cake à la chantilly. Yes, I could do that. I could always guarantee that pastry would turn out well. And oranges were abundant here. An orange cream served in orange shells? That seemed doable, too. And for a third? I thought of a bread and butter pudding, to remind them of home, but alas we had no stale bread. This was one of the disadvantages of being in someone else's kitchen. So I decided I couldn't go wrong with profiteroles—who doesn't like them?

Everything turned out to my satisfaction. I stacked the profiteroles into a tower and drizzled them with chocolate. Chef Lepin walked past and nodded. Mr Angelo seemed to approve, too, although he didn't say anything.

The dinner party went smoothly. We were even sent a message of congratulations that the queen found the whitebait to be particularly tasty and that Lord Salisbury had commented on the clever oranges. I was too worked up, and too relieved, to feel like eating anything at that moment and went out through the servants' door at the back of the hotel into the cool of the night. A great canopy of stars hung overhead, such as I had never seen since we left Hampstead Heath. A pall of smoke always hung over London. One never knew if there was a moon or not. I stood gazing at the stars, trying to remember constellations my father had shown me. Suddenly I was aware of voices coming from directly above me.

I looked up. A balcony ran around the rooms on the first floor, and several gentlemen were standing on this, smoking. The scent of their tobacco wafted down to me.

"Doesn't she see he'll have to go?" said one of the voices. I thought I recognized it as that of Lord Salisbury. It had that fruity, hearty quality of a politician used to speaking loudly in Parliament.

"He's an embarrassment. An utter disgrace."

I thought I recognized this voice, too. I had definitely heard it before. There was a slight Scottish hint to it. Dr Reid, the queen's doctor, maybe? "Claims his father was surgeon general in India. Why, the man was no more than a hospital orderly. This munshi person is completely lower class. In his own country, he would be despised and shunned by polite society. And here she is, taking him everywhere with her. It's a complete embarrassment. We all threatened to resign, you know. It didn't faze her one bit. He has her bewitched, if you ask me."

"She always was influenced by a handsome male," a third voice pointed out. This one was higher in pitch and staccato in delivery.

"This man is not even handsome. Exotic at best, and thoroughly objectionable."

"Not to her. With her, he puts on a different face. As sweet and charming as the ices she so loves. What can we do to make her see that she is making a fool of herself and of her country?"

"I gather the local people here think he is some kind of captive Indian prince," the second man added.

"Gentlemen, I fear it is worse than you imagined." This was Lord Salisbury again. "He is not just an embarrassment but a danger to our national security. You've heard of Rafiuddin Ahmed?"

"The barrister chap? The one who heads the Muslim Patriotic League?"

"And what is that?" the third man asked.

"A group that's actively working against our nation. Wants to drive the British out of his country. Wants self-government for the colony."

"Good God. And this munshi is connected with him?"

"He is. Great friends, in fact. We have information that the munshi has been privy to top secret documents and has passed along their contents to this Muslim League person."

"Privy to top secret documents? How is that possible?"

"She allows him to stay in the room when she opens her dispatch boxes." The voice sounded disparaging. "And she's soft enough that who knows what she discusses with him, or what he peeks at over her shoulder."

"But that's a treasonable offence. The man is a damned foreign spy."

"So it would seem."

"Has the queen been told this?"

"She has, but refuses to believe that her dear munshi would ever do such a thing."

"At least we can say we are safely away from the British court."

"On the contrary," Lord Salisbury said angrily, "I have received information that this Rafiuddin Ahmed is on his way to Nice, if not already here. Clearly planning to meet with the munshi."

"But this must be stopped at all costs."

"I agree," Lord Salisbury said. "We will do what we can to make sure the two do not meet. I'm sure it can be arranged that our men intercept him and quietly escort him on his way. But if the munshi still has access to secret documents, what is to stop him from communicating in writing to all and sundry?"

"The queen must be made to see sense." The higher voice snapped out the words.

"And who will accomplish this?"

"Perhaps the Prince of Wales. He dislikes and distrusts the man as much as we do. For all his philandering, he's a sensible chap and has our country's best interest at heart."

"He likes to stay well away from his mother when he's on the Riviera. She doesn't approve of his mistresses."

"Protocol demands that he comes to pay his respects. I'll have a chat with him, and perhaps he can make her see."

"It seems to me that there is an obvious solution," the higher voice said, this time speaking slowly and in measured tones.

"And that would be?"

"To do away with the munshi."

There was a nervous chuckle. "And how do you propose to do that?"

"There are all sorts of strange diseases down here, you know. The water is notoriously bad. Put something in his food, for God's sake."

"You are not serious, surely?"

"Deadly serious. The man has to go. It's up to us to make that happen."

"And how do you propose to bring this about?"

"You're a doctor. You must know what can kill a chap and how to make it look like food poisoning."

"My dear man. I'm a doctor. I've taken an oath to preserve life, not end it."

"Not when it is in the best interests of your client, of the public good."

"Not even then. I'm sorry. I should go and see if the queen needs me before she goes to bed."

I heard a door shut above me.

"He'll come around," the higher voice said. "If not, we'll just have to find someone else."

I waited for a while before I dared to move, but hearing no more voices, I crept back inside the servants' entrance and into the kitchen, where the scullery maids were clearing away the last of the saucepans.

"Sit down and eat," Mr Williams called to me. "You look worn out."

I pulled up a chair beside him, and he ladled me a bowl of chicken soup, made from the less desirable parts of the capons and the offcuts of the garnishes. It was just what I needed, slipping down without effort, and I gave him a grateful nod.

"Rather strange, isn't it?" he went on with his pleasing Welsh lilt. "Being so far from home. Everything's a bit different. A new kitchen, new challenges. It's no wonder we feel a bit topsy-turvy." Then he gave me an encouraging smile. "I expect it will all work out. I think you're doing just fine."

I felt tears welling in my eyes. The yeomen cooks had hardly acknowledged my existence before this trip. Now he was not only keeping a fatherly eye on me, he was actually complimenting me.

I made my escape as soon as it was polite to do so and went up to my room. Once I had safely closed the door behind me, I sank on to my bed. I tried to put the conversation I had overheard from my mind, but could not. Several important gentlemen, including the prime minister and the queen's doctor, were plotting how to do away with her Indian servant. Talk of intrigue, foreign plots and treason! If someone had told me about it, I should not have believed them, thinking it a wild exaggeration. But I had heard with my own ears. And I could tell nobody.

Why should you worry? I said to myself. *It does not concern you. You are certainly not fond of this munshi. And if he is a foreign spy, he must be removed some way or another.* But the talk of poisoning his food had unnerved me. After all,

I was one of Her Majesty's cooks. One of those who handled the food. If anything happened to the munshi, the suspicion would fall on my colleagues and on me.

CHAPTER 21

In the light of morning, the scene I had overheard did not seem real. I almost wondered whether I had dreamed it. I breakfasted, enjoying the taste of the still-warm bread and the tart sweetness of the apricot jam, then went to work. I made a batch of little cakes, maids of honour, and brandy snaps for tea. All of these kept well in tins. I had just finished the brandy snaps, rolling them when still warm around a spoon handle, when Chef Lepin came up to me. "What are these?" he asked.

I told him. "They are filled with cream before they are served."

"May I try?"

I held out the one I had just finished. He took a bite. "Ah, they have spices. Ginger, I think, and a touch of cinnamon?"

"And brandy, of course," I replied.

He savoured the one bite. "And an interesting texture. Lacy. Crisp. Perhaps you could share this recipe? There are now guests at the hotel who expect the English teatime."

"Dear me," I said. "An English recipe you consider worthy of cooking? Wonders will never cease."

He looked at me and laughed.

"I'll trade you. My brandy snaps for your octopus."

He held out his hand to me. *"D'accord,"* he said, meaning he agreed.

I was unprepared for the jolt of electricity I felt when his hand touched mine. I must have stammered something about getting back to work. I could feel my cheeks flaming, and I suspected he was chuckling at my discomfort. *He is teasing you, Bella,* I told myself. *He is using his French charm to make you uncomfortable. You mean nothing to him.* But all the same, it was exhilarating to know that a man's touch could have this effect on me. I had begun to wonder whether I was strange or cold because I had not been thrilled by Nelson's kiss. Now I knew that I had just been waiting for the right man.

I soon discovered that working at the hotel was very different from being in the palace kitchens. There we were shut off from the life of the royal family. We had no idea who came and went, what small dramas unfolded. We cooked the meals, sent them off with footmen and mostly had no idea whether they were well-received or not, unless there was a complaint—which was rare. Here we were in close proximity to those we served. Our narrow passageways passed behind their rooms. Windows were open, and we overheard conversations. And we got glimpses of their lives.

After what I had heard the night before, I over-heard another strange conversation that morning. I had just come out of the servants' entrance for a breath of fresh air after putting various cakes and pastries into hot ovens. I walked around towards the front of the hotel, enjoying that breeze that came up from the seashore with a hint of salt to it. I was just rounding the turret at the end of the hotel when I heard a shrill voice saying, "But you must give it to me. I order you to."

I glanced up and saw that windows were open on the floor above me. I thought at first that it was one of the royal children, but a male voice replied, "Your Highness, I am only thinking of your well-being. You know that your mother would not approve. She would be horrified if she found out."

"You are not to tell her. I absolutely forbid you to tell her," came the female voice, now even more shrill and with a note of panic to it.

"Then I urge you to be sensible and to stop this nonsense while you still can."

"But I don't want to stop. It is my one pleasure in life."

"That is your choice, but I will do nothing to aid it. Good day to you, Your Highness."

This conversation left me as shocked and

intrigued as the last one. One of Queen Victoria's daughters, unless it was one of her grandchildren, and the voice had sounded too mature to be the ten-year-old girl. What did she want? And was that Dr Reid who was refusing her? Life was definitely more interesting in Nice, I decided. I was about to turn around and go back to keep an eye on my baking when I heard the strangest noise. It was part cry for help, part someone choking. I could not for the life of me place it, so I had to run around the building to see for myself. What was standing outside the queen's entrance at the front of the hotel was a tiny cart, pulled by a white donkey, which was now braying and making those extraordinary sounds. *A peasant selling vegetables?* I thought, but I was sure that such a vehicle would not be allowed to stand in the forecourt beside the smart carriages. Then I realized.

How sweet, I thought. *It must be for the queen's grandchildren.*

"Guess what I have just seen," I reported on coming back into the kitchen. "There is a cart being pulled by a donkey outside the hotel."

"Oh, that donkey cart, I heard about that," Mr Angelo said, giving Mr Phelps a knowing grin. "Rumour has it that the queen came upon a peasant ill-treating his donkey. She was so shocked and upset that she paid for the beast on the spot. And now she keeps it stabled here so that she can ride around the area in a little cart." He grinned as he turned back to me. "It's outside now, is it? Let's go and have a look. I'd like to see for myself."

The other cooks decided they would like a peek, too, so we piled out of the back door and hurried around to the front of the hotel. As we came around, we heard an imperious voice saying, "No, not like that, you fool. Hold the beast's head while I assist Her Majesty."

It was the queen's munshi, and Queen Victoria clung on to his arm while she came forward, using her stick. Two of her grandchildren followed her, their mother keeping a watchful eye on them.

"Surely there is not room for you all," Princess Beatrice called as the queen was helped into the seat. "And is that poor little donkey strong enough to pull you all in the cart?"

"Nonsense. They are tiny scraps. They don't take up any space at all," the queen said. "Come on, children. Let's go for a ride, shall we?"

The two children climbed in eagerly, squeezing in beside their grandmother. And they set off. A groom walked at the donkey's head, and the munshi at the queen's side. Mr Angelo turned to us with an amused grin. "What some people will do for entertainment. Still, I suppose if you are empress of half the world, it makes a change to live like a peasant for a moment."

He headed back to the kitchen, and I was about to fall in behind him when a voice said, "You, girl."

I turned around to see Princess Helena beckoning to me.

I went up to her and curtsied. "You wanted something, Your Royal Highness?"

"Yes. I want you to run a small errand for me. You are to take this paper and find a chemist's shop in the town. Hand the paper to the pharmacist, pay him and bring what he gives you directly to me, do you understand?"

She thrust a sheet of paper at me.

I felt myself blushing bright red with confusion. "But Your Highness, I can't go into town. I have work to do here."

"Nonsense. I am sure your work here can wait. I need these items immediately."

"But Your Highness, I am one of the cooks. I have to prepare my part of the luncheon, and I have cakes that need to come out of the oven directly."

She was looking at me as if I was some strange kind of insect she had never seen before. "You are one of my mother's cooks, you say?"

"Yes, ma'am." I nodded. Then I added boldly, "I am currently the pastry chef."

"A female chef? How quaint. How novel." She sighed. "Well, in that case I suppose I cannot tear you away from your endeavours. My mother would not be at all pleased if luncheon were not served on time."

I curtsied again for good measure. "I'm very sorry, Your Highness. Cannot your maid fulfil this errand for you? Or a hotel servant?"

"My maid, I fear, reports back to my mother. But you are right—there must be a hotel messenger boy who can carry out this commission. I'll go and see."

And she strode off across the forecourt. I watched her go, realization dawning. It had been her voice I had heard coming from that window, arguing with the doctor. Now I understood. I had caught a glimpse of what was written on that sheet of paper when she had tried to thrust it at me: *2 bottles Bayer Heroin. 1 Bottle Laudanum. 1 packet needles.*

I had no experience or real knowledge about these things, but I had heard rumours, and my mother, before she died, had taken to using laudanum to the point that my father had become concerned for her. So now I understood the desperation in her voice. The needles were not for sewing—they were for injecting substances into her body. Princess Helena was addicted to drugs. Another fact I knew but could tell nobody.

I was hurrying in before my cakes burned when I overheard my name—at least, my adopted name. "Barton?" said a man's voice. "No, I don't recall anyone of that name in Her Majesty's employ." He repeated this in French but with a strong English accent.

I turned around to see one of Her Majesty's gentlemen talking to what looked like a messenger boy. I took a deep breath and went over to them.

"I am Helen Barton," I said. "I am one of Her Majesty's cooks."

"You are a cook for Her Majesty? Remarkable," the gentleman said.

I saw that the messenger was holding a letter. "Is that a letter for me?" I asked in French.

The messenger boy nodded and handed it to me. "From the Viscount Faversham."

I took it, my cheeks burning. "I'm afraid I have no money on me . . . ," I stammered.

"My master has paid me well. Do not concern yourself," he said, gave a little bow and then took off.

The gentleman was staring at me in a way that made me most uncomfortable.

"Since when do servant girls receive letters from viscounts?" he asked.

"We met at Lady Crozier's party," I replied. Oh, how I would love to have told him that Giles Waverly was my cousin. "I was invited to be part of the tableau."

The gentleman shook his head. "This is not a wise thing, young woman. Liaisons outside of your class can only end in tragedy, especially for the girl involved."

"Oh no, sir," I said. "It is nothing like that. I quite understand. Viscount Faversham promised to show me the beach by his villa. That is all. I have no intention of anything more."

"Make sure you stick to that," he said. "Young aristocrats tend to think that servant girls are easy pickings, if you get my meaning."

"Sir Arthur, are you free?" a man called from the hotel steps. "A word if you don't mind."

"I hope you'll take my warning to heart, young lady." Sir Arthur gave me a little nod and left me standing there. I watched him go with interest, not because of what he had just told me, but because I recognized his voice. His was the higher-pitched, clipped speech from the balcony that night. And he was Sir Arthur Bigge, the queen's secretary.

I waited until I was safely inside the building before I opened the letter.

Dear Miss Barton,

I hope you won't think it impertinent, writing to you, but I did so enjoy our little talk the other evening and would like to see you again. I know you told me you are at Her Majesty's beck and call, but my time is my own. Any moment you are free

*I will come with the carriage to sweep you
away for an hour or two. I would so like
to show you the area around our villa. It
is so beautiful.*

Yours sincerely,

Giles Waverly

I shouldn't reply, I told myself. As Sir Arthur
had said, no good could come of this. When Giles
Waverly found out I was merely a cook, it would
be an embarrassment for both of us. But the truth
was that I had enjoyed his company. He seemed
like a nice, harmless young Englishman. And
what could be wrong with a ride in the carriage,
in broad daylight? Then a wicked thought came
to me. If he tried in any way to get fresh, I would
reveal that I was his cousin. Surely that should
make him stop and consider.

I had done so many things that were not wise or
sensible lately, and they had all worked out well.
Maybe this was another of my father's occasions
to carpe diem. I resolved, if the occasion arose,
that I would write back to Giles Waverly and
accept his invitation.

Our next royal encounter came that afternoon.
We had finished the luncheon service and were
just sorting out the items that had come back

uneaten. Of these there were usually plenty, as the queen liked enough choice of items in each of the courses.

"I see they liked your fried fish, Mr Williams," Mr Angelo said. "Not a morsel returned."

"Too bad. I was hoping for a little of that myself. The fish looked rather tempting," Mr Williams replied.

We looked up as the kitchen door opened, and in came Count Wilhelm, the betrothed of Princess Sophie. He swept in, stood looking around him. "You are the English chefs, *ja*?"

"We are, Your Highness. Can we help you?" Mr Angelo asked as I dropped a curtsy.

"I very much hope so," the count said in his strongly accented English. He strode right up to Mr Angelo. "I am most disappointed in the food that you serve to my royal relatives."

"In what way, sir?" Mr Angelo was not easily cowed and stepped forward to confront the count.

"*Fleisch*!" the count said. "There is not enough fleisch."

"You mean meat, sir? Lamb cutlets were served at luncheon. And squab."

The count waved his hands dismissively. "This is food for old ladies and delicate vomen. I am a man. I must have my fleisch to keep up my strength. Where was the pork schnitzel? Where was the Rindfleisch? The famous English roast beef?"

"I'm sorry, sir, but this is France. You won't find English roast beef here."

Count Wilhelm frowned. "Are you being disrespectful? Are you mocking me?"

"Not at all, sir, but what I say is true. I'm afraid the hotel has not been able to find a joint of beef that meets my high standards yet," Mr Angelo replied. "You have to understand we are at the mercy of what the French butchers can send us. In France, they do not eat big hunks of meat. It is expensive here, so it is not so easily obtained. But I have put out word that they are to have some shipped from England if necessary."

"And in the meantime, I starve," the count said.

I doubted this. For a young man, he was awfully round. His yellow satin waistcoat only just met across his belly.

"You must make sure I have enough good meat at every meal," he said. "If not the roast beef, then liver, kidneys, brains. Fortifying food. Food fit for a healthy man like myself."

"Very good, my lord," Mr Angelo said. I could tell he wasn't quite sure how to address a German count. Was he a royal or merely an aristocrat?

"And another thing." The man wagged a finger in Mr Angelo's face. "Who is responsible for the *nachspeisen*? The pudding as you call it."

"That would be Miss Barton," Mr Angelo said.

Wilhelm turned to me in surprise. "A voman? You let a voman make the dishes?"

"Miss Barton is an accomplished cook," Mr Angelo said. I could have hugged him.

"Very well." He turned to face me.

"Was something not to your liking, Your Highness?" I asked.

"These puddings—the creams and the ices and the delicate little pastries—they are for the vomen. And yesterday you served the mehlbrei, such as we give to children in Germany. Where are the *knödel*, the dumplings, the English suet puddings? The things that really satisfy."

"I am sorry, sir," I said. "The queen is not too fond of heavy puddings. And mehlbrei is her favourite, especially after travelling. You surely understand that meals are planned to please her. At home, she must approve all menus. I'm sure she will here, too, once she has settled in."

"Then make her the mehlbrei, make her the frothy creams, but for the love of God make me a proper pudding."

"I will do my best, Your Highness," I said and gave him another curtsy, which he obviously approved of.

"Excellent. Carry on. Carry on." He waved a hand in our direction. Then, on the way out, he stopped. "Vat are these?"

"Brandy snaps for today's tea," I said.

He picked one up and popped it into his mouth. "Not bad," he said, his mouth still full. "And this cake? Is the icing chocolate or coffee?"

And to my horror, he ran his finger across the top of my cake and spooned up a big dollop of icing. He sucked on his finger. "Ah, chocolate. Good."

He looked around once more, and his gaze fell upon Jimmy. "And vat do you cook, young man?"

"Jimmy is our apprentice," Mr Angelo replied. "He does all the basic preparations. He is still learning."

"Very good. Carry on." The count nodded, then swept out. The door swung shut behind him.

"Ruddy cheek," Mr Angelo said. His face was bright red. "Coming in here like Lord Muck, as if he owns the place."

"And look at my cake," I said. "I'll have to scrape off all this icing and make a new batch."

"Miss Barton, I am so sorry that you have been insulted in this way," Mr Phelps said. "I've never seen anything like it. Have you, Mr Angelo? Never in all my years in the kitchen."

"I have not. And I don't think Her Majesty would approve of such behaviour," Mr Angelo said. "She is always most courteous with her staff. I think I'll have a little word with Sir Arthur, her private secretary. We're not having that fat bloke coming in and out of our kitchen when he feels like it!"

"Can one of us be of any assistance, Miss Barton?" Mr Angelo said. "Jimmy, get down the icing sugar and the chocolate powder for our pastry chef."

There was a joint effort to rescue my cake. I was still seething with annoyance, but at the same time I felt a warmth inside. We were a team. We cared about each other.

CHAPTER 22

As it happened, my chance to see Giles Waverly came sooner than I had expected. We were informed that the following day Her Majesty was to dine with her cousin, King Leopold of the Belgians, who had a villa just outside Nice. The members of her household would be content with a cold supper, and we could have the afternoon off.

"I'm glad he's not coming here, dirty old man," Mr Angelo muttered after he gave us the news. "We'd have to keep our Miss Barton safely locked away in the kitchen." He gave us a knowing look. "He has an inclination for young girls, so we understand. You may be a bit old for him, Miss Barton, but you still have that bloom of youth about you."

"Didn't I hear that he has his mistress with him?" Jimmy asked. I don't know how he managed to find out all these titbits of scandal. Mr Angelo obviously thought the same thing.

"Where do you find out all this rubbish, Jimmy? I hope you are not mixing with the wrong type of person."

"Oh no, Mr Angelo. I was chatting with some

of the footmen. They were telling me stories like you wouldn't believe. They said he has a predilection for little girls. Imagine, an old man like that. Disgusting, that's what it is. Oh, and another thing . . ." He paused, his smile broadening. "They say he lets his fingernails grow ever so long, so it's impossible to shake hands with him without getting stabbed. Can you imagine it?"

"I'm surprised Her Majesty chooses to associate with him, even if he is her cousin," Mr Williams said in a disapproving voice. "You know how particular she is about correct behaviour and marital fidelity."

"Well, I'm just glad Her Majesty is going there and we don't have to feed him," Mr Phelps chimed in. "I would like to put a big dose of cascara in his food."

"Mr Phelps, I'm shocked at you," Mr Angelo said. There was a pause, and then they both laughed. "He wouldn't be able to open the lav door in time with those long fingernails," he added.

We all joined in the laughter.

"Do you think all the royal persons are creepy in some way?" Jimmy asked. "Do you think they behave badly just because they can?"

"I have to point out that Her Majesty is a perfect example of decorum," Mr Williams said, giving Jimmy a hard stare. "And her daughters, too, I am sure."

I said nothing about Princess Helena. But Jimmy was not about to be silenced. "She had that John Brown fellow for a while, didn't she? And now that Indian bloke goes everywhere with her. That's not normal, is it?"

"There is nothing suspicious about their relationship," Mr Angelo said. "He is a wily snake who is playing upon her loneliness and desire for attention. And she likes young men around her, and she likes the exotic. Why else would she travel with Highland pipers when she could bring perfectly ordinary soldiers to guard her? But her relationship with them is only that of sovereign to subject, I am sure."

"I'll tell you who else gives me the willies," Jimmy said. "That Count Willie."

"I agree, his behaviour is not acceptable," Mr Angelo said, "but I don't know why it should worry you."

"I'm not talking about messing with the food," Jimmy said. "He came out of the dining room after dinner last night, and he asked me to come up and see him in his room, later. Well, I wasn't born yesterday, Mr Angelo. I got a whiff of what that might mean, so I said that I was sorry, but I had to report back to do the washing up."

"You were quite right, my boy," Mr Angelo said. "We servants always have to keep our guard up. We never know where the next impropriety is coming from." And he looked at me, clearly

269

remembering what I had told him about the Prince of Wales.

I was still thinking about this when I went upstairs to my room to write a note to Giles Waverly. Sir Arthur Bigge had said that we were easy pickings. Was that how Giles Waverly saw me? What if the carriage stopped at his villa and I was invited inside—would I go? How could I refuse? But if I turned down anything that might be dangerous, what a boring life I would lead. So I took up my pen and wrote that I would be free the following afternoon and would await his carriage at the entrance to the hotel grounds. I certainly didn't want anyone observing me getting into a carriage with a strange man!

Then, of course, came the question of what to wear. I certainly could not sit in a carriage in my cotton blouse, or my evening gown. I wondered if my new dress might be ready, or if Claudette's mother had found the fabric impossible to work with. How would I get a chance to find out? I resorted to a little subterfuge.

"If we are to serve a cold supper to the household, may I go to the market early tomorrow morning and buy fruit and vegetables to make salads? They are so much fresher there."

Mr Angelo raised an eyebrow. "If I didn't know better, I'd think you'd met a boy at the market you were sweet on," he said.

This made me blush, thinking of my encounter

with Chef Lepin. But I said, "Oh no, Cook. Absolutely not. But I have to confess, I do enjoy the atmosphere at the market—the flowers, all the bright colours. And I'll go without my breakfast so I won't waste any of your time."

"All right then," he said. He reached into a pocket and produced a coin. "You're a good girl, and you work hard. Who am I to deny you a little pleasure? Buy yourself a sprig of flowers while you are there."

"Thank you, Cook." I beamed at him.

I rose extra early the next morning. To my annoyance, it was cold and a fine drizzle was falling. That might spoil my plans for a carriage ride. I presumed it would be an open carriage as they mostly seemed to be around here. But undaunted I grabbed a cup of coffee, put on my cape and off I went down to the town. I had learned by now not to count on the trolley, so I walked, encountering various tradespeople on their way to work. But even at that hour, when the sun would have been visible had it not been for the heavy clouds that hung over the ring of hills around the city, the market was in full swing. I did my shopping first, selecting various vegetables and grapefruit, apples and oranges for a fruit salad. I was about to make my way to Claudette's mother when I saw Chef Lepin. He was standing at a stall that seemed to be laden with objects I didn't recognize: dirty brown earthy globes and what looked like bits of dung. I couldn't think what they were or what he might do with them. Curiosity got the better of me.

"Excuse me, Chef," I said.

He turned, and I was gratified to see that he looked pleased. "*Alors*, the young lady is up bright and early. My compliments. You are buying fish again?"

"No, today it's items for salads. The queen is out tonight, and her household will have a cold supper."

"Ah." He nodded.

"May I ask what these things are?"

"Different types of mushrooms. You do not have mushrooms in your country?"

"We do, but just the round, flat variety. Nothing like these." I pointed at some bright-orange little bells that looked lethal to me. "Are they all edible?"

"I would not be serving them to the guests if they weren't," he said. "These chanterelles, they have exquisite taste. These are straw mushrooms." He pointed to a cluster of thin white stalks. "These we call cèpe. These big ones are trumpet royale. And these, morels—although you must never pick these for yourself. The false morels look very similar and can be fatal. Try the chanterelles. You must cook some for your queen. She will approve."

"But that thing you were going to buy. How does one cook that?" It looked like a dirty ball of earth.

He rolled his eyes. "That, chérie, is worth more per gram than gold. It is a truffle. You do not have truffles?"

"No."

"Then let me instruct you. The truffle is a fungus that grows on the roots of certain oak trees. Under the soil, you understand. They can only be located by specially trained dogs, oh, and by pigs if they can get at them. They have a deliciously different flavour. We make the truffle oil for cooking, or we use a small amount to raise the quality of the dish. I will give you a taste tonight, and you will see. Only a tiny taste, you understand. More expensive than gold, eh?"

"Thank you," I said. "I have to take some of the orange ones—chanterelles, did you call them?—and try them at luncheon."

Chef Lepin handed a piece of truffle to the stall-keeper, who weighed it and mentioned a ridiculous price. He waited while I chose the more modest chanterelles.

"So do you head back to the hotel now? If you wait a while, we will walk together."

"I have another commission in the town," I said. "I'll see you back at the hotel."

"I understand," he said.

"No you don't," I wanted to say. "I really do have another commission." I could tell he had taken it as a brush-off. Oh, why did men have to be so complicated?

"Mademoiselle," he said as an afterthought. "It is well that you buy your mushrooms here, from this stall. Here I know they are picked with care and are safe. Other mushroom sellers are not so careful, and one bad mushroom can kill you very quickly."

"Thank you for the advice, Chef," I said. "I will watch how you cook tonight."

"Very well." He nodded, gave me a little bow and walked in the opposite direction.

I made my way to the house that clung to the edge of the castle hill. I knew it was still rather early to make a call, but Claudette's mother came out of her front door, just as I was approaching, paused and smiled when she saw me.

"Oh, it is the young English lady. I was wondering when you would return for your dress."

"It is finished?" I asked.

"I may have to make some minor adjustments," she said, "but I don't think so. I have been doing this for long enough that my measurements are usually correct—unless you have been eating too much for the past few days."

"Oh no, madame." I laughed.

"Then come inside." She held open the door for me.

"Were you not on your way somewhere?" I asked. "I don't want to hinder you."

"It can wait. Just to buy bread. Come." She ushered me into the dark little room.

"There," she said. "What do you think?"

On a dressmaker's dummy was a dress. A really pretty dress. "But that is not mine," I said wistfully.

"It is. Try it on."

"But no—my fabric was plain blue green."

"Your fabric was not strong enough for a whole dress," she said. "See I have used it in the skirt panels and the sleeves."

I picked up the skirt. The other fabric had a sheen to it and was sprigged with a flower design in a royal blue and gold. "But the rest of the fabric? It is lovely."

"It is. It was a marquise who brought it to me. She has good taste."

"I can't use another woman's fabric," I stammered.

She grinned, revealing that mouth with many missing teeth. "These rich people, they bring me metres and metres of fabric. There is always much left. They don't care. I say to them, 'What do you wish that I do with the remaining fabric?' and they say, 'Whatever you like. I am happy with my dress. I don't need the rest.'"

While she spoke, she was removing the

dress from the dummy. Then she helped me off with my blouse and skirt and slipped the dress over my head. It fitted perfectly, so slim in the waist it did look as if I was wearing a corset. The neckline was prim and demure, as befitted someone in my position. I turned around, examining myself in the speckled old mirror.

"It's wonderful," I said. She was grinning as if she had performed a magic trick for me.

"It is worth the effort to make a dress for a pretty young girl like you. And you will tell your friends that Francine DuBois makes good clothes, *non*?"

"I will," I said, regretting that I didn't have any friends to tell. Once I took it off, she packed up the dress in tissue paper, and I paid her what seemed quite a modest sum. A quick calculation made me realize that I should spend some of my wages on more clothes while I had such a talented dressmaker at my disposal.

"I would like you to make more clothes for me," I said. "What do you suggest, and where should I buy the fabric so that it is of better quality? I know nothing."

She patted my hand. "Let me see what I can do. Come back in about a week, and I should have something for you to try on."

I couldn't thank her enough, and I think I floated all the way back up the hill.

• • •

By midday, the clouds had rolled away and the sun was peeking through. Mr Angelo was apparently familiar with chanterelles and had prepared them on previous occasions on the Continent. He cooked them in butter to be served as a side dish at luncheon and heard back from the queen that she was so delighted he had found the little orange mushrooms again.

"You've got a good eye, my girl," he said.

"And Chef Lepin is going to show me how to use truffles tonight," I said.

"That French johnny seems to be getting rather familiar with you," he said. "I'd watch out if I were you."

"Cook, he's just pleased that I take an interest in his cooking."

"Oh, is that what he tells you?" He paused, then added, "He's a handsome man. He's foreign. And you've been sheltered all your life. Just keep it to the cooking, all right?"

"Of course," I said.

My world seemed to be full of men with good intentions about my virtue.

CHAPTER 23

As soon as luncheon was over, I rushed up to my room, washed myself carefully to get rid of possible cooking smells, splashed on a little rose water and put on my new dress. Thank heavens Madame DuBois had made it to fasten at the front. She must have guessed I had no maid to do up hooks at the back. I brushed my hair and carefully pinned it up. I was going to take my shawl, but I decided that it looked old and worn and I'd rather freeze if necessary. I came down the stairs, crept around the other side of the building, where ordinary guests were housed (or, rather, non-royal guests, as the prices here were too steep for ordinary people), then made my way successfully through the gardens and out to the front gate.

I hadn't been waiting long before a smart carriage came up the hill towards me. It was open, as were most of the vehicles I had seen here, a light gig pulled by a handsome bay horse. Giles was holding the reins himself, and his red-blonde hair was blowing out in the breeze. He actually looked rather dashing. He pulled the horse to a halt beside me and jumped down.

"Well, this is a treat," he said. "Hello, Bella. It was so good of you to agree to come out for a spin with me. Don't you look terribly nice?" And he helped me up on to the padded leather seat. "It turned out to be a lovely day for a spin. I was quite depressed this morning when I saw the weather, but it has cleared up beautifully."

He was doing what we English do when we're a little awkward and tongue-tied. We talk of the weather.

"It promises to be a lovely afternoon," I agreed.

"Yes, it does!" he said with enthusiasm, and I realized he wasn't talking about the weather.

We made our way slowly down the steepest part of the hill, then skirted around the back of the old town, coming out to the little port where fishing boats bobbed at moorings and fishermen sat mending nets. On the other side, the road started to climb again, this time hugging a cliff beside the sea. Below us was a spectacular drop to blue water, and to our left the hillside rose steeply, now dotted with occasional villas and gardens. We came around a corner, and I gasped. Giles grinned as if he had put on this view especially for me. Below us was a narrow bay. This time the boats at mooring were large pleasure yachts. Green hills dropped sharply on all sides, dotted here and there with occasional pastel villas, surrounded by lines of dark cypress trees or tall palms. A little town clung to the hillside with a busy port below us.

We had exchanged a few pleasantries along the way: how I was enjoying Nice so far, whether I had attended any other parties, what I thought of French food. Mostly Giles had pointed out places of interest. He did so now.

"That's the town of Villefranche-sur-Mer," Giles said. "It's a free port. It helped the French king once against pirates or Italians or something, and now they don't have to pay any taxes."

"How convenient," I said, making him laugh.

"I must say the idea appeals to my father, and to me, too. The death duties on our estate are going to be crippling when he goes. I only hope that I can afford to keep it on." He gave a little shrug. "Like most men in my position, I'm not much use for anything else."

I thought of my father, being sent out to the army in India—a profession to which he was completely unsuited—and then being at the beck and call of guests at the Savoy. He must have suffered, knowing that had birth order been different, he would have been living a life of leisure, just the way I had suffered on finding myself as a servant to a nouveau riche family. How I would have liked to tell Giles the truth. How interested he would have been to know. But I couldn't risk it. He'd only have to let slip one word at the wrong time to the wrong person, and it would get back to the Excelsior Regina and I would be dismissed.

Instead I chatted on pleasantly as we skirted the side of the bay. "That road takes us out to Saint-Jean-Cap-Ferrat," he said. "Lots of lovely villas out there. Lots of money. Rothschilds and the like. And that old devil King Leopold has bought up all the property he could get his hands on. I suppose you've met him?"

"I haven't," I said, "but the queen is dining with him this evening."

"They say he's quite repulsive," Giles said, "and with depraved habits. So it's lucky you've managed to avoid him so far. But I presume you've met the Prince of Wales?"

"Oh yes," I said with more emphasis than I meant. "I have met the Prince of Wales."

"I feel sorry for the chap myself," Giles went on. "I mean, stuck waiting for his mother to die, having no real role in life. But actually I suppose I identify with him. I have no real role either. My father won't let me take over any of the running of the estate. He thinks I'm going to drag it to ruin when he dies. I'm afraid he doesn't think too much of me. I'm somewhat of a disappointment."

"Why?" I asked.

"Oh, I don't know. I prefer art to hunting, and I hated boarding school, not being very good at rugger. He thinks I'm a weakling. I'm not. I'm just not like him, that's all. He comes from a long line of bullies. In fact, it is required of the oldest son to be a bully."

"But you're the oldest son?"

"Only son. Only heir, and I promise I will never be a bully, not even to my dog. Especially not to my dog."

His eyes met mine, and he smiled. *I like him,* I thought. *He's kind. He's gentle.* Then I reminded myself: *This cannot go anywhere. A pleasant carriage ride on a fine afternoon. That's all.*

Instead of taking the road out to the cape, we continued straight ahead, dipping down to a charming little bay edged with palm trees. Here he brought the carriage to a stop and motioned to a boy loitering nearby. "If you watch the horse, I'll give you a good tip," he said in French that was not as bad as he had portrayed.

"Certainly, monsieur," the boy replied eagerly and went to stand at the horse's head. Giles helped me down, and we walked through a little park until we came out to the beach. There was another small harbour to one side, a stone jetty and a perfect curve of pale-yellow sand around the bay.

"You see." He gestured to it as he took my arm down a flight of stone steps. "Not at all like Nice, which is absolutely horrible. Stones that cripple you, and a steep drop-off once you're in the water. Here you can stand or float to your heart's content. Do you swim?"

"I'm afraid I've never had the opportunity," I said.

"Pity." We started to walk across the sand. It was a novel experience for me, feeling the softness under my feet.

"I gather the queen loves to bathe whenever she gets the chance," Giles said. "I'm surprised she hasn't ordered her household to join her. It is a trifle early in the year, I'll grant you, but in a month or so you should give it a try. I'll teach you if you like."

"I don't even own a bathing costume," I said.

"I'm sure a local seamstress can run you up one between now and April. You'd love it. It is chilly in the spring, but bracing, and one feels so much better for being immersed in saltwater."

"You've been here before, have you?" I asked.

"A couple of times. We stayed at Menton once in a rented villa, and once at Cannes, but this is definitely the nicest. My father is thinking of buying a villa here. Naturally, I'm encouraging him."

We walked along the edge of the water. Small wavelets rushed up towards our feet, then receded again, but the whole bay was remarkably calm.

"Is your mother with you?" I asked casually.

His face clouded. "She died when I was only six," he said. "She was expecting another baby, and it did not go well. She was such a sweet, gentle being. She liked to take me on her knee

283

and read me stories. I still miss her, isn't that strange?"

"Not at all strange. My mother died when I was a child, and I certainly miss her."

"Is your father still alive?"

"No, he died, too. I have one married sister, but apart from that, I have no one."

"Ah, hence being put under the queen's protection. Very wise."

Working in her kitchen was hardly the same as being put under her protection. "I work for my living, you know," I felt obliged to say.

"Of course you do. It's well known that the queen is an absolute slave driver. You're not one of those maids of honour whom she keeps up until one in the morning, are you?"

"No, nothing like that. It'd be a disaster." I grinned. "I get sleepy by ten."

"The queen is quite remarkable, isn't she?" Giles said. "Nearly eighty years old and still stays up past midnight, bosses around her prime minister and has her hand firmly on the reins of the empire." He glanced up. "Speaking of reins, I don't suppose I should trust my horse to that boy for too long."

I gave a reluctant look back as we left the beach. Giles must have felt the same because he said, "Maybe next time we could arrange for a picnic. If you would consent to a next time, that is?"

Again I hesitated. Then I heard myself say, "Of course. I would love to have a picnic next time."

His face flushed with joy. "Jolly good. I'm so glad. Most girls I meet find me a bit of a bore, I'm afraid. I'm not dashing like the rest of the chaps."

"Oh, I think dashing would be very hard to take in the long run," I said, and he laughed.

"I say, there is a splendid little patisserie in Beaulieu. Would you care for a pastry and a cup of coffee before we return—if you must go back, that is?"

"I really must. I was given permission for a free afternoon, that's all."

"Even though the queen is dining out?"

"I'm afraid so. They really are quite strict with unmarried girls in the household."

"Of course. I understand. But how about that pastry?"

"I wouldn't say no to that," I said. "The sea air has given me an appetite."

He smiled again as if I had given him a present. We returned to the carriage and proceeded into the little town. Again Giles found someone to watch the carriage, and we walked up a small high street to the pastry shop. The array of cakes and pastries was dazzling, and so intricately made. I chose a chocolate-covered oblong with caramelized hazelnuts and chocolate curls on top. Giles went for a baba au rhum.

"What is that?" I asked him.

"It's like a doughnut but soaked in rum. Awfully good. Are you sure you don't want to try one?"

"Not rum in the middle of the afternoon, thank you," I said.

"Oh no, of course not. You couldn't return with your breath smelling of alcohol, could you?"

"Probably not the best idea."

We were laughing as we carried our pastries to a little table, and the shop owner brought over cups of milky coffee. The pastry was beyond delicious. I'd like to have asked for the recipe, but that would have seemed rude. As I glanced at that glass counter with its myriad pastries, I realized how much I had to learn. I could make a passable dessert, but I still lacked skills in decoration and presentation. I resolved, while I was in France, to learn some of the finer points of pastries. And I paused to consider how passionately I felt about this. Did I really want to become a real chef? Even if the prospect of marriage was offered to me? I glanced across at Giles, who was tucking into his baba au rhum. Viscountess Faversham—I tried out the idea in my head.

"You must come down to the casino sometime," Giles said as we left the café and headed back to the Excelsior Regina.

"Which is the casino?"

"You must have noticed it. That building on the pier, with the big glass dome. It's awfully jolly and ridiculously formal, too. They won't let you in unless you are properly dressed. I understand they turned away Lord Salisbury because he wasn't dressed well enough." He chuckled. "Can you imagine, telling the prime minister to leave?"

"I don't suppose they knew he was the prime minister," I said. "He doesn't look very stately, does he?"

"He doesn't. Have you seen him walking around Beaulieu with that shapeless old hat on his head? One could mistake him for a tramp! I wonder the queen doesn't tell him to shape up. She's usually a stickler for people looking the part. I say, is it true about that Indian chap she has with her?"

"Is what true?"

"That he's . . . more than a servant, would you say?"

"You're implying their relationship isn't quite proper?" I asked. "She is seventy-seven, you know. I'm told she likes to have handsome young men around her."

"But there has been talk. I overheard at Lady Mary's party. They were saying he thinks of himself as one of the gentlemen of the court, when in fact he was sent over as a table servant."

"You're quite right in that," I said. "There is a lot of discontent. The gentlemen of the household all threatened to resign if he came here with the queen. But they backed down, I'm afraid, and he's here, trying to lord it over everybody."

"And the queen allows this?"

"She won't hear anything against him. He has become far too familiar, with her all the time. And he's most disagreeable to everyone else— dictating that special food should be cooked for him and riding in his own carriage when the real gentlemen are all crammed in together."

"I wonder where it will lead?" Giles said. "Somebody will have to do something about him, surely?"

"I think they are trying to," I said. *One way or another,* I thought, but didn't say.

"I say, I've had a most spiffing afternoon with you," Giles said as we came around the Corniche and descended into Nice. "I hope we can do it again very soon, or perhaps you can escape for an evening and we could go to dinner somewhere? There's a perfect little restaurant out on a rock, surrounded by sea. I've been dying to try it."

Alarm bells were going off in my head. This was madness. If it was discovered that Giles had been courting a servant, I'd probably be dismissed, and Giles would be in trouble with his father. I knew little of the ways of men. I was just the means of spending a pleasant afternoon. He might enjoy outings with any number of young ladies and have a potential wife lined up at home in England. I could not risk my future for something that would probably lead nowhere. I paused in mid-thought. Did I want it to lead somewhere? I glanced across at him. He had a nice enough face, and he was sweet and amusing. And I had to admit that the prospect of being Lady Faversham, of righting the wrongs to my father, was rather tempting. But I really was leaping ahead here.

Giles deposited me outside the Regina. I thanked him for the lovely afternoon; he said he should be thanking me and looked forward to seeing me again when the queen could spare me.

"Just drop me a note," he said. "I'll be waiting anxiously."

"I'm not sure that I'll be able to meet you again," I said, hesitantly. "We are not supposed to have assignations with young men."

He laughed. "I wouldn't call coffee in Beaulieu an assignation, would you? We have been so frightfully proper. And I am a perfectly respectable chap, you know. You can look me up in *Burke's Peerage*. Good old family. Solid stock." Then the smile faded, and a worried look came to his face. "Unless you don't want to see me again and you found this afternoon horribly dull. I'm not the most scintillating of conversationalists, so I've been told."

"Oh no. I really did have a lovely time," I said. "It's just rather complicated in my current situation."

"Then we shall correspond in secret." He gave

me an impish grin. "You shall drop me a note when you might be free, and if I respond, I shall send it to the hotel rather than to the queen's party. And they never need to know."

He jumped down from the trap and came around to take my hand, assisting me down. His hand lingered too long in mine, and I think he was considering whether to say more or even kiss me. I avoided this by giving him a bright smile. "Thank you again. I must go before I'm seen and given a lecture."

I went inside feeling horribly awkward. I had encouraged him, misled him. When the queen could spare me indeed. The queen didn't even know I was part of her retinue here in Nice. And nothing could come of this, even if I wanted it to. But I had to admit it was nice to be treated like a lady, to sit beside a young man in a carriage. *This is what my father and mother would have taken for granted in their youth,* I thought, and felt a tinge of that anger and resentment that had haunted me since I was sent into service.

CHAPTER 24

There was great excitement at the Excelsior Regina. The famous French actress Sarah Bernhardt had come to stay—not with the queen, I hasten to add, but in the hotel proper. In fact, it was rumoured that the queen disapproved of her because of her loose ways. Therefore, we were all surprised when it was announced that the queen had requested Sarah to give a special performance just for her and her household at the hotel. What is more, we were all to be invited. The vast pillared dining room was turned into a theatre for the evening, the dais at one end surrounded by potted palms. We servants had to wait until the entire royal party was seated, then we were ushered in and allowed to stand at the back.

The grande dame came on to the stage and performed several monologues, all in French. But she was so good that one didn't even have to understand the language. The whole audience watched, transfixed. She finished to tumultuous applause. Someone rose from the crowd to escort her down from the stage. It was the Prince of Wales! Of course, I remembered that I had heard a rumour that she was once his mistress. He led her over to the queen to be presented. I decided this was a good time to leave the room, before the prince could notice me.

You really do flatter yourself, Bella, I said to myself once I slipped through the door at the back of the dining room into the narrow hallway leading to the kitchens. "The prince flirted with you once. Do you really think he'd notice you when the great Sarah Bernhardt was present?" And I had to laugh at my own vanity. I had almost reached the kitchen when I heard a male voice behind me calling my name—or at least the name by which I went these days. I stopped and turned around, thinking it was Jimmy with some witty comment about the actress. But it wasn't. It was Ronnie Barton.

"Well, well," he said, smirking as he came towards me. "We meet again, Miss Helen Barton." He said the words with great emphasis.

"What are you doing here?" I demanded.

"The same as you, I'd imagine. Taking my chances when I get them."

"You're here with the Prince of Wales?" I could hardly make myself say the words.

"I am. I'm doing rather well for myself, actually, thanks to you," he said. "Shall we go and talk somewhere? Catch up on old times up in Yorkshire when we were lads and lassies?"

"I don't think we have anything to say to each other," I said haughtily.

"Oh, but we do. I'd love a good chat with someone from home," he said. "Bringing back old times up on the moor."

My one thought was that I didn't want to risk bumping into anyone from the queen's household or the French chefs. It would be all too easy for Ronnie to say the wrong thing and give me away. He'd enjoy that.

"Come outside," I said. "The servants' entrance leads to the back of the hotel, where nobody can disturb us."

"Are you ashamed to be seen with your poor old brother?" he teased.

"Mr Barton," I said as soon as we stepped into the crisp night air. "Ronnie—I did what you asked of me. Apparently, you are well situated with the prince, so you should want nothing more of me."

"Maybe I should, maybe I shouldn't," he said. "My old long-suffering mother always did say I was greedy. She said I had ideas above my station and would come a cropper in the end. But it was Helen, the good child, who came a cropper, wasn't it? And I've landed on my feet."

"Are you one of the prince's footmen now?" I asked.

He grinned. "Better than that. Much better. I'm his chauffeur."

I couldn't have been more surprised. "Chauffeur?"

"I told you I always take my chances when I can. Well, I heard that the prince was going to buy one of these new automobiles, see. So I went to him and told him I wanted to be his driver and I knew all about those combustion engines."

"How did you know that?"

"I didn't. But I figured by the time he got the automobile delivered from Germany that I could learn. So I found a bloke in London, and he taught me a thing or two about automobile motors. I've always been mechanically minded—I took to it like a duck to water. And the chauffeuring part, too. Once you get the confounded thing started, it's quite easy, knowing how to shift gears and all that. You can't ever go too fast because it spooks the horses when you encounter carriages. I haven't run anybody over yet." He started to smile, then seemed to remember what had happened to his sister and winced instead.

"I'm glad for you that you have found your profession and a good situation in life," I said politely. "Now, if you'll excuse me, I should get back to the rest of my party."

"Hark at her. 'The rest of my party.' You give yourself airs now you work for the queen, don't you?"

I felt my hackles rising. "I don't give myself airs, as you put it. I was brought up in a refined family. I've always spoken this way. Remember that I told you before that I was put into service as a child and have worked my way up by being good at what I do."

"Either that or someone in the household has taken a fancy to you." His eyes were challenging me now. "You're a fine-looking lass. Too bad you're my sister, or I might make a pass at you myself. And speaking of making a pass . . . the prince is very upset with you."

"With me?" The words came out as a squeak.

"When he told you he'd give me a job, you promised you'd come to see your dear old brother. And you haven't been once."

I tried to keep the tone light. "Mr Barton, I hardly think that the prince is interested in a lowly cook when he can have his pick of women."

"Oh, but you're wrong. You turned him down. He loves a challenge. He's said to me several times, 'Where's your sister, then? Why doesn't she come to visit you?' and I had to lie and say that you couldn't get time off. But that's all right. I can tell him now that you're right here and available."

Before I could stop myself, I reached out and grabbed his arm. "Please don't do that."

He really was smirking now. "You don't know a good thing when you see it. You become the prince's mistress for a while, you move in high society, then he tires of you and you're left with enough money for life and prospects for a good husband, too. You'd be out of working in kitchens for good."

I gave him my haughtiest look. "Mr Barton, my body is not for sale. When I love a man, I'll let him touch me, and not before."

"Oh, hark at her. Prissy little miss, isn't she?"

"You won't tell him, will you? Please don't." I regretted it instantly. He was the sort who fed on fear. "Anyway, the great Sarah Bernhardt is here now. He'll only have eyes for her."

"She's yesterday's news," he said. "He likes them young and fresh. Poor old prince. He don't have much to make him happy, does he? No job, nothing to do except amuse himself. His mother won't share any responsibilities with him, won't let him in on foreign affairs or government briefings. She thinks he's weak and he'll make a bad king, so she intends to go on living as long as she can."

"Well, wouldn't you?" I asked.

"To my notion, he'll make quite a good king," Ronnie said. "He's not stupid, you know. And he gets on well with people. And when he does, all the better for me, eh?" He stepped closer to me, even though we were alone in the darkness. "Between you and me, he thinks his old mum is losing her mind. Going a bit senile."

"Oh, I don't think . . . ," I began, but he went on.

"That Indian bloke, the munshi. She's besotted

with him, isn't she? And you know what we heard? She shows him her important papers—confidential papers, things she won't even share with her own son. The prince has been talking to doctors about having her certified as insane now. Not fit to make decisions regarding the safety of our country."

"You seem to know a lot about what the prince says or thinks," I said. "I don't expect he discusses his doings with a lowly chauffeur."

He touched the side of his nose. "You'd be surprised how much you overhear when you are driving a motor car. You're invisible, see. They talk as if you are not there. And it's a good place for a really confidential chat where he can't be overheard. Oh, I've heard things that would make your hair curl, believe me. And I know he's just about had enough of the way his mum is behaving. He's ready to take some kind of action."

I knew the Prince of Wales wasn't the only one who was upset with the munshi, but I wasn't about to share anything I had overheard with a person like Ronnie Barton.

"I should go in," I said. I turned away.

This time he was the one who reached out and grabbed my sleeve. "You know, I've been thinking," he said. "You could be quite helpful in your way."

"I've already helped you, Mr Barton. I owe you nothing more."

"Not to me. To the prince. For the good of the country."

"In what way?"

He leaned closer. "You're a cook. You could maybe add a little something to Her Majesty's food."

"Are you saying I should poison the queen? Are you out of your mind?" I said the words louder than I intended, I was so shocked.

"Not poison her, as such," he said. "I'm thinking more along the lines of something that might upset her stomach, give her the trots, make her weak so that she might catch any disease that's going around. Even a simple grippe could finish her off. You'd be well rewarded, I promise you."

"I wouldn't dream of doing such a thing," I said. "And for your information, the queen seems to have a cast iron stomach. She eats and drinks enough to make you or me sick."

"There are certain patent medicines . . ." He paused.

"Did your employer say these things? He'd really do something to kill his mother?"

"No, the idea just came to me, while we were talking. But I know how fed up he is with his current situation. I know what he thinks about her carrying on with the Indian, and if she happened to pop off, he wouldn't grieve too much. So I thought I might do him a little favour."

It was my turn to smile. "You've just made a wrong move, Mr Barton. I now have something to hold over you. If you ever say one word about me to the prince, or to anyone, I'll be only too happy to spill the beans that you asked me to poison the queen. I believe that might be a hanging offence, don't you?"

"I never said . . ." He was now rattled. "I only suggested . . ."

"Let's just stay well away from each other in the future," I said. "If I see you anywhere near our kitchen, I will let the head cook know what you were planning."

"You wouldn't." He glared at me. "Because if you did, I'd tell them the truth about you and what you did to my poor sister."

"Then we'd both hang. Is that what you are saying? I think we both have every reason to stay silent, Mr Barton. I'm going in now, and I don't expect to see you ever again." I turned and walked back into the hotel, leaving him standing there.

CHAPTER 25

I tried to put the encounter with Ronnie Barton out of my mind. I was off the hook now, I thought. If I told anybody what he had suggested to me, he'd be in serious trouble. I felt the load of worry I had been carrying was finally lifting from my shoulders. But I did worry for the queen. If someone as lowly as Ronnie Barton had thoughts like that, maybe others might have the same ideas. Maybe even the prince himself might not be averse to helping his mother to join her beloved Albert in the great beyond. I resolved to keep a strict eye on everything that went to her table.

Actually, I suspected we were quite safe. Our kitchen was a private world. We rarely saw outsiders, and the only members of the royal party we encountered were the obnoxious munshi, who came in regularly to complain that he could not eat any of the food served at table, and the equally obnoxious Count Willie, who seemed to think he could wander in and help himself whenever he felt hungry between meals, which was often. Mr Angelo tried in vain to complain about him to Sir Arthur, but Count Willie was a law unto himself. And apparently his visits to the kitchen were not entirely about food.

"I've had enough of that bloke," Jimmy muttered to me when we were slicing vegetables together.

"Which bloke?"

"That German idiot. He caught me in the hallway again last night," he said. "Pinned me against the wall, if you can believe. He told me I was a pretty boy and he was sure we could have a little fun together. I told him I wasn't that way inclined. He wouldn't believe me. He said most people enjoy a bit of both ways, if you get my meaning."

I didn't actually. I had only the vaguest idea of what went on behind bedroom doors, but I had been too proud to admit my ignorance to Louisa.

"I suppose this is a hazard of working with the royal family," I said, giving him a commiserating nod. "They think they are above the laws that govern normal people. I had the Prince of Wales proposition me."

"Well, that's a lot better than that blasted Villie bloke, isn't it?" he replied, grinning. "At least he's not perverted, and he's British."

"And he's also a fat old man with a beard," I replied. "I can't imagine anything more revolting than being touched by him. Besides, I intend to choose my own mate, when the time comes."

"I suppose I'm out of the running for that

position?" He gave me that cheeky grin again. "Nelson's made it quite clear that we're to stay away from you."

"Nelson's a really nice boy," I replied, "but I'm not ready to be anything more than a friend to him."

"Blimey, Helen. From what he says, he's already planning who's going to play the wedding march on the big day."

"Oh no! Not really?" My heart skipped a beat. "I really haven't encouraged him, Jimmy, I promise you."

"He said you let him kiss you."

"That's true," I admitted. "But it was under the mistletoe on Christmas Eve. I could hardly say no, could I?"

"Then I think you better set him straight when you get home," he replied. "And in the meantime, do you fancy going out with me? I hear that Carnival is coming up."

"Carnival? Like a fair, you mean?"

"Oh, much more than that. They celebrate before Lent."

"Like Pancake Day, you mean?"

"From what I've been told, it's an absolute riot. Thousands of people in the streets all dancing and drinking, wearing costumes and masks, and there are big floats and bands, unlike anything you've ever seen before."

"I'd like to see it, since we're here," I said.

"And I'd appreciate being chaperoned by a sturdy lad like you, but I don't want you to get any ideas. We're going as friends."

"Bob's your uncle," he said, reverting to a cockney expression.

And so we agreed we were going to Carnival together. Then the queen's secretary let it be known that Her Majesty would also like to experience Carnival in Nice. This meant we were all to have the evening off. So I'd be going in a group with other members of the household, which made me feel much better. Jimmy was a nice enough boy but younger than I and frankly not what I had in mind for a potential suitor. I found myself wondering if Giles Waverly might be attending Carnival.

A few days before the big event, the weather turned especially mild, and the queen announced she wished to have a picnic in the park which adjoined the hotel. It was a fascinating place. I'd only had a chance to explore it briefly, but it contained a Roman amphitheatre, rows of old olive trees, a children's carousel, and on the far side an ancient monastery from which we heard bells tolling at regular intervals. Since I was officially the pastry cook, the preparation for the picnic fell upon me. Tiny finger sandwiches, biscuits and cakes, grapes and tangerines and of course my scones with jam and cream. Mr Phelps and Jimmy came to help me as I made shortbreads, ginger biscuits from Germany that were a favourite of the queen, macaroons and lemon curd tarts. At the last minute, we prepared cucumber, egg and cress, and smoked salmon sandwiches, wrapping them immediately into damp linen napkins to keep them moist. Flasks of tea were prepared. Everything was packed into hampers and loaded on to carts. Mr Phelps and I went ahead to help set up a serving table in the shade of a big eucalyptus tree. For a casual event, it certainly took a lot of planning!

Footmen spread rugs and a chair for the queen to sit, since it would be deemed too undignified to see her lowered to the ground. The queen's Highland pipers were assigned to keep curious onlookers at bay. However, naturally robust men in kilts had the opposite effect and drew even more bystanders. At three o'clock the first of the household members walked from the hotel and stood in groups chatting and awaiting the arrival of the royal party before they could sit. At three thirty the first of the carriages arrived, containing Princess Sophie, Count Willie, Princess Beatrice and her children. This was followed by a dashing open carriage pulled by two white horses, in which rode Her Majesty, Princess Helena, and, to our horror, the Indian munshi. The latter jumped down, offered his hand to Princess Helena, who rejected it, and then together they assisted the queen to the grass.

The queen was all smiles as she sat on her appointed chair, and a nod was given to us to begin serving tea. We poured the cups, and footmen handed them around. The various sandwiches were passed. The queen, I noticed, ate heartily and rather too quickly. I wondered she didn't suffer from indigestion. Next came the scones. She took a bite or two, then looked over in my direction.

"Ah, my little cook who makes the delicious scones," she said and beckoned me to come forward.

I approached nervously and dropped a curtsy.

"I didn't realize you were part of our small gathering here," she said, "but I should have guessed because I suspect your light touch is behind some of the cakes we have enjoyed."

"Thank you, ma'am," I replied.

"We must make sure we save some of the scones for my son," she said. "He has promised to join us today, although as usual he is not punctual."

I tried to keep my face composed. I gave another curtsy and backed away. I was wondering how quickly I could return to the hotel. But I hadn't even reached my serving station when the queen exclaimed, "Ah, here he comes now, the laggard."

And a smart carriage came into view—a small affair just big enough for two, rather like the carriage I had shared with Giles. I was relieved to see it was not the automobile and Ronnie Barton was not in evidence. Thankful for small mercies, I supposed. The prince had been driving himself. He hopped down with surprising agility for one of his bulk, handing the reins to a servant.

"Ah, here you are, Mama," he called in his big voice, striding towards her.

"You're late, as usual," she said.

"It's only a picnic. I didn't think there was an appointed hour for such things," he said, giving her a kiss on the cheek. "Besides, I was going to bring the automobile, but it does not like steep hills. So I had to revert to the carriage."

"You're lucky that we've saved you some food," she said, "including the scones that you liked so much."

The prince looked across in my direction. "Ah, my little scone girl," he said, and I saw his eyes light up for an instant.

I gave a demure curtsy.

"I am absolutely famished," he said. "I require sustenance in the form of scones immediately." And he beckoned me to come forward.

I had no alternative. I put scones, jam and cream on to a tray. "Bring him tea at the same time," I said to Mr Phelps. Safety in numbers.

We came forward together, and I held the tray while the prince helped himself. He was the model of decorum, with his mother so close beside him. He merely nodded and I retreated, my hands shaking a little. I was safe. I had worried for nothing. I was the little scone girl, nothing more. At least I now knew one thing—the prince had been surprised to see me. Ronnie Barton had not spilled the beans that I was here in Nice with the queen. That was one thing to be thankful for. I realized that I now did have power over him. It felt good.

The queen had had enough to eat, which meant that nobody else in her party could have any more. The moment she finished any meal, that meal was deemed to be over, much to the annoyance of her guests, I suspected. We packed up, and the remnants were loaded on to a cart waiting at some distance. The royal party began to amuse themselves with various outdoor activities. Racquets and shuttlecocks were produced for a game of badminton. Count Wilhelm tried to get Princess Sophie to join him, but she refused. Words were exchanged, and she walked away in a huff. Two ladies-in-waiting and one of the gentlemen made up the foursome instead. The young grandsons played games of tag, shrieking like normal children everywhere. Little Princess Ena, trying to be more stately and ladylike, went picking flowers. It was really the first time I'd had a chance to see the royal family acting like any normal family.

"Look, Mama. I've made a bouquet for you." Princess Ena came up to her mother, presenting her collection.

"Very nice, Liebchen," Princess Beatrice said. "But you should ask which flowers can be picked. I understand those pink ones are oleander and very poisonous. Throw them away, and ask Nanny to wash your hands."

"Yes, Mama." The little girl looked crestfallen and worried.

I turned to Mr Phelps. "If we have nothing more to do, I'm going for a walk," I said, wishing to distance myself from the Prince of Wales as soon as possible. "I've been wanting to take a look at that monastery." And off I went into the park. I paused to watch the children's carousel then headed towards the monastery that loomed over the far side of the lawns. I ascended a flight of steps and found a little churchyard to one side. It was so different from the Highgate Cemetery where my parents were buried. Tall marble mausoleums so close together it was like a small city. As I wandered between them, I heard the sound of crying. I came around a corner, and there was Princess Sophie, leaning against a tomb, sobbing softly.

Forgetting my place, I went up to her. "What's wrong?" I asked. "Is there anything I can do to help?"

She looked at me, not knowing who I was.

"You are part of the queen's household?" she asked in her strong German accent.

"I am, ma'am. One of her cooks. I know it's not my place to speak to you, but I hated to see you in such distress."

She gave a little shrug. "There is nothing you can do," she said. "I am to be married to a monster. A man I can never love."

"Surely you do not have to marry against your wishes?"

She gave me a pitying look. "You do not understand how it is for us. Marriage is not for love. It is for power, for political motivation. My father and the queen feel that Wilhelm's state is too closely linked with the Austrian emperor and that he is too friendly with the German kaiser."

"But the German kaiser is her relative, surely?" I said.

She shrugged. "Wilhelm has ambitions of his own. A new German empire, you know. Quite dangerous. They would like to lure him into the queen's fold. Therefore I must marry him, and he will become one of us. That is how it works."

"I'm really sorry for you," I said. "But if you refuse, can they force you?"

"Would you dare to refuse and go against your father and the queen's wishes?" she asked. "You must know how terrifying she can be."

"I would remind her how much she loved

Prince Albert and tell her that you feel that you cannot love the count."

"I did try something of the kind, and she said that love comes with time and I am so young and must be patient." Then she shook her head, making her curls dance. "But Albert was a good, kind man from what I have heard. Wilhelm is a bully—selfish, rude, critical. He will dominate my life." She leaned closer to me. "But it's worse than that. Do you know what he said to me? He said that once I have given him an heir, he will not bother me again."

"I am very sorry for you, ma'am."

She gave a sad little laugh. "I suppose I should be thankful that he will not bother me. But I want a man to love me. I want to be held in his arms and feel safe. Is that too much to wish for?"

"No, not at all. Is your mother still alive? I'm sure she would understand your feelings."

She shook her head. "She died when I was only five. My father has had a string of mistresses. I've hated them all. Common, vulgar women. I have been to stay with Cousin Victoria many times, and I have enjoyed being at the palace until now. But she will not budge on my marrying Wilhelm. I am doomed to a loveless life ahead of me."

Then she seemed to realize that she was speaking with a servant and had said too much. "You will not repeat a word of what I have told you?"

I reverted to a subservient mode. "Of course not, ma'am. You can rely on me."

"I should return to the queen. It was rude of me to wander off. They will come looking for me."

"You can tell them you are fascinated with old tombstones," I said, "or that cemeteries remind you of your dear mother." And she actually laughed.

"You are a devious and wise person," she said. "I wish you were closer to my station in life. I think we could have been friends. I am sorely in need of friendship right now."

"I am available any time you wish to talk, Your Highness," I replied.

"I don't think the ladies would understand."

I gave her a little curtsy and let her go ahead of me, back to the picnic.

I lingered up at the monastery, watching the princess walk back through the trees and across the park. Then I made my own way back and found the party was still sitting and talking. Mr Phelps had disappeared, so I headed back to the hotel, pausing to go into the Roman ruins. They were quite impressive—a large amphitheatre with arches still intact with spring flowers growing from cracks in the masonry. I was lost in contemplation until a gust of wind brought me back to the present and made me realize I should return to my duties. There was dinner to think about. As I approached the archway, a figure stepped out of the shadows.

"There you are, you little minx," said the Prince of Wales.

I swallowed back a small gasp. He was a large man, and he was blocking my escape. He put a finger under my chin and stepped closer. Too close.

"You have been a bad girl," he said. "You did not come to visit your brother. I was most put out. I only gave him the job because of you, you know."

"I'm sorry, sir," I said. "It is not easy to get time off when one works in a royal kitchen."

"I shall make sure my mother is invited to dine with relatives frequently while she is here," he said. "Then you will have no excuse when I send a carriage for you."

"I'm sure you have very fine chefs of your own, sir," I replied, deliberately misunderstanding.

He laughed at this. He had a big, hearty laugh. "You know very well it is not your cooking I am interested in. You fascinate me. I've always had a penchant for redheads, and you have this air of . . . purity that I find quite seductive."

The finger was still beneath my chin. He pulled me closer to him and planted those big lips on mine. His beard was prickly, and his lips were moist. It was all I could do not to slap him or push him away. That one hand held my neck while the other started to explore my body. I was beyond shocked as his hand lingered over my breast. As soon as he broke away, I put my hands on his chest and tried to push. "Please, sir. I beg of you. I am an innocent girl and wish to stay that way until I marry."

He was looking at me with amusement in his eyes, rather relishing my panic, I thought. "Oh, the blushing virgin. How delightful. How irresistible. Now you really have whetted my appetite."

"I can't understand your interest in me," I said. "You can have any woman in the world. Sarah Bernhardt is staying at our hotel."

"She was amusing for a while, I'll grant you. But it is such a chore having to speak French all the time. You know, I can ask Mama to lend me her cook."

"In which case I shall go to her and ask her to refuse your request," I said. After the initial shock, my fighting spirit was returning. "I know that your mother does not approve of your behaviour. She would not want me to be forced into a situation where I would be so compromised."

He was looking at me with interest now, as if he was seeing me as a person for the first time. "You're an eloquent young thing," he said. "Educated. How did you become a cook?"

"I was orphaned and had no family to take me

in," I said. "I went into service to support my young sister."

"Commendable. A martyr as well as a virgin."

"Please do not mock, sir," I said. "You can't imagine how abhorrent it was for me to find myself as a servant. Through my cooking skills, at least I've been able to rise a little."

He stroked my cheek. "You silly girl, don't you see what I am offering you? I'm offering what you have been looking for. A way out of servitude. I'll set you up with a nice little villa here if you like. I'll come and visit when I'm on the Riviera. The rest of the year, you do what you like. Find any man who tickles your fancy. Even marry him. I don't mind. I'm generous. I'm willing to share. And when we tire of each other—why, the villa is still yours to keep. What could be fairer than that?"

What could indeed? The thought did flash through my mind. Why was I being so noble and prudish when I had no honour? I was a servant girl, after all. King Leopold of the Belgians had bought his mistress a villa. I would indeed never have to work for my living again. Except that the thought of that man touching me, holding me, forcing himself on me was more than I could bear.

"I'm really sorry, sir," I said quietly, "but I prefer to wait for a man that I can love."

"I'm sure you'd come to love me," he said.

"I'm a loveable sort of chap. Ask any of my mistresses. They'll tell you how well I treat them."

"I'm sure you are a very nice man," I said, "but that's not the sort of life I want for myself."

His gaze turned suspicious. "You're not one of those women, are you? You know—a damned sapphist?"

I didn't know.

He chuckled. "You really are a little innocent, aren't you? Women who like other women."

"Oh no." I blushed with shock at such a suggestion. I hadn't even known such people existed. "I want to have a husband and family one day, when I meet the right man. But until then . . ."

"Until then, you are turning down the heir to the throne of the most powerful country in the world. I have to say I admire your integrity, young woman. I find you damned infuriating, but I respect your decision. Never let it be said that I have forced myself on a woman." He stepped back from me. "Well, I'd better let you get back to your kitchen pots and pans, hadn't I?"

"Thank you, sir."

He must have heard the relief in my voice. "I'm not really that repulsive to you, am I?"

"Not at all, sir," I lied. "I think you are a handsome man. But . . ."

"Not the man for you, eh?"

I nodded, gratefully.

"Go on then. Off you go." He slapped my behind and shoved me ahead of him through the archway. I don't think I breathed again until I was safely inside the hotel. I went up to my room, splashed cold water on to my face and rinsed out my mouth.

CHAPTER 26

The day of the Carnival procession dawned bright and clear. This was good news as apparently the year before there had been constant rain during the pre-Lenten days and the parade had to be cancelled. We cooks all made our way down to the town together at twilight. Mr Williams and Mr Phelps gave the impression that they really didn't want to attend such a foreign and pagan event, but felt they should to remind themselves how civilized we were in England. But they seemed to warm to the prospect as we neared the centre of town and passed booths selling all kinds of flags, trinkets and foods. "A genuine Italian gelato," Mr Angelo exclaimed. "I haven't had one of those since I was a boy. Of course we are only a few miles from Italy here, aren't we? Do you fancy one, Mr Phelps?"

"I think I might," Mr Phelps agreed, looking at the mounds of brightly coloured ice cream. Mr Williams and Jimmy both thought they'd like to try one, too. But the temperature had dropped, and I was already feeling a little chilly, so I declined, regretting it later as I watched their expressions of ecstasy. The Place Masséna, that big square with adjoining gardens leading down to the seafront, was brightly lit with flares and torches as well as the usual gas lamps, and already packed with people. The crowd was a delightful melange of peasants in their bright striped skirts and shawls mingling with loud drunken working men plus well-dressed families. There were also many people wearing outlandish costumes: Pierrots and pirates and Red Indians. Stands had been erected for those who wished to pay for a better view, and there was a special one of these, right at the front of the parade route, reserved for the queen and her party.

"The queen likes to be part of things," Mr Angelo muttered. "They throw flowers from some of the floats. She likes to collect the flowers and throw them back at handsome young men!"

We were smiling at this as we tried to find a spot where we would have a good view of the procession. Eventually we forced our way through the crowd and took up our places, packed in like sardines. The large woman standing next to me smelled strongly of garlic and unwashed body.

As darkness fell, the queen and her party arrived. There was polite clapping as she was half escorted, half lifted to her viewing platform. The rest of the royal party took up their positions around her. I was interested to see that they were sitting on ordinary hard benches, like the rest of the stands, although a couple of cushions were provided for the queen to raise her high enough to see. I noticed that the Indian munshi was not being allowed on to the seats near her. Count Wilhelm was blocking him, perched at the end of the narrow wooden bench. It certainly wasn't the sort of accommodation that the queen was used to, but she didn't seem to mind. I could see her face, and she seemed as excited as a young girl, waving to people and pointing things out to her grandchildren. There was no sign of her Highland guards. Tonight she really was just Lady Balmoral, enjoying herself like everyone else.

No sooner were they settled than we heard the sound of a brass band in the distance. Shouts and cheers greeted the band, looking impressive in their bright uniforms, adorned with lots of braid. Behind them came the first of the floats. I don't know what I expected, but it was enormous: a hideous caricature head of a man, some twenty feet high, on top of a cart dragged by a team of men. His mouth was open, and legs were protruding from it as if he was eating people. It was quite terrifying.

"Germont," the woman next to me said, grinning and giving me a dig in the ribs. Then a young man on the other side of me explained. The floats were often political comments. Germont was a politician who was intent on making money at the expense of the little people. More floats followed: a giant crocodile, more enormous heads, floats decorated with flowers, more bands and beside them men on stilts, clowns, tumblers, dancers in scanty costumes.

"I bet she's chilly," Mr Williams commented as a young woman wearing nothing more than feathers passed us.

The crowd around us cheered, jeered, shouted, and drank wine straight from the bottle—passing it around between them.

The parade seemed to go on forever. I was growing tired of standing, of being shoved, and of being enveloped in the garlic odour of my large neighbour. Suddenly a loud popping noise was heard over the raucous din of the crowd.

"Fireworks," Mr Angelo said. "There are always fireworks after the parade."

But then there were screams. Someone else was shouting, "The queen! They've shot the queen!"

Chaos ensued. I tried to see what was happening, but the crowd panicked, pushing this way and that, trying to flee from gunfire, wanting to gain distance from the royal stand. I tried to free myself and get to the queen, but I was borne forward in the crush of people. It was surreal. *The queen's been shot.* The words were screaming inside my brain. *I must see if I can help.* But at this moment, my main worry was that I would trip and be trampled. When at last the momentum of the crowd slowed, I was no longer on the

Place Masséna, but in a dark and narrow side street. I had no idea where I was. People were still streaming past me, and I caught snatches of conversation, "Anarchists! They shot the queen of England!"

I wanted to make my way back. I looked around me, but there was no sign of the other cooks, no sign of anyone I knew, and I wasn't even sure which way we had come. The crowd was making it impossible for me to retrace my steps. All I could do was to wait in a doorway until they had dispersed. Then a group of rowdy men approached, singing loudly. I shrank into the doorway, but they had spotted me.

"Hello, chérie," one of them said, looming up over me. "All alone, *ma petite*? Oh, that's too bad. You need company. You come with us. We'll give you a good time."

His speech was slurred. He was grinning like an idiot. They pressed around me. One of them took my arm. "*Allons*," he called out. "Let's go."

"No. Leave me. I don't want . . ." My French was failing me in a moment of panic.

"But we are such nice boys." Another one stuck his face in front of mine. "You will like us, I promise you."

I didn't know what to do. There were five of them. The rest of the crowd streamed past as if we didn't exist. They were now propelling me along with them.

"Leave me. I do not wish . . ." I struggled to free myself.

"Ah, Colette, ma petite, there you are." A man's voice boomed as a figure emerged from the darkness. "Take your hands off my little sister immediately. I have a knife, and I can assure you I am very good with it."

"We were looking after her for you, my friend," one of my captors said, releasing my arm. "A woman should not be alone in a crowd like this. No offence."

"You should not have wandered off alone, little sister," the newcomer said, addressing me now. He grabbed my sleeve roughly. "Come. We go home now."

I couldn't think what to do next. This really was a case of out of the frying pan and into the fire. Clearly I must resemble this man's sister in the darkness. If I said I was not his sister, then I had no idea what might happen. He could release me back to the drunks. And he had a knife . . .

He took my hand and dragged me forward. "Don't struggle. Come quickly with me now," he said, and finally I recognized the voice. In the darkness, I could make out his face. Jean-Paul Lepin, and his hand was grasping mine. Together we hurried away, out of the main stream of the crowd and into a quiet backwater of a residential square.

"I have to stop. I can't breathe," I said at last.

We had been going at a great pace. He stopped.

"That was a foolish thing you were doing, alone on a night like this," he said, glaring at me. "You were lucky I came along."

"I wasn't alone," I said. "I was with the other cooks. There were gunshots and somebody screaming and they were saying the queen had been shot then everyone started running and I was forced along with them and suddenly I didn't know where I was and those men came."

The words came out in a great rush. I am not sure whether my French was grammatically correct or even understandable. Without warning, a great hiccup of a sob came out of my mouth. "And if you hadn't come and saved me, I . . ." And I started to cry.

Immediately his arms came around me, and he was holding me close to him. "It's all right, ma petite. You are safe now. You are with me. All is well."

"But the queen. They shot the queen." Tears cascaded down my cheeks.

Jean-Paul stroked my hair. "Don't cry. I don't think she was struck."

"Are you sure?"

"No, but from what people were saying, the bullets missed her."

I looked up at him. His eyes were sparkling in the light of a street lamp. Then suddenly he was kissing me. And to my amazement I was responding to his kiss, my body pressed against his, feeling his heart beating against mine. When we broke apart, gasping, he was smiling down at me.

"Listen, chérie, we do not have to go back immediately. My cousin has a little hotel nearby. Why don't we go there for a while?"

"Why would I need a hotel when we can make our way back to Cimiez now that the crisis has passed?" I asked.

He chuckled as if I had said something amusing. "But you have had a shock. Would you not like a place to recover with a cognac, perhaps? And you and I—we could get to know each other better, away from the Regina."

All I could hear in my head was the Prince of Wales saying, "We could get to know each other better." And those awful men, grabbing at me. I took a step back. "No!" I exclaimed. "You have formed the wrong impression of me, monsieur."

He looked puzzled. "Forgive me if I misunderstood," he said, "I had no wish to insult you, but you certainly did not repulse my kisses. In fact, I got the impression that you would like to spend time alone with me."

My cheeks were flaming with embarrassment. "I was carried away. The fear, the chaos. I didn't know what I was doing."

"Oh, I think you knew and were doing it very well, too." He couldn't resist a grin.

I heard my voice, high and cold. "I am shocked that you would think I am the sort of girl who would dream of going to a hotel with a man she hardly knows. I was raised in a good family. Or is it just because I am a servant now that I am seen to be easy pickings?"

He took a step away from me. "But mademoiselle, you misunderstand me. I had no wish to . . ."

"Of course you had a wish. You are like all men. You prey on us innocent females."

"I apologize, mademoiselle," he said, stiffly. "I assure you I will keep my distance in the future."

"I must get back to the Regina," I said. "The queen. The queen may need me."

"The queen needs you? And why might that be?" he demanded. "I think if she needs anyone, it would be her doctor, not a sous-chef."

The words felt like a slap in the face. "Thank you for saving me, monsieur," I said coldly. "If you would just direct me to the quickest route up the hill."

"I will escort you."

"There is no need," I said. "I am sure you do not wish to waste your time with a mere sous-chef."

"Nevertheless, I will not let you wander about alone tonight. I know my duty as an honest Frenchman," he said. "Come. This way."

He took my arm and marched me off at a great

pace. We did not speak a word as we went up the hill. I was out of breath and terrified that I might cry at any moment. When we reached the forecourt of the hotel, Jean-Paul gave me a curt little bow. "You will be safe now," he said, and stalked off into the night.

CHAPTER 27

I stood in the darkness, trying to catch my breath and compose myself before I made my way to the hotel. The forecourt was bustling with activity. Lights were streaming out, illuminating two police wagons standing outside with what I presumed to be French policemen beside them. There were newspaper reporters and a curious crowd, comprised of hotel guests as well as local citizens who must have followed the royal procession up from the town. I looked around for the queen's carriage, wondering if she had been taken to a hospital instead of coming here, but to my relief I saw it being led around to the stables. I was dying of curiosity and worry by this time and searched for a familiar face. Off to one side, several of Her Majesty's footmen were standing.

I made my way over to them.

"Is there any news? Is Her Majesty all right?" I asked.

"Lucky, that's what she is," one of them said. "This must be the fourth or fifth attempt on her life, and every time they miss."

"They didn't exactly miss this time," the other said. "She might have been killed if that German count hadn't pushed her to one side to shield her and taken the bullet himself."

To hear that Count Willie had been a hero was remarkable news indeed. "Count Wilhelm was shot? Is he dead?"

"Nah, the bullet just grazed his shoulder. The shooter wasn't much of a marksman, if you ask me. One of these fanatical students who want to change the world order."

"Is that who it was, a student?"

"They haven't caught him yet," the first man said. "And I doubt they will. With a crowd that size, nobody saw anything until there were gunshots. And then there was a right panic, wasn't there? Everyone running and screaming. Weren't you there?"

"Yes, I was, but I got swept away with the crowd."

"You're lucky you weren't trampled. Quite a few people were, weren't they, Tom?"

The other nodded. "These foreigners, you know. Too excitable. That would never have happened in London."

I bade them goodnight and went up to bed. It was only when I was alone in my room that the emotion of the evening overcame me. I had a good cry and realized something: since the day I had become a servant, I had never allowed myself to cry once. It had been a matter of pride that whatever was thrown at me, it could not break me. Now it was as if something had snapped, and I had finally allowed myself to have feelings. And with that came the realization that I had felt something for Jean-Paul Lepin and I had driven him away.

When I came down to breakfast the next morning, there was no sign of my fellow cooks. Henri and several other French chefs were already working away in their part of the kitchen. Jean-Paul was not amongst them.

"Have my compatriots already eaten breakfast or not yet arisen?" I asked Henri.

"I have not seen them today, mademoiselle," Henri replied. "Perhaps they oversleep after too much merrymaking last night. Did you go to the Carnival procession?"

"I did," I replied.

"Your queen had a lucky escape, so I hear."

"Yes, so I heard. You didn't go yourself?"

He shook his head. "I've seen it all before. Too many people for my liking. Too much wine drunk."

"Has Chef Lepin gone to the market?" I asked, trying to keep my tone casual.

"Yes, he left early. I told him we had enough supplies because nobody ate at the hotel last night, but he wouldn't listen. He was in a bad mood for some reason. Maybe he consumed too much wine last night."

I left him to his preparations and helped myself to bread, jam and coffee. Still there was no sign of Mr Angelo and the others. I was beginning to feel annoyed. If they didn't show up soon, then the queen's breakfast would be left to me. I was just leaving the table when Dr Reid came into the kitchen.

"You're Miss Barton?" he said in his soft Scottish accent.

"Yes, Doctor. Can I help you? Does the royal party require something different for breakfast after last night's shock?"

"I understand that the queen wants no breakfast today. The incident has really upset her. She doesn't feel like eating, which is unusual for her, and she will remain in her bedchamber. Count Wilhelm wants his breakfast to be taken up to him on a tray as soon as possible. 'A good nourishing breakfast' was how he put it."

"How is the count? Was his wound severe?"

"No. Merely a graze. He will make a full recovery soon. But this was not what I came to see you about. Your fellow cooks, apparently they ate Italian ices from a stall last night?"

"Yes, they did. I chose not to because I was already feeling cold."

"Then I'd say you had a lucky escape, just like the queen."

I paused, digesting this. "Are they ill?"

"Very ill," he said. "I hope it is only food

poisoning, but I suspect dysentery from bad water. And I just pray it is not typhoid or worse."

"Worse? What could be worse than typhoid?"

"Cholera. We now know that it comes from contaminated water. I don't know what they were thinking, eating ices from a street stall in a strange city. The water probably came straight from the river, which also serves as the town sewer."

"This is terrible news," I said.

"I agree. You'll have more work than you can handle."

"I wasn't thinking of that. I was worried about my colleagues. Typhoid? Cholera? It might spread through the whole hotel."

"I'm taking precautions and keeping them isolated. If they can keep down fluids, they will come through—although at the moment I can't guarantee anything. Naturally I'll do my best for them. I suggest you boil some rice with cinnamon in it, and we'll give them the rice water to drink. That is settling to the stomach. And later some beef tea."

"Very good, Doctor," I said.

"And I will have a word with the queen's secretary. I'll ask him to requisition a couple of French cooks to help you." He paused. "There is no way a young girl like yourself should be left to face this amount of responsibility alone. But you seem level-headed and capable. I expect we'll all get through it, one way or another."

With those comforting words, he gave me a little pat on the shoulder and left me.

I stood like a statue, trying to digest all this. My fellow cooks were so sick they might die. They might have brought cholera or typhoid to the hotel and put the queen and her party in danger. And I . . . I had scarcely considered my role now. I was the sole cook left to cater for a party of royal persons and their retinue. Well, there was nothing for it but to get going, I decided. They'd have to make do with simple meals and few choices until I had help. I got to work, putting on the rice and cinnamon to cook, then sent in an order for beef bones and calves' feet for our invalids.

I cooked scrambled eggs and bacon to be sent up to the royal dining room and managed a kedgeree and more bacon for the ladies and gentlemen of the household. I piled both on to a plate for the injured Count Willie and sent it up with a footman. I was just wondering what Mr Angelo had in mind for luncheon when I looked up to see Jean-Paul approaching me.

"Your royal doctor has informed me of the distressing news," he said in a most formal voice. "I am most sorry for your colleagues. I have told your doctor that I will put two of my reliable chefs at your disposal. I suggested that they take care of all the meals for the household while you confine yourself just to Her Majesty and her royal relatives, knowing your great devotion to your queen."

"Thank you, you are most kind," I replied. "Your consideration is much appreciated."

Even as I spoke the words, I could sense the sting in the tail of his own speech. My great devotion to my queen indeed! He was mocking me for last night. But at least he was making my task bearable. Maybe he genuinely was trying to help me out.

I decided on a simple poached fish dish and saffron chicken over rice for the royal luncheon, as we had cold chicken from the previous day. As accompaniments, the creamed celery of which they were so fond, and a mushroom soup. There was sponge cake left from the previous day's tea. I soaked it in sherry and made a quick trifle. It might be nursery food, but I'd never found anyone who didn't like a good trifle, especially if one added enough cream. Once that was all under control, I went to find one of the ladies-in-waiting and asked about the queen. Could I not prepare her something to eat?

"She says she wants nothing," Lady Lytton said. "She is still in distress. It is useless trying to talk to her when she is in one of her stubborn moods. I rather suspect she is determined to make us all see how upset she is over this latest affront."

I went back to my kitchen. I didn't like to

think that the queen was refusing to eat. That was a bad sign at her age. It meant she was giving up on life. And if there was a deadly disease like typhoid in the hotel, she'd be more susceptible if she was in a weakened state. My latest encounter with Ronnie Barton flashed into my mind . . . his outrageous suggestion that I cook items that would make the queen weak and therefore a simple grippe might finish her off. Suddenly I remembered times in my own childhood when I had been ill in bed. My mother had taken care of me and fed me tempting little morsels. I had an idea. I set to work and then carried out the tray myself to the queen's bedroom.

The dreaded Indian munshi was standing on guard outside her door.

"What is this?" he snapped when he saw me approaching.

"It is for Her Majesty," I replied. "It is something to tempt her to eat and regain her strength. Will you take it in to her, please?"

"I have been instructed to leave her alone. She wants to see nobody, and she needs to rest. So go away." He waved at me as if I were an annoying fly.

"I would like her to eat this while it is still warm. If you care about your queen, you will want her to make a speedy recovery, which she will not do if she refuses to eat." I took a deep breath because he was quite a big man and he was blocking my path. "If you will not take it to her, then I will."

"You will not enter Her Majesty's presence," he said angrily. "You, a common servant."

"As you are," I replied. "I know all about you, Mr Karim. I know you did not come from an educated family. You were sent as a table servant, which is several levels below a cook. Now step aside, or I shall have to find Sir Arthur and Dr Reid to assist me."

"Upon your own head be it, stupid girl," he said, looking daggers at me.

I tapped gingerly on the door, then opened it and stepped into the queen's bedchamber. It was not a large room and rather overly furnished with the bed she had brought out from England as well as a large wardrobe and several chests of drawers. And being on the first floor it did not have the commanding view over the bay that my windows did. The queen was lying back, looking like a small doll against all those lace pillows.

"Your Majesty," I said softly.

She opened her eyes. "What do you want?" she asked. "I said I was to be left alone."

"Forgive my presumption," I said, coming closer, "but when you have had a shock, you should be reviving your system. I've brought you hot sweet tea, which is supposed to be the best thing for shock, and I've made you what my mother used to make me when I was sick as a child. It's a boiled egg with soldiers."

"Soldiers?" she demanded, sitting up now.

I put the tray down in front of her. "That's what my mother always called the thin fingers of toast. Because they stand up so straight."

"Soldiers." She gave a little smile. "It's been a long time since I've had a plain boiled egg."

"Please try a little," I said.

She took a sip of tea. "This is not a China tea," she said.

"No, it's an ordinary British tea, but it's strong, and that's what you need right now."

She looked up at me. "You're a rather forceful young woman, aren't you?"

"Not usually, ma'am. It's just that I was so concerned about you. And when they said you wanted to be left alone and not eat, I was worried that you might have given up on life and that you would just slip away."

She looked at me and laughed. "Can you see me just slipping away? My dear young woman, I was born to duty, and I do not intend to relinquish my role as empress and ruler of our great empire until the day that God calls me home. Which I hope will be many years from now. Besides, I have a jubilee to celebrate this year."

"I'm very glad to hear it, ma'am." I noted with

satisfaction that she had taken a finger of toast and was dipping it into her egg.

"To tell you the truth," she said, after she had taken a bite, "I was tired of all the fussing over me. My daughters were screaming and fainting and behaving like hysterical females. I just wanted to be left alone, to think. It makes one pause, when one faces one's own mortality. It's not the first time I've been shot at, you know."

"I heard, ma'am," I said. "There have been several attempts on your life."

"All of them terrible marksmen, fortunately," the queen said with a small grin of satisfaction. "But I have to confess this time it did rattle me more than I thought it would. In the past I had my dear Albert to comfort and protect me." She sighed. "I still miss him after all this time. It's a wound that will never heal until I am joined with him again."

"I understand that Count Wilhelm saved your life," I said.

She gave a derisive snort. "More by luck than heroism, I suspect. I think he was trying to get out of the way and accidentally pushed me aside. But we shall let the world think of him as the hero, shall we not?"

I wondered if I should dare say anything about Princess Sophie, then did not have the courage to do so. She ate more bites of her breakfast, and to my delight she finished her boiled egg.

"This was an excellent suggestion," she said. "Were you instructed to prepare it for me, or did you do it of your own initiative?"

"I am all alone in the kitchen at the moment, ma'am. The other cooks all ate Italian ices at the Carnival and have come down with stomach complaints." I thought it wise not to mention that these complaints might be of a serious nature at this moment. I'd leave Dr Reid to impart that news.

"You certainly can't handle an entire kitchen alone?" She looked at me with concern.

"I have two of the hotel chefs seconded to me, and I will be handling just your personal meals until the men recover. So if there are any particular dishes you would like, please have your table servant let me know."

"I did like those mushrooms the other day. Very tasty."

"Very well, ma'am. I shall go to the market tomorrow and bring back a selection for you," I said.

She was frowning at me now. "You seem to be a young woman of good family," she said. "How is it that you became a cook? Was this an ambition of yours?"

"Not originally, ma'am. I was orphaned as a young girl, alone in the world, and had to provide for my sister, so domestic service was my only option. Later I developed an interest in cooking

338

and found that I had a certain amount of talent for it."

"You had no extended family to take you in after your parents died?"

"I'm afraid my father was estranged from his family, and my mother had no close relatives." I realized as I spoke that I was giving details of Bella Waverly's family, not Helen Barton's. Should I have invented a cottage in Yorkshire instead? Except that it was impossible to lie to the queen.

"You poor child," she said. "But I trust you are happy in your current situation?"

"I couldn't be happier, Your Majesty," I said. "The chance to prepare fine foods and exotic dishes is the dream of every cook. And to be cooking for you—well, that is the proverbial icing on the cake."

She actually patted my hand. "Then I hope you shall stay with us for a long time, although I shall put some thought to finding you a suitable husband. I cannot think it would be the right thing for you to marry at your current level in life."

"I am in no hurry to marry, ma'am," I said.

"Nevertheless, a young woman is not fulfilled until she has a husband and children. I was not thrilled to be a mother to begin with. I found my babies tiresome. But look what I have now achieved. I have placed my progeny in all the great royal houses of Europe. If there were ever a conflict, I can call upon allies from many powerful nations—although I have to admit my grandson in Germany seems to have big ideas and is not showing the amount of respect one would expect for his grandmother, the empress." She paused, considering this and presumably whether it was right for her to impart such thoughts to a lowly servant, but then she went on. "Which is one of the reasons I have invited Count Wilhelm into the fold. He seems to be a devoted lapdog of the kaiser. So the marriage to my young cousin is fortuitous at this moment."

"I understand that Her Highness, Princess Sophie, is not happy about the marriage," I said.

She looked surprised that I should have dared to mention this. "And how do you know of these things? Does Sophie frequent the kitchen?"

"Oh no, ma'am. I came upon her crying one day, when we were in the park. She was most distressed. I tried to comfort her."

"Sophie tends to be rather dramatic and too emotional, I'm afraid. Bad blood on her mother's side. And she has been raised to be a rather spoiled young woman. Used to getting her own way. I can see that she is resisting marriage to a man who will clearly wish to dominate her. But alas, she will have to learn to compromise. Maybe she can even learn to tame her husband."

"But if she doesn't love him?"

"Love?" The queen shook her head. "I'm afraid that love does not often enter into royal marriage arrangements. They are solely for political reasons, and every royal person knows and accepts this. Sophie will learn to accept her destiny as we all have." She paused, and a little smile crossed her lips. "I was one of the lucky ones. I was able to select my own spouse, and I married a man I could love with all my heart."

She pointed to the tray. "You may take this now. It was a thoughtful gesture on your part, and I much appreciated it. I shall take my luncheon up here, but this afternoon, if the weather remains fine, I may take a turn in the garden. You shall bring me my tray and talk to me again. At my age, I appreciate a fresh young face."

"Yes, ma'am," I said. I took the tray, curtsied and backed out of the room, only once bumping into the corner of a large dresser.

The munshi was hovering outside. "You were there a long time," he said.

"Yes, we had a lovely chat," I replied. "She will be taking her luncheon in her chamber, but after that she may want to be pushed around the gardens."

I gave him a triumphant smile as I walked away.

CHAPTER 28

It was only when I was back in the safety of the kitchen that I realized what I had done. If the queen wanted to chat with me again, she might well ask me questions about my family, my childhood. And I would presumably have to lie. All I knew about Yorkshire I had gleaned from reading *Jane Eyre* and *Wuthering Heights*: bleak moors where the wind whistled through chimneys. And I'd have to explain why my folks had chosen to live there and why I had no Yorkshire accent. Either that or come clean. Would the queen understand and appreciate why I took this one chance, or would she see it as trickery, sending me packing straight back to England? It was a risk I couldn't take.

I poached a fillet of sole for her, with a parsley sauce, then added a bowl of mushroom soup, a bunch of grapes and a small dish of trifle. When I presented it to her, she stared at it for a moment. "You obviously think I'm back in the nursery," she said. "Next it will be bread and milk or gruel."

"Oh no, ma'am," I replied, flushing with embarrassment. "I was merely thinking that when one doesn't feel like eating, one needs food that just slips down without much effort."

"You are a thoughtful young woman," she said. "And you may be right. You may leave me now. I don't wish to be observed slurping my soup. I'll ring for a servant when I am finished."

"And for tonight, ma'am? A lamb cutlet? A little chicken?"

She looked up at me, her eyes remarkably young and twinkling. "No, I think I have languished long enough. I shall be eating with the family tonight in the dining room, and I rather fancy duck."

I smiled. "This is good news. I'll see to it, ma'am."

She returned my smile. "And you won't forget about my mushrooms tomorrow, will you?"

"Of course not, ma'am. I'll go to the market first thing."

As I backed away, she said, "Don't work too hard. We shall understand if the fare is less elaborate than usual. I realized from my boiled egg this morning that sometimes we appreciate the taste of simple things, rather than when good ingredients are disguised under myriad sauces."

"Absolutely right, ma'am. If the ingredients themselves are top quality, they should speak for themselves."

I curtsied, and as I opened the door, I saw the munshi hovering right outside.

"Is Her Majesty recovering? Does she need me to assist her with her papers?" he asked.

"Your Indian servant is here, ma'am," I said. "Do you wish him to come in?"

"Absolutely not," she said. "I've already told him that. It is not proper that any man observe the queen in her night attire, and certainly not a man whose religion covers up their own women and keeps them locked away in harems. Tell him I will summon him when I am ready to go out later."

How I wished I could say something to her—let her know how anxious her household members were about this man and his ties to dangerous Indian agitators. But a cook does not advise a queen. I closed the door and turned to the Indian.

"She says it is not proper that you should attend while she is in bed. And it is not acceptable that you should want to see any official papers." I added the last part myself.

I went back to the kitchen and started to think about dinner preparations. I had never cooked a duck in my life. I flicked through our cookery books. There were hundreds of ways to cook a duck, but also warnings that ducks were very fatty and that the skin was not appetizing unless crisp, but that the meat beneath the skin should not dry out. In the end, I had to swallow my pride and went over to Jean-Paul.

"I am sorry to disturb you, Chef," I said, "but

the queen has requested duck tonight, and I'm afraid we do not eat duck often in England. I wondered if you could recommend a dish for me to prepare."

Those dark eyes studied me for a moment. *He's going to turn me down,* I thought. *To make me fail.* Then he said, "I, too, have put duck on the menu tonight. Go and get two more birds from the meat safe, and you shall prepare it with me."

"I can't thank you enough," I said.

"It is my duty to assist new cooks," he said stiffly, "especially visiting cooks from abroad."

I fetched the ducks, already dressed and ready, thankfully. I was not very good at taking off heads and feet.

"A simple roast duck, with an orange sauce, might be a good way to start," he said. "The secret is to prick the skin in a thousand places, place it in a moderate oven for an hour, bring it out, let it stand for the fat to run off, then baste it, put it back in a hot oven to crisp the skin."

"Is this how you are serving it tonight?"

"No, that would be an insult to my talent," he said. "I serve the traditional magret de canard. The breast of the duck cooked in its own fat until the skin is crisp, and then I shall serve it with figs and balsamic vinegar and local honey."

"And you do not think I am capable of this dish?" I demanded angrily.

"I wish to save you from too much work," he

replied. "It is not easy the first time one has to run a kitchen alone."

"You're right," I admitted. "I will stick to the roast bird tonight, and perhaps later you will show me the secrets of the duck breast."

"Maybe," he said.

I wondered what I might serve to accompany the duck, something that would not require too much preparation or finesse, then I decided that I would treat the royal party to a bouillabaisse—that rich seafood soup of the region. I'd even risk putting garlic in it. Jean-Paul noted the smell of what I was cooking.

"Ah, so now you have decided that our local food is worth eating," he commented.

"I'm trying to keep the menu simple so that there is not a lot of last-minute preparation," I said. "I've made chocolate pots de crème for their dessert."

Even though the dishes were not complicated, I found I was quite tired and decided that I needed fresh air. I had been working since dawn. I took off my cap and apron and went out into the garden. It was a heavenly day, warm with the promise of spring. I stood beneath an umbrella pine tree, breathing in its scent, until I heard voices and realized that Her Majesty's party was also in the gardens. How silly of me to have forgotten that she had said she wanted to take a turn outside. The voices were coming towards me. The one thing we had had drummed into us as servants was that we should never be seen by our masters. And the last thing I wanted was for the queen to talk to me in the presence of her family. She might ask more questions about my childhood. I shrank back behind the pine tree as the royal party approached, the queen being pushed in a bath chair by the munshi, her grandchildren at her sides and Princess Beatrice following dutifully behind with the queen's doctor and one of her ladies-in-waiting.

The trunk of the pine tree was not broad enough to hide me if they came closer. I tried to retreat through a shrubbery of tall bushes, oleanders, gardenias and camellias in full bloom. The scent of the blossoms was heady. As I pushed my way between bushes, there was a metallic clunking sound, and something dropped to the ground. I pulled a branch aside and peered down at the soil beneath. It was a gun.

Trying not to get scratched or have my eye poked out, I bent to retrieve it, picking it up cautiously in case it was still loaded. *Who might have dropped a gun in the bushes?* I wondered, then it dawned on me that the anarchist might have followed the queen up here last night, wanting to finish off what he had attempted in the square. But perhaps there were too many people milling around. Perhaps someone had recognized him, causing him to throw the weapon deep into the bushes and flee. I should hand it over to the queen's secretary, and it would be up to him to decide if it should be turned over to the French police. I wondered if they had recovered the bullet that struck the count and if so, whether the police could identify whether a bullet was fired from a certain gun. In any case, there was probably no way of tying a weapon to a certain person.

Sir Arthur was not in the sitting room, and one of the gentlemen of the household said he had not seen him since luncheon. He had probably escaped for a snooze, the man said. I realized I was carrying a gun and hid my hand in the folds of my skirt. I hesitated, then decided this was important enough to wake him up if necessary. I had to tap on his door several times before a tousled head appeared, glaring at me.

"What do you want?" he demanded fiercely.

"I'm terribly sorry to disturb you, Sir Arthur," I said, "but I was walking in the garden, and I found this gun. It had been thrown into the bushes. I wondered if it was the same weapon that shot at Her Majesty yesterday."

I handed him the revolver, and he stared down, examining it as it lay in his big hand. I watched his expression change. "Could well be. The chap came up here to get another shot at her but didn't get a chance, or was recognized and beat a hasty retreat. Thank you, my dear. You were wise to bring it to me. There is a Scotland Yard man on his way out to take charge of Her Majesty's security from now on. He'll know what to do."

"You don't think the French police should have it?" I asked cautiously. "After all, they are the ones who might know of anarchists in the region who might have had a plan to assassinate the queen."

"We'll see what Inspector Raleigh decides to do. Personally, I fear the local police will be a bunch of bumbling idiots, but that's just my prejudice against the French." He gave a little chuckle and closed his door.

As I started down the staircase, I could hear a woman's voice, shrieking. Yes, "shrieking" was the only word for it. "Where is it? You must know. It's gone. Vanished. Did you take it? I'm sure you did. You're in the pocket of that doctor, aren't you?"

I didn't dare linger any longer. Servants are not supposed to eavesdrop on the conversations of their betters. But as I went down the narrow hall back to the kitchens, I was dying of curiosity. One of the women in the royal party was missing something valuable. And it could not be Princess Beatrice or Lady Lytton. They were both in the grounds with the queen. Princess Helena, then? The unstable princess who had wanted me to buy drugs for her. Is that what she was missing? Her supply of drugs? But she had used the word "it." I paused in mid-stride. Could the item be a revolver, by any chance? Could someone staying here at the Excelsior Regina have borrowed the princess's revolver to take a shot at the queen?

This was none of my business, I knew. I was a mere cook, not in charge of Her Majesty's safety, but I found that I felt a fierce loyalty to her. She might be the queen, but she was an old woman. She was vulnerable. Perhaps that was why she wanted to be incognito when she came to the Riviera. Nobody should want to assassinate a mere Lady Balmoral. If she'd only come with a small party and rented a villa, she could have passed this off. But ordinary women do not bring regiments of pipers and outlandish Indian servants with them!

I went back to my work and followed Jean-Paul's directions for the roast duck. By the time it was finished, the skin was brown and deliciously crisp. The orange sauce I made to accompany it was sharp and tasty. And the bouillabaisse—I took a little taste, and it was delicious. I accompanied these with roasted potatoes, puree of Brussels sprouts and a macaroni pudding. The dinner was apparently met with approval; the footman who brought back the dishes reported that the queen had had a hearty appetite and commented on the fish soup!

The only one who didn't approve was Count Wilhelm, who was still recuperating in his bedchamber and who sent down a footman to report that he had complained bitterly that the dinner did not contain any good, healthy fleisch. Why was he not served the full scope of the dinner, and why was his tray not brought to him by the good-looking boy, Jimmy? I wondered how long he would remain in his room if he felt he was missing out on the full meal served in the dining room.

Sir James Reid came into the kitchen just when I had finished clearing up.

"I have just checked on our invalids," he said. "And it is good news. I think we can rule out typhoid or cholera. It is a case of dysentery, although that disease is not to be sniffed at. At least it is not highly contagious. If they have a satisfactory night, I think maybe they might try a little beef tea in the morning."

"Certainly, Doctor," I said. "I have had beef bones simmering all afternoon. I'll clarify and have some sent up to them in the morning."

"I congratulate you," he said. "You are a most competent young woman. Most females would panic at the thought of having to feed a royal party alone, but you have pulled it off."

"Thank you, Doctor." I blushed bright red.

I went to bed basking in the doctor's words. I had cooked for the royal party single-handedly, and apparently they were all satisfied. Maybe I would soon be a confident enough chef to run my own kitchen or even open my own restaurant? Pride comes before a fall, my mother always used to remind us. I should be thankful for what I had at this moment.

CHAPTER 29

In the morning I rose early, remembering the queen's request, and walked down the hill to the market. A stiff wind was blowing off the sea, buffeting me as I descended the steep street. Clouds were building on the western horizon. It promised to rain later. I should get my shopping done quickly and return to the hotel before I was soaked. I heard footsteps coming up behind me and stepped aside to let the person in an obvious hurry go past. It was Jean-Paul Lepin. He reacted with surprise at seeing me.

"So, you brave the market on such a blustery morning? You are indeed dedicated, mademoiselle. I salute you."

"The queen requested a repeat of the mushroom dish I served to her. Perhaps you would be good enough to recommend which mushrooms I should buy?"

"Of course," he said. "And if you decide to make another bouillabaisse, then I recommend that you start with the freshest fish from the stalls rather than that obtained from the hotel's suppliers. I would not serve a fish dish if I had not personally picked out items from that day's catch."

"I don't think I dare serve them a fish stew two days in a row," I said. "There was a complaint last night from the German count that I had not served any red meat."

"He was the one who was shot?"

"Yes."

"A brave man. He took the bullet to protect the queen, I hear."

"There are two different accounts to that," I said. "The queen said she thought he was trying to get out of the way and bumped into her, thus saving her life."

He chuckled. "We should let the former story stand. It may be his one chance in life to be considered a hero."

We walked on in silence, then he cleared his throat and said, "Mademoiselle, I should like to apologize for the other evening. I realized immediately that a well-raised English girl like yourself has certain standards. You English do not share the passion of the French race. And perhaps you were right—it was the fear, the heat of the moment that made you respond to me when I kissed you."

I didn't quite know what to say. "I have had very little experience with men," I said at last. "But I do know that I was raised to believe that a young woman waits for marriage before . . ." I couldn't go on with that sentence, so intense was my embarrassment. "I was shocked when you invited me to a hotel with you."

He was frowning. "But mademoiselle, I fear that you misunderstood my intentions. I suggested we should go to my cousin's hotel because I could see how upset you were. I did not think you were ready to walk all the way up the hill, and I thought a cognac and a chance to recuperate might be beneficial for you."

I looked up at him, not sure whether to believe this or not. "You said you wanted to get to know me better," I pointed out. "With men, it seems that means only one thing."

A smile crossed his face. "You are right. Perhaps it does for some men. But the demands of my profession mean I have had limited experience with women, especially with women from a good family. I do not always have the right words to phrase things correctly. But on that occasion, I really did intend to limit it merely to conversation—and perhaps another small kiss or two." He shot me an enquiring glance, then went on. "I assumed, wrongly, that you felt something for me, as I felt for you. And I confess I had joined in the celebration with a little too much wine. Can we forget it happened and wipe the slate clean?"

"We can." Conflicting emotions were fighting within me. I wanted to believe that his intentions had been honourable, but had they? And I wanted to let him know that I, too, had felt something for him. But the encounters with the Prince of Wales and with those awful men in the street were all too raw in my mind. And I still wasn't sure that his intentions had been as honourable as he claimed.

He gave a curt little nod. "That is good. From now on, our relationship will be only professional."

"Only professional," I echoed.

We came to the market, and Jean-Paul instructed me on which mushrooms were best for which kind of dishes. I bought some of each and even dared to add a small piece of truffle—to be grated over fowl or fish, Jean-Paul said. Then he bought a small piece of truffle for himself.

"Do you have more commissions to fulfil?" he asked.

"I thought I would get more whitebait, as the queen is fond of it," I replied.

"I, too, must visit the fish market," he said. "And I would be happy to escort you back up the hill. However, first I promised to bring some of this truffle to a certain lady. She is very fond of such delicacies." He paused, then added, "Would you like to accompany me to visit her? She lives nearby, and after we can be extravagant and take a cab together up the hill."

I was still flustered and confused. "Oh, I'm

sure you do not wish my presence when you visit a lady friend," I replied stiffly.

Amusement flashed in his eyes. "Ah, but you see this lady friend is over ninety," he replied. "She is my grandmother. She lives nearby."

"Oh, your grandmother," I said.

"So will you accompany me?"

Again I hesitated. "I should be getting back for my food preparation," I said. "I find myself in charge of breakfast as well as the other meals."

"Of course. It was thoughtless of me to suggest this. But my chefs are at your disposal when you need assistance, you know." I could tell he was disappointed.

"I really would like to visit your grandmother with you," I said, "but I feel the responsibility very strongly. One does not wish to make any errors when feeding a royal party."

"I understand completely. But I have to tell you that I am very impressed with your cooking skills and with your organization. For such a young woman, you seem very calm."

"Except for the other evening," I said. He looked at me and laughed.

"So why do you not stop at my grandmother's house with me for a small second? The cab will whisk us up the hill speedier than we could walk."

How could I say no?

"Very well, if you really would like me to accompany you," I replied.

He looked pleased. We went to the fish stalls, and Jean-Paul made sure I was given the freshest whitebait, while he himself selected wings of skate and a big bag of mussels.

"So tell me how you cook this fish," I said as we walked together. I didn't know the French word for skate.

"*La raie*?" he asked and told me how he prepared it.

I was expecting his grandmother to live in the old town, like Claudette's mother, but instead we walked until we came to a handsome white building surrounded by a garden. His grandmother lived on the ground floor. She was a tiny, delicate creature wearing a white lace cap. She kissed Jean-Paul many times, calling him her angel. Then she wanted to kiss me, too, but Jean-Paul said hurriedly that I was just a colleague from the hotel—a fellow chef. She seemed really interested in this. A woman as a chef? Whatever next? And I saw her giving him an enquiring glance. He refused a coffee and a pastry, telling his grandmother that I was needed to cook for the English queen. She was suitably impressed and took my hands as I made to leave.

"Come to visit me again, any time," she said. "Life is lonely for an old woman, although my grandson comes whenever he can. He is a good boy. He cares for his family. Very important, don't you think? Family?"

I agreed that it was. When she learned that my parents were both dead, that my one sister was married, and that apart from that I had nobody, she smiled up at me. "Then I shall be your new family, no?"

"Your grandmother is delightful," I said as Jean-Paul led us to a taxi rank.

"As are all of my family. A race of delightful people." He gave a cocky little grin.

"They are all here in Nice?"

"All of them. My parents. My father owns several businesses, including a patisserie. My three sisters are married, and I have twelve nephews and nieces. I am the youngest. They despair of me."

As we went back into the hotel, I sensed that something had somehow changed between us. A barrier had been broken down, and I wondered if it was intentional that he had wanted me to visit his grandmother. Had he wanted to show me that he was a good, reliable man after all? The thought that he had wanted to reassure me was a comforting one.

I cooked breakfast for the royal party, including another boiled egg for the queen, as she had so enjoyed the first, then sent up more rice water and warm beef tea to the four invalids and set about preparing luncheon. I would serve some of the mushrooms in an omelette and save the more robust ones for a meat dish in the evening, maybe a steak and mushroom pie? I was pleased with that idea as it allowed me to show off my pastry-making skills.

Luncheon went smoothly, but I was sitting down to my own meal when the dreaded Count Wilhelm came into the kitchen. I have to say he did look rather pale and unsteady on his feet, and I immediately felt a stab of guilt that I had thought he might be exaggerating his wounds.

"You, girl, where is the chef?" he demanded. "I wish to speak with him instantly."

"I am the chef, Your Highness," I replied. "My colleagues are indisposed. Can I help you?"

"The food does not agree with me," he said. "Last night—that stew of fish that was sent up to my room. My home state is far from any ocean, and my stomach is not used to fishes. Vat is more, the bay leaves should have been removed."

"I'm most sorry, sir. I thought I had removed all of them."

"There were pieces of bay leaf, quite indigestible. Don't let it happen again," he said. "And today's luncheon? Finally I am brave enough to come down and eat with the family, and vat do I find? I find an omelette and a chicken dish.

Again no fleisch. No good meat. I have lost much blood. I am dizzy and weak from blood loss. I should be eating meat."

"I am cooking a steak pie for dinner tonight, Your Highness," I replied. "That should satisfy you." Then I had a brilliant idea. "And I do have some beef tea, if that would fortify you for the present?"

"Now we are talking sense." He looked quite pleased.

I had the pan on the warming stove, so I ladled a cup for him, and he drank it down, making little lip-smackings of satisfaction. He put the cup down on the table.

"*Ist gut*," he said. "I shall be requiring more of this beef tea at intervals. Make sure some is available."

"I certainly will, Your Highness. And I trust you are making a good recovery from your wounds?" I asked.

"It will heal with time," he said. "And I will bear the suffering patiently."

As he turned to leave, he staggered a little, banging into one of the tables—a bit too dramatically, I thought. "You see, the blood loss has affected my balance," he said. "I must rest again."

It crossed my mind to wonder whether he was drunk. I went back to my own meal, which was now cold. I was just helping myself to a little trifle when one of the hotel porters came into the kitchen. "Are you Mademoiselle Barton?" he asked.

"Yes, I am," I replied.

"A man is outside asking for you."

"A man?"

"An Englishman. He comes in a smart equipage."

Oh goodness. It had to be Giles Waverly. And I was hot, sweaty and in my cook's apron. I was going to say that I was not free to see him at this moment when the bellboy went on, "He says he is very worried about you, since he heard of the queen's misfortune, and could wait no longer for your note. He begs you to spare him two minutes of your time, just to reassure him you are safe and well."

I took a deep breath. "Please tell him I will be with him as soon as I can. And please do not mention that you found me in the kitchen. He does not know that I am a cook."

"That was clear." He grinned. "He said you were a young lady of the queen's household."

"Which is true. I am. Just not what he thinks," I replied. "I will hurry and change."

I ran all the way up the flights of stairs, put on a clean blouse, splashed water on my face and stuck pins in my hair, then ran all the way down again. Giles was standing beside his horse and trap under one of the large palm trees, away from the hotel entrance. His face lit up as I went to join him.

"Thank heavens. You are safe. We read the terrible news in the English newspaper, and it only said that the bullet struck a member of the queen's party, so of course I feared the worst."

"It was Count Wilhelm from Germany who was struck, but luckily the bullet only grazed his shoulder. As you can see, I am quite unharmed."

"Do you have a few minutes to talk? We could walk in the gardens, or go across to the park?"

I glanced back at the hotel. "A few minutes, maybe, but not the gardens. We could be seen from hotel windows."

"Is the queen so strict with all her ladies?" he asked as he tied his horse to a railing and then started to walk away from the hotel to the park with me. "She does not want any of you to meet young men, or only the young men of her choosing?"

I hesitated. I really hated this. *Tell him now,* I thought. *Put an end to this.* But I glanced at his hopeful face, and I couldn't say the words. "Meeting young men while in her service is frowned upon," I said.

"Would it help if I went to see someone in person? Her private secretary maybe? And assured him that my intentions were honourable?"

"I don't think that would matter," I said. I turned to face him. "Please give me a little time,

Giles. I need to work out how best to handle this."

"So you do want to see me again? I really can hope?"

"I really enjoy being with you," I said, weighing every word, "but I can't jeopardize my current position in the household."

"You know, I told my father about you, and he's frightfully keen to meet you," Giles said. "Perhaps we can invite you to dinner, with one of the other ladies as a chaperone?"

Now this was getting too awkward.

"I'm usually required to be present at the dinner hour," I said with great tact.

"I'm going to find a way around your stuffy regulations." He gave a determined nod. "Now look here. Here's a healthy young chap of good family wanting to spend time with a young girl of similar good breeding. Who could possibly be against that?" Then he paused, and that worried look returned. "Unless . . . oh, I see. Unless the royal household has someone else in mind for you. I know they go in for arranged marriages. You are probably promised to some frightful German count. Maybe even the one who got shot."

I had to laugh at this. "Giles, I can assure you that I would refuse to marry any German count, especially that one. Look, all I ask for right now is a little time. Let me think how best to handle this, then I'll write to you again."

He sighed. "Well, I suppose that's better than nothing. Gives a chap a modicum of hope."

"And I have to get back," I said. "They will have noticed that I slipped away."

"It's like being in a glorified boarding school," he said.

"Exactly."

"I don't envy you," he said. He took my hands. "Bella, take care, please. Someone has taken a pot shot at the queen. I don't want anything to happen to you."

"Don't worry, I'll be very careful," I replied. "Now, I must go."

And I almost broke into a run in my haste to return to the hotel.

My mind was in a state of turmoil. *I must tell Giles the truth right away,* I thought. *He is bringing disgrace on his family by paying attention to a cook.* I wondered what would happen if I told him the real truth. Wouldn't his family want to rescue me from the lowly state in which I now found myself? I would marry Giles and become Lady Faversham. But what if they decided this episode of my life was too shameful? And the most important question of all: Did I want to walk away from being a cook? Would I be happy sitting in a drawing room, sipping tea and making idle gossip while someone else cooked my meals and reared my children? It was a question I couldn't answer.

I went back to work and produced a glorious steak and mushroom pie for the royal dinner. I decorated the pastry crust with leaves and vines. It was a work of art, and I was immensely proud of it. I fried the whitebait that Jean-Paul had selected for me as a first course, made a salad with the remaining duck, added a bean soup and ordered ices for dessert. I felt rather proud of myself when I collapsed on to the bed at eleven o'clock. I decided I would not attempt the market in the morning but allow myself a good night's sleep. In the middle of the night, a storm blew up, rattling my windows and howling around the hotel.

The morning dawned equally unpromising, and I was glad I had decided not to go to the market. I should have been drenched.

As I came down to breakfast, I noticed an air of tension. The French chefs looked up from their rolls and coffee. "The English doctor is looking for you," one of them said.

"Oh dear. Is it bad news?"

"I think it must be. He had a grave look on his face."

This was awful. One of the patients must have taken a turn for the worse. Or perhaps Dr Reid's tests had revealed typhoid after all. I found it hard to eat anything. I could hardly go looking for him, and I had been forbidden to go up to the rooms of the stricken men. What if one of them had died? I had not felt a particular attachment to any of them: Mr Angelo had always treated me fairly; Jimmy was a funny, cheeky boy; but the two men had ignored me until this journey. But now I felt almost as if they were my family. I couldn't lose one of them.

I managed to nibble a little bread and drink a cup of milky coffee, then I went to work on breakfast. The hotel had procured lambs' kidneys, and I made a kidney and bacon dish I knew the queen was fond of. No sooner had the footmen taken the trays when Dr Reid came in. He had the gravest frown on his face.

I stood up. "Bad news, Doctor?"

"Very bad. I'm afraid Count Wilhelm is in an extremely grave condition."

"Oh no? Is it blood poisoning from his wound?"

"No, I think it is something intestinal. I fear it's something he ate."

"Something he ate?"

"Yes, can you tell me what he ate yesterday?"

"I can. I sent a tray up for his breakfast and lunch, exactly the same food as went to the royal dining room. The luncheon was a mushroom omelette and a chicken fricassee. He came into the kitchen and complained that there was no good red meat. So I gave him a cup of the beef broth I'd made for the others. And for dinner he joined the queen in the dining room. The menu was bean soup, steak and mushroom pie, whitebait, duck salad and ices from the hotel confectioner."

"So he was served no special meals?"

"No. The only thing he had that the rest of the party did not eat was that cup of beef broth." I paused. "Do you think it is a case of food poisoning? Or has he perhaps caught whatever has stricken my colleagues?" The thought did cross my mind that he might have been to visit Jimmy. He wasn't one to give up easily on something he wanted.

The doctor shook his head. "No, I don't think it's a simple food poisoning."

"Then maybe it was the whitebait. He did say when he came into the kitchen that fish does not agree with his stomach, having grown up so far from any ocean."

"But the fish were fresh?"

"Could not have been fresher," I said. "They were bought from the market that morning. So were the mushrooms."

He frowned again. "Ah, yes. The mushrooms. That is my fear, that he ate a bad mushroom. You did not obtain these through the hotel's supplier?"

"No, they came from the town market," I said. "But Chef Lepin picked them out for me."

"That was probably not wise," he said. "These

peasants, they do not always know what they are picking in the woods, and a poisonous mushroom can look a lot like an edible one."

"Oh, surely not," I said. "And anyway, Chef Lepin would know the difference. He serves them to his own diners."

"All the same, accidents can happen, and this does seem to present itself as a case of severe poisoning of some sort."

"I'm really sorry," I said. "Is there something I can do?"

"Nothing. I'd say we try and flush out his stomach, but too much time has already passed. The toxicity is in his system, and his organs are starting to shut down."

"Then it's possible he will die?" The words came out as a whisper.

"I fear it's quite likely. There is no antidote that I know to mushroom poisoning. And as I said, too much time has elapsed. If we'd washed out his stomach or made him vomit immediately, we may have had a chance to reverse the damage. But now, we can just watch and wait—give him fluids and hope that his constitution is strong enough to come through this."

He left, taking a bowl of the beef tea with him. I felt terrible. What had I done? I had not liked the man, but I did not wish him to suffer at my hands. And I realized that I did not know one mushroom from another. I had trusted Jean-Paul, but had he let me down? And then another worrying thought crept into my head: What might happen to me if it was found I had poisoned a member of the royal family?

CHAPTER 30

Before the end of the day came the news that Count Wilhelm had died. His heart had given out. The household was instructed to go into mourning. Most of us had no black clothing with us, so black armbands were supplied. I cooked a simple roast capon and a rice pudding for dinner, thinking this was in keeping with the mood. But I felt so worried and so guilty that I was hardly able to concentrate on preparing even the simplest of dishes. The count had died. I had killed him. The French chefs were naturally curious, and I told Jean-Paul what had happened.

He frowned at my suggestion. "A poisoned mushroom? This is not possible. I have dealt with that man for years now. He is quite reliable. He would not make a mistake. Besides, I myself selected those mushrooms. I know a good mushroom from a bad one."

"The doctor is quite sure the count was poisoned, and there was nothing else in the meal that could have had that effect."

"I'm really sorry." Jean-Paul was looking down at me with concern. "I don't know what to say. It has put you in an unenviable position."

"I know. I feel terrible. What will happen to me now? Will I be blamed?"

"I do not see how anyone can hold you responsible for an accident," he said. "If anyone is to blame, it is I. I selected the mushrooms, but I would swear on my reputation as a chef that there was no poisonous variety amongst them."

I nodded, trying to reassure myself. "All I can think is, what would have happened if the queen had eaten that mushroom?"

I could see that this thought had not occurred to him before. "We can thank the good God that she did not. She is a lucky woman. She seems to live a charmed life. Twice in one week, she has escaped death."

"Would it be an imposition to ask if your chefs could serve the royal party until this unfortunate matter is resolved?" I asked. "I am clearly under suspicion, and I would hate to make them uncomfortable with their food. Since we are all in mourning, it only needs to be a simple meal."

"But of course," he said. "And do not worry. I am sure tests will be carried out and all blame will be removed from you. It is possible this person took his own life with some kind of medicine."

I did not think that Count Wilhelm was the kind of person who would take his own life. He had thought too much of himself for that.

I spent a miserable day. The four invalids were not making much progress. They were past the critical stage but were all very weak. I could hardly eat a thing myself and went to bed as soon as I could. In the morning, I had scarcely finished my cup of coffee when I was summoned to a sitting room on the first floor of the hotel. Dr Reid was there, also Sir Arthur Bigge and a man I had not seen before.

"Come in, Miss Barton," Dr Reid said. "This is Chief Inspector Raleigh. He is in charge of the queen's security. He was called from London immediately after the attempt was made on Her Majesty's life. He would like to ask you some questions."

I nodded, not taking my eyes off the newcomer. He was sitting in an apparently relaxed position in an armchair, but he was observing me with shrewd little dark eyes. With his head tilted to one side and a beak-like nose, he reminded me of some kind of bird—a bird of prey. "So you are the young woman who cooked the mushroom that killed the German count?" he asked.

"I cooked two meals containing mushrooms," I said, meeting his gaze with what I hoped was confident defiance. "I don't know if it has been verified yet what exactly killed Count Wilhelm."

"It very much appears to be poisoning, and the way the count's organs shut down does seem to indicate that it was not a simple distress to the digestive system but that a mushroom was to blame," Dr Reid said.

They were all three staring at me. It felt like a trial in a court of law. I tried to remain calm.

The newly arrived inspector cleared his throat. "I am told that you obtained these mushrooms not from the hotel supplies that were at your disposal, but from a different source?"

"Yes, sir. A stall in the town market."

"And why did you do that?"

"This stall specializes in mushrooms and truffles. It has many interesting varieties, and the hotel chef here at the Regina always buys his mushrooms at this stall. He selected a variety for me on this occasion since I had prepared mushrooms for the queen on a previous occasion and she requested them again."

"I see." There was a long pause.

"So you had no way of knowing whether these mushrooms were good or bad?"

"No, sir. I trusted the expert opinion of a local chef—a well-respected local chef."

"I would put this down to a tragic accident, a misjudgement," Chief Inspector Raleigh said, "except that an attempt was made on the queen's life so recently. I ask myself whether maybe this chef was also an anarchist, or an anti-royalist. Perhaps he was the one who pulled the trigger in the failed assassination attempt and then resorted to more subtle means."

"Oh, surely not," I blurted out.

"How well do you know this man?"

I thought I detected sarcasm in his voice. I wondered if someone had seen us kissing in the town and he was hinting at a relationship that didn't exist.

"Only in a professional manner, working side by side in the kitchens. Chef Lepin has been most helpful to me, instructing me in the preparation of new dishes. And I can't believe he would wish any harm to the queen. In fact, he told me how glad he was that she had chosen to come to Nice because it meant that the new hotel had opened and given him a chance to cook for foreign visitors."

"All the same, we cannot rule out that someone with evil intentions might have used an innocent young woman to perpetrate his scheme," Sir Arthur said. He was looking at me with kindly understanding.

"Or not so innocent," Inspector Raleigh said, and again there was a smirk in his voice. "How long have you been in Her Majesty's service?"

"Since September, sir."

"Ah, so you are a newcomer to the household. And you came from where?"

I suddenly realized that I was in an awful trap. If I lied, they could well find out the truth, and I'd be under further suspicion. If I came clean and told the truth now, then they'd see me as an imposter with hostile intentions. They were staring at me.

"From Yorkshire, sir." I mumbled the words. "From Lady Sowerby's estate."

"Why did you leave your former situation?"

"Lady Sowerby was old and had decided to close up her own household and go to live with her son."

"But London—that's a long way from home for you, isn't it? What made you come to London?"

"I saw the advertisement, sir. And who would not want a chance to cook for the royal household?"

That seemed to satisfy them.

"I think that's all for now, Miss Barton," the policeman said. "We won't know more until we receive the results of the toxicology tests on Count Wilhelm."

I had only taken a couple of steps before he added, "We will need your full particulars, young lady. Place of birth. Employment history. References."

"Those are all at the palace, Chief Inspector," I said. "I submitted full particulars when I applied for the job."

"Precisely," he said in a clipped voice. "They are not here for me to check on, are they? Write everything down for me."

I decided the time might have come to stand up to them. "I don't know why you think I would have deliberately put a poisoned mushroom into a pie," I said angrily. "If you really believe I wanted to kill Her Majesty, that would be a really stupid way to attempt it, wouldn't it? It was such a random thing to do. The chances of the queen actually getting that mushroom were small, and why would I want to harm any other member of the royal party?"

"We were not suggesting that there was any evil intention on your part," Sir Arthur said hastily. "Please do not distress yourself, Miss Barton."

"If I had wanted to harm the queen, I have had perfect opportunities," I went on. "She took to her bed after the attempted assassination, and I carried up her meals on a tray. I sat alone with her while she ate them."

"You will be good enough to write out a list of all the food served to the royal party on that day, Miss Barton," the inspector said. "Was there any occasion to your knowledge when Count Wilhelm might have eaten something that other members of the royal party did not?"

"Not on that day," I said. I forgot to add "sir." I was so rattled by now. "But the first day after he was shot, he did remain in his room and meals were sent up to him. However, he had exactly the same food I had prepared for the royal dining room." I hesitated, as something occurred to me. "Count Wilhelm had a habit of coming into the kitchen—"

"Coming into the kitchen?" Sir Arthur asked, horrified.

"Yes, sir. He had frequent complaints about meals, and he helped himself to anything he liked the look of."

"That is most unseemly," Dr Reid said. "Was this reported?"

"I understand that Mr Angelo, our master cook, did complain about it. To no avail."

"Yes, now that you mention it, I did hear something about it," Sir Arthur said. "But I felt that the count had a perfect right to visit the chef and complain if the food was not to his liking."

"So did the count come into the kitchen on the day in question? The day he took ill?"

"Yes, he did. He was upset that there was no red meat with his luncheon. And he had not liked the fish stew from the night before."

"Did he sample anything in the kitchen on that occasion?"

I frowned, thinking. "No. In fact he still seemed rather weak from his gunshot wound. He seemed unsteady on his feet." I paused, then added, "Oh, I did give him a cup of the beef broth I had made for the other invalids. He seemed to like it."

"That must have annoyed you, Miss Barton," the chief inspector said. "Having this man wandering into your kitchen at will."

"I found it very annoying, sir."

He gave a satisfied little nod. I stared at him incredulously.

"But if you think I poisoned his food to stop him from visiting the kitchen, I'm afraid I find that ridiculous."

"Nobody is suggesting that you deliberately poisoned the count," Dr Reid said hastily, but I could see that was exactly what Chief Inspector Raleigh wanted to suggest.

"Did anyone else visit your kitchen?" he asked.

"Only Dr Reid, when he came to inform me on the condition of the patients."

"We shall need to speak to the servant who carried up the count's tray," the inspector said, addressing the other two gentlemen.

"But that was the day before Miss Barton purchased the mushrooms," Sir Arthur said, looking confused now. "On the day in question, we are told that the count ate his meals with the rest of the party."

"But he did visit the kitchen." The inspector was not going to let this go. "Can we think whether anyone might have had a grudge against the count? Is it possible that someone from his part of Germany is working at this hotel? Someone who might see this as an opportunity to get rid of an unpopular ruler?"

"If that were the case, then this whole sad business can have nothing to do with Miss Barton.

I don't think we need to detain her any longer."

"Maybe not," the inspector agreed, "but we shall need all those particulars, Miss Barton. Just in case."

"Very good, sir," I replied stiffly.

As I went to leave, the inspector added, "You understand that we want to keep this matter strictly between ourselves. Consider yourself lucky that it has not been turned over to the French police. I can assure you that their methods of interrogation would not be as gentle as mine."

"There is nothing to interrogate, sir," I said. "If the mushroom I cooked into the pie was indeed poisonous, then it was a tragic accident, for which I am genuinely sorry." I gave a little nod before I left the room. I had not mentioned that Princess Sophie would be the one who was now rejoicing that the count was dead.

CHAPTER 31

I don't know how I stumbled back to my bedroom. Once there I stood at the open window, taking in big gulps of fresh air. I had always despised women who fainted, but at this moment my head was ringing, and I felt I could easily pass out. It was clear to me that the inspector from London was anxious to wrap up the case quickly. He would be looking into my background, and as soon as he contacted Sowerby Hall, he would learn that Helen Barton had died. So I was an imposter, up to no good, someone who had joined the palace with an ulterior motive. I could see how easily a case against me could be built. Disgruntled gentlewoman, father cheated out of inheritance, sacked from job, raising his daughter with a chip on her shoulder against all aristocrats.

But if I told the truth now, maybe went to Dr Reid or to Sir Arthur, who seemed to have taken kindly to me, I wouldn't fare any better. At the very least, I would be dismissed from service immediately. I was damned if I did and damned if I didn't. I couldn't think of anyone who might speak on my behalf. Mr Angelo would say I was a good worker, but so what? I desperately needed advice, a female companion. I realized I had been so horribly alone since my mother died and I was sent to the Tilleys' house. There I had shunned closeness to other servants, thinking myself to be above them. When I moved to the palace, I had enjoyed chatting with Mrs Simms but again had not allowed myself to open up to her, since I had to carry the burden of my enormous secret. And my little sister, Louisa—I was fond enough of her, but we were so different, and I was the older one, the responsible one. I had never once told her how I felt. Now I sank back on to my bed, longing for my mother, longing for a woman's arms around me, telling me that everything was going to be all right. For the first time in my life, I was truly frightened.

As I lay there, a thought came to me. Lady Mary Crozier had seemed to be a kind and sensible woman. If I went to her and told her the truth, perhaps she could advise me on what course to take. I couldn't ask her to speak on my behalf, since she didn't know me, but at least I could have the advice of a woman, and I could tell my story to someone who would listen with sympathy.

I washed my face, tidied my hair, put on my new dress, then looked at the time. Still only ten o'clock. Was it done to call upon an aristocrat this early? I thought not, but at least I could probably guarantee that she'd still be at home. I had to risk it. The day was mockingly fine. Birds chirped in the big pine trees. Dappled sunlight played across the path. The sweet smell of spring flowers wafted on a gentle breeze. It was a day for a picnic, for a stroll in the gardens, for a ride in Giles's carriage. I paused, considering. Was he a person I could go to? But I had deceived him, hadn't I? He might find that a cook who had acted as if she was a legitimate member of the royal household might make him a laughing stock if the truth came out. I took a deep breath and walked resolutely towards Lady Mary's villa.

The maid who answered the front door looked startled to see a caller on the doorstep this early in the day.

"The marquise is not ready for visitors," she said in her prim French voice. "If you leave your calling card on the tray, I will present it to her at the appropriate time."

"It is a very urgent matter, mademoiselle," I said. "I would not usually disturb my lady so early, but it is very important that I speak with her. Could you please tell her that Miss Barton begs for a few minutes of her time?"

"I will tell her," she said, implying that she wasn't hopeful for a good outcome. "Remain here."

I waited in the marble foyer, examining the statues and potted palms. Everything was so perfect, so elegant, and people like Lady Mary took it for granted. Eventually I heard voices coming from the rear of the villa, then a voice from the balcony at the top of the stairs said, "I don't know what this is about, and my maid was still completing my toilette, but curiosity got the better of me." She came down the stairs, still in a peach silk robe trimmed with feathers. Her feet tapped in silk slippers across the marble floor.

"You'd better come into the music room. My husband is in the morning room reading the newspapers, I expect. And bring us coffee, Yvette."

"Of course, marquise." The maid hurried off in one direction. I followed Lady Mary into a sitting room dominated by a grand piano. The carpet was dark blue with a lighter blue silk wallpaper, and the view was on to the fish pond and the gardens beyond.

"Take a seat." Her voice had no warmth in it, and the friendly smile of our last encounter was missing. "Now," she said, "what have you to say for yourself, miss?"

It was such an aggressive outburst that I was taken aback. Had she already heard about the poisoning of Count Wilhelm, and was she blaming me?

"Well?" she went on. "I only agreed to meet you because I am dying to know who you really are and why you thought it was acceptable to deceive me that you were a member of Her Majesty's household."

Again I wasn't quite sure what she was getting at. "I am here as part of Her Majesty's retinue," I said.

"I don't think so. I was chatting with Lady Lytton and mentioned you and what a success you were at our party. She said there was nobody called Helen amongst Her Majesty's household." She looked up as the maid came in with a tray of coffee. There was silence as the coffee was poured into two cups and hot milk was added. "So was it a joke for you? And who are you in reality?"

"I assure you it was no joke," I said. "You approached me, remember, Lady Mary. You didn't ask for any details, only that you wanted my red hair as part of your tableau. What you never gave me time to tell you was that I did come from the palace with the queen, but I am not a lady-in-waiting. I am her cook."

Her eyes opened wide, and without warning she burst out laughing. "Her cook?"

I nodded. "I'm afraid so. I only agreed to take part in your tableau because I didn't want to let you down."

She looked confused. "But you are a girl of good family. One can tell breeding. Your speech. Your behaviour. You can't be a cook."

"I am," I said. "You are right that I am from a good family, but we suffered a series of reversals of fate, ending with my parents both dead and my being responsible for a little sister with no means of support. I had to go into service, which I can assure you was highly painful and embarrassing for me. Then I discovered an aptitude for cooking—one might even say a passion for it."

"How extraordinary," she said. "What an extraordinary story. And so your cooking skills came to the notice of the royal household?"

"Not exactly," I said. "They do not know my true story. I have shared it with nobody so far. That is why I've come to you. I have to tell someone the truth, and you seemed to be a wise and kind woman."

"My dear, do go on. I am all ears." She leaned forward in her seat.

So I told her the whole story, from Mrs Tilley refusing me a reference to Helen Barton being killed, my reading the letter and taking the terrible risk of applying in her place. "It was my one chance, you see," I said. "I didn't see the harm in it at the time. Helen was dead. They would need another cook to take her place, and I knew I was good enough."

"So why the need to tell the truth now?" she asked. "If you are accepted and respected in the royal kitchen, what harm is there that you work under an assumed name?"

"Because of what has just happened," I said, and told her about the count dying of mushroom poisoning. "So I don't know what to do,"

I finished. "I would not have troubled you, but I am desperate, and I have no friends here to turn to."

"Let me understand this," she said, staring past me out of the window. "You bought mushrooms from a stall. One of those mushrooms was apparently of a poisonous variety, and this German count died as a result."

I nodded.

"A tragic mistake, I agree," she said, "but I don't see how you can be blamed. You bought the mushrooms from a stall that specializes in them. Exactly the place one would go to if one wanted mushrooms. I am sure my own servants would shop there. You bore no malice or evil intent."

"That's the problem," I said. "A police inspector has come out from London, and he is trying to build a case that the mushroom was intended for the queen and that I am somehow part of an anarchist plot."

"How utterly ridiculous," she said. "If that was your intent, what were the chances that the queen would actually eat the poisoned mushroom, and not another member of her household?"

"That is precisely what I said. I told them that the queen stayed in her bedchamber on the day after she was shot at, and I carried up her food. I would have had every chance to poison her then."

"Except you didn't already have the mushrooms," she pointed out.

"That's true."

"But what on earth would make them think you might be connected to an anarchist plot?"

"They have asked me to supply all of my particulars—my birth, my previous employment, my references . . . Don't you see, once they find that the real Helen Barton is dead, they will know I'm an imposter. And they will fabricate a reason that I used subterfuge to infiltrate the royal kitchen."

Lady Mary continued to stare out of the window. "Yes, I can see that is a knotty problem for you."

"Even if I go to Sir Arthur or Dr Reid and tell them the whole truth, it would mean instant dismissal, I'm sure. And that London inspector is itching to make a case against me. I can see him saying that I planned this whole thing—he'd point out that I was raised by a disgruntled aristocrat who wanted vengeance."

"So what is your real name?" Lady Mary asked.

"Isabella Waverly," I said.

"Waverly? Related to the current earl? And young Viscount Faversham?"

"Their cousin."

"Do they know that?"

"Absolutely not," I said.

"Young Faversham was rather smitten with you, I seem to remember."

"Yes. And I've seen him a couple of times. We

went for a carriage ride together. I felt bad about deceiving him and kept trying to tell him that I couldn't meet him again."

"He'll be most disappointed when he finds out—"

"That I'm a mere cook? I know."

"No, my dear. That you are his cousin, and therefore off limits." She laughed.

"I'm only a second cousin," I pointed out. "My father and the earl were first cousins. My father's branch of the family had no money and no inheritance. My father was born in India and then sent back into the army there."

"That's the way it goes with our sort of family, isn't it? The heir gets everything. The spares are sent into the army or the law or the church. Not fair, one might say. But my dear, why didn't you appeal to the earl for help when your parents died?"

"My father had gone to the family for help once and been turned down. He let us know that no assistance could be hoped for in that quarter."

"But Isabella"—she reached out and put her hand over mine—"this might be a blessing in disguise for you. Giles is already fond of you. If you went to them now and told them of your predicament, you would have powerful allies. I'm sure you'd be welcomed into the bosom of the family, and the London policeman would know that you have a good pedigree and no reason to want to harm any member of the royal family."

"Do you really think so?" I asked cautiously.

"Darling, look at you. You have the sweetest face. Who could turn you down? I wouldn't be surprised if Giles didn't propose to you on the spot."

Oh gosh. I felt my cheeks burning. "But the fact that I have been a servant—surely that would bring disgrace and embarrassment to the family?"

"Much has been overlooked for a pretty face before now," she said. "Your character Nell Gwynne lived a very comfortable life after King Charlie discovered her."

"But he didn't marry her," I pointed out. "I have already had an offer to be someone's mistress."

"Really? Do tell." She gave an excited little shrug.

"The Prince of Wales actually."

"And you turned him down? My dear, I am impressed. You certainly have integrity."

"I couldn't . . . you know . . . with a man I don't love."

"Quite right."

"So you really think that I should go to see the Waverlys and tell them my whole story?"

"I do."

"And if they don't believe me or don't want to accept me?"

"What have you lost at this point? It seems to

me that you'll have to tell the truth to someone in the queen's party."

"And be dismissed. Then what? I'll have no reference and nowhere to go."

She took my hand and squeezed it. "Silly girl. You shall come to stay with me. I'll introduce you as a young cousin home from the colonies, and we'll find you a suitable husband in no time at all."

I looked up at her. "You are very kind, but I'm sure your husband would not approve of me."

"My husband adores me and would not question anyone I invited to stay. Perhaps he can find a suitably handsome French aristocrat for you. They are much more fun than the English in many ways, even if they have ridiculously strict social etiquette." She paused, thinking, then added, "But I still think Giles Waverly would be a good match for you. He's a rather flimsy lad and needs a sensible girl like you to keep him on the straight and narrow."

"You really think I should go to see him?"

"I really do. Or better yet, I'll invite him and his father over for tea. You can join us."

"You really are a fairy godmother," I said.

She gave me a sweet smile. "The moment I saw you sitting in the gardens, I knew we should be great friends. That's how it is with me. I see a person, and either I adore them instantly or take a dislike to them."

I started to stand up. "I should go back to the hotel in case they want to question me some more. Do you think I should tell someone the truth immediately?"

"I'd wait and see which way the wind blows," she said. "They haven't actually proven that a mushroom killed the count, have they?"

"Not yet."

"Well, there you are then. It seems to me that nobody is asking the right question."

"And that is?"

She gave me a knowing look. "Who might have wanted to kill the count."

"I believe the police are looking into that aspect," I said. "The inspector from London surmised that someone from the count's state in Germany might have gained employment at the hotel for that very reason."

"Well, there you are, then," Lady Mary said. "They'll find someone else with a motive, and you'll be in the clear."

"I do hope so," I said.

"So run along now. I have to finish dressing for a luncheon appointment in Cannes," she said, "but I'll send word as to when the Waverlys might be coming to tea."

"I can't thank you enough," I said.

"Nonsense, you did me a good turn the other night, and I'm repaying the debt. And we women have to stick together, especially when dealing with thick-headed and narrow-minded men."

She gave me a little hug, then rang the bell for the maid to escort me to the door. I walked back in a daze, hardly daring to feel more hopeful. Was it possible that I could marry Giles? And the other question: Did I want to marry Giles? Of course I did. He was a sweet boy, gentle, amusing. And he was a viscount who would inherit an earldom someday. I'd be set up for life, safe, secure. Isn't that what every woman wants?

CHAPTER 32

As I walked through the gardens, I found my thoughts had turned to the interesting question that Lady Mary had raised: the count had been the intended victim, not the queen. If I could find out who wanted him dead, I'd be able to prove my innocence without having to reveal my name. I supposed it was possible, as had been suggested, that a person from the count's home state had come here with the intention of killing him. In that case, I could understand shooting him. That is the usual anarchist's method, isn't it? But putting a poisonous mushroom in a pie in the hopes that the count would choose the right slice? That was downright stupid. Anyway, the policeman from London would already be checking into that, as he probably would into my own background.

I paused, shivering even though the sun was warm on my shoulders. I had to think and get to work quickly, before a reply could be received from Yorkshire stating that Helen Barton was dead. Very well: Who wanted the count removed? Princess Sophie was the obvious suspect. She had made it very clear that she did not want to marry him. But a princess could hardly have tampered with the food, certainly not put a poisonous mushroom into my pie. And she had never come into the kitchen. I thought about the attempted assassination of the queen. Were the two in any way linked? It seemed unlikely, except that they happened so close together, and the gun was found in the bushes at the palace. So the shooter had been nearby at some point. Why hide the gun here? Why not take it with him and throw it into the ocean?

Then I remembered the other strange happening: a woman's voice screaming that something had been taken from her. I had assumed that it was the queen's daughter Princess Helena, the one who took drugs, and that someone had removed or hidden the drug she depended upon. But what could that have to do with the count's death? Was it possible that the thing the princess was searching for was her revolver? Might she fear that someone had taken it to try to kill her mother? And that she might now be implicated? I knew that she felt her mother disapproved of her habit and was trying to break her of it, but might she be unstable enough to have tried to kill her mother? Taken a pot shot at her when there was chaos and darkness and a swirling crowd? It seemed unlikely. And she had certainly also never been anywhere near the kitchen.

But what if the count had not been the intended

victim? I remembered other conversations I had overheard: those gentlemen discussing how to remove the despised munshi. It had been suggested that Dr Reid might be able to poison him. The doctor had laughed it off, but he was the only one who came into the kitchen. Had he somehow tainted food designed for the Indian? He knew we made vegetable dishes that would be acceptable to the Indian's religion—spicy dishes not meant for the royal family. What if one of those had been poisoned? The greedy count couldn't resist helping himself to anything that took his fancy. For the first time, this seemed like a viable line of reasoning.

Except there was another one. Ronnie Barton had tried to bribe me into tampering with the queen's food, on behalf of the Prince of Wales. I didn't think for a moment that the prince would actively work to bring about his mother's demise, but Ronnie Barton had few scruples. I could quite see him sprinkling some poisonous substance into a dish designed for Her Majesty, and not having too much of a conscience if the dish accidentally poisoned someone else first. The only thing against that argument was that to my knowledge Ronnie Barton had not come into the kitchen at any time—certainly not recently.

The problem was that these two suppositions actually put me in more danger, not less. If Dr Reid had tried to poison the munshi, he certainly wasn't going to confess to it and would have every reason to make me seem to be the guilty one. Servants were always expendable. He could not risk his plot and his fellow conspirators being revealed. The fact that one of them was Lord Salisbury would bring down the government. Perhaps Dr Reid and I could have a small private conversation in which I told him what I had overheard and that I didn't want my background checked into. We would agree to call the whole matter an unfortunate accident and let it drop. We would buy each other's silence.

I shifted uneasily as a strong wind suddenly sprang up, sending blossoms flying. I had been raised to do the right thing. The use of a false name still hung heavy on my conscience, but this thought was one giant step beyond. It was hiding a crime. I didn't think I'd go to hell for using someone else's name. God would surely understand my desperation at that moment, but deliberately looking the other way when someone had been killed? I could never stomach that, however advantageous it would be for me.

I broke off my reverie as I heard footsteps coming towards me. I was in no mood for conversation and looked around to see if I could make another escape into the shrubbery. But I was in a part of the grounds that was all open lawns. The footsteps were moving fast towards me. Princess Sophie came into view, walking at a great clip. She was dressed all in black, with a black lace veil draped over her head, which made her fair hair and complexion look almost ghostlike. Her face showed great distress. She was looking down and hadn't seen me. I stepped off the path, and she was about to pass when she became aware of my presence. She looked up and gasped.

"I'm sorry if I startled you, Your Highness," I said, even though I had done nothing except move out of her way.

"You?" She almost spat out the word. "You're the one, aren't you? The one who poisoned my betrothed?"

"If the mushroom was indeed poisonous, I am afraid I was the one who baked the pie, Your Highness. But it has not yet been ascertained whether that was what killed the count."

"What else could it be?" she demanded, glaring at me. "Of course it was a mushroom, and they are saying you were stupid enough to buy food from a stall in the market. From a common street vendor."

"I am really sorry," I said. "I bought food from a man who was presented to me as a reputable vendor by the hotel chef, who buys all his own mushrooms from that stall. I am no expert on mushrooms. There are varieties here I have never seen before. I trusted his judgement."

"I have told Her Majesty's secretary that I

want this stall owner prosecuted and driven out of business," she said. "He should never be allowed to make this terrible mistake again. And this chef—who is he? He must also suffer for his mistake."

"Highness, I can see that you are upset," I said. "I can quite understand. You've had a terrible shock. In fact, two shocks in such a short time. To see your betrothed shot and then to learn he has died is more than any woman should bear." I did not add that this was not the sentiment she had presented to me the last time we met. But women are strange creatures, aren't we? We only realize what we treasure when it is taken from us.

"At least I was fortunate not to witness the shooting," she said. "I did not attend the procession. I had a headache that day, and I thought the noise of the bands and the crowd would be too much for me, so I stayed behind."

"Probably very wise. It was noisy and the crowd was rambunctious. But it was interesting for someone who has never witnessed such a show before."

"We have Fasching—Carnival in Germany," she said. "And many parades. For me it was not worth sitting on a hard bench without even a cushion, right where one can be ogled and pressed upon by the common people."

Then she seemed to realize she was talking to a common person. "I must return to the other ladies. I will be missed. We are supposed to be sitting in silence, in mourning, but it was too sad and depressing to be in there, so I escaped for a few moments."

"I'm sure nobody begrudged you some fresh air," I said.

"It is not fitting to be seen out in public," she said. "We must bear our grief and suffering locked away from the world."

Before she could leave, I reached out to her. "Your Highness, in your grief, I beg of you not to seek vengeance against the stall-keeper or the chef."

"But they must pay for their deeds, as must you," she said. "I shall ask my cousin to have you dismissed. It is not right that you ever cook for my family again."

"I am sure the French police will be checking into the stall-keeper and where he harvests mushrooms," I said. "But as to the chef and myself, we had no way of knowing that one of the mushrooms was of a poisonous variety. It was an honest mistake."

"Nevertheless . . . ," she said, glaring at me.

"Have you never made a mistake in your life?" I asked softly. "And were you punished unjustly for it?"

"No," she said defiantly. "Never." She was looking past me, and suddenly I saw her expression change. I saw hesitancy on her face and a look of fear in her eyes. Then she turned back to face me. "I must go. I am sorry that you must suffer for this mistake. But someone must pay."

She turned away and broke into a run across the lawn. I watched her cross the forecourt and disappear into the queen's private entrance to the hotel.

I thought about that sudden change of expression on her face. Sudden realization and fear. Had she remembered a time when she had made a mistake? Or had she seen someone in the garden who had alarmed her? She had, after all, been staring past me. I turned to look in that direction, but it was nothing but an open stretch of lawn, ringed by bushes, and there was nobody in sight. I couldn't think why anyone might be following her or have alarmed her, but just in case I headed across the lawn to those bushes and peered around them. Nobody. The grounds were deserted except for myself. The bushes were just coming out into bloom—pretty open flowers, pinks and whites. I went to pick a flower, then drew my hand back at the last moment. I recognized them for what they were: oleander. And I heard Princess Beatrice's voice saying to her children, "Those pink ones are oleander and very poisonous."

CHAPTER 33

I stood there like a statue, staring down at the flowers as they stirred in the breeze. So pretty and yet so deadly. And the leaves of the oleander, smooth and slim, not unlike those of the bay tree—I had put bay leaves into my fish stew. I remembered the count complaining that bay leaves had been left in his bouillabaisse, when I was sure that I had removed them all. Actually, now that I came to think of it, I would swear that there were no stray bay leaves in the soup. I had cooked the herbs in the usual muslin bag, so they were easy to remove. What if someone had sprinkled oleander leaves on to the portion of food I had sent up to the count's room? I had to find Dr Reid immediately.

I crossed the lawn as speedily as Princess Sophie had done. Princess Sophie, who had been so sweet and gentle before and now demanded punishment for everyone connected to the count's death. She had been there at the picnic; she had heard when Princess Beatrice had warned her children about the oleander.

Chilling thoughts were racing through my brain. Princess Sophie had claimed a headache and not attended the parade. So how did she know that the benches were hard and the royal stand was right at the front, with the crowd pressing in on all sides? Perhaps one of the ladies had described the scene for her. Or perhaps she had seen it herself from across the street, as she waited to fire the revolver and kill her betrothed. What better time and place when everyone was in disguise, wearing masks, jolly from too much wine? She could have fired the gun, watched the count fall, whipped off a mask and suddenly been a frightened girl asking what had happened. Which was why the gun had ended up in the bushes here at the hotel. She had to get back before the royal party, so she did not have time to hide the gun anywhere else.

All of this was pure supposition, of course. But oleander leaves? Well, at least they could be proven to be the source of the count's demise. I went in search of Dr Reid and found him coming down the stairs from visiting the four cooks.

"How are my colleagues today?" I asked.

"Finally we see the light at the end of the tunnel," he said. "The young lad is almost ready to be up and about. The older men are still weak, but at least they are keeping down nourishment now, which is a good sign. I rather feared for their lives at one stage, I can tell you."

"That is good news," I said.

"Was there something you wanted, Miss Barton?"

"Yes. I wanted to ask you what you knew about oleander poisoning."

He looked puzzled. "Oleander? Not much. I know it's supposed to be toxic."

"But would you know what the symptoms would be?"

"I can't say I would. Why the interest?"

"Because I believe that the count was not killed by a poisonous mushroom at all, but by oleander leaves, put into the bouillabaisse I sent up to his room when he was recovering from the gunshot wound. I need to know whether the poison would take more than one day to kill a person. You see, the count came into the kitchen, as he sometimes did, to complain about the food that had been sent up to his room. One of his complaints was that I had not removed the bay leaves from his bouillabaisse. Well, Doctor, I remember clearly that the bay leaves were in a muslin bag, and I know I removed it. And in the garden just now, I noticed how oleander leaves can resemble bay, especially if they are broken up."

He gave me an incredulous stare. "And who could possibly do such a thing?"

"I have my suspicions, but I won't say more until you can examine the body and find out if I am correct."

"Very well," he said. "I am sure that the

inspector from Scotland Yard would say you were clutching at straws to try and clear your own name, but I think you seem to be a trustworthy and sensible young woman, and I can see no reason why you would want to harm any member of the royal family. So I'll do what you say. I shall need to visit a French colleague, as I'm sure my own medical textbooks do not deal with oleanders. I think it's too cold in England for them to grow."

So off he went, and all I could do was wait. I was not cooking. I stayed clear of the kitchen just in case any further suspicions fell upon me. And I found myself wondering about Jean-Paul. He was the one who had selected the mushrooms. He could also have had every opportunity to put oleander leaves into my bouillabaisse. And he had been at the Carnival, where, he confessed, he had been drinking. I knew nothing about him other than that he was a talented chef and his kiss had been incredible. But what if he was an anti-royalist? What if he had taken the job at the hotel with the intention of doing away with the royal family? I shook my head. I didn't want to believe that. I also didn't want to believe that I was so attracted to him—that he was the first man who had ever made me feel alive.

I took my meals in the staff dining room with the other employees, but they avoided contact with me, as if they didn't want my current disgrace to rub off on them. Jean-Paul tried to offer a kind word. He saw that I was toying with a bowl of consommé and brought a plate over to me.

"Here," he said. "Try some of these noodles. I made them myself. You need to eat and keep up your strength."

The thoughtfulness brought tears to my eyes. "I can't seem to swallow anything," I said. "It's just like waiting for the stroke of doom to fall."

He put a hand on my shoulder. "You'll come through this. You are strong, and you have done nothing wrong. The truth will come out, I assure you. Myself, I do not believe that it had anything to do with a mushroom. I would swear by all the saints that the stall-keeper is an honourable man who knows his trade. I am sure they will find that the count died of another complaint. Maybe he caught the same disease that has felled your colleagues."

"Maybe," I said. I couldn't tell him that every minute we had to wait meant it was all the more likely that information would come back from England stating that Helen Barton was dead and I was an imposter. Then nobody would believe me. The situation felt hopeless, until I reminded myself that I did have allies: Lady Mary was on my side. Giles Waverly, too, I hoped. But what could they do if a policeman from Scotland Yard got it into his head that I was guilty of murder?

A whole long day went by in which I received no form of communication. The doctor did not report back on the effects of oleander, and Lady Mary had not yet managed to arrange a tea party for the Waverlys. The hours dragged on. The weather changed. A storm came in, bringing blustery rain and making escape to the gardens impossible. I sat alone in my room and wondered if I should write to my sister, telling her the whole truth of what had happened to me. Would she care? And even if she cared, what could she do about my current predicament? A butcher's family is not likely to have influence in royal circles, and Louisa might even be on her way to Australia by now.

Then an idea came to me: Had the count's room been cleaned since he was found dead? Was it left intact for the police to go over? If so, might he have removed a fragment of oleander leaf from his mouth and thrown it to the floor in disgust? I decided to risk taking a look for myself. I went up to visit Jimmy, who was now sitting up in bed, looking pale, but with eyes that lit up as he saw me. The window was wide open, but even so the cloying odour of sickness lingered, and I swallowed back my revulsion.

"Well, if it takes nearly dying of stomach poisoning to make a pretty girl visit my room, I'm all for it," he said.

"I'm so glad you are feeling better," I said.

"The doctor was really worried about all of you."

"Me too. I thought I'd had my chips," he said. "Never felt worse in my life. I think that's put me off ice cream forever."

"Maybe stick to reputable ice cream parlours in future," I said. "I shall be so glad when you can all come back to work."

"I know. I've felt so badly for you. You must have been run off your feet."

"It hasn't been too terrible. Chef Lepin had his men take over the bulk of the cooking, and I just prepared the meals for the royal party. With dire consequences, as I'm sure you must have heard."

"No. We've heard nothing shut away up here. The doctor was so worried it might be catching. He had one hotel footman bring our meals, and that was a bloke who had survived typhoid."

"Well." I took a deep breath. "Your favourite count has died, and I've been accused of poisoning him."

He gave me an incredulous look, then burst out laughing. "Lucky I was shut away up here, or I'd have been a suspect myself."

"It's not funny, Jimmy. There is a policeman out from London who is determined to find that I poisoned the count deliberately."

"How are you supposed to have done it?"

"With a bad mushroom, they think. But I'm not so sure. So I thought I'd take a look at the count's room. I thought you'd know which room it is."

"Oh, so you only came up to see me because you wanted the count's room number, eh?"

"We were not allowed anywhere near you until today," I said. "I've been asking about you all the time."

"Fair enough," he said, "but a fellow can hope, can't he? And you're right. The count did give me his room number. He wanted me to bring up a night cap. Of course, I didn't obey that one. I wasn't born yesterday."

"He was quite persistent, wasn't he?"

He nodded. "A pain in the you-know-what. I can't say I'm sorry he's kicked the bucket. So anything I can do to help you clear your name, just let me know. It's room twenty-four—two floors above the queen's."

I thanked him and hurried back down the stairs. It was mid-morning. I suspected the royal party would be in one of the sitting rooms. They would not have gone out in such weather. I walked slowly along the corridor leading to the count's room, listening for any sign that a room might be occupied. *I'd better have a good excuse,* I thought. *I was sent to find Sir Arthur as the London policeman wanted him. Yes, that would do.*

I came to number twenty-four, tapped on the door, waited, and then turned the doorknob. The door was not locked, which I thought was lax on their behalf. It swung open, and I stepped into a darkened room. The heavy velvet curtains had been drawn across high windows, and the room smelled, as Jimmy's had done, of sickness. The count had vomited in here. I tiptoed across the room and pulled back one of the curtains. Suddenly it occurred to me that the count might still be lying in his bed. I spun around, heart racing, then gave a sigh of relief when I saw that the bed was empty and had been made up. But that also made me think that the room had been cleaned. Of course, if the count had vomited over his sheets, they would have been changed right away.

I went around the bed but could find no trace of a fragment of leaf. Disappointed, I was about to leave when my gaze fell upon an elaborate box of chocolates on the bedside table. I opened the lid. One chocolate had been taken. The rest of the box was untouched.

This struck me as strange. The count had shown himself to be a greedy person. If someone had given him a box of chocolates, would he not have eaten several at once? I picked it up and took it with me. One never knew when it might be useful, not to eat but as evidence. I took it up to my room without being seen.

CHAPTER 34

I was just coming down the stairs again when I encountered Dr Reid.

"Miss Barton," he said. "We were looking for you. Please come to Sir Arthur's sitting room. We need to talk."

I followed him and found Sir Arthur and the London policeman already sitting there. The room was heavy with pipe smoke and my eyes stung. This in itself was unusual. The queen did not approve of smoking, and even her relatives went outside to smoke at the palace.

Sir Arthur, a man of perfect manners, rose to his feet as I entered. The police inspector did not.

"Good of you to come, Miss Barton," Sir Arthur said. "Please do take a seat."

I sat. I detected that the tone had changed, their manner to me had shifted slightly.

"Miss Barton," Inspector Raleigh said, "what made you suspect that the count might have died from eating poisonous oleander leaves?"

"He came into the kitchen to complain about several things, including not being served any red meat for his luncheon," I said. "One of the things

411

he complained about was that I had left bits of bay leaf in the bouillabaisse."

"The what?" he asked sharply.

"It's a local fish stew," I said. "Very tasty."

"And did you cook it with bay leaves?"

"Yes, but in the customary muslin bag. I removed it before I served the dish."

"So you immediately jumped to the conclusion that these were not bay leaves but oleander?"

"No, sir. I only began to see the connection when I encountered Princess Sophie in the gardens. She had been talking to me in a most hostile manner—saying that she wanted the stall-keeper, the chef and myself all prosecuted for killing her betrothed. Then suddenly she looked past me, and her expression changed. I saw fear in her eyes, and she ran off. I couldn't think what she might have seen that produced this reaction. There was nobody in sight. And we were on a lawn edged with oleander bushes. That's when I remembered we had been on a picnic and Princess Beatrice had made a point of stressing to her children how poisonous oleanders were." I paused, waiting for a reaction.

"Princess Sophie—which one is she?" the inspector asked.

"She is a German princess, a young cousin of the queen," Sir Arthur said. "She was engaged to marry the count."

"So what is this young woman trying to suggest

here—that a princess killed her intended?" The inspector looked at Dr Reid for confirmation.

"Yes, sir. That is what I am suggesting."

"And what would make her do that?"

"I came across her on the day of the picnic. She was crying. I tried to comfort her, and she told me that she did not want to marry the count. She called him a monster. I tried to intervene with the queen, but the queen was adamant that the wedding was politically important and would take place."

The inspector had put down his pipe and was now leaning forward, glaring at me. "You're a cook, correct?"

"Yes, sir."

"And yet you console princesses and chat with the queen? That seems rather improbable to me."

"I suggest you ask Her Majesty for confirmation if you don't believe me," I said.

"But why? Why would people of their rank want to confide in the likes of you?"

"One can see that Miss Barton is a young lady of good breeding," Sir Arthur said.

"Coming from a cottage on a Yorkshire moor? Going into service at the age of twelve? How does that equate with good breeding?" the policeman asked.

Oh goodness, I thought. They had already checked into my supposed background that was on file at the palace. There was nothing for it but to bluff it out for now. "My father was an educated man," I said. "Unfortunately, I was orphaned at a young age and had no choice but to go into service." I decided to change the subject. "But what I want to know, Dr Reid, is whether the count did die from oleander poisoning?"

"It seems highly possible," he said. "It causes confusion, dizziness, nausea and finally the heart to fail, which was how the count died."

"So he was already suffering when he came into my kitchen," I said. "He stumbled. He couldn't focus properly, and his speech was a little slurred. I wondered if he had been drinking."

"You prepared this fish stew," the inspector said, "and then what? Was there an occasion on which someone could have added these leaves to it?"

"Not while it was in the kitchen." I was feeling more hopeful now, and my voice showed it. "A footman came in. I served a portion and put it on a tray. The footman carried it up to the count."

"This footman has been questioned," Sir Arthur said. "He says he was about to take it in to the count when Princess Sophie arrived. She told him she wanted a few minutes with her intended and he should leave it on the table outside the room."

"So she had plenty of opportunity to put the oleander into the dish and give it time to infiltrate the broth," I said.

They nodded.

"If it indeed turns out to be the princess," Sir Arthur said slowly, "and at this point all suspicion does seem to be pointing towards her, I have no idea how we could ever prove it, or what protocol would be. Should Her Majesty be told? Should the distressing news be kept from her?"

"And what of Princess Sophie?" the inspector asked. "Are you planning to let her walk away scot-free?"

"It needs careful consideration," Sir Arthur said. "We have to consider the ramifications of an international incident. Her father is a powerful man in his own right. He has allies across Europe. The Holy Roman emperor, the kaiser . . ."

"As you say," Dr Reid agreed, "we can never prove it. I don't think we'd get the young lady to confess."

"One more thing you should know," I said. "I think she tried to kill him previously."

"Really? When was that?" The inspector was now sitting up straight, leaning towards me.

"I believe she was the one who fired the shot. Not at the queen, but at Count Wilhelm. Not being a very good shot, she only struck his shoulder."

"How on earth did you come up with that idea?" the inspector asked.

"The princess did not attend the parade. She claimed she had a headache and stayed behind. And remember, Sir Arthur, I found the gun in the bushes and gave it to you. If it had been an anarchist, an outsider, he would have had plenty of chances to dispose of the gun somewhere far away—throw it into the sea. I believe she had to get back here in a hurry, giving her no chance to get rid of the gun."

"Goodness me." Sir Arthur looked quite disturbed now. Not so the inspector.

"You know what I find interesting," he said slowly, "is this young woman's role in the business. She cooks the pie but claims she knows nothing about mushrooms. She discovers the oleander connection but claims she didn't put the leaves in there herself. And now she tells us that she found the gun and deduces that Princess Sophie fired it because it was in the bushes beside the hotel. All a little too pat, don't you think?"

"What exactly are you hinting at, Chief Inspector?" Sir Arthur asked.

"That for some reason she is very keen to implicate Princess Sophie."

"And her motive would be?"

"To save herself, of course." He looked rather pleased with himself.

I had had enough now. "Chief Inspector," I said. "I don't know why you have this idea in your head that I am somehow against the royal family. It was the greatest honour of my life to come and work for the queen. And if I really had committed these crimes, would I have told you about the oleander? Would I have brought the gun I had hidden to Sir Arthur?"

"She's got a point there," Dr Reid said. I could tell he was on my side.

"Maybe," the inspector said. "Maybe not. It's just that something's not quite right. I've dealt with enough investigations and enough criminals during my long career that I've developed a nose. I know when something is not what it should be. And there is something about you, Miss Barton, that troubles me. I aim to find out what it is."

"I think you are being unnecessarily harsh, Chief Inspector," Sir Arthur said. "This young lady could not have been more helpful, nor more intuitive. Although I'm afraid you were brought out from London for nothing and we shall have to let the matter rest; at least it seems to me that we have hit upon the truth—thanks to Miss Barton's keen observations."

"If you say so, Sir Arthur." The policeman looked at him defiantly. He knew he was out-ranked. An ordinary policeman has to defer to a knight of the realm. His gaze moved on to me. "I'm going to find out the truth, don't you worry," it said.

Once outside, it took me a moment to compose myself. The inspector was going to find out the truth about me. That would actually not be too hard. But what happened after that? If he sought out Ronnie Barton, might Ronnie not enjoy telling him that I had pushed his sister under the omnibus, in order to gain her position? I could tell the policeman was anxious to find me guilty of something, and murder would be very satisfying for him.

I knew I had to somehow prove my innocence in the matter of Count Wilhelm, even though it seemed that Sir Arthur and Dr Reid were perfectly willing to accept my theory about Princess Sophie. If only I could make her confess. I thought about the box of chocolates with one missing. And Princess Helena screaming that something had been taken from her. I frowned. I had thought it might be a gun that had been taken, but it was more likely something to do with her addiction to drugs. I held my breath. Was it possible?

I lingered in the hallway until Sir Arthur and Dr Reid finally emerged from the room, then I followed Dr Reid until he turned towards his own suite, then ran up behind him. "Excuse me, Doctor. May I have a word in private?" I asked.

He stopped and looked back at me. "Why, of course, Miss Barton. This whole affair must have been most distressing for you."

I nodded. "Most distressing, Doctor. But I think I might have found a way to finally get at the truth, beyond a doubt."

He was frowning. "Go on."

"Were there any drugs found in the count's system?"

He was looking suspicious now. "There were. Opioids. Probably that new drug heroin— supposedly much cleaner and safer than the original opium. The German company Bayer has put it on the market this year as being beneficial to coughs."

"So the count had some of this in his system?"

"He did. That did not surprise me, nor raise alarms. I have found that the aristocratic classes are all too fond of such substances. Sometimes to the point of addiction."

"Princess Helena," I said. "I know about her."

"How on earth did you know that?"

"She asked me to go into the town for her and buy a list of things at the chemist. I recognized the names on the paper she gave me."

"Well, I never." He shook his head. "And you think that the count was also addicted to drugs?"

"No," I said. "I think they might have been given to him. Tell me, Doctor. If someone had administered heroin to him, at the same time as he was being fed oleander, and right after he had lost blood from a gunshot wound, would the combination of all three have speeded up his demise?"

"Most definitely," Dr Reid said. "Certainly con- tributed to the slowing of the heart and breathing. But what are you suggesting now?"

"If you're agreeable, I think we might be able to prove something."

I drew close to him and whispered. He looked surprised, then nodded. "Very well. We've nothing to lose in this case. I'm willing to give it a try."

CHAPTER 35

Princess Sophie looked composed and calm when she entered the small sitting room.

"You wanted me, Doctor?" she asked. "You say there have been further developments in the death of my beloved Wilhelm?"

"Please do take a seat, Princess," the doctor said. "All will be made clear, I promise you."

As she sat on an upright chair, upholstered in royal-blue silk, she looked across and noticed me, standing off to one side, behind the sofa.

"What is she doing here? Ah, I understand. You have brought her to make a confession. Excellent. So she did know that the mushroom was poisonous."

She gave a nod of satisfaction.

"Yes, I think we can prove that the death was intentional," the doctor said. "Shall I ring for some tea? A little refreshment?"

"No, thank you. Let us proceed. I wish to hear this girl's confession and see her handed over to the French police."

She was sitting very upright, her pale skin above the black gown making her look like a ghost. Her blue eyes seemed unnaturally wide.

"Or perhaps you would like a chocolate," the doctor said. He took the box from a side table and placed it in front of her. "I must say they look quite enticing."

She had gone, if anything, paler. I heard a little gasp. "Where did you find these?"

"They were in the count's room," the doctor said. "And since he will not be enjoying them any longer, I thought it was a shame to let them go to waste. My Scottish upbringing, you know, has taught me frugality. Do have one." He took the lid off the box and offered it to her.

"No, thank you. I am too distressed to eat, and especially could not touch something that had belonged to my dear Wilhelm."

"Then I hope you won't mind if I do," the doctor said in his most jolly manner. "I must confess to a horribly sweet tooth." He reached into the box, took out a large chocolate near the centre and brought it up to his mouth. I watched, fascinated.

As he was about to bite, Princess Sophie cried out, "No, don't."

The doctor looked up, holding the chocolate a few inches from his mouth. "Why not?"

"Because . . . ," she began.

"Because the chocolate has been injected with heroin?" I asked.

Her look now was pure venom. "How did you know this? You are a servant. What right do you have to poke your nose into the affairs of your betters?"

"So, Your Highness," the doctor said, "you do admit that there might be heroin in this chocolate? You stole your cousin Helena's syringe and her bottle of heroin, and you injected the chocolates?"

"Only some of them. The big ones in the centre. He was greedy. He always wanted the biggest, the best. I knew he would take them first."

"You wanted to make sure that the oleander did its job," I said. "Just in case he did not eat enough of it."

"I had no idea how much oleander it would take to kill somebody," she said.

"You were clearly desperate when the gunshot missed its target," Dr Reid said in his calm, even voice.

"I—" Her eyes registered surprise and alarm that this, too, had been found out. There was defiance as she stared at us. "What does it matter? There is nothing that you can do. My cousin Victoria will not take a servant girl's word over mine. She will believe me that the girl killed Wilhelm and tried to plant the blame on me. You'll see. You will suffer for this." She said the last words to me with great venom.

"But she will take my word, Princess," Dr Reid said. "She trusts me absolutely. And I believe what Miss Barton has said is correct and true.

Besides, we both saw you preventing me from eating the chocolate."

"Stupid trickery." Sophie spat out the words. Then she shrugged and actually smiled. "In any case, what do I care? My cousin will not let any scandal get out. She will not risk the reputation of the royal family. She will find me another husband. I will marry and live happily ever after."

Who will want to marry you when you have already poisoned one man who displeased you? I thought. It was not my place to say anything. She swept out of the room, her head held high.

"Well done," Dr Reid said. "You have a good head on your shoulders, Miss Barton."

"I wonder what will become of her," I said. "Will you tell the queen?"

"I rather fear that the queen must be told," he said. "Fortunately, that task will fall to Sir Arthur, not to me. But I also think that Princess Sophie is right. Nothing will be done. The reputation and honour of the royal family must remain intact. I actually pity the girl. To be so desperate not to marry that she resorts to the most violent means. You and I cannot understand what it must be like to be a pawn in an international game of chess."

"No, you're right," I said.

He gave me a long, hard look. "At least this means you are off the hook now. Completely exonerated of any misdoing."

"I rather fear that inspector from London does

not think so," I said. "I have the feeling he wants to poke and pry into my past until he finds something."

"Is he likely to find something?" Dr Reid asked.

I hesitated. He was a kind man, I was sure. I could tell him. But I couldn't. "I've not done anything criminal or illegal in my life," I said.

"That's what I thought. We'll make sure he is sent back to London, don't worry." He chuckled, as if this was amusing. It wasn't to me.

I went back to my room and waited. Still no word from Lady Mary. Perhaps the Waverlys did not like tea, or were not interested in a tea party with her. Or were otherwise occupied. Or were travelling. At the very least, she had promised I could stay with her and she would introduce me as a young cousin. I did have an escape—if I wanted to escape, that was. In truth I was happy in my current position, and I didn't want to leave it. I was just learning new skills. But I had to ask myself whether I wanted to be a cook all my life. Like Jean-Paul, I could never marry and carry on my profession. No man would ever allow his wife to work outside the home, especially not to all hours in someone else's kitchen. Would I want to be like Mrs Simms one day—called "Mrs" as a token of respect but having never had a husband or a home of her own? The truth was that I didn't know. I was young. I had so much to experience, so much to learn yet.

All I could do was pray that Chief Inspector Raleigh let the whole investigation drop now that the culprit had been found and had confessed. Perhaps he had more important fish to fry in London. One could only hope.

Another day passed with no news, except that my stricken colleagues came back to the kitchen, looking pale and weak—mere shadows of their former selves. Even Mr Phelps, usually brusque and picky, was extremely polite and grateful to me for every little thing. I was complimented on holding the fort so bravely. I decided to keep the matter of the mushrooms from them. There was no point in their knowing what I had been through.

I was making a batch of the queen's favourite German biscuits when suddenly a preposterous idea struck me. I would tell the queen the truth. If she decided to dismiss me, so be it. But if not she would be a protector with whom no Scotland Yard inspector could argue. I arranged some of the biscuits on a fancy doily, put them on the tray with a sprig of freesias and went boldly up the stairs to the queen's sitting room.

I was expecting to encounter the munshi outside the door, but the hallway was deserted. That probably meant that he was in there with her. Did I have the nerve to knock and enter? I stood with my hand poised for a long moment before I whispered to myself, "What have you got to lose, Bella?" and I tapped. The door was opened not by the Indian but by one of the queen's ladies. "Yes?" she said.

"I've just baked some of Her Majesty's favourite biscuits, and I thought she might need cheering up at this sad time," I said.

The lady frowned at me. "You are a cook?"

"Yes, my lady. Her Majesty knows me. We have spoken together on several occasions. May I bring the biscuits in to her?"

"You must be the one who—"

"Was falsely accused of putting a poisoned mushroom into a pie. Yes, that was me," I said, meeting her gaze with my head held high.

She looked a little unsure. "I'll take the tray then, although I don't think Her Majesty feels like eating at the moment. She has been distressed by the news."

"Who is it, Lady Lytton?" the queen's voice asked.

"A young woman cook with biscuits," the lady called back. "Your favourites, apparently."

"Ah, my sweet young cook. Have her bring them to me," the queen said.

Lady Lytton stepped aside and permitted me to enter the room. The queen was sitting in a rocking chair by the open window, even though the breeze was still quite chilly today. I suspected she might have been dozing, as her spectacles and a sheet of paper were in her lap.

I crossed the room and went up to her, giving a curtsy before I said, "I made a batch of your lebkuchen, ma'am. I know how fond you are of them, and I thought you might like some while they are still warm."

The queen looked up and smiled. "How thoughtful. Yes, I believe I might try one." Then she looked across at her lady-in-waiting. "Perhaps some tea would go well with these. Would you ask for some to be sent up, Lady Lytton?"

Lady Lytton curtsied and departed. The queen smiled at me, reached forward and took a biscuit. She ate slowly, savouring as she chewed. "Just how I remember them from my girlhood," she said. "But you have been through an ordeal yourself, have you not? Sir Arthur apprised me of the whole sorry business. Falsely accused of trying to poison me with a mushroom?"

I nodded. "Yes, Your Majesty. I told them I would never do anything to harm you, but they didn't want to listen."

She sighed. "Such a sad business. Poor Sophie. To be so desperate that she had to resort to such means. I blame myself, you know. She begged me not to have to marry him. I didn't listen. I was more intent on political gain, on making sure the empire was on firm footing when I hand it over to my wayward son. I can see Wilhelm would not have made an ideal husband. A rather bombastic young man, vain, probably would have been a bully."

"Worse than that, ma'am," I said. "He made advances to a male member of the household. He told Princess Sophie that he would never bother her again once she produced an heir."

"Gracious." The queen looked quite startled. "That is news to me. I can see why the poor girl was so desperate to escape. That side of marriage I always found so pleasurable. To be denied it . . ." She sighed and took another biscuit from the plate.

"Your Majesty, there is something else," I said hurriedly, as I sensed I was about to be dismissed. "I came into your service under false pretences and have lived in fear of being discovered ever since."

"What do you mean?" She was frowning at me now. "You are going to tell me you are really a Russian spy?"

I had to laugh at this. "No, ma'am." And I told her the whole story. She listened patiently.

"It seems to me," she said at last, "that all you did was to make the most of an opportunity. I needed a cook. You supplied one—a rather good one, as it turned out. And nobody is the worse off for it. So what is your real name?"

"Isabella Waverly, ma'am."

"Any relation to the Earl of Altringham?"

"His cousin, ma'am. I told you before that my parents died. My father made it clear that he had appealed to the family for help and been rejected, so I had no option but to go into service to support my little sister."

"Admirable. You have a sense of duty like my own. But I'm surprised at the Waverlys rejecting you."

"I didn't appeal to them personally, ma'am. I was too young at the time to know anything about my father's family."

"I understand they are also on the Riviera. Shall you visit them now, do you think?"

"Lady Mary Crozier wanted to arrange a tea party for me to meet them, but so far they have shown no interest in such an invitation."

"You should be back amongst your own kind," the queen said. "It is not right to have you working below stairs when you come from a good family. I gather you were instrumental in working out how the count was killed. Sir Arthur was quite complimentary of your powers of observation and deduction. It occurs to me that I could always use you as my spy." She gave me an impish little smile. "What would you say to that?"

"Your spy, ma'am?"

"Yes. You'd be a member of my household and keep your eyes and ears open for anything that I should need to know."

"I'm flattered, but I enjoy cooking, ma'am."

She looked offended. "I'm offering you a chance to move into the right circles, you silly girl. You'd be one of my ladies, with a chance to meet men of the right social standing. And you'd be doing me a service, too." She paused. "I could order you to, you know."

"I'm aware of that, ma'am," I said. "And I have no wish to upset you. I realize you are being extremely kind to me, and it's a wonderful offer."

"But?" She wagged a finger at me. "You'd prefer slaving away over a hot stove to becoming one of my ladies?"

"As strange as it may sound to you, yes, I think so. If word got out that I was your spy, I'd be mistrusted and avoided everywhere I went. Also, your ladies spend a lot of their time with nothing constructive to do. I have been working hard for so long now that I'd find it strange to be unemployed."

She actually patted my hand. "You and I are kindred spirits. I have worked every day of my life since the age of eighteen, when I became queen. I have read the dispatch boxes dutifully every day, made sure I knew what was going on in my government and in the world so that I could properly advise my ministers. They haven't always thanked me for it, of course." And she smiled again. "Very well, I accept your refusal, reluctantly. I, too, need someone to be on my side, strange though it may seem. And now that dear Abdul has gone . . ."

"Your Indian servant, is he indisposed?"

"He is gone," she said in a flat voice. "One of the reasons I have been feeling so depressed. I miss him. I was forced to send him away, you know. My gentlemen have been pressuring me for some time, trying to convince me he was unsuitable. I thought it was mere jealousy and prejudice against a lesser race . . . but it turns out they may have been right. It seems he has been meeting with a man who is engaged in trying to drive the British from India. Actively working against us! Abdul claimed this man was just a friend, but he has had access to my papers— to the most confidential secrets of the realm. I saw that I could no longer take the risk, for the sake of the empire. So I had to send him away." She paused, staring out of the window. The breeze had become stronger, swirling out the net curtains. I went over and shut it hastily.

"It pains me," she said. "He had become a special friend. A queen has few friends."

"But you have your family, ma'am. Your ladies and gentlemen, all of whom are very fond of you."

"That may be so, but he was different. He didn't stand on protocol. He scolded me when I needed scolding. He teased me. Made me laugh. Made me feel like a woman, the way my dear

John Brown did. And my beloved Albert before him." She looked up at me. "I enjoy the company of handsome young men. Is that so foolish at my age?"

I smiled. "Not at all, ma'am. You have lived a life bound by duty. You deserve any happiness you are offered."

She examined me for a long moment. "You are a sweet child," she said. "You shall come and chat with me when you bring up my special biscuits."

"I shall be honoured, ma'am," I said. "I should leave you and return to my kitchen. Is there anything special you might want for your dinner tonight?"

"I don't have much of an appetite," she said, "which is unusual for me. Some fish, I think. And maybe a fowl. But probably no mushrooms." She saw my worried face, then she chuckled.

CHAPTER 36

"It never rains, but it pours" was one of my father's favourite sayings. In his case it usually referred to misfortune or misery. In my case it was quite the opposite. All of a sudden, a burden had been lifted from my shoulders. The queen wanted me to be her spy—not a job I would ever have taken. Imagine the suspicion and distrust amongst the other ladies of the household if they thought I was listening to conversations and reporting back to the queen. And Lady Mary Crozier wanted to take me under her wing. Also my position as cook was safe at last. I wondered if I should tell my story to the other cooks and change my name. All in good time. I'd have to think of the right way to do it. But it was all rather heady for someone who had felt herself an outcast and unloved for so long.

And as my father also said, "Good things come in threes." That very day I received an invitation to tea with the Marquise de Crozier. I told Mr Angelo that I would be gone for the afternoon.

"Tea with a marquise," he said, raising an eyebrow. "My, we have moved up in the world while I've been away."

I realized as I went to change that I hadn't asked his permission. I had announced my plans to him, and he had not queried them. Somehow our relationship had changed now that I had handled the entire kitchen. There was a new layer of respect and gratitude. I just hoped it lasted. I thought about this as I made my way down to Lady Mary's villa that afternoon. I had choices now. Did I want to stay in the palace kitchen, where it would be years before I was promoted to anything above an assistant cook? Had I learned enough to make my own way in the world? Or should I really consider one of the offers that had been made to me . . . was it finally time to return to my proper status? It was a hard decision, and I realized that Giles Waverly might have something to do with it.

Lady Mary greeted me warmly as I was shown into the sitting room. The two men who had been sitting there rose to their feet. Giles Waverly gave me a delighted and surprised smile, and I realized that Lady Mary had not told them I'd be joining them. The older man, who I presumed was the earl, bore a striking resemblance to my father. The same fine bone structure and strong jaw, the same deep-set eyes, although the earl was now quite portly, and my father had remained painfully thin.

I observed the earl's face. He was staring at me with a puzzled frown. I wondered if he had heard something about me that had displeased him until he said, "You remind me of someone, young lady. I can't quite put my finger on it, but it will come to me."

"Your cousin Roderick maybe, my lord?" I said.

"That's it. Roddy, when he was young." He gave me a questioning look. "And you are?"

"Isabella Waverly, his daughter," I said.

"Good God. Fancy that. Is this the girl you've been talking about, Giles? Why didn't you tell me that she was a cousin?"

"I didn't know," Giles said, a confused look on his face. "You said your name was Helen Barton."

"That was the name I had to work under when I became a cook at the palace," I said.

"A cook?" the earl looked startled now. "You became a cook?"

"Out of necessity, my lord. My parents died. My sister and I were left with no money and no place to go. I had to support her, so I went into service."

"Why the devil didn't you come to us?" the earl blustered. "We didn't even know that Roddy had married and had children. We thought he was still in India."

"The answer to that is that I knew nothing about you. My father told us he had fallen out with his family and could not turn to them for help."

"Stupid boy," the earl said, glancing at his son. "Your father was not the easiest of men, I'm afraid to say, Isabella. He got into trouble at Oxford. Gambling debts, bad checks, that kind of thing. I gather he ran with a wild crowd, drank too much, lived high on the hog without the means to do so. His own parents were dead. My father was paying for his education. He told Roddy that he'd settle his debts, but he was sending him back to India to make a man of himself. He'd arrange for a commission in an Indian regiment, and then he never wanted to see him again. And we heard no more from him. Presumed he was still in India."

"He had to resign his commission and come back to England because my mother couldn't take the climate," I said. "I'm afraid that drink was his downfall in the end."

He nodded. "Sad business. But you seem to be made of sterner stuff. You have the proper Waverly blood flowing through your veins. Well done, Isabella. And you must call me Cousin George. Come and sit here beside me, and you shall tell us all about the royal household." He patted the sofa beside him. I caught Lady Mary's eye, and she gave me a nod of encouragement.

We chatted. We ate cucumber sandwiches and petits fours, and afterward the earl told Giles to escort me back to the hotel. I couldn't be sure, but I think he gave Giles a wink.

437

"Why didn't you tell me that we were related?" Giles said as soon as we had left the villa. "I felt like a fool, not knowing."

"Because I had to prevent my true identity from being known at that time," I said, and I related the story to him.

"Ye gods," he said. "That's quite a tale. You poor girl. You've been through a lot."

"I'm still here," I replied. "And things are looking up at last."

"So what will you do now?" he asked. "You can't go back to being a cook."

"I'm not sure. Your father has invited me to come and stay at Kingsbury, which is awfully nice of him. Lady Mary has suggested I stay with her, and the queen doesn't want me to leave. It's all rather overwhelming after feeling unwanted for so long."

"I hope you take up our offer," he said. He was looking at me like an expectant dog, hoping for a treat. "I want to see more of you, Bella. I think my father wants us to be better acquainted, too. I thought you were a splendid girl from the moment I laid eyes on you. And now I know how strong you are; I think you'd make a perfect wife for me. I need someone like you to keep me on the straight and narrow. Father has been pressuring me to settle down and marry, you know, and I think he might like to keep it all in the family, so to speak."

"It's a little early to be talking like that," I said. "You don't really know me, Giles."

"I'm the sort of chap who makes up his mind quickly," Giles said. "When I see something I like, I know instantly. And I knew instantly about you, Bella. I think we'd have a grand old life together. I'll inherit Kingsbury someday. The pater is not without cash. You'll finally be where you are supposed to be." He paused, took a deep breath, then said, "I may not be the brightest chap in the world, nor the most athletic, but I'm a good sort. Do you think you could be happy married to someone like me?"

"I think I probably could," I said cautiously, "but let's take it one step at a time, Giles."

"Of course," he agreed, nodding. "I don't want to rush you. At least say you'll come to stay . . ." He took my hand, holding it between his own. "And we can take it from there."

Wasn't this what I had wanted, dreamed of? Of course it was. Mistress of a grand house. All the leisure in the world. Money for clothes. Money to travel. And yet I hesitated.

"Carpe diem, Bella," said my father's voice.

"Of course I'll come to stay," I said. "But I can't leave the other cooks in the lurch here. You'll have to wait until we return to London."

"I can wait, as long as it takes, if I have you to look forward to," he said, squeezing my hand now.

I changed out of my good dress and stumbled back to the kitchen in a daze. I started making a pudding for dinner, mechanically stirring in ingredients . . . Was this what I wanted to do all my life? Cook for other people? Be a servant when I could have people to wait on me?

"Attention. Pay attention," a warning voice said sharply behind me. "You are burning the butter."

I jumped, pulled the pan off the flame and turned to see Jean-Paul standing behind me.

"I was watching you," he said. "You have your head in the clouds today. It's not like you to burn the butter." He was looking at me with concern. "What is wrong? Are you still worried? I understood that you are not being held responsible for the death of that nobleman. They are saying now that he took his own life. Drugs, so I hear."

"Is that what they are saying?" I asked. "I'm sorry. I'm a little confused today. I think I just received a proposal of marriage."

"You think?"

"It wasn't a formal proposal, but a proposal nonetheless."

"And did you accept?"

"I might have indicated my willingness to accept," I admitted.

"Who is this man?" His voice was sharp now.

"An English milord," I said. "I shall become a viscountess and live in a fine house."

"And what of your passion?" he demanded. "It has disappeared? You will no longer cook. You will have someone to do that for you. You will accept mediocre food, knowing that you could have cooked it better. You will sit and do embroidery or gossip to while away the time until the next meal. Is that what you really want?"

"You are shouting," I said. I realized the kitchen had become very still and the others were watching us.

"Come outside." He took my arm and forced me from the kitchen.

"Let go of me, you're hurting me," I said.

"We cannot discuss this in front of the others." He propelled me along the hallway. We came into the open air at the back of the hotel. Seagulls were whirling in the breeze, crying above us.

Jean-Paul turned me to face him. "Tell me this is what you want. What you really want."

"I shall miss cooking," I said slowly. "But I have to think of my future. I had to work like a slave from the time I was a young girl because I had nobody to take care of my sister and me. Who would turn down the chance for a life of luxury and security?"

"Do you love this man?" he asked.

"I hardly know him. He seems pleasant enough." Even as I said the words, I heard Giles's voice saying that he needed a strong woman to keep him on the straight and narrow. Did he have problems with drink and gambling, as my father had done? Was this something that ran in the family? I realized how very little I knew about Giles.

"Pleasant enough? Is that what you want in a husband?" His voice had risen again. "A milquetoast little Englishman who minces around with lace on his cuffs and doesn't know what to do with a woman?"

"How do you know what he is like?" I was shouting back at him now.

"Because I see the English milords. They are spoiled little boys, not real men. Will he ever kiss you like this?"

He grabbed me and brought his mouth against mine with such force that I couldn't breathe. I tried to push him away, but I realized I wasn't trying very hard. When we broke apart, he stood looking down at me with those dark eyes burning with passion. "Will he make you feel alive?"

When I didn't answer, he said softly, "Don't make a mistake you will regret for the rest of your life."

"What if it's my one chance at happiness? What if I turn him down and then one day I become sick or injured with nowhere to go and nobody to look after me?"

"Why should it be your one chance?"

"I am an under-cook. I sleep in a narrow little bed, and I do what I am told. Maybe I want more."

"You could always stay here," Jean-Paul said at last.

"What do you mean?" I looked up, seeing those dark eyes looking at me with intensity.

"When the queen and the milords go home. You like it here."

"You're right. I do like it. But I can hardly stay here and work at the hotel. You have no female chefs."

"I was thinking the time might be right for me to open my own restaurant," he said. "You could come and work with me."

I gave a nervous little laugh. "I don't think that would be proper. Where would I live?"

"We could get married, of course," he said.

"You and I?"

"You and I," he said. "Why not? You like me. I know you do. I did not see how I could ever marry, because it would not be fair to a wife to have a husband who is never at home in the evenings. But if I had a wife who worked beside me, who shared my passion—think what we could do together."

"You're only saying this because another man has asked me to marry him," I said uncertainly. "You don't want me to marry an Englishman. You don't really mean it."

"Chérie, I have wanted you from the first moment I set eyes on you," he said. "But I told myself that you were not attracted to me the way I was to you. So I said nothing."

"You'd really want to leave this position at the hotel?" I asked, still trying to come to grips with his proposal and my own building excitement. "Isn't this a plum job?"

"Of course," he said. "But more and more foreigners are coming to Nice now. There are good restaurants but no outstanding restaurants. No Cordon Bleu. No reason for fashionable people to come down from Paris or Berlin. The time is right. I think it could be a magnificent success."

"Starting a restaurant would take money," I said, still not wanting to trust my instinct.

"I am not without money," he replied with a proud toss of his head. "My father has done well. I have done well. You would not starve, ma petite, I promise you."

"You only want me to come and cook with you," I said.

"Why are you saying these things?" he demanded. "If you do not wish to marry me, say so now and put me out of my misery. But please accept the truth. I want you," he said simply. "I think we could have an incredible life together. I guarantee you would never be bored. So what do you say?"

What could I say? I, who had despised my sister for marrying into trade, who had the chance to become Viscountess Faversham, heard myself saying the words, "I think I would like that very much."

"You are leaving my service to marry?" the queen asked me. It was April, and her time in Nice was drawing to a close. "Is it the young Waverly boy?"

"No, ma'am. I'm afraid I'm going to marry a Frenchman and stay here."

"Gracious me. And where did you meet this Frenchman?"

"He is the head chef at the hotel, ma'am. We are going to open a restaurant together."

"You are full of surprises, Miss Waverly. I hope you know what you are doing, settling down so far from home."

"Lady Mary married a Frenchman and seems very happy," I said.

"Yes, but he is a nobleman. You will be working hard for your living."

"I told you once that I want to be occupied, and cooking beside my husband seems perfect to me."

"Then I wish you well," she said. "Having a good man at your side is the best any woman can hope for. May you be as happy with him as I was with my dear Albert."

And shortly after that, I had another encounter. I was walking along the Promenade des Anglais, admiring the incredible blue of the water, dotted with the white sails of yachts and the red sails of fishing boats. The light sparkled and danced. It was almost too heady to be real. And suddenly I found myself thinking about Helen Barton. If she had been alive and taken her rightful place in the kitchen, maybe she might have been standing here at this moment, not me. And a great wave of pity came over me that her life had been snuffed out so young and she never had a chance for love or happiness. I wanted to do something for her, something in her memory. But I knew she had no family apart from her brother. I turned away from the ocean, and coming towards me was Ronnie Barton himself. His face took on that sarcastic smirk I had so loathed. It was a face I had wanted to smack so many times.

"Well, if it isn't my long-lost sister," he said. "We heard there was a spot of scandal that involved you. Some bloke died? Something to do with poisoned mushrooms?"

I gave him a hard stare. "I'm afraid you have it wrong. It turned out to be nothing to do with mushrooms at all."

"Lucky for you, eh?" he said. "I bet they'd have been interested to know you were involved in another death before this. Do the French still have the guillotine?"

"Why don't you give up these silly threats?" I said. "There is nothing you can do to me."

"Really?" he said. "Actually I'm glad you were not found guilty of poisoning." He paused, then added, "You'd be no use to me in a French prison, or with your head chopped off."

"I will be no use to you whatever from now on," I said. "Now, if you'll excuse me . . ." I tried to walk past him. He blocked my path.

"I hear the queen's going home next week. I may be coming to visit you in London. I can think of a couple of little favours I may want from you."

"The queen may be going home, but I'm not," I said.

"Ah, so they found out about you, did they?" He was grinning now. "Kicked you out at last, poor dear. So what are you going to do with yourself?"

"I'm actually taking another name," I said. "I have grown tired of being Helen Barton."

"What did you do—push another girl under an omnibus?"

I was about to answer when I heard my name being called. I turned to see Jean-Paul running towards me. "A thousand pardons for keeping you waiting, chérie," he said and kissed my cheek. "But I have exciting news. A building that I think will be perfect for us." He stopped, noticing Ronnie standing in front of me.

"And who is this?" Jean-Paul asked me, still in French.

"An Englishman who has been annoying me for a long time," I said. I looked Ronnie directly in the eye. "I am about to be married, Mr Barton. This is my fiancé. He is a famous chef. And his family is very influential in Nice. His grandfather was mayor once."

Jean-Paul was sizing up the skinnier, slighter man. He stepped forward. "And I do not like anyone who upsets my bride," he said in surprisingly good English. "She is right. I am a famous chef, and I am extremely talented with a knife. If I can bone a duck in two minutes, just think what I could do to you. Do not let me see you again."

He took my arm. "Come, chérie. We have a restaurant to buy."

"Good luck to you, marrying a frog," Ronnie called as we moved past him. "You'll be begging to come home to England in no time at all."

I couldn't resist turning back to him. "You don't know me, Mr Barton. You've never known me. I can think of nothing more splendid than living here with a man who loves me. And one day I expect the prince will find out the truth about you and you'll get what you deserve. But I won't be the one to tell him. Good day to you."

Then we walked away without looking back.

On the third of June, I married Jean-Paul Lepin in the church of Notre Dame of the Immaculate

Conception, behind the old port. Lady Mary outfitted me for the occasion. The queen gave me a set of pearls. My fellow cooks were more practical and sent a set of jelly moulds, in case they were not obtainable in France. My sister and her husband came over for the wedding. She really was expecting a child this time and looked positively radiant.

"Billy has put off the idea of going to Australia until the little one is born," she said. "Maybe he'll have a cousin someday soon."

And that wistful look came into her eyes again as she realized that the cousins would be thousands of miles apart.

After we returned from our honeymoon on the Italian Riviera, we opened a restaurant that I insisted on calling La Belle Hélène just off the Promenade des Anglais. It was my small tribute to Helen Barton. It has large arched windows that look across gardens to the bay, and we designed it with intimate booths around the walls. We have made local seafood dishes our specialty, and I have learned to create a really good baba au rhum. As Jean-Paul predicted, it has been a magnificent success. People come from all over the Riviera to dine with us, including the Prince of Wales, with his latest conquest. (I wisely stayed in the kitchen, just in case.) And I am able to pursue my passion for cooking, but I have recently found a new love in my life. He is called

Louis, after Jean-Paul's father and my sister, and he lies contentedly in his cradle while his parents create timbales, terrines and soufflés. Sometimes I let him suck on my finger when I have created a particularly delicious batter or sauce. He is clearly going to inherit his parents' palate.

HISTORICAL NOTE

A few years ago, I was researching another book on the Riviera. I was on the hill in Cimiez above Nice when I saw a magnificent building. I asked a gardener if it was a hotel. "It used to be, madame," he said. "Now it is only apartments." Then he added, "It was built for your queen, you know."

"Queen Elizabeth?" I could not have been more surprised.

"No, Queen Victoria. She used to come here every winter, so they built the hotel for her."

I had known nothing of this. I started to research it and found that Queen Victoria visited the Riviera during her last years, first staying with friends in villas until the Hotel Excelsior Regina was built for her. Her party took over a whole wing with a separate entrance. During my research in Nice, I was shown the brochure featuring the original design of the hotel, and how the rooms were allocated. That was when I saw that she brought a team of cooks with her, and I wondered if one of those cooks was a young woman. And so I have acquired cookbooks and menus from one of the queen's chefs with recipes for those ridiculously fancy meals.

Many aspects of the story are true: her Indian munshi, Abdul Karim, his association with a leader of the Muslim League, and his final fall from grace are factual. The members of her party are also true, except for Princess Sophie and Count Wilhelm. The queen really did go out in her little donkey cart, pulled by a donkey she had rescued from a peasant. She loved to attend the Carnival and go on picnics. And throw flowers at handsome young men in the parades. I have many photographs of her enjoying her time in Nice.

When she was dying a few years later, she said to her doctor, "If only I could go back to Nice, I know I could get well again."

ACKNOWLEDGMENTS

My thanks, as always, to Danielle Marshall and the whole author team at Lake Union who make working with them such a joy. Also thanks to my brilliant and wonderful agents, Meg Ruley and Christina Hogrebe. You ladies are the best! Finally thanks to my husband, John, for his editing skills, his love and his support.

ABOUT THE AUTHOR

Rhys Bowen is the *New York Times* bestselling author of more than forty novels, including *The Victory Garden*, *The Tuscan Child*, and the World War II—based *In Farleigh Field*, the winner of the Left Coast Crime Award for Best Historical Mystery Novel and the Agatha Award for Best Historical Novel. Bowen's work has won twenty honors to date, including multiple Agatha, Anthony, and Macavity awards. Her books have been translated into many languages, and she has fans around the world, including seventeen thousand Facebook followers. A transplanted Brit, Bowen divides her time between California and Arizona. To learn more about the author, visit www.rhysbowen.com.

Center Point Large Print
600 Brooks Road / PO Box 1
Thorndike, ME 04986-0001 USA

(207) 568-3717

US & Canada:
1 800 929-9108
www.centerpointlargeprint.com